BLACK LIGHTNING

BLACK LIGHTNING

MARK JONES

VICTOR GOLLANCZ

LONDON

First published in Great Britain 1995
by Victor Gollancz
A Division of the Cassell group
Wellington House, 125 Strand, London WC2R 0BB

A catalogue record for this book is
available from the British Library.

ISBN 0 575 05899 4

Typeset in Great Britain by
CentraCet Ltd, Cambridge
Printed and bound in Great Britain by
Mackays of Chatham plc, Chatham, Kent

for Natalya

FOREWORD

I wrote this book in 1993, when public optimism about Russia was high. The rebels in parliament had been suppressed. Triumphant reformers proclaimed a liberal democracy.

Shortly after I finished it, new elections were held. A televised party was organized on election night in a glittering Kremlin hall. The celebrations did not last long. As the results came in, faces changed. Suddenly the lights were turned out and the cameras switched off. The reason soon became clear – the far right had won, together with the communists and their allies – and not the *democratia* (or *deremocratia* – shitocracy – as many Russians call the parties of reform).

I was in Moscow, and this result did not surprise me. I spent time on the streets, and did not see victory written on the faces of ordinary Russians. I saw, and heard, fear, anger, hatred. The reforms were failing. Endemic gangsterism had encouraged a cowed populace to vote for anyone who promised order and a strong hand. Ironically, it was the gangsters themselves who turned out to be the main beneficiaries of this mood.

It would be difficult for any leadership to modernize Russia. But Yeltsin's is breathtakingly corrupt. The rot starts at the top: the palace guard, for instance, has a squad of conscripts who share his blood group, to provide him with the transfusions that sober him up. Meanwhile his government is in the grip of organized crime. The oil mafia has acquired political power, but the trappings of state do not hide its leaders' predilection for coercion and violence. Gangsters do not understand democracy and their approach to international affairs is equally cynical. In the circumstances, the mindless optimism of some Western analysts is hard to understand.

Events since this book was written confirm its pessimism. Russia's dilemmas are insoluble, its very borders a conundrum. Millions of Russians now live beyond them, while countries such as Chechnya which wish to leave remain forcibly incorporated. Russia is still a prison of nations, burdened with an economy which does not fit our world. Its spiral of decline will continue.

Mired in corruption, enmeshed in the tragedies of history and geography, half-European, half-Asian – Russia's agonized contortions may embroil us all. In this novel rebellion is depicted breaking out among the non-Russian peoples of the Arctic north. In fact, the first war of national liberation began in Chechnya (the sequel to this book, which is in the hands of the publisher, is located in the Caucasus. It foretells that region's descent into chaos). But Siberia too is drowning in the same lethal brew of turpitude, ethnic conflict and the oil mafia's catastrophic, single-minded pursuit of its imagined self-interest. In Russia, rebellion can begin anywhere.

Its ill-educated, parvenu rulers invite it. They suffer from a collective inferiority complex which leaves them feeling beleaguered and insecure. And they drip with great-power nostalgia – modern Moscow's anachronistic *Zeitgeist* which Vladimir Zhirinovsky articulates so well. They belong in the nineteenth century, not an era so inimical to empire as ours. They are leading Russia to disaster. Under their rule, either it will disintegrate, or a new empire will emerge from the ashes, unstable, more dangerous and more determined to find its place in the sun than the Soviet Union ever was. The world should tremble before either prospect. But I do not see a third way.

How accurate is this novel? Its themes and many of its characters are drawn from life. The nationalist leader, Zamok, for example, is based on the baleful personality of Vladimir Zhirinovsky. I know him, and know that the West underestimates him. We should prepare now for the likelihood that he will rule Russia one day soon. The Chechen adventure is straight out of his strange autobiography, *The Last Push South*, a sort of latter-day *Mein Kampf*. KGB* men I know say that only the assassin's bullet can stop his ascent to power.

Many events portrayed herein are based upon actualities, including *Molniya* (some say the Russian army is only a shadow of its former self. They forget that underestimating Russian military prowess is historically speaking a common and generally fatal mistake).

Mark Jones
January 1995

* The Russian security services remain ubiquitous. Changes of name have changed nothing of substance. Ordinary Russians still refer to them as the 'KGB' and this book does the same.

They said, Lord wilt thou that we command
fire to come down from heaven and consume
them?

Luke, 9:54

An inexplicable feeling of fear, arrhythmia of the heart, and a sense of wonder, are feelings many share on seeing the Northern Lights. Barely noticeable to begin with, they first appear in the night sky as vertical or slightly inclined poles of light. Becoming more luminescent, they move closer together, merging and melding into pale green, iridescent ribbons. Quite suddenly they become inflamed with orange and with a harsh pink light, bathing one half of the sky in a fantastic, soundless fire. An enormous, fearful sky burns over a land grown suddenly small and unstable. It could be the Last Day, but this apocalyptic vision is an everyday phenomenon in the Arctic . . .

Rostislav Dormidontov
Soviet Naturalist

Genesis of the Molniya system

. . . In 1943 Peter Kapitza was exiled by Stalin to his dacha outside Moscow. To help him wile away the time a friend sent the presiding genius of Russian physics a memorial collection on the work of Nikola Tesla, who had recently died. Having nothing else to do, Kapitza read the book and became intrigued.

Tesla was an eccentric, a great inventor of practical electrical devices and a collaborator of Thomas Edison in the creation of high-voltage electrical systems. He was at odds with quantum mechanics, which was becoming the dominant paradigm in physics. Tesla preferred to believe that nature was not fundamentally particulate. He was a wave-theorist, placing himself in the camp of Werner von Heisenberg and hypothesizing that a system of electro-magnetic waves enclusters the globe. In his opinion, these waves formed a kind of beneficent envelope within which life on earth had first emerged.

Perhaps he was also influenced by the great Russian scientific philosopher, Nikolai Vernadsky, who originated the idea of the biosphere. Both speculated about what would happen if the earth's vast electromagnetic energy should be placed in the hands of man.

In the cold winter of 1943, when the Germans stood before Stalingrad and the outcome of the war still hung in the balance, Kapitza the practical scientist began to find out. He performed a series of experiments, aspects of which we still do not understand. Using little more than kitchen utensils for laboratory equipment, he tapped into the forces within the earth's magnetic field. His experiments came to a spectacular end when his dacha was destroyed by millions of volts of artificial ball lightning.

This much is public knowledge. What happened next is one of the great scientific puzzles of the twentieth century. Stalin was informed about Kapitza's strange activities, of course, and he encouraged him to continue.

13

But when the first atom bomb was dropped on Hiroshima in August 1945, Stalin acquired new priorities and Kapitza was conscripted to the Soviet nuclear-weapons programme. His flirtation with the ideas of Nikola Tesla seemed to be at an end.

Nonetheless in the decades which followed, rumours continued to circulate in the close-knit, incestuous world of physics, a world which scarcely acknowledged the existence of the Cold War. Something was going on – but nothing definite emerged until the 1960s when Soviet scientists began large-scale experiments. Our surveillance satellites observed preparations in the Arctic North. The experiments involved the Northern Lights – the Aurora Borealis – a phenomenon associated with the intense electromagnetic fields presented at the North Pole. A cryptic report on the first results duly appeared in an obscure scientific journal published by Tomsk University. And then nothing. No Russian publication ever again referred to the so-called 'Spolokh' experiments.

That should have been warning enough. Unfortunately we made a mistake at that time: we stopped monitoring them. We had good reason; we guessed that the Russians were trying to propagate Electromagnetic Pulse radiation – EMP for short – artificially and we knew that was impossible. The prevailing laws of physics decreed that EMP can only exist as a by-product of nuclear explosions.

Of course, if we were wrong – if any country devised a way to create EMP – they would own the most devastating, war-winning weapon ever invented, more dangerous even than the hydrogen bomb. Because an EMP weapon would be no mere deterrent: it would be capable of use. And its effects would be almost without limit, overwhelming to all adversaries.

To understand why, it is necessary to remember the chief characteristic of EMP – namely, that it does not damage buildings or kill people, but it does destroy electrical and electronic systems. Missile guidance, radar scanners, military communications and control systems – all are disabled by EMP, which can collapse entire electricity-supply grids like houses of cards and blanket out any electronic component. Even automobiles do not function.

Obviously an enemy who could wreak such havoc, and who could do so without the need to detonate nuclear devices, would soon enjoy strategic superiority. He would be able to play with us: to bring ordinary life to a standstill for an hour, or for a day – or for ever. He would be able to switch Western civilization on and off at will. Such a device for propagating EMP, if it existed, would be the ultimate blackmail weapon.

Our arrogance about the laws of physics proved untimely. Today we know that EMP propagation is possible. The work by Peter Kapitza so long ago was developed and perfected in the Soviet Union, at a human and material cost so great it directly contributed to the collapse of that state. But today an EMP weapon *has* been created.

Its name is **Molniya**. Its meaning is 'Lightning'.

It is the effect of Molniya on civilian life which is the most important factor. It can reduce multi-millioned cities to starvation in weeks. And we have no real answer.

If the new rulers of Russia adopt the programme of the ultra-Nationalist leader, Zamok, they will rearm and re-equip the Russian army, putting millions of men in uniform, restarting the tank factories.

They have declared their aim: to march south. How long will it be before Russian soldiers occupy Tehran and Istanbul, and, shielded by Molniya, turn up on the shores of the Persian Gulf and the Indian Ocean? Together with their Iraqi allies, they would dominate the Middle East, and their hands would be on the West's energy lifelines. Russia would emerge as the true victor of the twentieth century.

If ever they do use Molniya, we will have to hope that they allow the White House to keep one functioning telephone so that we can at least listen to their surrender terms.

CHAPTER 1

Winter had come early to Varta. Drizzle fell out of an inscrutable sky, blanketing the land. In late September the drizzle turned to arrows of ice which fell in millions on to the cold Siberian city which gave the region its name. The endless downpour intensified, scrubbed the autumn bronze off the region's vast forests, finally erupting in fierce electrical storms. Jagged lightning parried and slashed the forest, splintering its tall trees like matchwood, sending them crashing to the ground where the animals of the Siberian North hid in silent fright.

The storms were of unusual severity and caused many accidental deaths and much damage to property in towns and cities throughout central Siberia. In late autumn they intensified and then suddenly spread southwards. Magnetic disturbances swept over a giant swath of the Arctic Circle, 180 kilometres north of Varta.

The storms originated from within the Aurora Borealis, whose spectral curtains of violet light each winter flood up into the endless polar night. They arced over the Siberian air bowl, knifing thousands of kilometres south into Eastern and Central Europe. There, the damage and loss of life caused by these freak winter conditions was far worse than in the empty North. Whole cities were plunged into darkness; air-traffic control systems failed; on-board electronics blacked out and hundreds of lives were lost as giant airliners spun to earth.

Patients died in darkness on operating tables; trains collided; radio and television services were lost; computers crashed. And as the cost of the damage began to be calculated, hundreds of billions were wiped from the world's equity markets. In one single catastrophic fortnight, as the storms intensified, striking at the eastern seaboard of the US, ominous rents appeared in the world's telecommunications systems. Satellites were plucked from the skeins which web the earth and with them the data networks on which human society had learnt to depend in the last decade of the twentieth century. Governments declared disaster areas. Nation could no longer speak unto nation.

Then one day the storms suddenly stopped. The rain ceased. Apocalypse departed as swiftly as it had come. The world shrugged its shoulders

17

and went about its business. Loss adjusters worked overtime and normality returned as suddenly as it had left.

In the far North, too, the seasons resumed their normal course. The seamless mass of cloud that had been carpeting Siberia lifted, the fingers of mist and damp which crawled through Varta city disappeared. In October the wind died, the air became drier and even a little warmer, for a few days.

Then, just as they always did, the snows came. As winter proper began in Varta, giant snowflakes, abrading and ionizing the silent air, settled like butterflies on roofs and window ledges, on pathways and roads and vehicles, on passers-by, on the peaked caps of schoolboys.

Snow fell in straight lines into sheltered courtyards, rustled through the icy branches of birch trees, settled and froze. Mornings brought hard frosts to Varta, and as the temperature fell to minus 5, minus 10, minus 20, the air thickened and curdled and froze. Children were released early from school because of the cold and like children will, they played in the streets, throwing snowballs, heedless of the frost.

The same cold that stabbed through windows which were hastily sealed with strips of gummed paper, flailed at thresholds and entrance ways. The season of blizzards began and a dragon of ice howled off the taiga. Snakes of freezing snow whirled up tall buildings, clotting under gutters and around cornices. Each morning new drifts of snow covered streets where owners frantically dug out their vehicles; many abandoned their cars till next spring and only Varta's trams clanked through the gloom in their usual numbers. Snow and ice gripped the frozen heart of the city like a thrombosis, slowing traffic to a dribble, settling in drifts two metres deep and as thick as custard on the quiet squares where old folk had sat a month before.

Winter. Unusually early, unusually hard; but life went on – more or less.

For some in Varta, winter scarcely came at all. One such was a prisoner held secretly in an underground cell in a compound belonging to the Varta offices of the Ministry of the Interior (MVD). The cell was windowless, its walls rough concrete, the door made of solid iron sheets welded and bolted to massive frames and hinges, as strong and unburstable as the day they were installed sixty years before. Latterly the cells had seen little use – occasional residents included a drug-trafficker, two fraudsters wanted by Moscow, and a member of an illegal communist organization.

The prisoner, an American, had been detained for six weeks in total secrecy, on strictest orders from Moscow and at some inconvenience to the Varta Ministry of the Interior. A squad of Omon troops had been brought to guard him – the most feared paramilitary division. Six men mounted a round-the-clock watch in three eight-hour shifts, two men to a shift. They sat near the cell door, and communicated with no one, neither the prisoner nor the regular station guards – who also mounted a second guard by the sole entrance to the cells, on the ground floor of the building.

The prisoner had not been well treated. For much of the time his cell was left in darkness. His diet was restricted to sour bread, tea and occasional soup. No one knew why he was being held, and the order was strict – no communication *whatsoever*. Only the Omon guards knew he was a non-Russian. The man spoke good Russian in fact, but had soon given up attempts at conversation with his silent guards, who resisted promises and threats alike.

The prisoner grew resigned, abandoning the futile escape attempts of the first days and weeks of captivity and spending his time lying on the hard cot or pacing silently up and down the gloomy little cell.

He seemed a forgotten man, just a nuisance-value that required extra rostering among the station staff. Then in late November an order came from Moscow, marked 'Most Secret', for the attention only of General Sokolnikov, the head of the Varta Main Administration.

That same night the six men of the Omon squad went together to the prisoner's cell. They locked the door behind them. It took four of them to pinion, grab and throw him face down on the wooden boards of the cot; then while one of them struck his face on the boards until the blood ran, another tore off his coat and ripped the left sleeve from his shirt. They turned him over and only then did their leader approach; he stood over the prisoner, his eyes glinting behind steel-framed spectacles, lips set in a grim smile. 'Lie still,' he advised.

The leader knelt with his weight on the prisoner's forearm, which was extended over the edge of the cot, so that the joint cracked and the veins stood proud of the skin.

'Bastards!' the prisoner screamed as the needle found the vein. It was the last word he spoke before the amylo-barbitone flooded in him, and it was lost in the endless Siberian night.

The prisoner was carried from the cell block tied in a bundle of bedding. Two cars, both official black Volgas, had been parked outside and he was placed in the boot of the second car. Four of the Omon troops climbed inside. A few minutes later their commander followed them out of the cell block; with him was another officer, who wore an

MVD general's greatcoat and astrakhan hat. This was General Sokolnikov.

The two men walked in silence across the compound. When they reached the cars, Sokolnikov was the first to speak and he spoke in evident anger. 'He's still alive, Colonel Medved? He must be delivered *alive*. You know that.'

Colonel Medved removed his glasses to brush away a speck of snow. 'I have my orders,' he told the General. 'Your part is finished. What happens next is no concern of yours.'

'I am still in authority here and I don't like this business. Such measures should have a formal basis. I take no responsibility for this mad action.' He pointed to the black Volga in which the prisoner had been dumped. 'He's an American citizen. We are not at war yet. I advise you to be circumspect.'

Medved smiled. 'I have my orders,' he repeated.

'No mistakes,' the General said as Medved turned to go. 'Too much is at stake.'

'Goodnight, General,' Medved replied, then hesitated and turned to face Sokolnikov once more. 'Maybe you know *too* much about what is at stake, General Sokolnikov, to afford such attitudes.' He extended a gloved hand and brushed away a few flakes of snow which had settled on one of the General's braided epaulettes. 'Russia is at war: a secret war, still; but war nonetheless. Those of us privileged to serve the new Russia at such a time must be grateful for the opportunity.' A bleak smile crossed his face. 'I shall note the fact that you do not feel thus privileged. Goodnight, General,' he repeated, and climbed in the car.

'I do not need lessons in service to the Motherland from you!' Sokolnikov shouted, swearing under his breath as the Volga's doors slammed and it began to move off, leaving him to turn and tramp back to the compound.

The two black Volgas slowly pulled out of the compound's heavy outer doors, wheels crunching over the new snow. They drove through the city centre and out on to the main highway north. Then they sped on for six hours, stopping twice. Each time they stopped Medved had one of the men open the boot and check that the contents were still alive. The second time, the prisoner was groaning. He was returning to consciousness.

'Shall I give him another shot, sir?' the soldier asked Colonel Medved. 'To keep him quiet?'

'No point. We'll be at the changeover in half an hour. Then he'll need to be awake.'

The other man grinned. 'Awake to watch his own funeral arranged, sir?'

Medved leered at his subordinate. 'Don't let your zeal get the better of you,' he mumbled. 'Now let's get going; we're already late.'

They climbed back in as the engines returned to life, snarling on their diet of 76-octane petrol. Then the two black cars, grimed with the filth of Russian roads, set off again. There'd been no more snowfalls in the night and they were able to make up time, the Volgas running at a steady eighty kilometres an hour down the ribbon of white that slashed through the endless forest.

As light crept like a ghost over the taiga, at last they came to a turning – a narrow, concrete-paved track, closely bordered by impenetrable forest. It was six-thirty in the morning. The two cars crept down the track, the sun rising in front of them and gilding the silent, frost-rimed ranks of birch and pine. Other than occasional black-and-grey Siberian crows wheeling overhead, there was no sign of life.

They came to a clearing and stopped. At the far end of the clearing a small stockade enclosed two or three huts. Smoke was visible rising in vertical columns from the chimneys. The columns reached treetop height and then pancaked out in a horizontal smear.

The prisoner, hands bound to his ankles, was thrown out on to the frozen ground, and left. He was conscious and groaned intermittently, but no one paid any attention. There was no way to escape and nowhere to run to.

Some dogs in the settlement barked as the stockade gates opened and two men appeared. Wearing furs and the thick felt boots called *valenki* which are impervious to the deepest cold, each man carried two double-barrelled shotguns. Behind them came a small woman, pulling a sled on a string. On the sled were several bags and a cardboard box.

Medved shook the hand of the first man, an old hunter with the appearance of a Kalmyk. The hunter was smoking a *papiros*: the kind of short, pungent cigarette with its cardboard tube over an inch long traditionally beloved by Russian workers.

'Where's the *Gazik*?' Medved asked.

'Coming, Colonel.' The hunter pointed to the stockade from which a giant truck was lumbering. The truck was a three-tonne off-road vehicle, with enormous wheels more than two metres in diameter on its three axles. The cab was painted military green. Behind it an aluminium personnel cabin had been mounted.

'Your driver knows where to go?' Medved asked. 'We leave immediately.'

'Don't worry, Colonel. He knows.'

So saying, he handed Medved a gun, giving the other three to one of Medved's men. 'These are size twelve cartridges,' he added, opening a box. 'And *these* are real elk-stoppers.' From a second box he produced a cartridge, pointing to its single flat bullet over a centimetre in width. 'It'll halt anything; knock down a tree for you. Illegal of course—' he smirked up at Medved. 'But they work!'

'I know,' Medved said, taking the box. 'Tell the woman to put the rest of the stuff in the truck, and we'll be going.'

'Semiransk airbase called,' the hunter said as Medved watched two of his troops levering the prisoner up into the truck.

'And?'

'They'll meet you in a Mi-8. Sasha, the driver, knows where. At four o'clock. That's all I know.'

Medved smiled. 'OK, Volodya,' he said. 'We'll be back this evening.' Something like a smile passed momentarily across his face. 'And have the sauna prepared. We'll stop the night here, most likely.'

'Yes, Colonel.'

Medved climbed in the cab, motioning one of the Omon troopers to join him. The lad, a tall, unsmiling, square-framed NCO in his early twenties, shouldered his carbine and swung lithely up to the truck. The driver at once crashed into gear and the vehicle moved slowly off, its drive train whining. It had rolled less than fifty metres down the concrete track when, without warning, the driver swung the wheel suddenly to the left and they lurched through a ditch and then plunged into the forest. There had seemed no trace of an entrance to a path and nor did they follow a visible trail – any bushes and saplings in the way were simply smashed down, the taller trees avoided as the vehicle spun in a crazy pirouette, but always coming back to the same compass bearing.

While they drove Medved gave the soldier instructions. The prisoner was to be kept alive and conscious to the end. 'If necessary, warm him up with vodka – but keep him sober. I want him to be aware of what's happening – and what is *going* to happen.' Medved was emphatic. 'And you can issue the squad with vodka now – not more than a hundred and fifty grammes each.'

The NCO nodded and pushed through the hatchway into the rear cabin, where the four guards were sitting round a small table bolted to the floor, playing cards and shouting above the drone of the engine. The NCO ordered two of the men to untie the prisoner, pick him up from the floor and handcuff him to a latticed bench at the rear of the cabin. The filthy cloths binding his bloody head were cut away and his legs and arms

22

freed. The prisoner was barely conscious and the NCO slapped his face twice, hard, to bring him round.

The six-wheel drive pulled the *Gazik* through the deep ruts and recesses of the forest floor, and the truck lumbered on unremittingly for several hours before it finally came crashing into a wide clearing and stopped.

On Medved's orders the prisoner was left inside the cabin while the squad took it in turns to scratch a shallow pit in the frozen ground on one side of the clearing. To pass the time Medved took the driver and two men to act as beaters, stationing himself a half kilometre west of the clearing and sending the beaters further into the forest. An hour of hallooing and crashing through the underbrush produced no game whatsoever – no white-haired Siberian hare, elk or wild boar.

At 3.30 the prisoner was brought from the truck and carried bodily across the clearing to a stand of linden trees at the far side, against one of which the Omon troops propped him, securing the handcuffs to a rope tied around the bole.

At 4.30, as the light began to fade, the NCO approached the prisoner and waved a bottle of strong *Sibirskaya* vodka in front of his face. 'Want some, American?' he asked. 'You'll perish in this cold.' He laughed, but when the prisoner said nothing the NCO seized his head from behind, forcing it back and upending the bottle into his mouth. 'Drink, American! Colonel's orders. You have to live till he says you die.'

The NCO was retrieving the bottle from the prisoner's mouth when the unmistakable clattering of an approaching helicopter was heard. The sound brought sudden activity, as the truck driver ran to his vehicle, fired the engine and drove it away from the clearing, whilst Medved lined his men up.

The helicopter – a military Mi-8 – landed in a hurricane of snow whipped from the surrounding trees by its rotors. The two men who emerged, one in civilian clothes and the other in the greatcoat of a two-star general, were accosted by Medved who went forward to meet them. His salute to the General was perfunctory to the point of insult.

'Where's Comrade Sakharinov?' he asked them.

'He won't be here,' one of the arrivals replied. 'You're to continue as ordered anyway.'

'I won't take responsibility without the personal decision of Sakharinov. I already stated that.'

'The prisoner is to be finished with, *now*. We're here to witness it. *Do it.*'

'Don't give me orders!' The man was his superior, but here in the taiga it had no significance, and perhaps nowhere in Medved's world did it signify. 'I have *one* leader,' he rasped.

'We have the *same* leaders,' the General said. 'The *same* mission. Your insubordinate attitude is becoming famous; you should be more careful.'

'You general-staff scum have brought the country to its knees,' Medved whispered, his face pale with anger. 'You can always join the American in the *same* grave, if you like, *Comrade* General.' He leaned towards the other man, who was suddenly silent, afraid. 'Now or later; but the day of reckoning will come.'

When he spoke again his pencil-line lips curled in scorn. 'We'll send you very far – as they say, where Makar keeps his flocks.' Medved's laugh was dry like a death rattle. 'One day soon.'

He turned on his heel and tramped through the snow to where the prisoner was tied. The superior he had threatened slumped as though unseen strings had been cut, then turned and walked slowly back to the Mi-8.

The prisoner's face was deathly pale under the clotted blood, his breathing stertorous from the effects of his ill-treatment. He was still propped up on the huge linden tree. Medved stood in front of him, loading an elk-stopper into his shotgun.

'Don't worry, American,' he hissed. 'You won't feel anything.' His smile was a line drawn on tracing paper. 'Goodbye, American.'

Medved fired once at close range. He watched the prisoner's head snap back, the blood spattering the snow behind.

It was enough. He never missed.

He whistled to his men. They quickly untied the body and threw it into the prepared grave – no more than a foot of dirt scratched out of the frozen ground. Then they threw down covering soil, snow, branches. They were all tired, cold, perhaps a little drunk despite Medved's iron discipline. It was time to go. The helicopter's blades were already thrashing the air; in a few seconds it was airborne, in another minute it had disappeared over the treeline.

Medved's truck ground into gear and lumbered off through the snow-filled trees.

It was already dusk; the Siberian days are short in winter. A deadly silence fell on the forest and snow began to drift down; isolated flakes at first, then a thickening stream. Night fell. The forest watched and waited. Time passed.

A light flickered fitfully, shining without warmth, illuminating nothing. It was something primordial, protozoan, an ersatz, glow-worm sheen.

24

Then this luminescence faded and the snow ceased falling. The night sky cleared; it grew colder. High in the trees a branch snapped under the burden of snow, then another. The forest slept, but within it something else persisted. It was as if a terrible pain now filled its world, a sudden agony flooding horizon to horizon.

The protozoan wriggled, a trace in the dark. A soundless voice uttered: *I am between life and death. I am in the antechamber. I have dreamed of this. A dream of some ancient book. There, it is stated that the dreams that occur in the antechamber are only illusions . . .*

Another voice answered, calling a name – a woman's voice, soothing, kindly: 'Douglas. Douglas. Where are you? Douglas . . .'

Darkness invades me, seeping through wounds, battening inside my skull . . . I am not dead.

The prisoner's hand clawed the frozen earth, a broken thing grasping a pebble, a twig. Something soft, foreign, invasive, oozed up into the mouth from below, and the prisoner recognized his own tongue, probing the palate and teeth from the inside.

Then the prisoner was awake. There was no transition. Suddenly he was conscious, lucid, aware in every faculty and sense.

Feeling returned in stabbing waves of pain, crisscrossing his body pinioned under the earth and snow. His tongue was constricted in his own throat, bloated and swollen like a dead, sour fish. The pain knifed through his chest, a fire seared his eyes; cold tore at his hands and feet. The prisoner felt the earth groan and throb and roar beneath, felt the weight of snow and loose soil above; felt the silent enormity of Siberia everywhere around.

Hysterical, silent laughter rose from somewhere within. He lay still until the pounding of his heart slowly subsided. Then he thrust a hand *upwards*. Soil fissured a centimetre from his face; his breathing roared in his ears and when he forced himself to stop and to lie completely still, he could hear the crackle of the tiny ice granules frozen round his eyelashes.

In that shallow place, he lay savouring the pain of breathing, the pain of *being*. And all the while, the soundless voice continued to prompt: *Is it a predicament – life? Or are its predicaments only its attributes?*

Of course! Life stands alone, great, glorious, invincible, miraculous. And the prisoner was alive, had survived the unsurvivable. Now he was suffocating, not with fear but with excitement.

I do not know where I am. I am lying in a shallow grave God knows where, frozen, wounded, in a Siberian winter, and yes, I am not dead, but I am dying.

I am far from life.

Far from the assassins. Lie still. Here there is warmth, safety.

The prisoner moved his head, stuck one arm through the snow-and-earth covering which had insulated him in the same way as a bear's lair of leaves, earth and snow conserves its body heat for its six months of hibernation.

He pushed aside the debris, his heart pounding like a cannon.

One eye was blind, one clotted with dirt, both stinging. But he could see an indigo sky studded with solemn stars, untwinkling in the clear Siberian air.

Yes, he was alive! But cold, small rivulets from the ocean of Siberian cold crawled over him. Frost crackled in the hairs of his nostrils.

It must be twenty, thirty below, the prisoner said to himself.

I will die if I stay here. I will freeze in minutes if I leave.

Leave or stay?

The prisoner debated the question. Perhaps he blacked out, for suddenly he blinked and the stars had moved on, pinioned in their silent orbits, brushing the velvet sky.

Leave. Suddenly, galvanically, he rose up from the grave.

Leaf mould, rotten earth, mud and slime, thawed by his body heat, all cascaded to the ground.

The prisoner stood up.

Violent pains scalpelled his midriff. A star exploded behind his eyes, as fierce, biting pain slashed through the gaping wound above his temple. He gasped, and fell to his knees. The snow was dry as icing sugar. His hands had no feeling, unless burning ice constitutes a feeling.

I am going to die in this place.

He retched, violently, and a sour smell of bile and blood reeked in his nostrils. His head pitched forward into the snow. He could not remain still without certain death coming in minutes, seconds. But nor could he move. He fought the ache in his limbs, fought to still the shivering which seized him with such violence it prevented all other movement.

Again, he was sick; cataclysmic retching that wracked his body and threw him on the ground.

Get up. Now. Up – the voice told him.

The prisoner stumbled to his feet again. OK, now what?

Now, walk.

He put a foot forward and sank like a weighted rag into deep snow.

Up. Get up! The prisoner rose, walked. His shivering was uncontrollable, it was not shivering, it was a seizure, epilepsy.

A three-quarter moon had risen. The clearing was full of pale light. The prisoner could see the linden tree where they had tied him.

26

In summer this place must be a dream. Pale yellow linden blossoms, the air full of fragrance.

He heard the voice again, a woman's voice – one that he knew – and for a moment was back in a cool summer meadow, listening to his wife, his lost Lisa, laughing, calling to him.

The prisoner blinked fiercely and looked around. Every movement was agony. The blood above his temple had frozen to his skin in fragments that split and fell like crumbs when he turned his head. The fresh fall of snow had hidden most traces of what had happened that day, but even in the moonlight the direction taken by the *Gazik* was clear enough.

The prisoner fumbled by the base of the linden tree and found what he sought – a three-quarters full bottle of *Sibirskaya*. Too cold to drink, of course. But he had a precious item in his pockets. Trembling violently, he carefully put down the bottle, and began searching. The item was in his left trouser pocket, but his left hand was swollen and one finger broken. It took some minutes to retrieve what he sought, but at last he pulled it free.

'Kempinski Hotels,' he could read even in the moonlight. There were two matches left in the book.

The prisoner began to look around for fir cones and tinder: temperatures of minus 20 and more simply freeze-dried wood. He slowly built a bonfire, sprinkled half the viscid fluid over it and struck one of the matches. The fire flared at once and the resin-filled pine twigs soon began to burn fiercely. The prisoner had nothing better to do, so continued his labour, throwing larger and larger bundles on the flames, even wet logs which hissed and spat. He then warmed the bottle, and drank what was left in two gulps.

When morning came, the prisoner was still alive – just. His body was slumped before the embers, from which a column of smoke rose to the treeline, hit warmer air and pancaked out in a thick smear of smoke visible for miles around.

The prisoner was sleeping. In his dreams he heard the rumbling of vehicles, heard shouts and doors slamming. Someone touched him, was picking him up. Gently picking him up.

This is not a dream.

He awoke, thrashing in blind terror.

'Easy! Easy!' a voice said; then, 'Ivanich! Come and help!'

More hands gripping. Resist!

But he was blind. With his right hand, the prisoner tried to brush open the good eye. His hand was a log, senseless, numb. His eyes hurt. He could not see.

'Easy!' The voice was imperative.

The eye opened and through a yellow film he saw – they had returned! Again, the *Gazik*! Again, burly men in white paratroop survival uniforms . . . The prisoner began to thrash, to shout, in English: 'Leave me! *Leave me!* I don't *want* to die!'

It took three men to hold him still, as they half dragged, half carried him to the vehicle. Then the prisoner saw the white roundel and red cross blazoned on the side.

They had sent an *ambulance* for him!

Strong hands gripped him, lifted him. The prisoner slid back into the dark place. The hands were attending to him, removing his clothing. He was in the cabin, lying on a stretcher, hearing fragments of conversation: *'Ivanich, I don't believe this is the man . . . I told you when you turned this way – we should be two kilometres further east . . .'*

The next thing the prisoner heard was the roaring of the motor; he felt the *Gazik* start to move.

Something pricked his skin. He tried to look but his eyes wouldn't open. Again he felt the needle.

Warmth was flooding his arm, his side, his whole body. His limbs stretched out, relaxed. He heard a woman's voice, far off but clear and penetrating. It calmed him, but he could not say from where the voice came or whose it was. He smiled; he knew it was summer, again.

The voice said: *'It is necessary to live. To live.'*

Again he smelt the citrus scent of linden blossom.

Then the prisoner felt nothing, knew nothing. He sank deep into the dark place.

CHAPTER 2

What woke Renard was the fire which snaked in his guts and scorched his throat.

He yelled at the top of his voice and a frog croaked somewhere. After a while a bored-looking auxiliary came to him, urine bottle in one hand and fresh serum pouch in the other. She hooked the pouch on to the drip, checked the catheter in his arm, lifted the bedclothes and helped him with the urine bottle.

He emitted the snake, scale by serrated scale. It took a long time and when he finished he was sweating.

What he really needed now was a drink. An ice-cold six-pack of Beck's would do.

'Beer,' he croaked.

The auxiliary smiled grimly. She gave him two pills the size of dimes and a glass of pink fluid which smelt faintly of camphor and of oil of cloves and which tasted like brine. 'Your kidneys are a mess,' she said before she left.

Renard lay still and gazed for a while at the whitewashed ceiling, wondering where he was – in a hospital, or a hole in the ground? Then he fell asleep.

Next morning a busy, handsome female doctor arrived and told him his kidneys would recover from the effects of exposure. She changed the bandages that swaddled his head and smiled sympathetically when he asked where he was.

'You really don't know?'

'No.'

'You're in Varta, in the geological hospital.' She watched him go stiff. 'Surprised?'

'Only to be alive.' Renard was no longer delirious. Now he wanted to be inconspicuous and avoid questions. He waited silently while she plucked stitches from his face and made encouraging but noncommital sounds.

He was blind in one eye now, she said, but they would see the whole story in a few days when all the stitches were out. She was intense, with a smile that warmed like spring sunshine. He would have an interesting scar, she said and told him he was luckier/stronger/more foolish than he had a right to be, and more besides.

The doctor left and Renard lay quietly, in wait for the small hospital sounds of clattering trolleys and loud far-away voices. Days had passed and he had no idea why he was still alive, who had saved him and for what?

Then Olga Ivanovna – that was her name – came back with a consultant and they took away the last stitches, cracking open the encrusted lids of his eye like the halves of a walnut. He could see with it! He thanked her and meant it. She stopped by the door as they were leaving and came back in the little room, waving her colleagues on ahead of her, to smile more encouragement at him and to say: 'You'll be fine now, Mr Shadrin.'

She was tall, slender, grave and slow-moving, a woman in her early thirties and in the prime of life. He wondered why she called him by someone else's name and told her that he still didn't remember anything. 'How did I get here?'

'You were delirious when you were brought in, but that's normal. The degree of exposure you suffered was enough to kill most people; and you've been seriously wounded as well.'

Then she surprised him by saying: 'For a geologist you ought to know better. That kind of behaviour is simply shameful.'

'What kind of behaviour?'

'You really don't remember?' She studied his face, and told him how he was injured in a shooting accident on a drunken hunting party. 'You are lucky to be alive,' she said. 'What saved you was the cold, which stopped the head-wound from haemorrhaging. Without that you would have bled to death. Now all you have to worry about is minor frostbite on your ears and nose, and on the left hand.'

Her eyes were honest, but the story was absurd. 'My hand hurts like hell,' he said and held it up.

'Apart from that, you have concussion, and general exposure symptoms. But they're the least of your worries. The main problem is the head-wound.'

'At least I'm not blind.'

'No, you're not. But you've lost a tear duct. That means your eye will water freely, for example when it's cold or windy. You were grazed by a large-calibre shell and you lost a lot of blood, but fortunately the physical damage is all on the surface.'

Renard grinned which felt like unzipping his face, winced and laughed: 'I'll cry more often, will I? Jesus, I'm in pain!'

She leaned over him, laughed too, and plumped his pillows. 'Don't be so cheerful, then,' she told him. 'It's indecent.'

'I'm sorry, but indecently cheerful is how you make me feel. I think I'm in love with you.'

'I get about a dozen half-crazy geologists a year, brought here from mountain tops, river bottoms and frozen tundra. That's what they all say when they find out they're alive.'

'Who was it that's supposed to have accidentally shot me? I don't even know that.'

'Your General Director, Grigory Schmidt I think he's called.' Olga Ivanovna made way for the orderly arriving with breakfast; she told him she would come back later, in the quiet hour.

Then she said: 'Schmidt has called several times. He'll be visiting you as soon as you feel up to it. You should rest now, and don't waste your energy worrying. You'll get all the explanations you need in good time.'

Renard was in a single-bed ward, bare apart from a small washstand with a mirror, a locker and one chair. There was no lock on the door, as far as he could see. When the orderly left he stumbled from the bed, went to the mirror and inspected himself. Most of his head and one eye was bandaged. A four- or five-day beard covered yellow skin that was stretched parchment tight over the skull. He was unrecognizable even to himself.

He picked up the aluminium clipboard from the footboard and sat on the bed to read his medical notes. 'Shadrin, Ivan I.' they were headed. 'Geologist. Varta Main Survey Administration. Passport No. X-635478-VB. Republic of Latvia.' Renard sat back down on the bed.

He thought he'd been hallucinating when he'd heard Olga call him by that name; but no, they really thought he was Shadrin. He put the clipboard down, crawled back under the covers and closed his eyes; he needed to think.

Stray words came drifting back from some deep place: '*Ivanich, I don't believe this is the man . . .*' His rescuers had been searching for someone else. They had found him instead, which was miraculous luck, considering the remoteness of his burial place. Unless the mistake had been made earlier? When Medved had brought him to where Shadrin was supposed to come, and had not.

They had wanted him to meet Shadrin, then. They had set something up, had dragged him all that way, and in the end they had failed.

Renard remembered the scene in the forest. Medved had been waiting for someone; in the end a helicopter had brought some go-betweens, but not whoever it was he was expecting. After that, Medved had shot him.

31

Most likely, they had tried to fool Shadrin into a meeting with Renard, and had failed. Renard was not surprised because Ivan Shadrin was a fiction, the man who never was. The last role played by the greatest Soviet spy: Ivars Latsis.

Ivars was the best, but he had been betrayed. So he'd had to break the rules and call for help; if it had been anyone else the call would have gone unheeded, but this was the operative known as 'Baltic Tsar'.

That was why Renard had come early to Varta, unprepared and against every professional instinct, only to be imprisoned and taken to the very point of death.

Now he was in hospital and, God knows how, with Latsis' own cover. His *blown* cover.

But what had happened to Latsis on the day Renard was himself shot and dumped? Had he escaped and gone to ground, in some unfathomable twist of circumstances which had led others to confuse their identities? Had he somehow led the rescuers to Renard?

They had never met and Renard wouldn't have known him if they'd stood at the same bus stop, but he and Latsis were alike – mirror-inverses in that infamous wilderness of mirrors. When had Latsis changed his mind?

One day he had turned against Moscow, had openly avowed the Nationalist cause and that was the beginning of the end; a lot of people knew it and said it, even in Moscow's cocktail circuits. They had tried to kill him then, when the Omon were already loose in the sandbagged streets of Riga, and Councils for National Salvation had begun sprouting in Latvia's retired Russian officers' clubs. Even before that, all kinds of folk who dreamed of one day living in those blessed three republics had begun to dig through the archives for evidence of Baltic ancestry, because everyone knew that in future you would have to prove a blood tie to be a citizen. And that was in 1989, when talk of secession from the USSR was indictable, and even singing hymns in a public place in the Latvian language meant jail. But the centre held as long as the dark forces did; only when Ivars Latsis cut the first threads, and the *Baltikum* unravelled, did the whole thing start to come apart.

But Latsis had done more. And perhaps the most astonishing thing: he was among the first to understand the meaning of Molniya and the threat it posed. So that's why he'd assumed the role of 'Shadrin' as cover, and come to Varta to uncover the secret behind the Molniya conspiracy.

And he had been betrayed. Renard didn't waste much time speculating by whom, although his list of candidates was short enough.

Anyone could argue that the leak was on Latsis' side, but Renard doubted that. Latsis had used Sobor – old KGB hands they might be, but they were insiders who knew the rules and played by them. And they were people for whom there was no retreat. Latsis' fate proved it. If they counted the traitor among them, it was through pure carelessness.

The list of remaining candidates boiled down to the President, the Secretary of State, the Director of the CIA, and the three other people who knew in detail about the operation against Molniya. About Renard's mission. Of those three others, one was his liaison officer in Moscow. That was Claud Perkins. The two others were Bob Hill and Paul Gregory, both at base, at Langley. If one of them was the traitor, it no longer mattered because Renard was now officially dead, invisible, alone.

Renard's room was one cell of sickness in a vast 800-bed hospital, which served the needs of more than 30,000 employees of Varta Geological Administration and their families. Its routines continued, touching him when they needed to. He made friends with Olga Ivanovna but did not learn much from her. He got better, slowly he thought; remarkably swiftly it seemed to her. He continued to reflect on what had happened and to wait for the inevitable next development – rearrest, or worse.

Locate Molniya. Acquire the Molniya metacodes. That had been the mission. Find out what the damn thing was, what it was supposed to do, how it fitted in with the re-emergence of Russia which gathered pace every day. Could it be the biggest thing and the worst thing which had happened to the world since Hiroshima? After all it had happened in a Russia whose re-emergence had suddenly begun to frighten the pants off people. That new Russia had turned out to be, not the West's grateful handmaiden, supplier of markets and raw materials, which the pundits had proposed. That new Russia was a wild and wilful hooligan.

Anything would help, they had told him at Langley. Any scrap of data he could dredge up, because the blunders of five years' fatal misconstruction of events in Russia had left the West flat on its back. Ignorant. Blind. Unable to respond to the most miserable tinpot Balkan pan-Slav eruption, no more than a boil on Europe's rump. Unable to answer the frothings of mad Russian fascists who threatened a new World War and screamed about new secret weapons. Because of Western pundits, policy-makers and think-tanks who couldn't see the wood for the trees, the poor slobs at the sharp end had been left punching shadow-men in the dark. Renard knew that the Russia they all debated 'losing' had never existed in the first place. He had seen too much of the debate – of his masters' hubris. They trumpeted their victory in the Cold War and didn't see that all that had been achieved was the releasing of Russia from constraints which it had been the work of forty years to install. And *he*

33

had seen too much of Russia, too, not to be afraid of the place. Had seen the strengths as well as the weaknesses, saw how those strengths were going to be directed – and how the Russia of whole past epochs of expansion would live again.

When the first glimmerings about Molniya came filtering through, the reaction was a sensation. But the old Russia hands had uttered warnings enough: unheeded of course, until fear had become fashionable again, and the handful of remaining veterans like Renard were given new tasks and thrown pell-mell into the fray.

Locate Molniya. And then, should it be deemed necessary and/or feasible (feasibility was what Renard mainly doubted – he was sure it would prove necessary), prepare for a combined British–American Special Forces' assault on the Molniya base.

Military operations in Russian territory. Renard could remember the questions on the faces around the table the first time the notion was floated. *How? Where?*

'The Semiransk ice-rim,' Paul Gregory, Langley's one-man database on all the nastiest secrets in the Russian armoury, had informed them. 'Semiransk – that's where you'd have to go in.'

Renard also recalled the look on Admiral Duncan's face. *Not quite copy-book*, it had said, or something like that. No officer in the US Navy suggested attacking Russia. You were inoculated against it while still at West Point.

'Rendezvous with a submarine-borne assault group about here, at Maly Utinsk or thereabouts,' Paul had continued with the suicidal relentlessness which the three of them – he, Paul and Bob Hill – had grown to share. 'That'd be the way.' The Secretary of State had actually slopped his coffee at that.

Henry Washington had grown a sneer as wide as the Grand Canyon. 'May one know why *that* option is favoured,' he'd cracked his face to say. 'I mean, why not just nuke the whole North Pole?'

The Secretary of State had withered Henry with a look which said: 'Don't humour them; this isn't the funny farm. Not yet.'

But Bob said, since Henry had mentioned it, a nuclear attack on Molniya was something thought had been given to. He considered it was categorically impossible and for two reasons. He mentioned them and astoundingly they had nothing to do with political factors, like for instance how any President would get Congress to agree, let alone such secondary considerations as Nato, the UN, the SALT and START treaties, the President's limited power to make war, international reaction, whatever.

34

Obviously Bob Hill felt all that didn't count for much if you happened to believe that Molniya was real. Bob did believe and repeated that one day, soon, the West would have to deal with it or go under. Simple as that. It was ironic, he went on, that Russia's ICBM forces were now a defensive shield around Molniya. So a strike might produce a counter-strike. But there was more. Even if you attacked with a very low-yield warhead, say twenty or thirty kilotons, Hiroshima-sized, you might end up doing more than just destroy Molniya, which, Bob had said, moving the electronic pointer on the overhead projection of the Arctic, lay somewhere in the lee of the Semiransk peninsula. *We think.*

Renard had witnessed a collective dropping of jaws when they saw it. Semiransk turned out to be a sort of finger sticking out of the Russian landmass deep into the Arctic Ocean. *The Semiransk peninsula, they were told, is sitting on the world's largest reservoir of natural gas. It could blow up, and blow up half the polar ice cap with it.*

More than twenty per cent of the world's natural gas lies close to the surface. For decades the Russians tried to figure out how to take out the gas, but the peninsula rises only a few metres above sea level. Pumping out the gas might cause it to sink beneath the Arctic Sea. No one had figured out the consequences, but they would be pretty serious. Bombing the place would be even worse. The sudden release of such a colossal quantity of methane into the upper atmosphere would catalyze the process of global warming. And it might melt the ice cap straight off. Half of Britain and lowland Europe would disappear under the Atlantic Ocean for a start.

So the nukes were off. Even Molniya didn't warrant melting the polar ice cap, flooding Europe and precipitating global warming overnight. And that left Renard and the Baltic freedom group Sobor and the commandos, unless someone thought of a better way. No one had done.

Before anything else happened, Renard had been supposed to go and set things up in Varta. That meant dovetailing with the guys at Sobor, where things had somehow recently become more opaque instead of more transparent. Something was wrong somewhere, and Renard believed that the problem was in Langley or at State, and nowhere else. Sobor knew there was a leak because they were being hunted even harder than before and as a result they had quite naturally gone deeper underground. That was reasonable enough. As far as Renard could see, his own credentials, however, were still good. That was another compelling reason to come over himself and stand amongst them like a hostage. Then perhaps they would start to communicate again, although it would take time to rebuild trust.

All that had led straight to Renard's second task: acquire the meta-codes which were the keys to Molniya, to its use. The metacodes were equivalent to the famous briefcase which everywhere accompanies both American and Russian leaders, and which contains the launch instructions for each side's vast nuclear arsenal. The metacodes were also the keys to understanding, at last, the nature of Molniya: its capabilities, its operational parameters. Its targets.

Sobor, silent for so many months on the subject, had suddenly come to life, and had offered this material. The price tag was five million dollars. That was what Sobor would have to pay its sources. The amount was small in relation to the value of the product. For possession of the Molniya metacodes might provide not only the means to understand Molniya, but also to control it. No one knew for sure, but the chance was there and had to be taken. That was the enticement which had encouraged Renard to rush to Varta on a fool's errand to save Latsis. But all that was the past, over and done with. Whatever had happened to Latsis had happened.

Renard lay long hours thinking about it all while he watched the sunlight creep over the whitewashed walls of his small room. There had not been much sunlight in Varta jail.

That second night he slept deeply, but just as he was stumbling into wakefulness he heard Olga Ivanovna's agreeable voice say 'Let him rest' to the nurse who accompanied her. 'Today he'll get MVD visitors, I'm afraid.'

It was time to act, and Renard began to make his preparations.

Later in the afternoon Olga Ivanovna returned alone to his bedside, as she had promised.

Renard, propped on pillows, watched the low sun paint the wall primrose behind her. He said he felt better. She smiled and promised to arrange a massage: 'You Balts are like Americans – you don't understand the importance of getting the salts out of your joints. That's why you start to fur up before you're forty.'

Renard studied the clear skin, the eyes which were brown and warm, and asked her when the MVD would arrive.

'They came this morning. I sent them away – you need more rest.'

'You sent them away?' Renard said foolishly.

'I told them you were alive and – turn over, please – that was mainly what they wanted to hear. Did you want to see them? You should certainly file a complaint. Did that hurt? I'll help you if you like.'

'Thanks. I would.'

'You ought to.' She peeled the bandage from his head. 'Why let them get away with it, after all? No infection here.'

'Why are you so sure they'll be on my side? What if they're not? If they want to cover up the scandal? Then what?'

She stopped to look at him. 'Anything's possible, I agree. The bad old days have come back, without even the hypocrisy which used to smooth things over a bit. But I don't think you need to worry. Schmidt and the MVD colonel seem seriously concerned about you. They're good chaps, I'd say.'

'Perhaps they're fattening me up like a Christmas goose. I'm a Latvian; they can do what they like with me if they want to use the situation.'

'Meaning what?'

'What happened – when Schmidt fired at me, I mean – perhaps was no accident. I'm here on a contract; Latvian geologists have always worked here – we know the territory and they know us. There never used to be problems, but there are now, of course. Every time something goes wrong for Russia in the Baltic, they start looking for scapegoats.'

'I've heard some stories, it's true. Since we stopped supplying Latvia with energy—'

'That, and a million other things.'

'Then why work here?' Olga asked. She sat on the cane chair by the bed. She was serious; she liked him and she didn't give a damn about phoney patriotism. It occurred to Renard that he'd never met a Russian woman of child-bearing age who did.

He laughed sourly. 'I need the money. The alternative is to be an unemployed Latvian geologist. This is all I know.'

'Like lots of other homeless geologists I've met,' she said. 'I understand, but I think you're paranoid. The worst that can happen is they'll ask you to go home.'

'The best that can happen is if you ask me home.'

'Pardon?'

'I've been watching you. Professionally.'

'And?'

'The alluvial basin is broad and fecund. The foothills are flowing and svelte. And I want to put my hands on the peaks. They are studded with white quartz and pink jasper.'

She laughed out loud. 'You are the craziest yet!'

'I want to make a few seismic soundings, with your permission.'

'And if you're arrested?'

'I'll have some memories.'

'Look, I have a girlfriend at MVD headquarters. I'll make a few calls, see what I can find out. If things do look poor, we'll just have to get you out of here, that's all.' She was blushing now. 'In any case, I can discharge you into the care of a competent person now. You're well enough.'

'Are you competent?'

'I doubt it. You'll have to find out.' She stood up to go, straightening her white dress. 'I hope you know what you're doing when you make your test drillings. I'm not so young any more.'

'Now you're talking crazy.'

At two the next afternoon Olga came to him again. 'They're here,' she told him. 'Colonel Travkin and another MVD guy, I mean. Don't worry – I checked up. You're not at risk.' She left and returned in moments with two uniformed MVD officers.

'I've told them not to tire you,' she said to Renard as she went away.

The senior officer wished him a good morning and introduced himself as Colonel Leonid Travkin, of Varta MVD. He ordered the second man to wait outside the door against interruption. Travkin sat down on the chair by the bed, placing his Colonel's cap with its shiny red badge and sweat-seamed headband on the little table.

'How do you feel?' he asked Renard. His smile had a policeman's solicitude, the kind which is available to the outraged guilty party equally as much as it is to the fearful innocent.

'Better – a little.'

'Good. Frankly, we've been more than worried.' Travkin peeled off his black leather gloves and placed them carefully by the hat. 'We know more or less what happened.'

'I don't remember much myself.'

'Perhaps that's for the best. Really, Schmidt thought you were dead. It's a tremendous relief that you're not. None of us wanted a court case or any noise at all.'

Renard said, 'Please, come to the point. There's no need to play games with me. If you want me, here I am.'

Travkin gave him a penetrating look. 'If we want you? We want you to get better, that's all. They said you couldn't remember much and I see it's true. I'm very sorry you're so ill. It is a concern to us – we don't want to reinforce the negative image this region enjoys in the outside world. We are trying to civilize our oilmen, but it isn't easy!'

Travkin pulled out a pack of Marlboro. 'Do you mind?'

'Yes, actually, I'm allergic to tobacco smoke.'

'OK.' He put the pack away. 'Of course, nothing can put right the wrong that has been done to you. However, there is the possibility of compensation, and I should like to discuss this with you.'

Travkin looked expectant, but Renard was silent. He shrugged his shoulders. 'That's not all. The Varta Region Administration will formally apologize to you.'

Renard was inscrutable.

'Do you object to compensation? You want to sue?' Travkin asked nervously.

Renard saw the policeman's stolid indifference swing open like a door and he glimpsed the greed within. 'Tell me what form will the Region's apology take?' he asked. 'If I sue, it won't just be me, it'll be the Latvian government you'll be up against.'

Travkin smiled. 'That won't do at all, obviously. We have good relations with the Latvian Republic now, and neither you nor I want to jeopardize them, I'm sure. We must find an amicable way out.'

'I've been shot and beaten, and I'm lucky to be alive. What's more I've lost all my papers. It's not my main worry, of course. I should like to go home, frankly, but . . .'

Travkin said, 'You don't mean to press charges, then? Against Schmidt?'

'It depends on what I'm offered.'

'Your helpful attitude will be reported.' He leaned over the bed. 'Confidentially, I'm sure you will be satisfied with the proposal.'

'Make your offer. I'm tired and I'd like to get this over with.'

'I'm coming to that, my dear fellow. But do you need anything? Tea, perhaps?'

'Tea, yes, tea would be good.'

Travkin spent a moment in conversation with the MVD man outside the door, before returning to Renard's bedside.

'Ivan, let me tell you the situation as we understand it.' Travkin twisted his gloves like the throats of enemies. When he spoke again his eyes focused on an invisible speck on the floor. 'It was a hunting party that went wrong. Nothing more than that. Am I right? Everyone was drunk, *everyone*. Yes?'

'No.'

The gloves splayed out and were placed slowly on the hat. 'I'm not implying anything. You can hear me out. It's a question of how we make amends, given all the particularities. A wrong has been done and you—'

'A wrong bloody well *has* been done! The question is, how will I be compensated?'

'I'm authorized to make you an offer.' Travkin's eyes slewed round unwillingly. It was clear to Renard that the man had been given a budget to buy his silence – God alone knew why, of course – and wanted the percentage which any fixer, *commerçant*, or even passer-by, feels entitled to abstract from such a transaction. So this was a negotiation, and from the look of Travkin the budget was big. That meant someone in a very high eyrie was looking down on them.

'The amount would not be negotiable, of course. Understand me, please. *I* do not decide.'

'Tell me about it. Come to the point.'

'The offer is one year's salary, in cash, now, if you'll sign a disclaimer and leave Varta immediately you're well enough. Agreed?' Travkin gripped Renard's top sheet tightly between the forefinger and thumb of his left hand and peered at him. 'Agreed?' he repeated.

Renard looked sideways at him. He hated hasty hagglers. 'In principle I might agree. But what constitutes a year's salary? In *this* context, I mean.'

Travkin exhaled. He was about to speak when Olga Ivanovna came in with a tray bearing tea, and biscuits which had the hammer-and-sickle logo baked on as decoration. 'Of course. Tell me, how does forty million roubles sound?' he said when Olga had left.

It didn't sound much to Renard, but he supposed that the equivalent of $20,000 might seem reasonable to a Latvian geologist, and that's what he was meant to be.

'I need to think,' he said. 'I need to consult my government.'

Travkin reiterated, 'The offer is conditional on there being no noise. I already said that. The money is available now.' Renard watched his hand tremble. 'Think about it.'

Renard *was* thinking. 'And I already mentioned to you, I'm unhappy. I've been mistreated. I've lost my papers. I'll need something . . .'

'Don't worry, that's nothing. We'll give you papers which will get you to Moscow at any rate, and a plane ticket of course.'

'Tell me, Travkin, what will the agreed version be? What will the disclaimer say?'

'That you were on a hunting party which went wrong. Schmidt fired and you were accidentally hit. You ran into the forest – probably some kind of delirium made you do it. You'd just been shot. They couldn't find you. Later Schmidt had an ambulance sent – expecting the worst. By a miracle, you were still alive; mistakes were made, but that's what matters. Now you'll go home, for a rest. As far as anyone knows, your post here is open, the Concern will be waiting for you to return.'

'Which presumably I won't.'

'Good God, no. You'll never return. One more thing. You know Schmidt. He's a cautious man. He wants to meet you one last time. Just to hear you say to his face that bygones will be bygones and – to shake hands on it. Agreed?'

Olga Ivanovna came in again as he spoke. 'He's still too weak for this,' she told Travkin with smouldering eyes. 'Don't prolong this meeting, please.'

'We need him to meet one more person. Just for a minute,' Travkin was saying. 'Then that's the end. We won't need to bother your patient again.'

Renard was looking more than bothered. Unlike Travkin, Schmidt – whoever he was – knew the 'real' Shadrin. Alias Ivars Latsis. Renard did not want to face him. Not yet at any rate.

'No,' Olga said, reading Renard's eyes. 'That will not be possible. You must come back tomorrow.'

Travkin started to complain: 'We've come a long way, and we're speaking of a General Director—'

'No, and that's final. *Tomorrow*.'

'Very well, then. It is most inconvenient.'

'I have my orders, the same as you.'

Travkin was defeated. He accepted the situation, apologized and left, not however without pointedly telling Olga Ivanovna that *he* was the custodian of Mr Shadrin's future, not her. To Renard he could not resist sending a look full of secret anguish. Renard wondered how much the budget really was. Fifty million? Eighty?

After he was gone, Olga adjusted Renard's bandages and gave him a vitamin injection. Then she massaged him asleep, using an emollient pungent with birch and eucalyptus oil. He slept for more than sixteen hours. In the morning she came back and gave him two more injections. 'I'm discharging you this afternoon,' she told him. She was very close to him and for the first time he smelt her properly.

When Travkin came back he was alone. Schmidt was a big man; he didn't like waiting around in hospital corridors for a subordinate. He had returned in anger to his *Kombinat*. But Renard had agreed to meet Schmidt and that was enough to satisfy Travkin.

'All's well that ends well,' he told Renard. 'I'll bring the papers and the money, and if you like I can even arrange a new Latvian passport for you.'

'A *Latvian* passport? You can do that?'

'No problem.'

41

'Agreed, then,' Renard said.

Travkin left.

It was 7 November – the anniversary of the 1917 Revolution and still celebrated as a public holiday in Varta at least. In the afternoon, Olga Ivanovna came to take Renard home. 'You can leave everything here,' she told him. 'I'm only *informally* discharging you.'

They went to her two-room flat near the hospital. She fed him with black bread, smoked sausage, pickled wild mushrooms – fragrant white *boletus edulis* from the local forest – caviar and champagne. Then they went to bed.

Somewhere in the middle of it all, Renard asked about her family and she told him, 'I live by myself, except for the cat. My husband was killed eighteen months ago in an accident. He was a geologist, too. After his death I thought about going back home to Voronezh, but there's nothing there for me. So I'm still here. God knows why.'

They drank more champagne and talked a great deal, about her life and his. But she refused to listen to his would-be geologist's stories – she had heard them all, she said. 'This flat is still stuffed with memorabilia I can well do without,' she explained. 'But perhaps you'll come again and see for yourself. I should like to look after you till you get better.' Renard took her brown kindly hands and kissed them and said thank you, he'd like that.

He slept till late and she woke him when she returned from her morning tour of duty. 'Travkin will call again today; I guess you'd better be there.'

CHAPTER 3

Travkin brought with him two brown cardboard suitcases, a cloth bag and two envelopes. He gave one envelope to Renard. In it was the disclaimer summarizing the alleged events which had led to his being hospitalized. There were two copies, both already signed by 'A.V. Schmidt, General Director, Varta Neftegazprom', and witnessed by Colonel Travkin.

It described in police language the accidental shooting of Ivan Shadrin during a hunting party in the northern forests of Varta Region, one which had gone tragically wrong. All in less than one page of typing. But Schmidt's acceptance of responsibility was an indication of the weight of whoever was behind the whole thing – the 'oil generals' were the independent-minded bastions of local power.

'What's in the other envelope?' Renard asked Travkin, who opened it and spilled out a pile of notes and a Latvian passport. Travkin counted out: $20,000 in $100 dollar bills.

Renard opened the passport. He looked at the blurred picture. The face would not stand out in a crowd. That was the mark of Latsis' trade-craft: Shadrin was inconspicuous. The features were not Slavonic and bore some resemblance to Renard's own – wide-set eyes, a firm jaw line. But Shadrin was younger than himself.

'Where did you get the photograph?' he asked.

'Copy of a copy; it came from your personnel file.'

'It looks doctored.'

'It needed doctoring,' Travkin grinned. 'It's ten years out of date, I guess.'

'I'd like a sight of my personnel file. For old times' sake.'

'You've got some balls, asking for that kind of favour. But—' an idea occurred to Travkin. 'You're disappearing, anyway. I guess that losing your file might have some advantages, actually.' He paused. 'You've got money. You can pay. So it can be arranged.'

'How much?'

'A thousand bucks. Probably. We'll have to see right a few people in the MVD registry.'

43

Renard looked at the address: *3 Altmanis Street, Riga, Republic of Latvia.* 'OK,' he said. 'I agree.' He put the passport on the other side of the bed.

'Not so fast, *gospodin*. I'll take that with me. First you must sign. Then you get the papers.'

'Don't worry, I'll sign. When can I leave?'

'Whenever you like. Tomorrow.'

'Decided.'

Travkin gave him a hard look. 'Why be in such a hurry? You're not well.'

'Get me on a plane.'

Travkin suddenly stood, as though making up his mind. 'OK. I can understand how you must feel. You'll be on the morning flight to Moscow.'

'Bring me the ticket. Then I'll sign.'

Travkin swept up the money, but Renard clung to the passport.

'OK, I'll be back in an hour.'

With Travkin gone, Renard was left to rejig the parts of the puzzle. The pieces did not fit but the most important thing was this: Renard's identity had genuinely been mistaken. He was *not* going to be rearrested; Medved had *not* come for him in the hospital. Medved was only interested in Renard and as far as he was concerned, Renard was dead.

Renard knew that violent altercations between Siberian oilmen were not unusual. Lawlessness was rife in the oilfields and many oil workers carried weapons. Shooting parties were organized from a small number of available hunting lodges, which were mostly in the same general locations. His rescue could have been just a coincidence.

Or Latsis could after all be a double, whose primary allegiance was to the Russians. Renard thought about it and again dismissed the idea. It was nonsense, though repeatedly heard nonsense in Henry Washington's office at State, that Sobor was a Russian front. Sobor was anything but; it was the Baltic group which – since splitting away from the Latvian KGB at the time of the Great Collapse – had served the cause of Baltic freedom better than anyone. Sobor had tentacles in Moscow and Varta and God knows where else, but they were not working for the Russians.

Travkin believed in the Latsis cover – for him 'Shadrin' was only a geologist. Renard didn't think there was any undercover relationship between them. Latsis was close to Molniya and if he was dead it was an unmitigated disaster. No other verdict would do. Without Latsis and without the Sobor network, next to nothing remained on the ground on

44

which to base an operation against the thing called Molniya, whatever and wherever it was.

Renard was thrashing with frustration. He had to get to Moscow *now* and then get in contact with whatever remnants were left of Sobor. But the mission was looking spent, irrelevant. He couldn't even be sure of getting out of Varta, and if he did it could be a set-up. He tugged at his chin. He would have to lose the watchers, that was all.

Douglas Renard had already died and been reborn with another identity. That was the only solid, if strange, fact. The connection would never be made between his own 'death' and that of the man known as Ivan Shadrin. His own body would, of course, remain unfound. And the chances of anyone ever finding the body of Latsis – other than wolves or crows – diminished every day. Even if Latsis had improbably survived, Renard was in no danger as long as he could leave Varta.

Latsis was dead, Renard alive. And Renard had crawled inside Latsis' role of the geologist Shadrin like a hermit crab claiming a shell. It was a miraculous opportunity and Renard knew what to do with it.

He used the time while Travkin was away to investigate the contents of Latsis/Shadrin's two cases. Neither was locked. One contained a change of clothes and some personal items: an address book; a geological text book with photographs of different kinds of marble; a small silver-plated hammer inscribed 'Moscow State University. Geological Faculty. Class of 74'; a faded monochrome photograph of an attractive young woman with masses of blonde hair. Then there was a hard lump within a rolled-up pair of trousers; it was a .38 automatic, loaded, with a spare ammunition clip. The gun was clean, oiled, cared for.

Renard put the gun on the bed and wondered why Travkin had left it for him.

The second suitcase was bulging with rolls of paper which spilled out over the bed and on the floor when he sprung the rusty catches. They were geological survey papers: seismic analyses; test-drilling results; background reports; the detritus of a geologist's career which Latsis had been careful to assemble around himself as camouflage. Renard picked up a musty, blue-ribboned file and opened it. A label stuck on the first page was typed: 'Frunze Petroleum Geology Institute, Kirghiz SSR. Analysis of the feasibility of liquid-gas production in the Semiransk peninsula, Leninsk reservoir, pool R-36, Analysis Depth – 2293-2297 m; 2307-2315m, By Order of the All-Union Ministry of Geology, Moscow, USSR. Main Varta Order of Lenin and Order of The Red Banner Labour Industrial Geological Authority. Ratified (indecipherable signature) Chief Geologist. Varta. 10 December 1980.' He put the file back in its place, next to a huge roll of A3 listing paper covered in columns of numbers printed so faintly as to be all-but invisible, the result of some long-forgotten analysis of sedimentary layers.

Renard looked through the other papers, unpicking the blue ribbons whose knots had seized up with time. Whatever he hoped to find did not appear to be there. He stood on the case to close it. At the same time there were footsteps in the corridor outside and the door opened just as he climbed into bed and pulled the covers back. It was Olga Ivanovna, come to change his dressings.

As Olga finished working on him, Travkin also returned. Renard signed the disclaimer, managing a wobbly scrawl with his bandaged left hand, and Travkin counted out the money – $19,000, after the $1,000 in bribes for Renard's personnel file. Renard guessed that the true price would be around $50. Travkin would certainly keep the rest for himself.

Olga Ivanovna promised to come to Renard again that evening, but when the evening arrived and the door was thrown open, it was not Olga but two unknown men who entered. One of them, a tall, thin character with a corrugated face told Renard, 'I want to check the wound now that the stitches are out.'

Renard said: 'Who the hell are you?'

'I'm Sasov, the senior duty surgeon. I would have come before but I've been on a business trip.' He indicated his colleague, a small, thickset man. 'This is Dr Petrov.'

'I wasn't expecting you,' said Renard.

Dr Petrov went round to Renard's left, opened his bag and unfurled a sphygmomanometer. 'I just need to take your blood pressure,' he said. His black eyes were kindly behind thick-framed spectacles.

Dr Sasov meanwhile placed his own small black bag on the corner of the bed. 'You're a lucky man, at all events.' He picked up the patient's clipboard. 'Tell me how you're feeling.'

'Better, I suppose.' Renard watched as Sasov opened the bag and pulled out a hypodermic. 'There are obvious signs of improvement.'

Dr Petrov wrapped the elasticated ends of the sphygmomanometer around Renard's arm, gripping the ends in his right hand, then fishing for something else in the pocket of his gown. He smiled encouragingly at Renard. A thick white bandage appeared in his left hand. Renard smiled back.

Sasov leaned across the bed, syringe in his right hand, left hand bearing down on the covers, trapping Renard's right arm under the sheets.

'Ready?' he said.

'I guess so,' Renard replied.

The explosion when Latsis' gun went off was deafening. Renard had fired from the centre of the bed and Sasov froze as Petrov, the kindly eyes suddenly blank, slowly tilted over then crashed to the floor. Renard swung his legs violently to the right, and Dr Sasov keeled over, stumbling backwards but instantly straightening up, his jaw snapping shut as he took two paces back, braced himself and drew a gun from his belt.

'I wouldn't,' Renard said.

'Fuck you,' Dr Sasov answered.

Renard heard the safety catch click, registered shouts and running feet in the corridor outside, saw Sasov stagger back and jerk straight as he fired two shots which slammed into the wall behind Renard. As he climbed from the bed, Sasov was already outside and running down the corridor. He heard a scream but before he could get to the door, Olga flew through it and fell into his arms. She wasn't hurt, and neither was he. And that was to be their last encounter and only goodbye.

The militia captain who came half an hour later was the kind who can be found in any police force anywhere – overweight, pompous and apparently convinced that the victims are the most suspicious people left at the scene of a crime. He told Renard it was his own fault the attack had happened: he was too showy and a moneyed Latvian was a natural target in town. He even confiscated Renard's weapon, although Shadrin had had a licence for it.

When Travkin reappeared at five in the morning, he had the gun with him, promising to return it to Renard at the airport. Travkin's attitude had changed; now he, too, was in a hurry to get rid of Renard.

Renard had put on one of the two suits owned by Latsis/Shadrin; it fitted surprisingly well. He looked at himself in the mirror. Bandaged and bruised, and with a week's beard, he was a different man. Good: quite apart from the unknown quantity of people who sought the death of Latsis, there were plenty of people in Varta who would be interested in Renard if they thought he was still alive.

The two men slipped quietly out of the entrance foyer, Travkin's pass answering all questions, and left in the white Volga waiting outside. 'What did you learn about my attackers last night?' Renard asked as soon as they were in the car.

'They flew in from Samara two days ago,' Travkin said as the Volga slid away from the grey bulk of the Varta Geological Administration General Hospital. 'We found no papers on the one you killed and the other escaped, so it's impossible to say who they were.'

'You do surprise me.'

'I'm not responsible for your enemies. You seem to have enough of them. Perhaps you'd like to tell *me* who they were.'

'I've no idea, obviously.'

'I find that hard to believe.'

Renard twisted round to confront Travkin. 'Here are the facts: this is your town; I was attacked by people I've never seen and know nothing about; one of them somehow escaped. How?'

Travkin was silent, so Renard continued: 'You want to tell me that you didn't anticipate this attack. In that case, I'm indebted to you for leaving me the means to defend myself.'

Travkin ignored that. 'How did you know they weren't doctors?' he enquired.

'I didn't know. I just got sick of doctors, that's all. What was in the syringe, by the way?' Renard was curious.

'Some kind of sedative. They came to abduct you, not to kill you.'

Renard sat back in the seat. Nausea swept over him.

'Are you OK?' Travkin asked him.

'I'm all right, thank you. Unfortunately they neglected to point out that they only came to abduct me.'

'I don't know . . . maybe it never occurred to them that you shoot at doctors who try to take your blood pressure.'

'I didn't shoot Olga Ivanovna.'

'She stopped being your doctor.'

Renard couldn't help grinning. '*Touché.*'

Travkin smiled back wanly and handed him a large Manila envelope. 'Your personnel file.'

'Thanks; I'll read it on the plane.'

Travkin leaned close and said very quietly: 'I put a note in with the other papers. There are two phone numbers on it. Don't look now; you'll find them later. Call me on either of them when you get to Moscow. There's a little something you can do for me; I want to make contact with someone. There'll be something in it for you, too. It'll be worthwhile, and without risk. Please don't forget.'

'Why don't you tell me now? Why trust to the phone?'

'I've no choice; I don't know the name of the contact yet.' He scrutinized Renard's face. 'In any case, call me when you get to Moscow. I can help if you get problems. Where will you stay? You mustn't use your own address; better not even visit there, frankly, except with a trusted friend or a guard.'

Latsis has a place in Moscow, then.

'Thanks for the tip.' Renard took the envelope. 'I'll stay at the Ukraina

48

probably. I have a few things to do in Moscow. Then I'll go back to Riga.'

Travkin had further advice: 'Try to avoid airports. Railways aren't much better; but you can be more anonymous on a train: you don't need to show a passport. Go to Riga by train, therefore; that's my suggestion. Riga, by the way, also isn't safe for you, any more. And please, *call me in Moscow*. Before you go to Riga. That's all I ask. It's important.'

Renard looked out of the window. They'd left Varta and were passing through interminable white forest. It was already daylight. Soon they would be at the airport. His right hand slid into the deep pocket of his overcoat and found the butt of the gun.

'You'd better level; what do you want me to do in Moscow? Don't make a fool of me, Travkin.'

Travkin thought for a long time before he spoke. Then he said, 'There's a joint venture I'm interested in. A British–Swiss–Russian firm; in the oil business. They want to get a licence to do some recovery work in a disused oilfield. I said I'd help them; that's all.'

'What's the name of the firm?'

Travkin studied him like a mouse studies cheese. 'Molniya,' he said. 'Ever hear of it?'

'No.'

'Well, it's small.'

'I guess that's why, then. So, where's the oilfield?'

'Somewhere near Nizhnevartovsk.'

'And you want me to call someone, but first call you to get their number?'

'That's all.'

'Why take a risk, giving out a number on an open line? You can tell me now.'

'I could, if I knew it. But I don't, yet. Tomorrow I'll know. We'll do it like this – like two good conspirators. You call me and I'll tell you the phone number, and then you subtract a number from each digit, starting with the number two; then take three from the second digit, and so on. Clear?'

'OK, clear. I'll do it.'

Travkin's small tobacco-coloured eyes peered at Renard with sudden triumph. Before he could say anything more they'd arrived: the car lurched through a slalom of bollards and slewed to a halt beside a slab of concrete four metres high, which turned out to be a map of the USSR.

'Varta airport,' Travkin announced.

CHAPTER 4

'Where to? The general departures hall, or VIP?' the driver growled as the Volga approached the long glass-fronted terminal building.

'Deputies' Hall, of course.' Travkin turned to Renard. 'You'd better give me that gun. Put it in your briefcase and I'll take it through Security for you.'

Renard placed the gun in Latsis' flimsy case and handed it over. The Volga rumbled on, past the frost-bitten concrete globe with its dozens of red lines radiating like spokes from the rusty axle which was Moscow and telling of the greatness of Aeroflot, and over to the shabby terminal.

On the left Renard could see a line of Tupolev TU-154s parked on the hardstanding. The sturdy mainstay of the old Aeroflot, the jets had been gutted for spares and there would be no fuel for them anyway. Thick with hoar-frost and smeared with the grime and the spent kerosene which had spilled on them from a thousand take-offs, they were ghostly reminders of a different past.

Travkin left Renard in the Deputies' Hall and went to complete the paperwork. The flight was due to depart at nine but Renard knew it would not. He was the first passenger and but for him there would be no flight at all. His *abonyement*, an official MVD reservation, had forced the Aeroflot/Air Varta duty-shift to find fuel and a plane, because it meant the flight could no longer be cancelled. But a plane couldn't leave with only one passenger. A scheduled flight could still be a business opportunity, though a more tedious one than simply selling the allotted fuel on the black market. It entailed scrambling to find passengers to whom tickets could be sold at inflated prices. Both aircrew and the airport shift would compete to do this, with the inevitable result that when the plane did at last take off it would be overloaded – its passengers crowded into aisles, the hatch areas, toilets, and even the flight deck, where they would gratefully share vodka and sandwiches with the pilot.

There were plenty of intending passengers, since the flight – a scheduled daily service – had been cancelled for a week already. But finding them was difficult. Some were sleeping rough in the terminal, but most had returned to Varta, to the hotel or to stay with friends, after giving contact numbers to bribed airport staff.

Travkin took Renard to the VIP lounge. It overlooked the terminal on the runway side. The two men stood on the balcony watching preparations for the flight.

As the scheduled departure-time approached, an angry crowd formed at the barrier. Two Aeroflot ground staff arrived to negotiate with them. They began by explaining about the black market in kerosene, which simply *forced* them to put a premium on ticket prices.

An Azeri oil-worker shouted: 'You want us to buy tickets for three times the official price, you rascals! Monopolists!'

'That's right!' the crowd yelled. 'It's *you* who sells the fuel, Jewish tricksters!'

'While I've been waiting here my wife has had our baby in Moscow! I need to get back and you bastards are fleecing me to the last kopeck!' the Azeri shouted. The crowd roared its agreement.

An airport militia-man strolled up to give his Aeroflot colleagues support. The Azeri appealed to him for justice, which seemed folly to Renard, or perhaps it was evidence of collusion.

'Comrades, comrades,' the militia man was saying. 'You see the difficulties we have; now let's be reasonable. Why, our ground staff even have to buy engine parts with their own money nowadays!'

'Liars! Liars, all of you! Jews!' a furious old lady in an ancient astrakhan coat shouted. 'There's no order in this country! Disgrace! Disgrace! And foreigners are watching!'

This was true: two German businessmen were standing in the Intourist lounge doorway, to the left of the VIP lounge, laughing at the scene and taking photographs.

'National humiliation!' the old lady shouted, and began prodding the militia man with a long object furled in brown paper.

'No need for that,' the militia man mumbled, loosening the catch on his holster.

'Comrades, two hundred thousand roubles per ticket, take it or leave it,' the Aeroflot woman repeated. The masses groaned. The militia man went over to the Germans and confiscated their film, creating a crowd-pleasing diversion. The moment of drama passed, and the would-be travellers became a haggling queue as seats were bought and sold and resold.

'They'll call for you, just now,' Travkin was saying in the lounge. 'I've given your briefcase to the pilot. You'll get it back when you land.' Renard was silent, but he knew what it meant. *He got to keep the gun.*

51

A petite girl in a blue Aeroflot uniform arrived to take the VIPs to the plane. Renard and Travkin shook hands.

'Be careful in Moscow,' Travkin said. 'And call me. Goodbye.'

The girl led the VIPs out on to the tarmac. It was a long walk to the plane, and Renard listened to the Germans discuss plans to open a string of *patisserie* shops throughout Varta province. It was cold; the temperature had fallen to minus 26, a howling wind blew snow mixed with frozen drops of unburnt kerosene into the faces of the line of passengers snaking out of the terminal building behind them.

The Aeroflot girl led the VIPs to the front of the plane. While they made themselves comfortable, the other passengers – including babies and pensioners – were kept waiting at the foot of the jetty. Renard scrutinized the crowd through the window. No eyes stared back; but Renard was sure that somebody was there for him.

Someone touched his shoulder; it was the Captain.

'Shadrin?' Renard nodded. 'Captain Sidorov. Yuri Sidorov.' He offered his hand. 'I've got your case. Don't worry. I'll return it at Domodedovo.'

'OK, thanks. I'm obliged.'

'Think nothing of it. Have a nice flight.'

The other passengers flooded on to the plane, and the captain retreated to his cabin. They took off two hours late and overloaded. The jets howled and the ancient Tupolev lumbered like a pregnant sow over the pitted tarmac, crawling improbably into the air. Renard watched the airport terminal rotate beneath the wing, as the landing gear crashed back into the shuddering body of the plane.

At 2000 metres, the Tupolev's pressurization system began to give up its unequal battle with Boyle's law. Renard felt as though his eardrums would explode. Children howled with pain. At last, however, the plane lumbered through some kind of collective pain threshold. The howl of the engines became a petulant whine. People relaxed, warmed up, began to move around and tell stories to neighbours. A cheerful stewardess circulated sweets for the tearful children and brown plastic cups with pear juice to help adults wash down the cognac and vodka which began to flow. She startled Renard by giving him a complimentary copy of the English-language version of *Moscow News*.

Renard loosened his coat and stretched his legs and began again to think through what had happened.

Sakharinov.

At the killing ground, Medved had said: 'I won't take responsibility without the personal decision of Sakharinov.'

Which of the Sakharinov brothers was meant to be present at the illegal execution of an American citizen?

Whichever one it was, things were moving to a head faster than anyone supposed: the dark forces were openly emerging into daylight, and Russia was heading for revolution and war.

If the Sakharinovs were behind Molniya . . .

Renard shifted in his seat and accepted a glass of cognac from his neighbour, who was going to pass the flight telling stories. The cabin was hot and Renard was sleepy. He smiled at some joke about a drunk in Red Square who called the General Secretary an idiot and was given three months for rowdyism, and fifteen years for revealing state secrets. He was drifting, the cabin was hot and he closed his eyes.

Five miles below, the endless taiga slid by.

Latsis' cover was blown. Who, then, was the traitor?

Someone at the highest level of British or US government.

Someone who had been broken or bought or compromised into becoming party to a mad scheme to plunge Russia and perhaps the whole world into a new tyranny.

Only one thing was certain: his journey to Varta had yielded nothing and now, either as Renard or as Latsis, people were searching for him.

This was double jeopardy with a vengeance . . .

Renard accepted another shot of cognac from his neighbour, who had been a steelworker in Magnitogorsk for eighteen years but had since set up a company to import Italian sweet wine. The best seller, he told Renard, was Amaretto, which people add to vodka to make cocktails – but just recently he had been to a market-research seminar and the manufacturer had told them that seventy per cent of the stuff sold in Russia never got nearer to Italy than Odessa, and that some mafia circles used dilute cyanide to give the stuff its almond flavour.

Renard smiled and said that from choice he only drank Johnny Walker Black Label. You couldn't disguise the taste. Or the price, the former steelworker from Magnitka said.

Renard hunched down and entered a light sleep. When he woke up, the Tupolev was touching down at Moscow's Domodedovo airport. Good! He had dozed more than two hours. His neighbour was still telling jokes: *The Russian President wanted to do something for pensioners, so he gave them permission to cross the road when the lights are at green . . .*

The plane taxied interminably and Renard had time to flick through his copy of *Moscow News*. An article described some 'Do's' and 'Don'ts' for foreign businessmen. 'Remember when you come to Russia,' it exhorted, 'that every major institution reports to the mafia. Passport

53

control at the border sells them the computerized details of every visiting foreigner. The airport customs at your point of entry records any amounts of hard currency which you declare and sells that information too. When you check in at a hotel your passport details are registered with the police, who will also routinely alert the mafia to your presence. If you use your credit card to make purchases while in Russia, the clearing centre in Moscow will soon be able to tell the mafia what your credit status is, where you live back home, what your personal and corporate banking details are and even how many children you have (especially valued information). If, subsequently, you decide business looks so good that you want to open an office in Moscow or St Petersburg, fine, but you will not be able to avoid paying protection money to some local gang and that's only the beginning. All your Russian staff will be pressured to part with confidential company information and finally to join in whatever scheme the mafia hatch for filleting you. In general,' the journalist concluded, 'the safest way to make business in Russia is (a) to have yourself declared bankrupt *first*; (b) dress down and (c) finance all your activities only with undeclared hard currency . . .'

As the Tupolev came to a halt Renard wondered when the mafia would take the next obvious step and reinstate the censorship of newspapers. Through the porthole he could see the L-shaped terminal building nearby and as the engines died Captain Sidorov emerged into the saloon, stopping at Renard's seat to return with a friendly smile the attaché case with the gun inside, which Travkin had given him for safekeeping.

The crew disembarked and the python of passengers followed obediently behind. The two Germans headed towards the VIP baggage reclaim at the far end of the building, facing the runways. Renard set off in the opposite direction, to where the terminal buildings abutted a service road. A five-dollar bribe to the gatekeeper could get a wily passenger with no bags to reclaim straight out of the airport. Renard had the two suitcases to collect – but he wanted to identify the watcher.

He'd walked a few metres when a voice called to him from behind. '*Gospodin* Shadrin!' Someone was running, feet crunching over the ice. He turned; it was a crew member – Sidorov's second in command. He was shouting: 'This is the wrong way!'

The crewman grabbed the attaché case and said: 'I'll help you; your injuries – you know!'

Renard looked at him. He was a young flight officer, someone who could be found in airline messrooms the world over.

Renard smiled politely and unresistingly parted with the case. 'I did

54

forget the way, actually. Thank you; you're very kind. I'd have lost my cases!'

They set off back towards the VIP lounge.

'Will you be staying in Moscow?' the crewman asked.

'A few days. I have some matters to see to. I'll stay at the Ukraina hotel,' Renard volunteered. 'And you?'

'Oh, back to Varta tomorrow. I never get more than twenty-four hours here.' The man struggled to make small talk against the background of howling jets. 'A pity, because I have family here – my sister.'

'Really.' They were at the VIP lounge. 'Thank you – er—'

'Bultov. Ivan Petrovich.'

They shook hands; Bultov's was cold, like a fish. 'Thanks, Ivan Petrovich. Really, I never saw such politeness! From Aeroflot crew!'

Bultov grinned. 'Times are changing.' He paused. 'Are you being met? Perhaps I—'

'Thanks, but don't worry. I'll manage. Goodbye.'

Renard turned and walked smartly into the lounge, where Bultov, he knew, would not follow. His cases arrived within minutes. He gave a dollar bill to a porter, instructing him to bring a taxi to the door of the VIP lounge, against all the rules.

A white Volga taxi arrived. The shift leader, an obese woman who had not benefited from the transaction, began shouting. Renard pacified her with another dollar bill.

He would be followed, and he could be attacked on the road to Moscow. But he was sure that this taxi was straight – unless the whole terminal staff were involved in some charade aimed at exterminating Latsis/Shadrin.

'Wait,' he said, as the driver started the engine and prepared to move off. He held up fifteen dollars. 'I need to go here and there; it'll take four or five hours, probably. What's your hourly rate?'

'Thirty dollars.'

Renard reached for the door handle.

'OK, OK, let's say fifteen.'

'OK, and a bonus if you get me everywhere on time.'

'Done.'

'Head for the service access.'

'They won't let us through, we're not authorized.'

'Don't be silly, this is Moscow.'

The taxi crawled over the ice and slithered to a halt by a heavy motorized metal gate which crossed the service road where it entered the airport perimeter. The gatehouse keeper controlled the gate from inside a small cabin. Renard knew that five dollars was always enough to get through.

As they crossed the tarmac to the gates, he saw a car spin snow off its back wheels as it sped from the rear VIP area. The car was foreign – a Mercedes. It ought to be, could only be, the Germans from the plane. But he could see only one passenger, sitting behind the driver and guard. So it wasn't the Germans. The car was following him.

'What's your name?' Renard asked the driver.

'Sasha.'

'Sasha, what were you, before—'

The driver laughed. It was a very short laugh. 'I was an officer. Paratroops. Fell out with the army.'

'You're not afraid of a little trouble, then.' He gave the driver a fifty-dollar bill.

'Depends.' Sasha palmed the bill.

'There are some people following me. See that Mercedes?'

He watched the driver's eyes flick in the mirror.

'I'm not looking for that kind of trouble.'

'They're business competitors, that's all.'

Sasha nodded. 'If you say so.'

Renard gave him an extra ten dollars. 'This is for the gatehouse keeper. Tell him not to let the Merc through. He must delay them as long as possible. He can make up a story. Let him say that you showed him a special *propusk*.'

'Leave it to me.'

They stopped outside the gatehouse. The Mercedes was less than a hundred metres behind. The taxi driver opened the driver's side door and left the car at a run. He was already in the gatehouse when the Mercedes pulled up. Renard watched the German car in the Volga's interior mirror. The driver made no move but simply waited for the gates to open.

The gatehouse keeper came to the door of the hut, gesticulating and shouting at the driver of the Mercedes. He pointed to the 'No Exit' sign above the gate, but the driver simply shrugged his shoulders.

Impasse. The keeper went back inside his hut, Sasha with him. Minutes passed and Renard watched the three occupants of the Mercedes begin a heated discussion; at last the driver got out and walked casually over to the gatehouse. He peered in at Renard on the way. *There's no hurry*, his look seemed to say, *because you are mine. You have nowhere to run to.*

Renard peered back. The driver was tall, fit, a martial-arts trained guard and he was armed – the bulge of a weapon clearly visible under the Daks coat. He walked with the assurance of those who know there can be no real opposition. As he climbed the steps to the gatehouse, Sasha emerged and came racing back to the Volga. The gates ground open and they inched through. Renard looked back and saw the well-dressed driver running back to the Mercedes as the gates clanged shut again.

'They'll be there for half an hour,' Sasha said as they pulled away.

'We'll see,' Renard said. 'Don't leave the airport – pull in behind the old Ilyushin.'

Just beyond the service entry, abutting the main access road to the front of the terminal building, an Ilyushin-18 turboprop of 1950s vintage was mounted on a plinth. The monument celebrated the achievements of Soviet civil aviation. They parked in the lee of this huge machine, the dirty white Volga taxi anonymous among twenty others. In less than a minute they saw the Mercedes speed past, out into the main access road. Renard saw the man next to the driver speaking on a cellphone; the man in the back looked like Bultov.

'Jesus,' Sasha said in disbelief. 'I gave that guy ten bucks to stall them, just like you said.'

'I believe you. They're professionals, that's all.' Renard was looking at Sasha's eyes in the mirror. 'Do you know the scenic route to Moscow?' he asked.

'The scenic route?' The driver laughed shortly. 'Of course!'

'Then let's go . . .'

The Volga sped off down the access road and on to the Moscow highway.

'No need to rush,' Renard warned. 'Don't let's be noticeable.'

'Understood.'

They joined the steady stream of traffic bearing people and freight from the provinces to the capital. After five kilometres they came to a turning signposted 'Sovietskaya Collective Farm.'

The Volga slewed down the access road. As they approached the turn, Sasha slowed then pulled on to the verge and killed the engine. He left the car and opened the bonnet.

Good. He's thinking.

Renard looked around; there was nothing to see except the usual flow of heavy trucks which constitutes more than half the traffic on Russia's roads, an endless stream of mud-spewing machinery.

To the left of the highway a wide expanse of snow-covered pasture gave way abruptly to the forest which spread over the horizon like black ink on a blotter. Only the line of a wire fence running away towards the forest identified the farm track from the surrounding fields. There was no sign of life on it.

Sasha slammed the bonnet shut and climbed back into the driver's seat. 'No one and nothing,' he said, and started the engine. The Volga inched forward on to the farm track.

Renard opened the attaché case. The 9mm automatic had been wrapped in a clean linen cloth. He pulled out the clip, and ejected the bullets. They were blanks; someone had switched them. Renard put the clip in the case and replaced it with the spare clip which had been digging into his left ankle the whole way from Varta.

Sasha wound down the window, and air cold with snow blew in. 'I'm a judo black belt, by the way,' he said.

'Then why . . .?'

'Why am I doing this crummy job? I could be a guard, like that prime beef in the Merc. But after the army I got real difficulties, and I ended up doing time and it's in my labour-book. You know what that means!'

'Sure I do.'

'There are plenty worse off. God knows what's happening in this country.'

'What *is* happening?'

'Oh, come on. The country has been sold to Jewish speculators and American businessmen. We need a strong hand; someone to give us order. Russia doesn't even have proper borders any more. The frontiers are bleeding, and twenty-five million Russians are on the wrong side of them.'

Sasha wound up the window. The car sped on through the poor settlements and farms south of Moscow, and Renard turned to the papers in his attaché case and then closed it.

They were soon approaching the outskirts of Moscow. They passed through an industrial zone studded with the sightless concrete shells of abandoned factories and emerged suddenly from behind the Kashirskaya Metro station into a modern residential area. Then they rejoined the main highway and Renard watched to see what would happen as the stream of traffic began to bunch and slow as they approached the next GAI checkpoint. Nothing. A red-faced GAI-man, grandiose in huge felt *valenki* boots and a suede coat the size of an aircraft hangar, waved on the traffic with his white night-stick. He looked bored – but Renard saw him peer at the taxi's plates and as they sloshed past he sauntered back to his guard-post.

In another fifteen minutes Sasha announced that they were being followed. 'A white Moskvich; four guys inside. They've been two cars behind for the last five minutes.'

'I don't believe it,' Renard said, believing it absolutely. 'You're imagining things.'

In another thirty minutes they had arrived outside the huge bulk of the Ukraina hotel, near the river Moskva. The taxi crawled into the car park opposite the administration offices.

'The Moskvich has gone,' Sasha told him. He swung round in his seat and grinned at Renard. 'What next?'

Renard handed over his brand-new Latvian passport. 'Take this and book me in. Here's fifty bucks for tonight.'

Sasha studied the passport photograph. 'You want me to say that I'm you?'

'Exactly. Good man. I want a semi-luxe for three nights, on the side facing the river if possible. Get the name of the girl who serves you. Give her this—' this time he parted with a twenty-dollar bill. 'Check if anyone has been asking after me, if there are any messages, and ask her to make a mental note if anybody comes looking for me later tonight.'

'OK.'

Sasha left the car. Renard watched the people walking around the forecourt: militia men, girls, passers-by swooping on occupied cars to buy or sell God knows what. He tried to look inconspicuous, and was rewarded when no one took any notice of him.

In ten minutes Sasha returned with a hotel pass and the key. 'Room 14108. The floor-girl's name is Irina. Her extension is 2347. Yes, some guys were here looking for you. From their description it was the two at the airport. There are no other messages.'

'How did she look? Nervous? She take the twenty bucks?'

'No hesitations.' Sasha grinned at him. 'So they didn't say they were the law.'

'Well, what are they?'

'You tell me. It's you they're following. But – I guess they're *not* the law. I'm sure of it. Moscow's MVD don't look or dress like that. If they *are* official, then they're KGB – or worse.'

'When do you go off duty, Sasha?'

'In an hour.'

'Who does this taxi belong to?'

'A co-operative. I have to take it back at the end of my shift. Or make a call and warn the driver not to come till a prearranged time.'

Renard gave Sasha a long look.

'I do own a car,' Sasha volunteered at last. 'Only it's a Lada.'

'Even better. OK, how long will it take you to get your Lada and come back?'

'Hour and a half.'

'What colour is it?'

'White. Old model. The number is 2785.'

'OK. Call my room from the lobby. Let it ring three times. Then hang up and immediately dial again. Then I'll answer.'

'Right.'

'Now drive round to the basement entrance. There's a service lift. Five bucks will get you in. Take the baggage up to the room and come back for me.'

'Too dangerous.'

'Why? No one's looking for *you*. They'll be looking for someone wearing bandages.'

'They could be in the room, waiting.'

'Hey, how you do enter into the spirit of things! But rest easy; we've only just booked in. Even if Irina *has* called someone, it'll take them half an hour at least to come back.'

'OK, OK.'

Sasha left with the two cardboard suitcases and Renard watched him disappear into the hotel. He got out of the Volga and wandered across the car park. On the far side were three rows of cars and the back row was deeply covered in snow; they were cars belonging to long-term guests or staff at the hotel. He disappeared among them, bending down and ripping off the first loose-looking front number plate he found. He then levered off the same car's back plate, stuffing both trophies inside his coat and returning to the taxi. Sasha was already there.

'You were quick; I thought I'd take a breather.'

'Let's go,' Sasha said, leading the way into the service entrance and from there to Room 108 on the fourteenth floor which consisted of a cramped suite.

After Sasha had left, promising to be back with his own transport within an hour, Renard went to the wardrobe and found a spare blanket. When he had finished stuffing it under the door so that no light could be seen from the corridor, he wrapped the number plates in a towel; they were thick with grease and dirt.

In the small lounge was a cocktail cabinet; he took a tumbler and half filled it from the litre bottle of export-strength Johnny Walker Black Label he'd bought at Domodedovo airport. He downed it in one gulp, turned on the television and then went to the bathroom for a shave and a bath. He inspected his chest. The massive bruises were starting to fade and his breathing was easier now. The swelling in his broken finger had largely subsided, too.

He carefully unravelled the bandage around his eyes. There was no sign of infection where the stitches had been. He exchanged the bandage for a simple plaster.

Renard lay in the bath for a long while, wiggling his toes, drinking a second tumbler of Johnny Walker and reflecting on the fact that under some conditions, even Moscow can seem civilized.

He dressed slowly, half watching the news. The lead story concerned the coming Duma session: German parliamentary observers were shown arriving in Moscow. A man named Döhlen, leader of the German Nationalists, was being interviewed at the airport.

'We have forged unbreakable ties with our comrades in the Russia First Party,' he said. 'We stand for the unity of the Russian and German peoples, the strongest nations in Europe. We must never repeat previous mistakes, we should never have allowed the international Jewish conspiracy to make us enemies instead of allies in two World Wars.' The interviewer nodded approval.

It was 7.30 in the evening; 9.30 in Varta.

Time to call Travkin.

Renard dialled the trunk code and almost immediately heard a ringing tone. After two rings a male voice said 'Yes?'

'Colonel Travkin, please.'

'Colonel Travkin is not here at present. Perhaps someone else can help you?'

'When will Travkin return?'

'Wait a moment, please.'

A silence, then a different voice, hard, unpleasant. 'Who wants to speak to a Colonel Travkin?' it enquired.

'When will he return, please?' Renard asked politely.

'You've made a mistake. There's no Travkin here. This is Colonel Petrov speaking, head of shift. Who wants to know?'

Renard put down the phone.

It rang immediately, three times, then stopped. A few seconds later it rang again. It was Sasha. 'You've got company,' he said. 'And I think they recognized me.'

'Where are you?'

'By the main entrance.'

'OK. *Wait for me by your car. Don't worry if I don't come for ten or twenty minutes.*'

Renard put down the phone, grabbed his coat and hat and picked up the attaché case.

Fourteenth floor. The Finnish-made lifts took less than three minutes to ascend. His room was on the far side of the hotel. But they would be running. Not walking.

Renard left, quietly locking the door to his room and walking quickly to the fire escape less than thirty metres away.

He opened the fire-escape door and ran one floor up. On the next floor he stopped and leaned over the railing, rasping for breath, his chest in agony.

The door below opened, as he had thought it would. One man appeared: the driver of the Merc. The other would be waiting in the room.

The first man was in no hurry. He stopped to listen for the sound of Renard's running feet.

He can probably hear my heart pounding, damnit.

Up or down? Renard could see him thinking.

Down, the man decided. It was logical. His quarry was running for his life. He would try to leave, somehow, anyhow.

The man slowly descended via the fire escape to the floor below, pausing at the door to the corridor and then opening it.

Renard went back down the fire escape and returned to his room. There was not much time. He pushed the door open and saw Bultov standing by the bed, opening the second of Latsis' two cases.

CHAPTER 5

Extract from the US Joint Chiefs' weekly summary of Intelligence reports. **Not to be copied, removed or referred to in any third-party communication.**

> *Biographical summary.*
> *Vadim Medved*
> *dob 06.07.54*

. . . during service in Vietnam as adviser to the Hanoi regime, he became widely known as 'the Acupuncturist.' His skills as an interrogation officer were deployed in Afghanistan, and he is known to have worked in Iraq training Saddam's torturers.

Vadim Medved is a sadistic torturer and killer in the mould of Stalin's great butcher, Lavrentii Beria. During the early 1970s, while still a young officer keen to win his spurs, Medved served as Soviet adviser to the North Vietnamese. He impressed his superiors with his zeal and especially with his aptitude for interrogation. Many American prisoners passed through his hands. Some went mad, many died; none ever returned. He learned the gentle art of acupuncture from a Chinese physician, but he applied it in his own way.

His specialty is the exact physiological and psychological assessment of his subject. No one could break men down quicker than Medved, whose reputation was for prising information out while it was still of maximum operational value. His apparatus of acupuncture needles, connected by wires to a variable voltage transformer, was scarcely original in itself. His genius was in the application of the needles. He always used a rope hammock in which his victims were suspended. A trained acupuncturist who knows all the human body's pathways of pain is potentially the perfect holistic torturer. Medved was able to orchestrate pain so that the victim, bound, penetrated with long electrodes, inhabited a furnace of exploding torment which, however, did not result in death except when Medved wished.

He is known to be a close supporter, aide and confidant of the Sakharinovs.

Renard stood in the threshold of his room at the Ukraina and pointed his gun at Bultov's forehead.

'Don't be a silly boy, Shadrin.' Bultov slowly lowered his hands, palm outwards. He was smiling. He took a step forward. 'Give me the gun. No games, please. It isn't loaded.'

He took another step forward.

Renard backed around the bed, squeezing between it and the wall next to the en-suite bathroom. Someone was running down the corridor; it was the other man, the bodyguard.

'He's got away, but he'll be back,' the man said as he came in the room. Then he turned, saw Renard and stopped. He also smiled, and held out a hand the size of a shovel.

'Give it to me,' he said softly. 'Or I'll have to smack you.' He stepped forward and so did Bultov.

Renard shot the bodyguard through the head. The bullet smashed into the wall mirror behind him, showering the guard with glass as he fell. Renard went over to the door and closed and locked it, keeping the gun pointed at Bultov, who had screamed once and now stood quite still with his mouth open, gaping at the body on the floor.

'Sit,' Renard said, pointing to the bed.

Bultov sat.

'Amateurs,' Renard pronounced. 'You disappoint me.'

Bultov's face was ashen. 'This is nothing to do with me,' he mumbled.

'Really?' Renard said. 'Turn over and lie face down.'

Bultov obeyed.

'Hands behind your back.'

'You're going to kill me,' Bultov whispered.

'Maybe you'll just die by yourself and I won't have to bother.'

Renard wrapped a long coil of the bandage Olga Ivanovna had given him around Bultov's wrists.

'OK, sit up.'

Bultov sat up. Renard put the barrel of the gun inside his teeth.

'I'm growing to dislike you,' he said pleasantly. He sat down on the bed next to Bultov. 'OK, question time. Wrong answers *will* result in my killing you. Now, who sent you?'

Panic had risen like a flood tide through Bultov; any second now he would start to scream again. Renard slapped the crewman's face, hard.

'Who sent you?' he repeated in the same mild voice.

Bultov's mouth opened and closed, but no sound came out. Then, in a deathly whisper he said, 'Kill me now, please.'

'OK,' Renard theatrically clicked the safety catch.

Bultov's eyes swivelled like gimbals, but he kept silent. Either he didn't believe that Renard would fire or he didn't care. Renard thought it was more a case of the latter. He could not spare the time to find out why. He would have to deal with the guy elsewhere.

Renard stood up and took the bottle of Johnny Walker from the cabinet. It was still three-quarters full. He poured out a treble for himself and then filled a tumbler to the brim for Bultov. He took him by the scruff of the neck and poured the whisky down his throat, giving him time between gulps to stop gagging. He did that several times until the bottle was finished.

'Cheers,' he said, drinking his treble. Then he made Bultov drink two bottles of effervescent *Essentuki* mineral water which he found in the fridge, and then waited for the results. They were not long in coming. Fear, adrenaline and shock combined with the alcohol catalyzed by the carbonated water to turn Bultov into a stammering wreck in five minutes. Renard told him to lie face down on the bed again.

Renard went through the pockets of both Bultov and his dead comrade. Bultov was unarmed, but the guard carried a silenced German-made automatic. He took the weapon, then polished his own automatic clean of fingerprints. The guard carried a pass which announced he was an officer of the Russian Ministry of Security, Varta Region Security Administration. Renard pocketed the pass.

He took out the ammunition clip from the butt of the weapon and sat down on the bed again and waited for the inevitable. Sure enough, within a few minutes Bultov had fallen asleep, snoring peacefully. Renard twisted the man's limp fingers around the gun which had killed the guard. Then he replaced the clip, and threw the gun under the bed.

The next thing was to find Sasha.

The little white Lada was parked by the slip road off the car park. Sasha saw Renard in his door mirror as the latter came limping down the ramp. There was curiosity in Sasha's eyes but he was silent until Renard spoke.

'One of them's in my room,' Renard said. 'The other left.'

Sasha lit a cigarette. 'Yeah?'

Renard smiled. 'I'm allergic to tobacco.'

Sasha put out the cigarette. 'What now?' he asked.

'The guy had too much to drink. I need to get him out of there.'

'They live at quite a pace, your business competitors, don't they? OK, let's fetch him down. But where are you taking him?'

'My place.'

'*Your* place?'

Mystified, Sasha started the Lada, and drove it round to the service entrance. 'The doorman doesn't know your room number, but if it's all the same to you I'll stay here while you collect your friend. My advice is to bring the luggage first.' He opened the door, came round to Renard's side and opened his. 'Don't worry. I'll be here.'

'I know you will, Sasha.'

Five minutes later, Renard returned half carrying the shambling form of Bultov. 'Get my cases,' he ordered Sasha, face pale, voice hoarse with pain. 'They're in the foyer. No one will see you.'

Sasha claimed the cases, threw them in the boot, and they left.

'Where to?'

'North. I'll show you.'

The Lada stuttered away from the kerb, slid in the slush, then gathered enough speed to join the serpents of traffic snaking through Moscow's snow-ridden streets.

By eleven on that evening, the 10th of November, they were at Renard's place, the Lada nosing through a rutted, slush-filled archway which led into a small courtyard. It was an apartment block in a dormitory village some ten kilometres north of the Moscow city boundary. The courtyard was surrounded on all sides by crumbling five-storey flats which had been built in haste in the 1950s. There were two entrance doors in each side. Renard told Sasha to pull up by the first entrance on the left.

Renard looked behind: Bultov, sprawled over the back seat of the Lada, was mumbling, somewhere between sleep and the pain of wakefulness.

'Wait here,' he said to Sasha. 'I won't be long.'

Renard left the car and walked through the new snow. He stood for a while on the threshold of the apartment block and listened to the familiar sounds of Moscow's crowded tenements. Somewhere a baby cried and a mother soothed. In the flat by the entrance the concierge yelled at her husband, as she did every night.

Renard watched the snow patter down. Through it fell shards of music from a high window: a Chopin prelude, manically played by the pianist living on the fourth floor.

Long live Chopin!

His flat was on the third floor. He went up the stairs and discovered, as usual, the corridor light was out. He fumbled behind the meter and located the spare key kept there, opened the door and entered.

The flat was as he had left it two months before – down to the cup of coffee abandoned on the kitchen table when he'd left in haste, hurrying

66

to Varta, to a subterranean cell, to a killing ground. But his professional inspection of drawers and cupboards showed that the place had been thoroughly and expertly searched in the interim.

Renard opened the kitchen cupboard, rummaged in an old shoebox and pulled out a Soviet-made ultra short-wave radio receiver. The batteries were dead, and it took a few minutes to rig up a cable long enough for his purposes. When the set was working, he began methodically sweeping the walls of the flat. Twice the apparatus howled with feedback from transmitter microphones. One had been placed behind the heavy frame of an oil painting, in the main room. The other was inside the telephone extension socket in the flat's only bedroom. It was a bad sign. He flushed them both down the toilet, then left the flat and returned to Sasha waiting in the Lada.

Renard asked Sasha where he lived – out in a village, north of the beltway, he learned.

'But I won't be going there now,' the driver grinned. 'My girl is an expensive habit, but I can afford her tonight.'

Renard thought for a moment, then told Sasha to be sure and return not later than seven the next morning. He had little choice but to trust him.

How long could he stay at the flat? A few hours, a day at most. Removing the bugs meant he was safe until an over-zealous neighbour reported the return of his presence to the local militia, or until he made or received the first phone call. Obviously someone – most likely Medved's men – had already been here. They would find Sasha, or follow his car for sure. Telling the cheerful taxi driver to come back in the morning had probably been a mistake – Sasha would lead them to him, if they were quick enough to track him down tonight.

Back in the flat, Renard had to prop Bultov over the toilet so that the man could be violently sick. Renard untied his hands, and went to make coffee. In a little while, Bultov appeared at the kitchen door, ashen-faced.

'Coffee?' Renard gestured to one of the two available chairs. 'You look green.'

Bultov slumped down. 'Where am I, you bastard?'

'You could be in prison by now. Breaking into hotel rooms is against the law.'

'You're crazy.' Bultov's face twisted in a grimace and he plunged back into the toilet. Renard listened for a while, then closed the door.

It would be a long night. Somehow he needed to start a dialogue with this Aeroflot crewman who had accepted a mission to spy on him, and who feared someone else more than death. He went through the file on Shadrin again, trying to glean whatever he could.

According to the personnel file supplied by Travkin, 'Ivan Shadrin' was a Latvian-born geologist seconded to a Siberian-based oil exploration firm – a subsidiary of the giant Sibinternefte corporation run by the Sakharinovs. His secondment was from the Riga Geological Institute on a two-year contract to co-ordinate a programme of survey work in the Arctic North. It was an important job. Latsis' cover had been flawless.

Renard decided that the file was not pure legend. He already knew of Latsis' Latvian origins. Maybe some details were true. At all events, Travkin wasn't in Latsis' group, Sobor. He knew of Molniya, perhaps, but not of any connection with Renard and he couldn't have known the truth about Latsis either. One way or another, the file was indeed a blind. Whatever fragments of the truth about Latsis it contained, they had been melded together in a tissue of falsehood.

Bultov would add little, of that Renard was sure, and so it turned out. He was what he appeared to be – an Aeroflot flight lieutenant. He told Renard of his life in Varta, sharing his father's apartment with a young wife whom he loved, and their baby son. He tearfully showed him their photographs.

Bultov had been called into the offices of Varta KGB – the place where Renard had been a prisoner – three days before. A KGB Colonel had interviewed him, showing Bultov his service record, which contained one or two inconsistencies which could easily be prejudicial to his future career as an airline pilot. Then the Colonel had told him the name of his wife and son. Without mincing matters, he had explained to Bultov that their lives hung by a thread; they would *assuredly* be executed, if he, Bultov, now refused to carry out a simple task, one which involved nothing criminal and was necessary for the security of the Russian state.

Bultov said that at first he had been outraged, shouting at the KGB Colonel that Russia was now a democracy, that such things were impossible. The Colonel, he said, had smiled at this speech, merely taking off his spectacles to polish them.

'Tell me about this Colonel. What was his name?'

'Why should I tell you anything? I've already sentenced my wife to death.' Bultov shouted, hysteria running his speech ragged. 'I shouldn't be here! They will kill me, and the fault is yours.'

Renard poured more coffee and told Bultov to calm down. He repeated his question: the Colonel's name?

'Really, I don't remember.'

'Try. It's important.'

Bultov dabbed tears from his eyes and told Renard he couldn't keep him prisoner. 'Perhaps you need me, after all. I have friends – powerful friends. Let me leave. I will tell no one. Perhaps I can even be of some use, in whatever you are doing.'

'Bultov, I don't really believe in you,' Renard told him at last. 'I think you betrayed your wife.'

The Aeroflot man twitched and looked at Renard sidelong. 'You're crazy,' he said, his yellow eyes darting.

'Let's look at the evidence. You were in the hands of the KGB. You knew what it meant. Even in these enlightened times. Your chances of getting a pilot's licence were on the line, perhaps more than that.' Renard leaned over him, looked in the frightened eyes. 'I know what kind of person you are. I know what people like you do in situations like that.'

Bultov was sweating; beads of moisture began to roll from his brow. 'You're not making any sense,' he whispered hoarsely.

'Try this for sense, then. You betrayed her, didn't you? That's what a worm like you would do. You offered her as a pledge for your own behaviour. Let me guess, Bultov. *She's there now, isn't she? At Varta KGB centre?*'

Bultov's eyes bulged like a frog's. His lips worked but no sound emerged.

'You are a traitor,' Renard whispered. 'You never seriously expected to find me and bring me in, so you bartered *her* life for mine, didn't you? She was the wager: she and the child—'

'No!' Bultov shouted. 'Not the child! Not the child!'

Renard shrugged. 'OK. Not your life on the line, but hers, right? And they had to agree, didn't they?' Bultov was puce. He could not speak. 'They offered you that because they know you, what kind of creature you are – just as I know.'

He knelt down so that his nose almost touched the Aeroflot man's. 'Only your own death could save her, yes?' He saw the look on Bultov's face, and nodded bitterly. 'Your mafia is everywhere, like carbon dioxide, choking the life out of the country. But they found it easy enough to break you. Well, listen to me.' He leaned lower. 'You will never claim my life, funny boy. Never! Because I will take what's mine from this goddamn place, come what may.'

Renard placed the silenced automatic he had taken from Bultov's driver on the table before him. 'I don't know who this belongs to; not to me at any rate. It's up to you: you can be found with this in your hand, a bullet in your brain and a very interesting suicide note. And the militia won't take long to connect you with the killing of your driver. Your fingerprints were on the gun with which he was shot—'

Bultov gaped as he recollected the events of three hours earlier.

'I see you'd forgotten that little matter. No, I think on the whole that it is you who needs help.'

Now Renard stroked the table, again speaking in a whisper. 'I need the answers to some questions, and I need them now. The sooner we finish, the sooner you can go. You've nothing to lose, now. In any case, no one will connect anything you say back to you. I merely want some facts corroborating, that's all. You don't have much time. Let's begin. The Colonel's *name*, please.'

Bultov was broken, the answers began to come.

'I think his name was Medved. Colonel Medved.'

Renard's jaw clenched shut. He couldn't prevent an involuntary shudder, and Bultov noticed it.

Medved! The room fell away and for a moment he was a prisoner back in a forest clearing, watching the sunlight gleam on the rims of those steel spectacles as the shotgun swung up to fire . . .

Renard opened his eyes and looked wearily down at Bultov's frightened face. 'Are you all right?' the Aeroflot man had asked him.

'The name was *Medved*, you say?'

'Yes. Yes, I'm sure of it.'

Bultov was plaintive, wallowing in self-pity. He told Renard of the unspeakable things this Colonel had promised to do to his father, wife, son, and about the film they had forced him to watch, where he had seen exactly such things done to some poor, helpless creature whom Medved had reduced to quivering bloody meat in minutes.

Again, a shudder shook Renard.

'He was trained as a doctor. I heard a story about him in Varta,' Bultov said woodenly.

'Tell me! Now! Whatever you know!'

But Bultov had gummed up again, and Renard had to shake out of him what he had heard while in the KGB compound.

'They call him the Acupuncturist,' he said in a while. 'I was told a few stories about him before I met him. He's fouler than anyone I ever encountered.'

'Why did Medved want to use you? Why *you*?'

Bultov laughed, a dry rattle that died in his throat. 'Why me? Why not? I'm hardly on my own.' He leered at Renard. 'I have the impression that *many* are searching for you. My role is very simple; I was to try to cultivate you, to make contact with you in Moscow, provide access to your circle.'

'My circle?'

'Exactly. The Latvian traitors. Those who will stop at nothing to bury Russia, to prevent Russia's rebirth.'

Renard told Bultov to be quiet for a while. He needed to think. Bultov sat back and looked almost pleased with himself. He watched Renard pace up and down, and took the chance to look around the flat and try to work out where he was.

For six weeks, Renard was thinking, *they kept me in a dark cell, and did not interrogate me. Many times the guards gave oblique warnings of what was to come; referring to the Acupuncturist. But nothing happened. I didn't meet Medved until the last day, the day of the forest, of the killing ground. Why? Why didn't Medved touch me before?*

The answer was obvious: Medved had not been in Varta. He was expected, but did not arrive until the end of my captivity, and by then it was too late: new orders had come, orders to waste no time, to execute me at once. Why? How was what happened connected in Medved's mind with Latsis/Shadrin?

Renard heard Bultov's querulous voice, interrupting the flow of thought. But the words made no sense.

'What did you say?'

'I asked you where I am. Is this your flat?'

'Stupid question. You can answer it yourself. The Latvian circle.'

Again Bultov spoke and Renard understood at once what had happened. He stood motionless in front of Bultov and waited. Looking triumphant, Bultov repeated himself, but this time in Russian: 'I said, the flat looks more Russian than Latvian. But it would do, wouldn't it? Because you're no Latvian, are you? You don't speak the language. I think,' Bultov said the fatal words, 'that you are actually an American.'

Renard looked at him. 'You are either braver than I thought, Bultov, or more stupid. If you are right then you know something no one else does, and you know that means I shall have to kill you.'

Bultov went very pale. He hadn't thought of that.

'Tell me,' Renard said easily, 'how did you learn Latvian? I tried.'

'My family lives there. You have to learn it to get citizenship; we're all trying.'

Renard grinned. 'So that's how you really feel about Latvian traitors.'

A queer light came into Bultov's eyes. 'I wanted to live, like anyone else. That's how I know you are not a Russian; you don't understand what it means.'

71

'You should be ashamed of yourself, if you even have a self. But tell me, Bultov, how would killing me in a hotel room in the Ukraina have helped your Varta bosses?'

'We didn't intend to kill you. You were too quick, too drastic. It's just as they warned me; you're a hard person to get close to. You made a fool of us at the airport. But we knew, or suspected, you would try to hide at the Ukraina – I received a radio message while we were in flight. You must have told someone in Varta of your plans. Foolish; you have no friends there.'

'Go on, please.'

'Once you gave us the slip at Domodedovo, we had no choice. On no account were you to be left unsupervised in Moscow.' Bultov smirked. 'Those were our orders.'

'You had no other contact names in Moscow? Who else am I supposed to be connected with?'

'I don't know anything more.'

'You're lying.' Renard picked up the gun. 'You're in too deep, Bultov. I can't leave you to go roaming round.'

Bultov was very still, only the eyes revealing the panic within. 'I don't know anything more,' he repeated.

Renard put the gun down. He was tired and it was already early morning. The sky outside was lightening. He decided to waste no more time on Bultov. He took a roll of Scotch tape and trussed him. It made the Aeroflot man giggle. 'I wasn't going anywhere anyway,' he said. 'There'll be no flights today.'

'What do you mean, no flights?'

'We were warned yesterday. Russian airspace will be closed. It's supposed to be a secret.'

'Why?'

'Oh, not only Russia, I guess. Half of Europe will be closed, but *they* won't be forewarned. They don't have the technical means.'

Molniya. *It was beginning.* Renard felt ice inside. 'What the hell are you talking about?' he asked.

'It happened twice already, last month. Some kind of freak magnetic storms; probably due to the close proximity to earth of some asteroids which supposedly swoop through the solar system once every two or three millennia. Or maybe not; nobody really knows.'

'*What* happened last month?'

'I just said, magnetic storms. The storms take place in the upper atmosphere; they seem to originate in the polar North. They're very intense – they may last only a few minutes but they have a devastating

72

effect on communications systems, radar, electronics. Last month there were three civil air disasters in Western Europe as a result. The whole of the European air-traffic control system went down, and not only that. The same thing is forecast to happen today and tomorrow. All Russian flights are grounded. No one will notice, of course; half the time we don't fly *anyway*, because of kerosene shortages.' He giggled again. 'They mock us for our antique systems, but in fact we can fly when they can't. And our Russian science can predict these occurrences, while theirs hasn't a hope in hell.'

Renard decided the interview was over. Bultov was spent. He took a sock and while he stuffed it in his captive's mouth, he said: 'One more thing, Bultov. Yes, I am not a Latvian. Now I'll tell you a secret, and if you blab this then you'll be killed for sure, because *no one* wants to know that you know it. I'm flattered you think I'm CIA, but you're fantasizing. I'm from the Ministry of Security. We're investigating the Varta political authorities. Keep this secret, and the President himself will reward you.'

Bultov began to grunt, but Renard was through with him. He Scotch-taped his head. 'You get used to the feeling in time,' he said. 'Have a nice day, as the Americans say.'

Renard closed the bedroom door. The front-door bell had rung; somehow it was already seven a.m. and Sasha had arrived. Renard sent him away to find eggs, milk, tea, bread, *kefir*.

Time was short. According to what Bultov had said, it was shorter than he had supposed. Molniya was operational.

'Our cities will face starvation; we would have no defence.'

That was what Bob Hill had said to the President that last weekend before Renard had left for Russia on what was the most unwelcome and unplanned mission of his entire career. And the most critical.

CHAPTER 6

Moscow 11 November: 8 a.m.

'This is the best I could do at short notice,' Sasha said. Renard looked up from the mass of papers culled from Latsis' suitcase and saw a triumph of Russian logistics. Foraging, haggling, concocting, slicing, frying and boiling had resulted in a Tsar's breakfast.

'Man, you're in the wrong job.'

'Ah! You think I should be a *dvoretski* – a – wait a minute – I know the English word. *Butler.*'

'The very thing. A Man Friday. Retainer, wrinkled, old. Confidant. Chaperon. Sentry. Mr Fix-it.'

'Serf, then. Like Tolstoy's Gerasim. Actually I don't mind. Did some valeting in the army. The officers were swine unfortunately.'

'I should like to employ you, but—'

'But frankly there's no point in my working for you, *gospodin*. I'm better off driving a taxi.' He began spooning cod livers on to a small saucer. 'You'll be here for a month or two, not more. Westerners cannot live in Russia, Old Scrotum or no. Coffee? Or beer? It's full strength *Zhiguli.*'

'My God, you *are* a genius. Beer!'

'Then you'll go back to your adoring wife and you won't need me. And I'll be unemployed. No one wants a butler in this country.' Sasha mixed a little *smetana* with acacia honey and spooned it on to *borodinsky* bread, pungent with rye. 'Even mafia lords are still too Sovietized in their outlook for that.'

'Well, firstly I'm not married. Not any more, anyway.'

'Ah, you're divorced.' The Russian's look grew serious. 'Maybe I can help,' he said, gazing at Renard with the cataclysmic earnestness of the *biznisman.*

'How?'

'I have several beautiful sisters.'

Renard laughed. 'These are real Niyezhinsky cucumbers?' he asked, prodding the fat vegetables nestling among a pile of fresh rough parsley.

'Of course.'

He took two, together with a tomato the size of a baseball, its deliquescent flesh a definition of the colour crimson. 'Thanks, but no thanks. Or anyway, if you plan to introduce them to me, just do it. Preferably one night when I'm already drunk. But I'm not divorced. My wife was killed in an accident.'

'Your wife died? I'm sorry to hear that. And you still so young.' Sasha shrugged expressively.

'My wife was much younger than me.'

'It's tough, but I'm sure you can't blame yourself.'

'I know that, of course.' Renard stared at the cod livers. 'She didn't want to die, she fought for a long time.'

'What happened?'

Renard shook himself, then said, 'Let's skip that. But I'll tell you this, I spent a lot of time in hospital with her. I observed the routines, and I occupied myself trying to decide who they were meant to benefit, patients or staff. Then I understood that the people exist for the routines; everything else is incidental.' He smiled ruefully. 'Recently I proved the point. I was treated in a Russian hospital. Now I know that even in the nineteenth century it was the same. Slower, that's all.'

'You're right about hospital routines,' Sasha said thoughtfully. 'For example, Doctor Ivanov at the Ismailovo hospital was on his rounds and he saw that patient Petrov had unfortunately passed away in his bed. "Did the patient have a good sweat before he died?" he says to the nurse. "Yes," she says. "Ah, excellent," he says.'

'That's a joke?' Renard grinned.

'Yeah. And why don't you eat?'

Renard's spoon hovered over the *embarras de richesses* before him then lunged into the raisin-filled *tvorog* cheese, piling it on to the Byelorussian smoked ham and eggs.

Sasha watched him eating with undisguised pleasure, at last producing the *pièce de résistance*: a half litre of *Moskovskaya Osobaya* vodka which he swore on his sister was genuine. Renard decided to keep it till later, then opened it anyway.

'Why not? After all, this is a Russian breakfast,' Sasha said earnestly, tugging at the Soviet Army belt which held up his ancient pinstripes. 'Start the day right, eh?' He poured out fifty grammes of *Osobaya*. 'When did it happen? Your wife, I mean?'

'A few years ago.' Renard swilled down the vodka and sucked in air. 'We'd been married less than six months.' He sliced the omelette into slivers. 'I still can't forget her,' he said.

Sasha spread pale unsalted butter and red caviar on the *borodinsky*

75

bread. 'You should have started with this, you do everything back to front.'

'Give me beer.'

'Done already. Here.' Sasha chinked two of the bowling-pin-sized bottles. His grin was as wide as the Grand Canyon.

Renard looked up at him. 'I know a true story about this beer. A few years back, in Brezhnev's time, they started exporting it to the West. Everything went well and the Party was satisfied with the initiative, until one day a high-up bureaucrat was shown the advertising poster, which read: "Catch a Russian – Buy Zhigulis." *What does it mean*? he asked. They explained it to him. End of exports.'

'I don't get it,' Sasha said.

'OK, OK, I've got work to do. Thanks, Sash.'

He folded the serviette Sasha had found and which the flat's previous brief tenant, Paul Gregory, must have left. For about a month Gregory had used the place as a safe apartment, while setting up a fake arms deal to trap Chechen gun runners. Renard smiled. One month had been long enough for Paul to make sure that the household linen, and the cutlery and crockery, were all up to scratch. He wasn't sure what else had been achieved.

'No problem,' Sasha mumbled.

Renard went back to rummaging through Latsis' two cases. The contents were all stage-props for his Shadrin persona. It was unlikely, to say the least, that they would yield any clues about Latsis himself. But there wasn't much else to go on.

The first case yielded nothing; he closed it, and placed it in the small cupboard by the front door. The second case was full of clothes. Nothing in the pockets. He looked hard at the one good suit Latsis had seemed to possess. He felt all the seams and checked the linings. Again nothing.

The suit was made of good London worsted; there was a label to that effect. Yet it had been tailored in the Baltic: another label proclaimed in English 'Rigas Fashion House'. Some more words embroidered underneath were in Latvian. Somewhere in his bookcase there had once been a Latvian–Russian dictionary: Renard went to look. He found it on the second shelf down behind a twelve-volume Soviet history of the war. He translated the inscription. It said: 'Personal tailoring. Finest Quality.' So the suit had been made to measure. It wasn't new; maybe five years old. But someone at Rigas Modes had measured Latsis; made notes, discussed the client's requirements. Maybe that someone would remember. It was a start. He had nothing else to go on – unless he decided to go and meet his Langley contact, Claud Perkins.

Renard sat down again, picked up his beer, and began to think: he could go to Riga; or he could find a way to meet Claud. He had nothing to go on in Moscow. He could trust Perkins, but a meeting with him wouldn't guarantee a meeting with Sobor. Nothing else really mattered now. And Claud would have to report the contact at some stage. Claud was on the other side of the wire. Of course *any* contact risked jeopardizing what still seemed to Renard to be his most precious asset – the fact that he was counted dead. *That* cover was perfect. He had hardly begun to exploit it. No, he would try any other means of locating Sobor but he would not blow his cover by contacting Perkins. Not yet.

Travkin had said that 'Shadrin' had a flat in Moscow, but Travkin had disappeared. Without him, Renard had no way to find the address, and he certainly couldn't stay for more than a few hours more in this apartment. He had to go to Riga.

He was still eating his way through the ham and eggs thinking about this when the phone rang. It rang for a long time before he picked it up.

A man's voice spoke, without waiting for a greeting; '*Ivan, this is for you. You must leave the place now. Take only the lists you brought from Varta. Whoever is with you, leave them. Go to the Metropole Hotel, the usual spot. You'll be met.*'

The line went dead.

Renard sat for a long moment. In the kitchen, Sasha washed the dishes, whistling tunelessly. From the bedroom came the mewling of the Aeroflot crewman.

The hell with him!

He went to the hall cupboard and opened Latsis' case, yet again.

Take only the lists you brought from Varta.

Which lists, and why? There was only the geological survey results, which came in two parts – the bundles of charts and closely typed seismic reports neatly tied in blue ribbon, and the wad of A3 listing paper which bore what he amateurishly supposed was the crude data.

Almost certainly it was Latsis' people who had called. Renard thought of taking the whole case to them but it was too heavy for what he had to do. He compromised and stuffed the roll of listing paper into an 'Aeroflot Duty Free' carrier bag he found at the back of the cupboard. Then he went into the kitchen. 'I owe you for this morning,' he said to Sasha. 'Here's another fifty.'

Sasha began to protest, but Renard pushed the money into his shirt pocket, saying, 'By the way, I need to borrow your car for an hour; to visit a friend.'

'Sure, no problem. Here's the key. It's parked at the back.'

'Thanks.'

Sasha watched with round eyes while Renard peeled off more hundred-dollar bills – ten, twenty, forty, sixty.

'Insurance,' Renard said. 'In case I have an accident. You know.'

He gave Sasha the money. 'Thanks again. And, Sasha – don't hang around here when I'm gone.'

Sasha grinned lopsidedly. He'd heard the phone ring. Anyway he wasn't keen on the idea of keeping company with Renard's Scotch-taped house-guest.

'Clear enough. And here's my number. I mean – my sister's number. Maybe I'll rest there for a day or so.'

'Wait a minute.' Renard hunted around for a pen, found one in the shoebox by the front door and hastily wrote the number on the palm of his hand; he was desperate to be away. 'How related are you to your sister?' he asked the driver.

'Not close enough for it to be written down anywhere. She's a "voluntary" sister. No one will find me at her place.' The grin broadened. 'At least I hope not.' They shook hands. 'Any time I can help. Call me at Tanya's,' he said. 'Tanyushka between ourselves.' He let go of Renard's hand, but motioned at it with his own. 'Write it down. *Tanyushka*. You might forget.'

Renard laughed, and wrote down the girl's name. Anything to oblige. 'I have to go,' he said at once. 'Thanks for everything, Sash. Especially for the breakfast!'

'No problem.'

Renard put on a heavy leather overcoat, took the silenced gun and the carrier bag, and went to the bedroom. He picked up the towel with the spare number plates wrapped in it. Bultov glared at him from the bed. He was terrified; it looked as though he had been to the toilet. Renard made a face at him. 'I ought to kill you.' Bultov twitched. 'Really, I should. But you remember what I said?' The taped head nodded convulsively. Renard laughed. 'Keep your mouth shut as long as you can, old lad. That's my advice.'

Renard left him and went to the big window and inched it open. He *ought* to kill Bultov; this was bad tradecraft. They would find him and within an hour it would be Renard they would be looking for, not Shadrin. He paused for a moment, reaching for the automatic.

The hell with it.

Instead he went on to the balcony and peered under the railing. His bedroom window looked out on a small parking lot and a row of garages. Beyond that was forest. He could see nothing unusual. In any case if anyone was waiting for him, they'd be round at the front. Moscow's hitmen were normally employed to kill bankers and other people who keep regular hours and leave by the front door. Such work had made them lazy.

Renard had wrapped an elastic bandage around the two fingers of his damaged left hand as tightly as he could bear. To test it, he uncoiled a length of nylon rope he kept on the balcony floor, took a bight around his waist and gripping it with the injured hand he leaned back from the balcony, pressing against the rail with his foot.

The left hand would hold.

His flat was on the third floor, sixteen metres above ground level. He threw the rope over the balcony and abseiled to the ground. No one saw him. Sasha's ancient Lada was parked a few metres away; it started first time. He secured the stolen plates with waterproof Scotch tape and drove off.

As Renard nosed out of the courtyard archway into the street, a black S-class Mercedes Benz turned left into the entry. The driver flashed the car's headlights, indicating Renard should give way. Renard ignored him, inching the battered Lada through the narrow space between the Mercedes and the bollard set in the wall by the entrance. He pulled out into the road and headed south into the city, just another Russian going about his business. The Mercedes disappeared into the courtyard.

It was fifteen kilometres to downtown Moscow. The little Lada drove steadily south, through powdery snow that fell like icing sugar from a bleak sky. While he drove, a question worried at him like a terrier at a bone. Why had Travkin let him go? What did he hope Renard would do for him in Moscow?

Latsis had acquired the metacodes in the last days and hours of his freedom. He'd had the metacodes – and he had given them to Travkin.

Then the truth screamed at him. Suddenly Renard understood what had happened in Varta – why he had been saved, and by whom.

Travkin was the answer! Before he met his end, Latsis had somehow passed the precious material on to him. Had told him the price tag.

He still didn't know what had happened to Latsis – or indeed if he was really dead. But it seemed clear that someone had tried to rescue him, and had found and saved Renard instead. And the mistake had been covered *because Travkin had wanted it covered.* And now Renard knew why.

He swerved the Lada without warning into the side of the road and stopped. The driver of a giant *Ural* truck pounding along behind blasted his horn but his intended target heard nothing. Renard wrenched the handbrake and with trembling hands grabbed frantically at the carrier bag stuffed behind the front seat.

Travkin was a double; but he was working for us. Because the papers, those heaps of obscure seismic surveys, are in fact the keys to Molniya; the keys to world peace.

Latsis had the control metacodes. *And now I have them.* Travkin gave them to me!

A searing pain stabbed Renard's eyes and his hands shook as he released the rolls of paper into a heap on the seat beside him. And then it was obvious, *so* obvious what they were, those endless streams of four-digit number groups. He stared blankly, even as a dark shadow passed around the Lada and he heard the squeal of brakes. The black Mercedes had swooped into the kerb in front of him.

Even as Renard frantically tried to start the Lada, two men were already out of the other vehicle and lunging towards him; he could see one of them crouch to fire, see the big Russian automatic rear up. The Lada's windscreen dissolved into fragments as the accomplice raced for Renard's door. Renard gunned the engine, and as the Lada slewed forward he handbraked violently, so that the car spun on its axis. He could hear the crackle of the automatic; hear the bullets slamming into the engine block, hear the screams of the second Russian who had lost his footing and fallen backwards, his legs underneath the Lada as the car spun back. Renard threw the car into reverse, the shattered gearbox groaning as the wheels sucked the car down on to the Mercedes. The gunman leapt aside and rolled to the ground, coming up instantly, crouching to shoot, this time the automatic a mere three metres from Renard's head.

Renard froze. The gunman slowly straightened up, steadying his aim. The gun was now inches from Renard's forehead, motioning him out of the car.

It would be better to die now. Better for everybody.

It is necessary to live, and to win.

The gunman pointed the automatic through the shattered windscreen, his eyes round with concentration, the mouth drawn open over tobacco-stained teeth.

'*Now! Out!*' He screamed the words. From the ground to Renard's left where the second man lay, came a long, low moan of pain.

Renard swung the door open, an inch at a time, crouching to exit, then swinging his legs slowly on to the ground, simultaneously firing through his overcoat: two shots which burst the door window and struck the gunman in the chest, throwing him like a leaf in a blizzard.

The gunman did not get up, and his companion lay under the Lada, his legs twisted like a pretzel.

'Amateurs,' Renard whispered. He leaned down to look at the man he had run over. There was little time. Thirty metres away another car had already pulled up and someone had emerged to investigate. Renard pointed the gun at the man's forehead. His writhing stopped instantly, eyes locked in terror on the gun muzzle.

'I'm going to take you to hospital. Dead or alive: it's up to you. *Understood?*'

'Yes, yes,' the man squealed.

He stood up, the gun held loosely at his side, not hidden. The newcomer came up to him; a big, gangly bear of a Russian dressed in a well-worn cotton quilted jacket and wearing a fox-fur hat. He saw the gun and froze.

'These men are mafia. The Merc is theirs. You've interrupted an undercover operation, fool. I'm from 38 Petrovka.'

The big Russian's mouth opened and closed. 'I thought this was a car accident,' he said. He was already backing away. 'I'll get the militia.'

'No you won't. Stay where you are. I want this man *alive*, can you understand me?' The man nodded.

Other vehicles were stopping; a crashed Mercedes meant easy pickings. From the corner of his eye, Renard could see people walking across to them, dodging the traffic. 'Help me pick him up. *Now!*'

Renard peered inside the Lada and scooped up the sheets of printout into the Aeroflot carrier bag, slipping it on to his wrist, then leaned over and gripped under the shoulders of the man trapped by the Lada, pulling him almost free. He squealed with pain; the big Russian bystander began to protest.

'Lift the car, you fucking idiot!' Renard shouted.

The big man at once squatted down like a weightlifter, both hands cupped under the sill of the Lada. The car came up, one, two, then five centimetres; it was enough. 'Pick him up by the legs,' Renard ordered as he dragged the gunman clear. 'You'll take us in your vehicle; the Mercedes is also out of action.'

The big Russian's eyes opened wide with fear. 'I can't possibly do that. You know we must wait for the militia.'

'I *am* the militia – 38 Petrovka – didn't you hear me?' Renard yelled.

'He's lost blood, he could die. You must help. Don't worry about the other guy, he's a goner.'

Two other passers-by had approached and both at once offered help, cupping their arms under the gunman's back; the instinctual solidarity of people on hand in a crisis. The big man seemed to accept the situation, and now concentrated on the problem of putting the blood-stained hospital-case in the back of his Moskvich *Kombi* estate car without smearing blood everywhere. As the four of them struggled to lay the injured party in the back, their efforts were rewarded by a howl of pain.

Fuck you, Renard said to himself.

In a few seconds they were off. Five minutes later they were passed by a militia vehicle speeding north, hazard lights flashing. It had been close, but at least Renard was now in a car which was completely anonymous in the Moscow traffic. Nevertheless, if the militia spoke to either of the two witnesses who had helped load the *Kombi* with its human cargo, that anonymity would be highly relative. The GAI – Moscow's traffic police – operated road-side stations every two kilometres or less on the city's main roads. They would be stopping every Moskvich estate which passed.

Renard gave his driver a sidelong look. It was obvious that the man was terrified, and probably of the belief that Renard was a more likely candidate for mafia membership than the casualty in the back. To stop him pulling in at the next GAI station they passed, Renard pulled out his gun and rested it on his lap, the barrel pointing at the driver.

'*No need for that!*' the man hissed between clenched teeth. 'I don't want any trouble, I don't care who or what you are. Just let me go, I won't say a word to the militia about any of this.'

Renard believed him, but it still wouldn't do. He waited until they were clear of the woods and had entered the city outskirts. As they passed through a dilapidated industrial park Renard ordered the driver into an entry between rows of concrete outhouses.

They pulled over and drove slowly down a pot-holed track. Each time the wheels of the Moskvich crashed into a pothole, the passenger groaned, but his groans were becoming fainter and less human. He was dying.

'Stop over there,' Renard said, pointing at a twenty-metre-high pile of concrete slabs amid a wilderness of coiled wire, scrap metal and heavy boards.

The driver was becoming hysterical. 'I have a wife and kids—' he was beginning.

'Save it,' Renard said. 'I'm not going to kill you or hurt you at all.'

The car lurched through a deep trough, eliciting a prolonged noise

82

from the man in the back. They stopped; the driver a study in frozen terror, hands glued to the wheel.

Renard leaned over and pulled out the ignition keys, then climbed out of the car, went to the driver's door, opened it and ordered the big Russian out. 'Take your belt off,' he said. 'Drop it on the ground, then turn over and lie flat on your belly. Here, where the ground is frozen.'

The man did as he was ordered. Renard strapped the belt tightly around his wrists, tying the end to the front bumper of the *Kombi*.

Then he returned to the car. The passenger was mumbling, delirious from loss of blood. 'Who sent you?' Renard whispered in his ear. The eyes, which had been closed, suddenly opened wide, but not with fear, and whatever he was looking at, it wasn't Renard. His lips twisted in a half smile, he coughed a small dry cough, and then the head fell back, the sightless eyes staring into something beyond.

Renard went through the man's pockets. He found an ID which bore a likeness and identified him as Lieutenant Strishkov of the Anti-Terrorist Squad Section No 3, Main Administration, Moscow Municipal Militia Headquarters. He was a detective from 38 Petrovka Street – the police headquarters.

They would now be hunting Renard as the killer of two police officers.

He finished searching the dead man's pockets without finding anything else of importance.

It would take the driver of the Moskvich estate not more than ten or fifteen minutes to get free, say another ten to get to a phone; twenty minutes before any policemen capable of debriefing him turned up. Say forty minutes in all.

They had parked close to Ismailovskii metro; from there it would take Renard thirty minutes to get to the Metropole as instructed. Then what? He would find out.

Renard said his goodbyes. 'The guy's dead. And you're right, I'm not militia. But I won't kill you unless it's necessary; I'm not the violent type. I'm going to make a call; there's a *taksofon* just by the main road. Don't try to escape though; or I really will shoot you. I'll be back directly.'

The man cringed as if struck. Renard decided his threat had given him an extra ten minutes to make his get-away.

There was a direct route by metro to Revolution Square, but Renard changed trains twice, stopping first at the Square of Three Stations, where he went to the twenty-four-hour left-luggage depot, said hello to the attendant, who recognized him, deposited the carrier bag and took the key. Directly opposite and less than 100 metres away, stood the

Leningradskii Hotel, a gothic pile built in the last years of Stalin's rule. He stopped to buy chewing gum from a kiosk then entered the Leningradskii. It was, as usual, the least well-guarded foyer in any Moscow hotel; no one observed him. He ascended the massive marble staircase on the right of the main hall; at the top of the first flight was a men's cloakroom where he entered the first free cubicle, flushed the toilet, and used the gum to stick the key to the deposit box high up behind the cast-iron cistern. As he left, he pushed open a small door on the landing which sported a garish sign, '$Casino$ – U$ $lot'. A big doorman was loafing inside. He saw Renard and immediately raised a hand, palm outwards. 'No tie, no entry,' he growled.

Renard gave him five dollars. 'I'm trying to avoid a woman. Let me out through the back entrance?'

The doorman grinned and silently ushered him through a corridor which led to a single door opening on to the street. Renard left and walked quickly back to the metro; he caught a train at once and in ten more minutes he was standing outside the gleaming entrance of the Metropole, the finest hotel Moscow could offer. Through the massive glass and steel doors he could see the brilliantly lit interior. Two doormen stood watchfully at the entrance; beyond them well-dressed figures, mostly foreign businessmen, were strolling to and fro. No one seemed to be waiting to meet Renard.

He turned and looked opposite, towards the great bulk of the Lubyanka. The afternoon was already gloomy; snow was falling and the area wasn't exactly over-populated. He walked back to the corner of the hotel building, and looked down the side facing Revolution Square.

Nothing.

Nothing but three old women, *babushkas* huddled in the lee of the Metropole, chanting the Orthodox church liturgy for the benefit of the few passers-by. It was a familiar sight in Moscow's main streets. Beside them stood a portable icon stand. The icons, wrapped in transparent polythene, were lit by guttering candles shielded in smoky glass bowls. The women were chanting a threnodic psalm. Renard walked past them, intending to investigate the other entrance to the hotel.

'*Brothers, you have sinned, and lightning shall scorch the earth,*' one of the women intoned as he walked by.

'*The earth shall give up its dead, and Judgement shall walk the ways of the world,*' the others responded.

Renard turned and stood in front of the three crones. They smiled up at him. 'Pray for me, mothers,' he said. He pulled out a 2,000 rouble note.

'*A silence shall shake the air, and the birds of the forest shall fall silent.*'

'*Jesu Christi, Son of Man,*' murmured one of the sisters, a plump woman with darting, bird-like eyes. '*Jesu Christi, Son of Man,*' the others repeated.

'*The Alpha and not the Omega,*' came the response.

Renard regarded the plump woman in silence for some moments. She was almost spherical, wrapped in several overcoats against the cold. Her smile was saintly. She took the banknote from him and offered him a candle in return.

'I am looking for a man,' he told her.

'Of course. We will show you the way.'

He received the candle; it was wrapped in a slip of paper.

'I have not confessed, Mother,' he answered.

'You must not confess, brother. It is not according to the True Word,' she said, her eyes shining.

'What am I to do, Mother?' Renard asked. 'To save the world from the lightning, I must first be saved.'

'Molniya is Satan. You must overcome it,' she said.

While they spoke the others quietly continued to chant a psalm.

'Father Pyotr awaits you. You must go now to the Novoyavlenskaya Church in Armyanskii Street. Near Artillery Square. Do you know the place?'

'Yes, Mother.'

'Go there now. You will be met.' The old woman made the sign of the cross. 'God be with you.'

'Thank you, Mother.'

'You are in great danger, my son. Go quickly. Now.'

Renard lit the candle and placed it in the glass bowl beneath the icon; it was a copy of Andrei Rublev's 'Madonna With Child', the Infant Jesus against the cheek which Mary inclines towards Him.

Renard bowed to the evangelists and they nodded back in triplicate. The afternoon had grown even colder and Renard shivered. He turned to go and a trolley bus loomed suddenly from the gloom and whined up the hill to Dzerzhinskii Square. The whole rushing and roaring of Moscow seemed to follow in its wake. He hunched into his leather overcoat, fingers jabbing deep in the pockets and strode across the vast empty space behind the Hotel Moskva to Revolution Square metro station. When he looked back to the Metropole, the three evangelists had gone.

The taxi stand by the *Teatralnaya* entrance was cordoned off as usual to stop assorted Moscow villainy – hawkers, beggars, limbless Afghan war veterans, prostitutes – from milling too close to Red Square, so Renard had to push and stumble his way through the underpass which led to Nicolskii Street. Here he found a cab at once and told the driver to go to Novoyavlenskaya. Renard sat with his head resting on the back of the seat, trying to apply reason to the last twenty-four hours. It must have been Sasha who had led them to him. They would have noted his taxi licence plate at Domodedovo. But he still had one over them: the men in the Merc had been militia, not KGB. Senior plain-clothes officers from 38 Petrovka, probably from the State Committee on Organized Crime. High-level police, but police just the same. That meant that Medved didn't know of the existence of the CIA 'safe' apartment because otherwise he would've had a helicopter-borne KGB division on his head that morning, not two stray policemen following a low-level lead. But someone *had* searched the place and bugged it. Who, then?

If not the KGB, it could only be Sobor. So it was Shadrin's group which had been checking up on him, and maybe trying to find him after his disappearance in Varta.

Medved thought Renard was dead and Latsis/Shadrin alive. How long did that give him? A few hours? Not more than that. A lot of people were looking for him. They were panicky, he felt it. Hyperactive. They would find Bultov soon enough and then they would make the connections.

Everything was indicative of the power of Alfredo Sakharinov – and of his fear.

Most of all Sakharinov was afraid to lose the Molniya metacodes. Renard's remaining task was simple enough: to hand over the codes. But how? To whom? Claud Perkins was the contact he'd been given during his briefing. They knew each other and had worked together before. He was the obvious person – the only person, in fact. The entire US presence in Moscow, down to the safest of safe houses, was under a spotlight. And Sakharinov had the priceless advantage of being advised by a high-level US traitor. Renard would leave a dead-letter drop for old Claud tomorrow. But first he wanted to meet Sobor.

Whatever was to be done, it had to be soon. Events in Moscow were reaching a climax. The politicians were acting out their roles, the country was waiting, and any day now Sakharinov must make his own move.

The cab churned slowly through the snow, eventually crawling into Armyanskii Street, a narrow alley running between the two- and three-storeyed buildings – mostly merchants' mansions dating from the last century.

'Novoyavlenskaya; five dollars,' spat the driver, extending a hand over the back seat without looking at his passenger. Renard paid and got out.

He found himself outside the Novoyavlenskaya Church, a building whose architecture and modest appearance, closeted between two ochre-coloured brick townhouses, would have made it indistinguishable from the profane structures surrounding it – were it not that the roof was adorned by three magnificent golden domes.

He opened the entrance door and went inside.

It took a few moments to adjust to the gloom; he watched the large crowd of worshippers swaying, chanting, crossing themselves in the half-light thrown from the many candles set before the altar. There were no pews so the congregation stood. They were mostly elderly women, tiny, hunched, dressed in black. There were others, too; younger women, and young men, some with long hair and beards, heads bowed in prayer. He recognized no one.

Renard worked himself through the crowd towards a side wall where he would be less observed. Service-goers constantly came and went through the heavy entrance doors which crashed shut behind them. Few had time to stay for the duration – which Renard knew could be up to four hours. He tried to scan the faces in the first circle of worshippers. Some of the old women held lay offices, pushing members of the flock to make space for newcomers; or for the officiating priests when they emerged from the sanctuary and walked amongst the congregation to bless individuals and cense the many icons which lined the walls of the church. Renard saw one of the old ladies move towards him, trimming and tending the candles placed before the icons by fellow-worshippers as she went.

Suddenly she came right up to him, muttering '*Move! Move, gospodin*' and prodding him in the stomach. He allowed her to push him to the left and down towards the side of the altar. Nearby was a small door set in the wall beside the icon screen. Renard looked around then turned back to face the iconostasis. The old woman had disappeared. A few moments later he saw her again, dressing the candles which sputtered and spat on an icon stand some distance away. Then Renard became aware of another woman watching him, standing half in shadow three metres away.

He pulled the great collar of his leather coat high around his neck, and set his fox-fur hat to cover his forehead. Even so, he could feel the woman's eyes crawling over his semi-hidden face, inspecting his form, weight, stature, her eyes darting from contact with his. An icon of Saint Vladimir was placed on the wall above her left shoulder. He half turned the better to see it. The gilded frame shone in the light of the icon-lamp hanging from a brass chain in front of it. Courtesy of this *lampada*, Renard saw that the woman wore an ill-fitting heavy astrakhan coat, shabby black lace-up shoes, khaki-coloured woollen stockings and a fur hat two sizes too small set upon a mass of raven-black hair done up in a beehive. She was peering at him through lenses as thick as cobble-stones set in brown acrylic frames. He sensed that her interest was malicious.

He had seen her somewhere before.

The choir was singing . . . *The Lord hath sent redemption to His people, Hallelujah!*

Renard gazed up at the great icon-screen. The ranks of the saints, lit by hundreds of glowing candles, gazed solemnly back at him. They had no answers.

. . . comfort all in sorrow, thou river of piety that sweetens the Russian earth with its streams.

The singing swelled over the sanctuary into the golden dome which signified the limitless boundary between heaven and earth. Renard looked up into the great hemisphere and then again to where the female figure had been standing. She had disappeared. He immediately changed his position, pushing through the crowd to where a small door opened into the sanctuary – there was nowhere else she could have gone. But as he approached, it suddenly opened. A priest in white robes emerged and the door clanged shut behind him.

This holy figure proceeded to bless the congregation, whilst pacing the length of the screen swinging a thurible on a long chain, filling the chamber with the scent of sandalwood and myrrh.

. . . Let all who hate Zion be put to shame by the Lord . . .

The priest censed the icons, the sanctuary behind the screen, then the worshippers themselves, row by row until he stood in front of Renard, gazing into his eyes. He censed Renard and made the sign of the cross, turning at once through the door into the sanctuary where the woman had certainly gone.

The choir was singing the Beatitudes from Christ's Sermon on the Mount. Renard waited a few minutes and then as the Liturgy of St John Chrysostom began, he pushed through the doorway. The priest was standing behind it as though waiting for him. He at once offered Renard his hand, ushering him into a small room which symbolized the transfigured world of the risen Christ but which from the inside looked like a changing room. Renard saw two other doors, one leading to another room and one straight into the street. There was no one else present.

'I'm very glad indeed to see you,' the priest said. 'My name is Father Pyotr; please, be seated.' He motioned Renard over to a small table.

The priest was young, no more than thirty years old. When he spoke he stroked the beard which extended to his chest and which in the fullness of years would certainly meet the belly which already bore evidence of a cheerful disposition. His wide-set, grey eyes were surrounded by laughter-lines; he was a picture of kindly benevolence.

'Shadrin. Ivan Shadrin,' Renard answered him, and saw the flicker of something – disappointment, irritation – behind Father Pyotr's smile.

'The service continues for several hours longer. I am not required for a while, so we can talk a little. Are you hungry? I will arrange something . . .' The father opened the other internal door on to a dimly lit scullery where a samovar could be seen steaming. The priest whispered a few words to one of several women in attendance and at once returned, seating himself on the opposite side of the small deal table.

'Your service is magnificent,' Renard said with feeling. The singing had filled him with exaltation. 'I was very moved. Especially by the choir.'

'Ah, the Moscow Philharmonia! They've been together since we opened the church two years ago.'

A woman appeared bearing a tray on which were placed glasses of tea and a plate of sticky cakes.

'Two years?' Renard said in surprise. 'I thought that—'

The priest laughed. 'You thought it the work of centuries? In a way it is, of course. The church has no beginning, and no end. Only a destination . . .'

He took an enamel mug of tea from the tray and said: 'Thank you, Margarita,' to the grey-scarved woman who served them. For Renard, the guest, there was a glass in a silvered holder.

'But I must tell you a small secret,' continued the priest, 'I am very afraid for my choir.' He leaned forward, smiled confidentially, and launched into an involved diatribe against the rival attractions of certain evangelical churches.

Somewhere in the middle of it all Renard found his head swimming, and sipped more of his thick, sweet tea. He was deathly tired. Very soon he was only half hearing.

'They think we are idol-worshippers,' Father Pyotr went on. 'Really, they are fools. Our icons are not graven images. They are sacred. Through their eyes the Lord looks out on His world. They embody the difference between our way and theirs. There is not much of the Holy Spirit in their churches. No living God, no grace, no truth.'

Renard nodded agreement, soothed by the tea, listening politely, trying to synchronize his host's lip movements with the words he spoke.

'Orthodox believers live in a state of grace,' the priest announced. 'Their religious objects surround them with the unmediated presence of God. At our worship, you do not see a congregation of agnostic do-gooders served by a clergy who think like religious accountants, keeping double-entry ledgers on people's lives. Our church bodies forth the mystery and wonder of the True Word.'

Renard nodded and jerked his head back up. He lifted the fragrant brew to his lips again. 'The tea is wonderful,' he mumbled, slopping it on to his jacket.

The priest looked at him intently. 'I'm sorry?'

Renard tried to repeat the words but his tongue wouldn't move.

'For the Orthodox the bread and the wine become the body and blood of our Lord not through the intercession of the hierarchy but through a central mystery: *metousiosis*,' the priest continued.

'I am tired, Father,' Renard managed finally, looking steadily at him. The thought slowly came to him that the tea must be drugged. It didn't even seem to matter. '—am tired,' he echoed.

For a moment there was a deathly hush in the room: the Novoyavlen-skaya choir had removed itself to another dimension from where its music was heard only dimly. 'I am in danger,' Renard added woodenly. 'In danger.'

Father Pyotr was sitting very silent and erect, as though absorbing the energy he had drained from Renard, whose fingers were aimlessly twisting the slip of paper given to him by the *babushka* back at the Metropole. He had opened it in the taxi. Pencilled on it were the words: 'St Paul mentions three graces, and the greatest of these is Love'.

'It is your soul that is in danger,' Father Pyotr said after a while.

'I have killed.'

The priest said: 'I know. They are looking for you.'

'I had no choice.'

'I believe that also. But it does not save you. Before God.'

The singing of the choir now seemed to have faded from Renard's ears altogether, and he had to adjust to the complete silence.

'I'm sorry, Father?'

'I said, you are not who you seem.'

'Which of us is?'

Renard was tired, so very tired; the room had begun to sway, the priest's voice came and went . . . *metousiosis* . . . not who you seem.

'Do you need counsel?' The priest was standing over him, shaking him . . .

Counsel, yes . . ..

Suddenly the glass-holder spun from the table, the glass shattering on the stone floor. At that moment a door opened, a figure had come into the room. It was the woman in the astrakhan coat, her eyes distended by the cobblestone lenses she wore.

Those eyes reminded Renard of . . . of . . .

The woman slapped him, twice, with all her strength, the blows whipping his head one way then another. He could hear a voice hissing: 'No! Not like that!' The voice was that of the priest, Father Pyotr. Renard wanted to protest but his lips would not obey. Instead he felt himself sliding into a long tunnel. He was glad of it. The struggle was hard, so hard. He wanted release.

'I say it is *not* him! Not him!' The woman's voice was angry, the timbre strong. 'I would *know!*'

Renard slipped deeper. Now he was in the tunnel. It was dark, cool. He slid gratefully down; many hands seemed to touch him, to press him gently in. A heavy cloth was laid on him; when it touched his lips, it was rough, like braided damask, and smelt of camphor. Then he heard voices, many chanting voices; but they soon receded into silence. That silence swallowed him. He slept.

At first his sleep was black, dreamless. Then there was motion, sometimes violent, sometimes soothing. And next came bright, stabbing lights. And questions – hundreds of questions, sometimes in Russian, sometimes in English; and once, a woman's voice speaking a language which had no meaning.

Always the same questions: *Who are you? Where is Latsis? Where are the metacodes? Who is your Moscow contact? Who is running you? When did you come here? Who did you meet in Varta? What happened in Varta? Where are the codes? Where are the codes?*

And on and on; and it seemed to him that there were answers, that he too spoke, though the answers made no sense at all. And always the questions came back to this: *Who are you? Where is Latsis? Where are the codes?*

CHAPTER 7

Extract from a letter to Douglas Renard, found amongst the papers of Ivars Latsis

... While still a young man, Alfredo Sakharinov had his finger in every business in Varta province. At harvest time, he provided the thousands of young people needed to work in the fields. Whole colleges, from the director and his staff down to the doorman, were expected to roll up their sleeves and dig for carrots and potatoes. None dared to refuse. Soon the region's entire food supply system was in his hands. And all this time, the oil industry was making spectacular leaps forward. Soon the USSR became the world's leading oil producer and the torrent of black gold which poured from Varta bankrolled the whole country.

Sakharinov developed links with the 'oil generals', who were just as unruly, clannish and ruthless as he. There were many clashes, some of them bloody, before some sort of order emerged. And then the circle was complete: Varta region had its own ruling class, completely impermeable to outsiders, accountable only to itself. The Kremlin had lost control of a region which produced more oil than Saudi Arabia, and was now accountable only to the Sakharinov clan.

Later the equally spectacular fall in oil production began. Varta's oil basin was like a big, rich cake, the centre of which had been brutally scooped out in an act of ecological vandalism and commercial suicide. But it did not matter to Alfredo Sakharinov: he reaped the benefit of the rape of the oilfields. No one has ever indicted him for the baleful legacy of exploding refineries, pipelines which leak half the gas produced, poisoning the upper atmosphere; phenols flooding half the Siberian water table, and a reduced human lifespan. (In the years of rocketing oil production, when Sakharinov was ordained Hero of the Soviet Union, average male life expectancy in Varta fell to less than sixty years – people did not live long enough to retire!)

The result? A resource that should have provided Russia with oil for fifty years was plundered in fifteen. No one knew where the money went. But Sakharinov was to move on before the full fruits of his crimes became evident. On the strength of his achievements he would become 'the man of steel', the 'anchor' on whom the post-Communist government came to depend. Within his stranglehold, organized crime stole Russia from her people.

Nonetheless, his elevation to the highest posts of government did not lessen Sakharinov's interest in the oil business, on the contrary.

Who would own what? Until that question of questions was decided, nothing else would progress. And that meant, in particular, foreign investment. Sakharinov was in a quandary. To begin with he knew only the Communist system, which was dying before his eyes. He had met American lawyers, and their talk of bonds and shares filled him with dread. He had twice visited America, and those experiences had also panicked him. It was clear that if American investors came in, everything would be lost. At all costs, that must be avoided. If it took ten years to create a system of private property which would give legal title to their own oil, so be it. There would be no foreign investment until then.

And now Sakharinov began to show true political genius, and a mastery of the techniques learnt under Stalin. What was more, after a while he began to discover that his methods could also bring success in the West. Secrecy, ruthlessness, political amorality, complete and utter lawlessness – plus blind clan-obedience, and an inexhaustible inventiveness when it came to intrigue – these were his tried and tested methods.

He had to tread a delicate path. First of all, it was necessary to display a warm welcome to Western white knights. And indeed, foreigners were welcome, in the same way that a psychologist welcomes rats into his maze: in order to learn from them by studying them at close quarters. Thus a constant stream of eager potential investors was encouraged to come visiting. A sanatorium was converted into a spacious complex for the sole use of foreigners, who never knew that it was built on one of Stalin's killing grounds, and that the leafy woodland walks around it were saturated with blood from the purges.

Sakharinov's clan learnt much about Western psychology, Western attitudes to business ethics, which rules could be broken and which could not. They learnt of the sanctity of the contract, which was a great surprise to them, and the lesson was at first very painful. There were many rich scandals in those years.

And Sakharinov began to find Western allies. He was delighted to discover some Americans were as hypocritical in their public utterances as he was. He found corrupt lawyers and businessmen aplenty. Accountants who worked for the most blue chip corporations spent long hours with him explaining just what really goes on in Wall Street. Above all, he found the advisers who would help him and his 'generals' to wind up, five years down the line, as legal owners of the oil in the ground of Varta province.

Now Alfredo Sakharinov controls Siberian oil, through the giant corporation Sibinternefte which he and his brother run. And from that he has built an enormous international empire. Most of it is still secret, of course. The West would be horrified to learn just how much has already been lost into the hands of this former Forest Brother. But Sakharinov is clever. He doesn't only own banks and corporations. He owns editors, politicians, even highly placed ministers in some Western countries.

And, in addition to all that, Sakharinov has Molniya . . .

While Sasha had been serving Renard his sumptuous breakfast, elsewhere in Moscow another feast was laid. Snow-white linen was spread over a long table set to one side of a large, ornate room. Two waiters in blue tuxedos moved silently to and fro. It was the Kremlin; the suite of Alfredo Sakharinov, Minister-Plenipotentiary in the Government of the Russian Federation.

Sakharinov himself was pacing up and down by the long window, deep in thought. Events were piling up and he'd had to work through the night, but there were few traces of fatigue in the lithe walk of this big man. He dealt with subordinates who came and went in his habitually calm manner. He'd had a massage, showered, and dressed in a fresh silk shirt and a single-breasted navy blue silk suit. Only one detail betrayed inner conflict – his habit of worrying constantly at the button of his jacket, which hung forlornly, revealing something else – there was no woman around him, no one to maintain the fabric of his life. In fact he was alone through choice. His wife had long been exiled to her own minor court, given an Amex Gold Card and told to get on with it; his two sons, both army officers, met him infrequently and in circumstances which only confirmed their estrangement. They were empty, parasitic, incompetent and barely tolerated. Only his brother Sergei was allowed to frequent Alfredo's world, and that was merely so that his miscreancy could be monitored, a habitual task with which no one else could be trusted. The alternative was to have Sergei disposed of, a possibility which Alfredo had thus far avoided because of a lurking feeling that it would be inequitable to eliminate one's own scandal-prone brother when the whole apparatus of Soviet power was full of bureaucrats who exercised their depravity unmolested by any law or custom. Like an enslaved Caliban, Sergei had somehow hung on, serving his sibling in his own deformed but occasionally effective way and eking out his perverted pleasures in the interstices of this servitude.

Alfredo's face, with its high, wide forehead, intense eyes and strong jaw, this morning as usual betrayed only the relentless determination, the controlled but apparently limitless energy, which fuelled his constant quest for power.

In an adjoining reception room three secretaries and Sakharinov's personal administrator shared space with two guards drawn from the paratroops, and with two KGB colonels attached to the Kremlin garrison. Over them all reigned an icy calm, disturbed by nothing more violent than the clicking of a fax machine or the muted buzz of the *Vertushka*, the special Kremlin telephone system. The reception office was a membrane which filtered out everything inconsequential; it was the apex of a vast system of filtration – the whole Sakharinov taxonomy of dependent organisms which served his needs. This system, whose nerves webbed the vastness of Russia, and much else besides, had its own ganglia, its subsidiary centres, its feedback mechanisms and its shut-off relays. It sieved out unnecessary input, shielding its higher centres from every shock, and transmitting back down to its lower levels every nuance of every command coming from above. The system not only worked to gather and sort information, refining the relevant from the dross, it also worked to amplify and direct the will of its controllers – screening out all external noise and anything injurious to them. It functioned like any nervous system – its complexity endlessly ramified, and its goal the achievement of clarity, simplicity, certainty.

The system, generally speaking, worked. But sometimes it overloaded. And the great machine's wheels would spin uselessly. Now, when the culmination of years of planning was in sight, such an overload seemed about to happen. Just when so much depended on the continuing smooth running of Alfredo Sakharinov's system the first tiny but ominous symptoms of unpredictability had begun to appear.

This meant that everything depended on the actions of one or two people and that's what seemed most dangerous to Sakharinov: that statistical outcomes had suddenly become subject to the profound uncertainties of individual behaviour.

He stopped pacing and stood by the great window. It overlooked the River Moskva by the Kremlin wall. On the opposite bank stood the elegant building housing the British Embassy – a constant source of annoyance for Alfredo. He thought of it as a nest of Jews – hyperactive Jews, whose fingers pried constantly into everything Russian. A Union Flag hung limply from the Embassy flag pole, as it had ever since the day in 1929 when the Embassy was opened. He had long ago decided that when power finally came into his hands, amongst his first uses of it would be to force the British to vacate the place. Not even Stalin had achieved *that*!

He turned away, and gestured to a waiter standing motionless by the table. The waiter, attuned to his master, brought the few simple dishes required. Sakharinov turned back to the window.

Latsis.

When would there be peace from these Baltic pests?

Ivars Latsis haunted him. You had him killed; he rose up and, like the dragon's tooth in the fairy tale, he was found in ten places at once. The other one, the American Renard, had been dealt with. Medved never failed in those kind of missions. But Sergei *had* failed with Latsis. He didn't blame him, although such lapses were not uncommon. Family is family. A younger brother must be forgiven. But this mistake was serious, and could even be critical. The Molniya metacodes! That was the stake.

Political events in Moscow were flooding his way; he was riding the cusp. Until now Sakharinov had played his hand cautiously. As the representative of the country's most important region – Varta – he had become the Kremlin power-broker and the President's *éminence grise*. But he had eschewed the highest posts. They were not stepping stones to what he really sought – the Presidency itself. When he was offered the Prime Ministership he had levered his brother into the post instead. It had taken some doing, even in Russia where promoting buffoons to high office had been elevated to a tradition. But he'd insisted on Sergei, and his position was strong enough in the bouillon of Kremlin politics to get his way.

Now his grasp on power was almost complete. But a worm had escaped into the broth and had begun to swim: Ivars Latsis, an old enemy. Latsis was clever, he'd avoided the assassins against all odds in Varta, and had done the same thing when he came back to Moscow. There'd been a noise about events at the Ukraina Hotel; quickly silenced, of course, but nonetheless a noise. Now Latsis had gone to earth. And if he should tunnel through to freedom . . .

The KGB were hunting him but with few results. Yet there was no doubt that Latsis had got hold of the Molniya metacodes. It meant that a danger now hung over Sakharinov's strategy. Two years of labour and of endless detailed planning and preparation were jeopardized by this one fatal matter.

A horrific image came to Sakharinov, and he uttered an involuntary groan; both waiters snapped their heads round to look. But they saw that the *Vozhd* continued to pace the floor, oblivious of everything around. They shrugged their shoulders at each other and soundlessly went on with their chores.

It was the image of Mother Russia, surrounded by enemies, her frontiers bleeding, that had appeared to Sakharinov. It was the image of his own life. In his nightmare vision he watched while his enemies toyed with him like cats with a mouse. They would wait until Sakharinov revealed himself, until he made his play. Then they would ask to see his hand; and they and he would know that the joker was gone, the hand empty.

For if Latsis escaped, Latsis would give them Molniya. Then Russia would be lost.

Find Latsis! Heal the frontiers! Nothing else mattered now.

Sakharinov grimaced. He would see. His KGB stalwarts would find Latsis, kill him, retrieve the precious metacodes.

Alternatively, delay was possible, while Molniya was recoded. Then Latsis' gift to the enemy would be so much worthless paper. But Sakharinov was so deep in this business that to stop or turn back was as dangerous as to continue. The machine had started, the clock was running. His forces were moving, openly now, in Moscow, Varta, through all Russia and the Republics. Ready to strike on the opening day of the Russian parliament – the Duma. The operation was still secret, despite the leaks to the British and Americans. And no dangerous signs had come from his Washington network; no hints that Latsis or the codes were located.

No, it was impossible to abort.

Sakharinov ground his teeth, striking his right fist into the palm of his left hand.

Latvia! He would bury the place! He walked over to the small table set for him and sat down. He couldn't eat, however. A bitter taste flooded his mouth. Instead he pressed the 'talk' button on an intercom placed on the table.

'Elena? When is my brother expected?'

'I've just been told that he's arrived at main reception; I'll send him in to you as soon as he reaches here. And Admiral Essen has been asking to speak to you.'

'On the video-link?'

'Yes.'

'Connect him now. Keep my brother waiting until I've finished.'

'Yes, sir.'

Sakharinov motioned the waiters to leave and then pressed another button. A flat screen rose up from the desk. A miniature camera was built into its frame. Now it displayed the head and shoulders of a man in his late fifties, wearing the uniform of an admiral in the Russian navy.

'Good morning, Admiral Essen,' Sakharinov told him. 'I'm glad to see you look relaxed; I trust you are?'

'Good morning, sir. Indeed I am; never felt better! Aching to begin, in fact.'

'Good; you'll get your chance soon enough. How is your countdown progressing?'

'Flawlessly. All our systems are responding better than ever. We're ready now, and Molniya is totally operational.'

'None of those little details which so spoiled your mood two weeks ago?'

'The bugs in AlphaScan have been ironed out – more or less. I dry-tested yesterday and again today, and I'm satisfied AlphaScan offers a magnificent new flexibility to the weapon.'

'Tell me about it.'

'Second-generation AlphaScan has transformed what was just a safety device into the true Molniya command centre – the cortex of the system. We've achieved full spoken communication with Molniya by developing a voice-activator mode and *not* in programmers' language. Molniya has a special fuzzy logic that works. And listen to this, sir, the system is intuitive. We've found in simulations that Molniya can respond much faster to hostile actions, and to new opportunities in the course of battle, if AlphaScan is used to control it.'

'Unfortunately it seems I still can't use it from here. And that my brother Sergei is unable to use it at all, because it won't accept his authority.'

'The optical fibre cable is being laid from Moscow. Then we'll install a parallel command centre for you.' Essen shifted uncomfortably. 'As far as your brother is concerned, we've discussed that matter before, and I—'

'Admiral Essen, you are sitting very comfortably, as far as I can see, in the middle of eighty thousand tonnes of steel and titanium which cost the Russian people much blood to put on the Arctic seabed. I do not have that pleasure. What is more, I'll still be here when operations begin. That's why I have to send Sergei to oversee everything on the spot. I'm pleased that *you* are pleased with your new AlphaScan toy, but you must understand that Molniya, which offers Russia perhaps her last chance to take her proper place in the world, must come under direct political control. At all times. This is not a matter of trust, Admiral.'

'Indeed I do understand, sir.'

Alfredo Sakharinov stood up and walked slowly back and forward in front of the desk, so that Essen could see him only when he passed through the tiny camera's restricted angle of vision. His voice went lower, harder. 'Yet General Medved tells me that AlphaScan is not functional in its intended form at all. That there's no fail-safe political control over the weapon. That you, and only you, have full control of Molniya.'

'Not at all. These are technical matters, sir—'

'They are *not* technical matters, they go to the heart of security. The first-generation AlphaScan utilized identity checks such as retina- and palm-print scans. Simple, but effective. It was a weapon that couldn't be used without political authorization. That's a principle that both we and the Americans have always accepted. We cannot possibly confess to them that Molniya is controlled exclusively by our own High Command; it would send them into overdrive.'

'I appreciate the risks, sir. But these are matters of diplomacy and I am a military man.'

'Essen, that's just not good enough. I repeat, we once had such control. Then some genius suggested alpha-wave scanning. I heard a lot of hot air about the need to make Molniya more fail-safe: how AlphaScan would do more than simply confirm an identity, it would let Molniya assess a controller's mental or emotional state. It would be given a database of brain scans taken at different times when the subject was in different moods. By comparing these, they said, it could determine whether the subject was unusually fearful. This, I was told, was intended to eliminate the possibility of an Authorized Controller initiating a Molniya attack while under duress, or having a nervous breakdown, for example. That was the sales pitch.'

Sakharinov's voice dripped with sarcasm as he went on, '*Then* I was told that AlphaScan operates exclusively within a human normalcy paradigm familiar to behavioural psychologists and based on psychometric tests. The idea behind the gobbledygook being that only sane people would be allowed to make war using Molniya.'

Admiral Essen silently waited for what he knew was coming next.

'Of course, it never occurred to me that my brother's personality – according to his so-called paradigm – is so diseased that Molniya won't acknowledge him. And on the grounds that he – the Prime Minister of Russia, remember – is allegedly a paranoid schizophrenic. Is that, putting it brutally simply, the position?' He stood in front of the screen and glowered down at Admiral Essen, who glared stolidly back. 'So now we have a simple charade,' he went on, not giving the Admiral time to answer. 'Sergei puts his head in the damn scanner, which then pretends to take orders from him, but in fact neither he nor I have any real control over the weapon.'

'Sir, that's absolutely wrong! Obviously I can't comment on your brother's promotion to the office of Prime Minister. No doubt he's the best choice; but I've never disguised my view that someone who suffers from mood swings, to the point where extreme lucidity alternates with what looks to this layman like just the opposite, is not the person best qualified to be in charge at periods of national crisis. However, the way that AlphaScan is now set up means that Sergei Sakharinov and yourself are the *only* people who can instruct AlphaScan to obey the commands of whosoever you authorize.'

'Idiocy! You are saying that because my brother is considered insane, which I repeat he is obviously not, he cannot command the system; on the other hand, only he can order the system to take instructions from anyone *it* might consider sane.'

Essen winced. 'I am not saying your brother – the Prime Minister – is insane, of course not.'

'Whatever his attributes,' Sakharinov said silkily, 'operational control is a matter for military, not political, regulation. As with any weapon system. With this proviso: the decision to use the weapon, and on what targets, remains exclusively ours. No military personnel must be able to utilize Molniya unless either I or my brother so authorize. That's what I want to ensure. In other words, you don't press the button before I or Sergei have authorized the Molniya system to accept your commands.'

'I repeat, that is exactly the case, sir.'

'But not according to General Medved, who says you're lying, I may as well tell you. He thinks there's nothing wrong with Sergei; not more than with most other political figures. And that you've invented this problem for your own purposes.'

'I don't follow you, sir,' Essen equivocated.

'Let me put it to you in the simplest form I can. It's Medved's responsibility to ensure the security of the political leadership in this country. That means, not merely physical, personal security, it also means *operational* security. In other words, it's his task to eliminate the danger of any politically unauthorized use of weapons such as Molniya. To ensure that the military – meaning you, Essen.' He paused and the two men glared at each other like bulls in a ring. 'That the military don't attempt a coup d'état. The fact is that AlphaScan for the first time makes it possible for *anyone* to fire Molniya. It's now about as complicated as playing with an arcade game. *And you don't like that.* It takes away your last authority. That's why you've invented this myth about Sergei's madness, to justify the fact that you refuse to allow Molniya to be operated *except by yourself*. AlphaScan didn't just make it easy, it made it too easy. And more or less put you out of a job! That's why you want to declare Sergei Sakharinov – the Prime Minister – unfit. And bingo! Effectively, only you would then have the final say, unless I left Moscow and came to supervise matters personally.'

'Technology is moving on all the time, sir. I'm not responsible for the fact that such a powerful instrument has been devised, or that there are certain paradoxes involved in its use. Yes, the Prime Minister is blocked from giving commands to Molniya. But that's not *my* decision. It is because he's considered unfit to do so.'

'"Considered unfit!" Pure treason! Medved's convinced you've made some kind of deal with Dmitry Zamok and his Nationalists. What do you say to that, Essen?'

'I am incapable of treason, sir. As for Zamok, he's a fool, a demagogue and a charlatan. As a responsible General Staff officer, I repudiate his wild plans for attacking the Middle Eastern states. He's a warmonger. And you're not. Certainly you plan to use Molniya, but only in a salutary way – as I understand it. To force the West to sit down and talk with us at last. I agree with that. I'm an honourable soldier, sir. I only obey orders issued from the constitutional authority.'

Essen was broken; he mopped his brow with a linen handkerchief.

'OK, Admiral Essen.' A grin appeared and disappeared on Sakharinov's heavy-featured face. 'I give you the benefit of the doubt. Maybe the General's being over-zealous. We'll test you out; but if Medved finds anything amiss when he visits you, he has my permission to shorten you by a head, there and then. I'm sending Sergei to you as well. He'll report to me on what he finds. In the meantime, please continue your rehearsals. And update me on progress with AlphaScan. The moment of truth is approaching. I expect to hear from my brother only that you are loyal. Goodbye.' He switched off the screen without waiting for an answer. It sank back into his desk, and he pressed the intercom button again.

'Is Sergei there?'

'Yes, the Prime Minister has arrived, sir.'

'Invite him in at once, please.'

'I'll see to it, sir.'

A few minutes later Sergei Sakharinov was shown in to his brother.

'Where's the Little Corporal?' Alfredo Sakharinov said at once.

'Zamok? I thought the plan was to meet him later, after the reception?'

'It seems to me I need to meet the little turd *before* he gets a chance to make any more idiotic manoeuvres in front of the world press.'

'As you say, then; I'll have him fetched—' Sergei offered.

'Well, before you do, I should prefer to discuss your achievements, or lack of them. What's happened with Latsis, for instance?' Alfredo left the table and stood in front of his younger brother. 'And have you prepared our people in Maly Utinsk? Are you ready to go to Molniya as soon as is necessary?'

'Alfredo, please, one thing at a time. Everything's organized. Don't waste your time on my problems, because there's no need.'

Alfredo flicked imaginary lint off his brother's shoulder. '*Everything's organized,*' he repeated mockingly. 'Dear little brother, when you arrive at Molniya, don't let Essen pull your leg this time. I'm going to send a special programmer with you. *We* must control the weapon: you, me and no one else.'

'Yes, Alfredo,' Sergei said. 'I think we can agree on the priorities.'

'So, now. What about the Jesuit? Is that organized too?'

'I promise you, it is.'

'And Latsis, whom you let slip away?' Alfredo's voice was icy. 'Do we continue our feeble efforts to find him and the Molniya metacodes? Or is our property already being offered for sale in some New York auction house?'

Sergei sighed. 'We know where he is. We could have taken him yesterday – but I want to use him a little longer. He's under a cup; we're watching his every move, believe me. The codes are safe, Alfredo, I promise you.'

'I do hope so, Sergei, but you speak in riddles.' Alfredo Sakharinov crossed the room and pressed a button on his desk. 'All I want is the return of the metacodes, and then the liquidation of this nest of Latvian snakes.'

'The question will be resolved, Alfredo.'

'Time's marching on, Sergei. Perhaps, indeed, you should have brought Zamok here,' he told him. 'We obviously need a final meeting with him.'

Sergei Sakharinov picked up the phone. 'I agree, there's no reason not to. I'll arrange it now.'

Sergei gave the necessary orders, heard them repeated and resumed, 'Zamok's been meeting the German neo-fascist parliamentarians, giving them breakfast.'

'He would! I feel physical disgust whenever I meet Zamok. Only in Russia would we be so crass as to make a Jew the leader of our Nationalist party. But we'll finish with him.'

'How? It seems to me he's already well entrenched, with his fans in the press and his Duma followers – not to speak of the Boys' Brigade he's organized. If he's assassinated now we might get a bigger public backlash than we bargain for.'

'I think not. We'll see him off. Next week, or the week after. I'm tired of his pantomimes. In any case he needs reminding that we didn't bankroll his demagoguery all these years just to see him steal the crown from us at the last. *We're* going to rule – not that jumped-up lawyer's clerk. I shall stop his mouth.'

'I hear he refers to you as "Grey Koba". I don't think he's really all that interested in our bankroll.'

'Zamok is a prostitute and *that* is what he's interested in. I'll show him "Grey Koba". Does he know who was first called that, and how he punished those that did so?'

Sergei Sakharinov grinned. 'I guess he does.'

'Let's waste no more time; today is 11th November. Molniya is scheduled to begin on 28th November; the decision is final. So we have little time to prepare.' Alfredo Sakharinov clasped his brother's shoulders. 'Sergei, you and I have discussed this before—'

'—many times, Alfredo.'

'Then you know my feelings. It's our task to put right the disasters which started with Gorbachev's madness. But we won't stop with the Near Abroad. And we're not going to build a wall of missiles around ourselves like Leonya Brezhnev did, and then spend the rest of our lives drinking and fucking. The country must expand, or die. We *must* recover east Europe, and we *must* find new allies—'

'—which means Germany.'

'—which means Germany, first and foremost. This is the future; nothing else. And we can't leave it to that clown Zamok. There's no more time to waste on nuances, on finesse. Today he must decide; he'll do it our way, or he'll be dispensed with. Sergei, make sure he understands what we mean. I give *you* this task.'

Sergei Sakharinov gazed in silence at his brother, frowned and paced a circle by the big picture window.

'Is that a problem? Do you need Medved to help?'

Sergei started. 'Good God, no. Not him! It's just that, frankly, I still don't see the need for a split. This alliance has served us well enough until now.'

'Sergei, in seventeen days we'll be eyeball-to-eyeball with Washington, and I mean without blinking. We've got to deal with this shit-filled stables before then.' He waved his right arm; presumably the stables meant the Kremlin. 'We can't have enemies at our back. It's always been our weakness, this endless quarrelling over the spoils.' He went over to his brother and gripped his shoulders. 'The time has come at last. We need to rally the people. No daylight must show between us and any other social group, or party or political trend. Russia cannot afford that kind of chaos. Let us prepare ourselves. Sergei, you have a role to play.'

'I will, I will. But it seems to me that Zamok can accommodate himself to your leadership. Which means his usefulness will be undiminished. He's a demagogue of great skill.'

'Well, I want him broken enough for it not to matter whether he agrees to serve or not. Call me after you meet him.'

The meeting was over. Alfredo turned his back on his brother and returned to his papers. Sergei Sakharinov left the premises overflowing with self-loathing, as usual. But this time there was something more: Sergei Sakharinov was in the grip of a deadly fear.

Nothing within himself matched the remorseless drive his brother showed, or the implacable will to win. He knew why. The watershed which had set their lives in different directions had formed when they were still children and he'd endured a brutal rape at the age of twelve. The perpetrators were three of the former monks who ran the orphanage where he and Alfredo had spent their childhood. But whereas he was the one who suffered the rape, Alfredo had been the one forced to witness the violation. And this had turned his elder brother into a man who had created his own justice ever since.

All of his life Sergei had wanted to wreak revenge on the human race for what had been done to him as a boy. He did it by humiliating others as he had once been humiliated himself. But that same crisis had had quite different meanings for his brother. Alfredo had responded by asserting himself in the world of men. Alone, he had redeemed the family honour. And he had come to dominate his brother, showing the patronage which still continued so many years afterwards. A patronage which humiliated Sergei every day of his life. Thus the very thing which had blighted Sergei's life had set Alfredo Sakharinov on the path to personal power, and therefore he had profited from the original degradation. Sergei knew this.

Perhaps that was why the person Sergei hated most in the world was his brother. That was why Alfredo Sakharinov's every forward step was pure torment for Sergei and why, also, the prospect of absolute power one day falling into Alfredo's hands filled him with horror. Absolute power meant absolute surveillance, control, patronage. The day his brother became ruler of Russia would be the day when Sergei would lose the last of his freedom.

The trappings of position secured for himself had meant nothing. To be made Prime Minister was just the latest cruel joke at his own expense, a humiliation not a victory.

Back in his suite, Alfredo Sakharinov dismissed all distractions and got down to the work which had preoccupied him for much of the previous night: the speech he planned to make to the Duma.

Russia had had enough of democracy, he would say. The people needed order, but someone must give it to them. A new power must arise, and that power must know how to defend itself.

The West would be taught a lesson, taught not to meddle, not to crush the new power. The West would be frightened into acquiescence.

Operation Molniya was the key: a brilliant scheme, combining a whole slew of Russian virtues – secrecy, scientific genius, strategic vision, and the raw power of the people in the hands of a truly strong, ruthless leadership. The world would see anew a very Russian phenomenon – blind determination and blind obedience, mobilized under the strategic umbrella that Molniya provided, to renew the greatness of empire, to recreate the nation's destiny. The destiny of world-leader.

Molniya had been tested, Molniya worked. The countdown had begun, and nothing and no one could stop it. Those who had tried were already dead, or soon would be – betrayed by their own side, by the political prostitutes who could be bought in any Western chancellery.

Alfredo Sakharinov was interrupted by the sound of the *vertushka*, the special Kremlin scrambler phone whose continuous whine could not be ignored.

It was Medved.

'Are you alone?' he asked Sakharinov brusquely.

'Yes. What's so serious that—'

'Latsis is dead! The man we're looking for is the American, Douglas Renard!'

There was a long silence. Sakharinov sucked in breath, then said in a whisper, 'Impossible. Sergei has just left me. We discussed it and—'

'Sergei shot Latsis personally, and he made damn sure he was dead. I've just spoken to the pilot who took him to meet Latsis, and he's quite sure. But we'll go back for the body.'

'You should have done that before.'

'I know. Your brother blocked us.'

'And Renard? You told me he was dead.'

'Evidently when I shot Renard, he somehow survived and ended up in Varta hospital, getting both treatment *and* Latsis' identity.'

'Colonel Medved, you make no sense. Why would my brother lie to me, pretend that Latsis is alive and make himself look a fool?'

'I don't know, but I can make a few guesses. One thing's for sure: the person we're looking for is an American. It can only be Renard.'

CHAPTER 8

Suddenly Renard awoke, sat up violently, panic flooding like bile in his throat. He was lying in a bed and something hurt. He looked down, saw the fingers of his left hand convulsively twisting. They were caught in the bedcover; he disentangled them.

For some reason a number came into his mind: *2134765*. He had no idea why, or from where, but he memorized it anyway.

He picked up the left hand in the right and inspected it. The bandage had been removed and the third finger ached dully when he clenched it. He laid his hands down on the old quilt, and found he was facing a small window; light poured through it in an intense stream which hurt his eyes.

The room was small, white-painted. It was morning; outside a cock was crowing. He looked around at the sparse furnishings: a bedside chair; a small deal table; and a ewer and bowl for washing. On the wall above his head hung a crucifix; on the wall opposite was placed a cheap print of an icon of St Nicholas, the patron saint of the poor, who glared reprovingly back at Renard.

Renard swung his legs to the floor and stood up. He was naked and the floor was ice cold under his bare feet. On the washstand stood a tiny mirror, splotched with brown where the silvering had peeled. He picked it up and examined himself. There was a three-day growth of beard. Apart from that, he looked good. The brown circles of fatigue had gone from round his eyes; a new plaster had been applied to his forehead, and when he peeled it back he saw that the scar underneath was already fading.

Renard replaced the mirror and went to the small window. He looked out on a muddy, chaotic yard, the kind which might be found in any collective farm in Russia. Two horses stood hitched outside a stables, their steaming flanks covered with heavy blankets. There was a milking parlour crudely made of concrete panels; he could see two farmhands mucking it out, throwing forkfuls of straw and manure on to the back of a small trailer.

Beyond the yard and the outbuildings, a landscape of gentle tree-covered hills stretched into the far distance. It was near the winter

107

solstice, and the low sun sheened off the glittering snow, filling with fire a million ice-garnished trees.

The window was screwed down, the screws rusted into its wooden frame. The planked door was secured by a big old-fashioned deadlock. He looked through the key hole; there was no key.

Renard sat down on the bed and pulled the covers around him; it must have been five below in the room and he was shivering. Confused memories of interrogation came back, but the voices which cajoled and wheedled and shouted at him had no matching faces, and the bright lights that had stabbed his eyes illuminated nothing else.

And now he remembered that the number 213–4765 had once been written on the palm of his own hand. It was the number given to him by his driver, Sasha.

What had happened after he had left the apartment?

The followers had evidently wasted no time on Sasha; that had to be because he'd left at the same time as Renard. But they would be certain to have picked him up later, unless the good *muzhik* had done the sensible thing and sunk, as the Russian saying has it, to the bottom of the river for a while.

Renard began to hear children's voices calling in the yard below. He went to look; perhaps ten children, boys and girls aged from about seven to sixteen, were milling about. Two adolescent girls were struggling from the milking-parlour with pails brimful. A few stragglers toting schoolbags trudged wearily to a classroom somewhere.

He turned back into the room. From the passage he had heard the sound of well-shod feet climbing a wooden staircase. There was no means of defence. Renard sat down again on the narrow bed and pulled the covers around himself, waiting.

A key grated in the lock, which was obviously a stranger to oil, and the door crashed open. Father Pyotr, the priest from Novoyavlenskaya, entered; Renard watched him pocket the key as he came through the door. He was alone. He placed a parcel wrapped in brown paper on the bed next to Renard and offered him his hand.

'Good morning, Mr Shadrin,' he said. 'Or should we call you Mr Renard? If it's to be Shadrin, then a miracle has happened and you are resurrected. Unfortunately such miracles are rare in our times, at least among the righteous.'

Renard sat motionless and silent. The priest said 'May I?' and without waiting for an answer, sat on the small chair facing Renard so that their knees almost touched. He arranged his black cassock, clasped his fat white fingers together and looked at Renard with a widow's air of expectation at the reading of a will.

Renard glowered and said nothing.

'You shouldn't be angry with us,' Father Pyotr said after a while. 'We had to find out who you are. We chose a gentler method than some would have.'

'What did you learn?' Renard asked.

'That you are not Ivan Shadrin; but we already knew that.'

'Was it worth all the bother, then?'

'Certainly it was. And is. We'd been looking high and low for you, Mr Renard. We were worried about you. Your colleagues in Washington were worried. They still are. They think you're probably dead.'

'Why don't you enlighten them then?'

'You didn't allow us to. We suggested the idea to you but you were opposed to it. It was one of the few times you showed much emotion. But perhaps you don't remember? Of course you don't.'

'I don't recall that, no. I remember some other things. Being slapped about, drugged, rolled in a carpet and more besides. It's not the first time, either.'

'I know about your experiences in Varta jail,' the priest said. 'I'm sorry for what *we* had to do, but our intentions were different. You do know that.'

'I don't know much at all, yet.'

'That is our fault, I'm afraid. But here am I forgetting my manners. How are you? How is your hand?'

'Why don't you tell me what's going on?'

The priest leaned forward and the chair creaked under him as he quite gently took Renard's hand – the injured one. Renard did not resist.

'I apologize for the discomfort you've endured. Try to understand our position. We had to know who you are.'

'And now you think you do?' he asked. Renard found it hard not to like the man, despite everything.

'Oh, yes, you are certainly Mr Renard. We asked Langley and they confirmed it.'

'*Langley* confirmed it? Who in Langley? And how?'

'They gave us details of some of your dental work. I'm sorry that we had to open your mouth to check. But you were asleep and not aware of the indignity. Perhaps that excuses it.'

'Now you know who I am, who are you?'

'You already know us. We are Sobor.' The priest sighed, flicked a crumb from his cassock. 'What's left of it. But forgive me again; I think

109

it's always a mistake to have explanations on an empty stomach, don't you? When the blood sugar is low, it leads to irritation and perhaps misunderstanding. I have arranged breakfast for you.' He stood up to go. 'Please get dressed, Mr Renard.' He gestured to the parcel on the bed. 'I hope everything is provided. We'll be waiting downstairs. The dining room is at the end of the passage.'

Renard washed and shaved. The water from the ewer was freezing, cathartic. It smelt of snow. He dressed, went downstairs and through a long corridor, on either side of which were numerous doors. Light shone through cracks in a planked door at the end of the corridor. He opened it and entered a small dining room in the centre of which was a refectory table made of unvarnished pine. To the left a wood-burning stove crackled and hissed. On the opposite side an open door led into a kitchen where he could hear female voices murmuring. The priest was sitting at the table with a woman, deep in conversation.

They stopped when Renard entered. The priest rose to greet him. The woman, who was dressed in outdoor clothes, remained seated. She was young, elegantly dressed in a white mink coat with a matching hat which, Tartar-style, surrounded her head in a great roll of fur, so that the face beneath was framed in snow-white mink. She was beautiful in a classic Slavonic way, with the somewhat Asiatic features that betray the history of the Russian aristocracy – the mixing of blood during the three centuries of Mongol rule, when the Golden Horde swept westwards at the dawn of the Middle Ages. The woman wore expensive perfume. Renard felt she was familiar.

The face was a perfect oval, the cheeks rosy from the cold outside, the green eyes almond-shaped, huge. The lips were set in a smile, but so full and red that even in anger they would form a cupid's bow. She laughed at his confusion and pulled out a pair of acrylic spectacles with cobblestone lenses, perching them incongruously on the perfect snub nose. Renard smiled, shook his head. He had guessed at once that she was the woman who had slapped him at Novoyavlenskaya. But that wasn't it. Only when she stood up and took off her coat and put aside the hat – when she shook free the coils of blonde hair – did it click: she was the woman from the photograph in Shadrin's case, the one Travkin had given him in Varta geological hospital. But that portrait, faded prematurely to sepia and ragged round the edges, only hinted at the truth. She was an astonishing beauty.

Father Pyotr showed him his place and Renard sat down. The priest glanced from one to the other and suppressed a smile. 'Allow me to introduce you,' he said and his smile was suddenly a satyr's in at the launch of a myth. 'Douglas Renard, mortal,' it said, 'meet Zidra Latsis, deity.'

Swain, meet goddess. Come out fighting.

The deity took his hand. 'You are the sister of Ivars Latsis,' he said.

'Yes, I am.' She took her hand back and said, 'I do not hate you as Renard. Only when you pretend to be my brother.'

Renard looked at the hand he had just relinquished. She wore three rings, two made of silver or platinum and set with large green stones – malachite probably. The third was a large old-fashioned ring of gold, set with three white diamonds. Each of them weighed at least a carat.

'I couldn't be more surprised or more pleased to meet anyone than I am you,' he told her with obvious truth. 'Your disguise was superb, but it was more than a disguise.' Renard rubbed his finger round the rim of his teacup. 'Such a disguise is like a metaphor for Russia.'

She laughed. 'Very poetic, Mr Renard.' She poured the tea; it was green, perhaps Georgian. 'You must be hungry,' she told Renard. 'I know I am, and I have eaten more recently than you.'

The table was spread with the simplest of meals. Carrot salad, rough brown bread and a bowl of broth were set before each place. The priest said grace, and began to eat. Famished, Renard finished the salad, ate the bread and drank the soup in moments, then looked up and saw the smile on Zidra's face.

She pushed her uneaten food towards him, told him to take it: 'You need to build up your strength.'

Renard didn't argue. He ate like a man possessed, while they planned Father Pyotr's return to Moscow and a gangly red-headed girl of thirteen or fourteen meanwhile came and went with the dishes.

'What is this place?' Renard surprised the girl by asking, taking the glass which she had filled with *Kagor*, the sweet communion wine beloved of the Russian clergy.

'The orphanage of the monastery of St Vladimir and All the Saints,' she told him as she left for the kitchen.

Zidra elaborated. 'We're at a place called Nivgorod. It's not far from Moscow – a hundred kilometres to the North. But very quiet. A little old-fashioned, I'm afraid.'

'The monastery was only reopened two years ago,' the priest added. 'We have poor facilities – a primitive power supply. No telephone.'

Renard ignored the obvious lie – there had to be *some* way to communicate after all. He had seen no guards or security of any kind; apart from the kitchen women, and the orphans themselves, he had noticed only some elderly monks. Which meant he could stop Father

Pyotr leaving if he wanted. But although Renard was desperate to get back to Moscow, he knew he had to work with these people. He needed help to retrieve the Molniya metacodes, hidden in a left-luggage depot at the Square of Three Stations. Renard decided to use the opportunity to unravel as much as he could about the workings of Sobor.

'The monastery is a happy community, not far from self-sufficient,' the priest continued. 'There are twenty-six children here at the orphanage, mostly saved from the streets of Moscow. Some are unruly. But it's to be expected. Maria—' he gestured to the redhead '—is one of the better ones. Maria, bring tea please,' he told her. The girl curtseyed and minced out to the kitchen.

When Renard boorishly asked the priest who he really was, Father Pyotr said, 'I am what you see: an overfed friar, cheerful beyond reason. And Zidra is – Zidra. Perhaps you will persuade her to tell you about our history and current intentions. But I should prefer to define Sobor, at least for the moment, as what it is *not*. We do not support Alfredo Sakharinov. We do not want civil war in Russia but nor do we want a new tyranny. But I have no special vision of Russia's future. We're striving to prevent certain negative outcomes, that is all.'

The priest cleaned his bowl with a hunk of bread while he spoke. He seemed in a hurry. He had swallowed the last of the wine and it coloured his voice deeper. 'That is what brings us together – to defend what little dignity we have. Keep the dark forces at bay. A modest enough goal in a land where every *muzhik* keeps a blueprint for Utopia in his back pocket.'

'I'm not really interested in your political philosophy,' Renard said. 'It isn't any kind of guide to whether you'll survive or not. Can we talk practicalities? For example, what happened to your brother in Varta?'

Zidra answered. 'Ivars is dead for sure.' Her voice had no tremor in it.

'He called me on an open line from Semiransk,' Renard explained. 'Told me to come straight away. We never met, of course. I was arrested off the plane.'

'Both of you were betrayed by someone in Washington. Ivars died trying to reach you. He wanted to give you the Molniya metacodes and he failed.'

'What was going on during the six weeks I was in Varta jail?' pressed Renard.

'After you were arrested our Varta operation was rolled up. We had nothing left, not even a courier. But Ivars went into hiding and he continued to protect our Molniya source. He protected that to the end.'

'Do you know the identity of the source?'

Her eyes met his. 'Yes, but I cannot tell you. Yet.'

Renard knew this was not the moment to challenge her. 'Go on with your story, please.'

'Ivars asked you to come to Varta to meet the Molniya source. In fact the source is not one person but three. The identity of one – the go-between – was known to Ivars. They had begun to grow frightened, not surprisingly considering the risks involved in what they'd been doing. They knew they were likely to be exposed and they wanted out. They asked me to meet a US representative to give them guarantees, otherwise they wouldn't part with the metacodes – the keys to understanding Molniya's technical capabilities and perhaps to defeating them. The source stipulated that the meeting had to be in Kalegut, the capital of the Semiransk region in northern Varta. That was why Ivars sent for you; by that time he knew how close Medved was to him.

'Your arrest was a catastrophe. It was weeks before we could get together with the Molniya source after that. At the meeting Ivars persuaded them to part with the metacodes, which were lists of four-digit numbers disguised as geological survey reports.

'In desperation, Ivars contacted Sergei Sakharinov. He wanted to make a deal – Sakharinov would help get you all out of the country in exchange for the metacodes – and also for something else – something which Ivars had and which was even more important to Sergei than the Molniya secret. That something was an incriminating tape recording of conversations between Sergei and Dmitry Zamok. It forms evidence of a conspiracy between them, aimed at destroying Sergei's brother, Alfredo. That was Ivars' ace. When Sergei understood what he'd got he was devastated. He went into shock, and it seems to me he's still in shock.'

'What was this conspiracy?' Renard asked.

'Sergei tried to explain it away as just an insurance policy against his brother growing too powerful. It was much more than that, however. Sergei didn't understand how far he'd fallen under Zamok's spell. He'd even shown him how to win over the Molniya base commanders; virtually given him the keys to the weapon. Sergei naïvely thought he could play Zamok and Alfredo Sakharinov off against each other, and end up the power-broker. In fact, he was just the meat in the sandwich. Zamok is a great politician, knows how to be everyone's friend. Now Sergei has no chance unless he agrees to be Zamok's creature and help him destroy his own brother.'

'So what happened when Sergei and Ivars met?' Renard asked.

'Unfortunately, Ivars' ploy was all too successful. Sergei was frightened out of his wits. He agreed at once to the deal, which was simple enough: you were to be brought from Varta jail and Sergei was supposed to provide a plane. You and Ivars would then be flown to Canada. That was the plan. It all went wrong because Sergei Sakharinov's only thought was to get hold of the tape and kill Ivars at once, because Ivars was a witness to his betrayal of his brother.'

'So let me guess what happened next,' Renard said. 'Sergei aborted the planned meeting, and Medved was left hanging around with me tied to a tree and staring into my own intended grave.'

'The grave which saved you, in fact.'

'True. So Medved didn't know whether he was supposed to kill me or what. That's why he began arguing with the representatives sent by Sergei Sakharinov. Meanwhile, Sergei had been meeting Ivars. He got the tape back and didn't wait to collect the metacodes. He just killed Ivars and left.'

'That's exactly what happened. It was a fantastic piece of folly! Ivars certainly wasn't stupid enough to meet Medved and Sergei Sakharinov alone in a forest carrying the metacodes. He had covered himself by leaving them with Travkin. But he died without revealing this act of safekeeping. And Travkin later passed them on to you.'

Her gaze was unblinking. 'Well, Travkin *did* get the metacodes to you, didn't he?'

Renard had been considering whether to tell her. She had no need to know in order to play her part.

She knew the rules. Her green eyes watched him steadily. She smiled at him and took his hand. 'Don't try to protect me, American. If you need our help, for anything, I'm ready to give it. We are also hunted now, so we have nothing to lose. It is the endgame. Alfredo Sakharinov and his allies in the army and parliament will take power. They have scattered all before them, ourselves included. Now it seems that the Russian nation must be liberated from without. Unless we are more lucky than Russian history usually allows.'

'The malignancy theory of history,' he said and grinned. 'Actually, I don't believe it. I love Russia. I'm an optimist. But tell me – how did Travkin come to understand the significance of the metacodes?'

'He didn't, of course. But he did understand five million dollars. That's what Latsis said the stuff was worth. But geological surveys can also be worth that kind of money, and Travkin knew of such cases. Sometimes Russian survey data only exists in one set of seismological graphs if the survey team had no access to computerized equipment or even to machines capable of photocopying metres-long graphs. It costs millions of dollars to drill one test bore or to detonate one seismic blast. If there is oil and the original seismic graph is the only evidence of the fact, then sure, that piece of paper can be worth a lot. In the chaos after the collapse of the Soviet Union there were occasions when geologists simply sold surveys for that kind of money to Western oil companies, and kept the proceeds themselves. That's what Travkin thought was happening here.'

'But he mentioned Molniya to me.'

'Doesn't signify. He didn't know anything, he was just fishing, that's all.'

Renard had been watching her clever eyes and had made up his mind. 'Well, of course I have the metacodes,' he told her.

'I know. But thank you for trusting us.' She hadn't even blinked. 'The question is what to do with the material. That's what Pyotr is trying to organize. But he's almost alone, now, and I daren't go to Moscow unless the reason is life or death.'

She went to the kitchen, calling to the women to bring tea. Father Pyotr looked businesslike. 'Zidra will show you the place,' he said to Renard. 'Tomorrow I will return, early in the morning. Is there anything you need from Moscow?'

The diplomatic pouch, Renard wanted to say. *Claud Perkins from the US Consulate. The head of Moscow's Delta Airlines office.*

'I need to go to Moscow myself.'

'You can't be serious,' Zidra said. 'We need to prepare a new cover for you. I understand the urgency but—'

'The metacodes. I need to collect the papers. Make a delivery. It can't wait.'

'Maybe Father Pyotr can do it for you? Either that, or wait until he's back tomorrow, then we can organize some papers for you. Otherwise you won't get through the first GAI station. You'll be arrested for sure. You have no one left.'

Renard protested. 'I had a driver.' But then capitulated, 'Yes, I know you're right. I've no choice. I have to trust you.'

'What driver?' Zidra said at once.

'No one particular, I was joking in fact. Just a taxi driver I picked up at Domodedovo.'

'You mean Sasha Vernov?'

Renard looked surprised. 'He was called Sasha, yes. But how—'

'There was a number on the palm of your hand.'

'213–4765.'

'Yes. Your driver is no fool. He saw what happened after you left and he skedaddled. We had some difficulty getting hold of him. We got the address which belongs to the number – I won't tell you how – and went to see him. His place, or rather, his girlfriend's place, is a cottage in a dacha village north of Moscow, near Strogino. He was feeding the chickens when we arrived.' She laughed at the memory. 'He assumed we were the police and left over the back fence into the woods. Father Pyotr went after him. I've never seen you run like that, Father. In fact, I don't think I've ever seen you run at all before. Fortunately for us Sasha tripped in the snow and the good father jumped and landed on top of him.'

'I guess that took the wind from his sails.'

'Not much. He's quite a guy actually. Fortunately Father Pyotr took one of his lay helpers with him. She hit him where it counts, with her umbrella. Then I had to deal with his so-called sister, who as it happened had just been sharpening the knife she uses to decapitate the chickens. She chased me round the orchard screaming like a banshee. It was quite a day, really. But in the end we all got to know each other. Of course, Sasha has his difficulties now. He can't work any more. But we've given him a new identity and some money. And we'll keep an eye on him, give him small errands to do. He'll be OK.'

'Good. I'm sure he'll be useful. And the other guy? The Aeroflot officer?'

'Disappeared.'

'Hmm. Then Medved took him. Nothing to be done about that. Coming back to Father Pyotr's tasks in Moscow—' Renard turned to the priest. 'You'll need to collect the papers from the Leningradskii left-luggage office. Then we need to copy them and deliver them on.' They discussed the practicalities and Renard told the priest how to retrieve the locker keys from the men's room in the Leningradskii Hotel. 'At the left-luggage office, you must find an attendant called Sergei Petrovich Timkov. You'll have to find out when he comes on duty. Once you've found him, the code word is *Maria*. Not very original, I'm afraid. There are several bags there – bring everything.'

'Mr Renard, it shall be done; don't worry. However, I don't think it's sensible to bring anything here. There is a Sobor safe house in Moscow. Better there.'

'Agreed. But one more thing. Can you organize a break-in to my offices in Moscow?'

'In principle, certainly.'

'Good. There are other things there which we will need.'

'Can you describe the lay-out of the place?'

116

'The office is in an *osobniak*, a small house in Alexei Tolstoi Street—'

'That's in the Diplomatic quarter, with lots of security. That complicates matters.' The priest looked worried.

'Of course. The place will be under surveillance anyway. Your man must be a pro, preferably someone on the outside, a simple burglar with no visible Intelligence connections.'

'That can be arranged.' Father Pyotr looked at Zidra and said a Georgian name; *Kavtoradze*. She nodded assent.

'The *osobniak* is in a guarded compound,' Renard went on. 'The building has a number of offices, all rented by western companies. The compound has a gatehouse, normally with one guy inside.'

'No problem.'

'No, I'm sure it won't be. Then there's the usual daytime security downstairs. Moscow militia. You can fix them with a bribe – but they'll make calls unless you have someone sit with them the whole time you're in there. You'll also have to get permission from the office administrator. The only person who can fix that is Claud Perkins at the US Embassy. I was told before I came here that Sobor know him?'

Father Pyotr and Zidra exchanged looks. It was Zidra who spoke. 'If you'd said that name at Novoyavlenskaya we could have saved a lot of time.'

'Well, I didn't. You know why. Now we know each other a little, it's different.'

'It can take time to reach Claud. Meetings usually take one or two days to set up. Meetings are last resort anyway.'

'He needs to be told that I'm alive and that we've got the Molniya metacodes. Get him on the phone and say the words "cricket fixture" to him.' Father Pyotr was taking notes as Renard spoke. 'He'll know at once that means me, means I'm still around. Tell him that after we've retrieved and copied the codes, one set will go to him for onward transmission to Langley. And tell him he needs to think of a way to get me out of here alive.' Renard looked at Zidra. 'You too, I guess.'

'I'm not leaving Russia yet, Mr Renard.'

He looked her in the eye. 'As you say, of course. But I'm sure you'll be prudent.' To Father Pyotr he resumed, 'OK, so, you'll get documents from Claud to fix security at the *osobniak*. He'll provide something that looks like a fax from Remex's head office in Houston, to say that the office equipment is being put in storage. And he'll put the consular seal on it, which won't make it official US government business but will show that the fax is considered genuine by the Embassy. They won't be able to resist that. The main thing is to show absolute no-nonsense certainty with both security and the administrator of the *osobniak*. Just be quick, don't let anyone stall you or start making calls.'

Father Pyotr interrupted, 'I'll prepare the fax from Houston before I meet Claud, give him less chance to procrastinate. Do me the text now and I'll have it typed out and then run it through a fax a few times to look kosher.'

'OK. I'll do it before you go. You'll have to break in the office door by the way – I have no keys, of course.'

'There are no staff?'

'No. It's a sleeping representation. It was part of my cover, but we never got as far as staffing it up. I went to Varta, and you know what happened next. So, to continue, you get in and you silence the alarm – the code sequence is 8372. You enter the code first on an alphanumeric key pad located in a small cupboard right by the main exit door. After that, you key in the password: *Macgevanny*. Got that?' He spelt the Latin letters out and Father Pyotr carefully noted them. 'But remember that meanwhile both the guard and office administration will be on the phone to the MVD and God knows who else.'

'No problem!' returned the priest. 'We'll have a couple of big boys sit in with them and entertain them while it's all happening. We're just going to arrive without warning. Our paperwork'll be OK. They'll have no reason to refuse us. They can make their calls when we've left. The only bother will be the watchers outside.'

'One thing more: there's two hundred and fifty thousand dollars in the Remex office safe. The safe works off a combination lock – the number is 376454. *But* there's a time-delay. You get round that by entering a second number: 879. At that point alarm bells will ring at the local MVD station unless you do a whole lot of other things which you won't have time for. So leave the safe till last: until you're already on the way out of the place.'

'Understood.' Father Pyotr seemed confident.

'There's also a Magnavox satellite transceiver which we'll use to transmit the metacodes. It's in two aluminium cases. The place will be bugged, so they'll know at once you're in there. You'll just have to be quick. In and out in not more than five minutes. As far as external surveillance goes, at worst there'll be one guy routinely on watch in a car outside, most likely not even that. Depends how excited they are about me—'

'*Very* excited. There will be someone watching, and maybe even a team. They are seriously looking for you, Mr Renard.'

'Well, it's up to you. If you can lose him, you're away. Change the licence plates, once you're down the road; maybe create a diversion in the *osobniak*.'

'That might be advisable. In any event, it will take a day or so to arrange all that. But we'll do it, Mr Renard.'

Renard questioned whether the portly priest *would* manage to do all that so easily and still return to the orphanage the next day. He doubted it, but the exercise would show whether Sobor was all there.

After the details were decided, Father Pyotr announced he was leaving. Time was short and he needed to be in Moscow early enough that evening to contact the Georgian, Kavtoradze. 'I'm leaving you with the leader of Sobor,' he told Renard as he stood up to go. 'Now that Ivars has gone, you can discuss everything with her. I'll be back tomorrow.'

'I'll see you out,' Zidra said and rose to her feet as well. She had spoken little during the previous discussion and Renard had been seizing on syllables, wanting to wash himself in her voice, to drink it in as if human speech had just come into fashion. At the same time he acknowledged that she scared the hell out of him.

They left, and he paced about in the dining room waiting, thinking about Zidra Latsis, while sunlight blazed off the snow outside, flooding into the room, warming him. He stood by the window, watching a bird, wheeling and falling in the white silence. *Zidra Latsis*. Christian name and surname were both pure Latvian – but the face bore clear signs of Russian blood. He watched the bird swoop behind a clump of birch trees mantling a hill half a kilometre away and wished he was there; it was skiing country.

The Latsis family was a legend within the Intelligence community, but no one had warned him about Zidra. Bob Hill must certainly have met her, yet he'd never mentioned it. An émigré great-aunt had once told him a Russian fairy tale about a princess made of ice. The ice-princess knows how she will die: one day she will meet a mortal man and their passion will last a day and a night; then she will melt and expire. That was Zidra Latsis. He did not see how you could keep her existence a secret, once you knew of it. Renard was thinking about this when he heard her speak behind him. She apologized for having taken so long. He turned, still blinded by the brilliant light, and could not make her out. Gradually she emerged from the gloom, her hair solarized with gold. The iris of her eye was gold too, inside the green; the lips that spoke to him blessed as the wound in the side of Christ.

'I'm sorry I was so long. I had to make a few calls,' she said, adding 'on the walkie-talkie,' as if to cover Father Pyotr's po-faced explanation to Renard about the lack of telephones at the orphanage. Her smile was full of complicity. She had changed into a V-neck sweater made of fine cashmere. Her skin was white and a small pulse was visible at her throat.

She told him everything had gone calamitously wrong, especially her own behaviour. 'I've had so little experience of working with foreigners,' she said.

Renard said inconsequentially that her English was flawless.

It came, she told him, from the Institute. She offered him tea and while they drank it she told him how the fledgling spies at IMEMO had been made to learn *Charley's Aunt* off by heart. 'It was Philby and Maclean in their time who showed our tutors table manners and English etiquette.'

'The Anglophilia of the Russians,' Renard laughed. 'A Langley legend.'

'Oh, Anglophilia is confined to us spies. But our boys were disappointed by the place when they actually went there. I think that was Donald Maclean's fault; he oversold England. He seemed to think it was on another plane of civilization. Still, one day I hope to see those dreaming spires.'

He asked her how old she was. *Ageless, endless, like any Immortal.* But she said she was twenty-eight, and would he help them please because now Ivars was gone and just when they needed him most.

'Where's the traitor?' he asked her.

She laughed, briefly. 'Try under any bush. Apart from your side of the water, someone in Varta certainly. A secondary figure; could have been Travkin but it wasn't. He's dead also. And he died without talking, much to my surprise. But we shall find out who it is.'

Renard regarded her through half-closed eyes. 'I hope you do.'

'Well, it can't be you. The proof is that you are Renard, and that everyone's looking high and low for you. They certainly think you've got the codes, even if Travkin perversely didn't admit it to them. If you were a traitor you wouldn't need to be here; Sakharinov would have won already.'

'Are you saying that Travkin saved me?'

'You were saved by accident; it was Ivars we were after. We didn't even know you were there. We thought you were two hundred kilometres further north, in Semiransk. But it made no difference; Ivars was already dead. We took a profound chance trying to save him; we exposed our Varta operation, which has had to be rolled up. I believe, hope, that the damage stopped with the death of Travkin. He played a hero's role actually, and quite out of character.'

Maria came in from the kitchen, saying it would be time for lunch for the orphans and asking permission to set the table please. She was twitching and Renard noticed how ill-fed she looked.

'Sure, Maria,' Zidra said. 'We'll be going in a few moments. Come on, Mr Renard; Maria has her chores to do here. We'll go upstairs. We can continue there just as well.'

Renard had a request first. 'Can one get a stiff drink in this place? Other than communion wine?'

Zidra Latsis half smiled, rose and went silently to the kitchen, returning with half a litre of Stolichnaya and two glasses. She was mercurial: now she laughed and tossed her mass of blonde hair. 'Vodka is as common as hens' teeth in this place, so this is a godsend.'

'Literally.'

They climbed the narrow wooden staircase and Renard asked, 'Forgive such a crass question, but how secure is this place?'

Zidra turned to face him on the landing, 'Well, it *is* an orphanage and not some kind of front so we are putting these people at risk. Everything is a hell of a struggle for them anyway, of course.' She waved him through her door ahead of her. 'No one in today's Russia is interested in places like this, and they are hardly aware of the outside world either. So it's as secure as anything in Sobor. As a matter of fact, apart from you, no one knows of our infrequent use of the place – except for myself and Father Pyotr.'

'Next obvious question – who exactly is Father Pyotr?'

'What he seems he is – as he's told you himself.'

'Then your church has a funny idea of the role of the clergy.'

She laughed her musical laugh. 'Father Pyotr is – or was – *also* a KGB officer; a full colonel. But the main thing is that he's a believer. A true believer, and therefore a true democrat. He doesn't want the Nationalists to take over his beloved Church. So, you can trust him. The Russian clergy is traditionally composed half of mystics and half of the KGB; and those halves overlap.'

'Who's left over, then?'

'Why, the *Orthodox* of course: neither mystic nor KGB.' She gave him a sidelong look. 'I'm joking, of course. I need to say that because I know how literal you Americans can be. The KGB no longer exists; it's been abolished—'

'Well, I heard about that.'

'—but abolishing the KGB is like a procreative act; you just end up with more than you started with. All KGB men are *former* KGB men. They've become a kind of freemasonry, helping each other and subscribing to certain values which they probably can't articulate, most of them, but which they instinctively share. Not all of them are bad, believe me. The KGB was a very broad church indeed.'

Zidra's room was on the opposite side of the corridor to his own and faced west. She waved him into the solitary chair. She herself sat on the bed, kicking off her boots and curling one foot under her knee. Her feet were slender like a dancer's.

'You're not a believer?' he asked her.

'The truth is that in my family we were opportunistic agnostics.'

'How come?'

'Expediency. Before the 1917 revolution, the Latsis line married into German blood. To hedge its bets, the family married a great-great-aunt of mine off to a minor Russian aristocrat. I got my portion of Russian blood through him. Very tactical. But the Germans were Roman Catholics and the Russians were Orthodox. This led to a split.' She sighed, 'Now you're looking at the Latsis family, or what's left of it I'm afraid.' She smiled at him. Her teeth were small and very white. 'After my brother, I am the last. And we were *barins*, Latvian aristocrats; but the bloodline must be passed from father to son. So my brother was the last *barin* Latsis.'

CHAPTER 9

Zidra poured out two glasses of vodka.

'To what do we drink?' she asked.

'To your brother, Ivars.' He leaned forward to touch her glass.

'Not like that,' she said. 'You don't touch glasses when you drink to a fallen comrade.' They each raised their glass, and drank it in one to Ivars. *Rest in peace.* Langley had warned him about blood-feuds, Renard told her, about the whole dark underside of the past which the new Russia carried as baggage.

Zidra's strange family history had been entwined with the Sakharinovs for nearly fifty years, like a thread running through Russian history. Her forebears were aristocrats, traders and bankers who had made their money a century ago, officiating over Germany's trade with Russia. So the First World War initiated an epoch of disaster. They lost everything and then the Bolsheviks came. The family split into Reds and Whites; some emigrated to the States where they still were. Her grandfather, Rainis, and his younger brother had become Revolutionaries, much to the despair of the family elders. They'd fought to defend Lenin's Revolution against the Germans. Rainis had stayed in Russia, married a Russian, and joined the Red Army. But his brother made the mistake of staying in Latvia, and when the Whites eventually won there, he and the rest of the family were ground into dust.

In 1940 Stalin took over in Latvia, as part of the deal by which he let Hitler have Poland. Rainis came back too, as boss of the Latvian NKVD. He helped supervise the mass deportations to Siberia. 'He wasn't a cruel man by nature,' Zidra told Renard. 'But it's not the most heroic episode in the family annals. There were some real scores to settle; even after the mass deportations, there were plenty of Latvians left who hated Russian communism and who were quick to take advantage of German occupation in 1941. They joined the *sonderkommandos* and exterminated the Jews more enthusiastically than the Germans themselves. They became *polizei* and informed on, tortured and shot their own neighbours.'

Zidra poured more vodka; they drank to families, the chance and circumstance that makes and breaks them. Outside, the shadows were already lengthening. They could hear children's voices, excited, shrill in the raw air.

'I have never discussed this – family business – with outsiders, Renard. It's against the training and habits of a lifetime.'

'Please, continue. I want to understand the connections.'

'I'm not very proud of most of it. But I'm part of it. The laws of commerce don't really apply in the Slav world, I sometimes think. The trade we seem to understand best is revenge, betrayal, lust, death. So I, too, have this private desire for revenge in the midst of what should be public duty. I mean to destroy the Sakharinovs. The only Latsis who didn't feel like that were the ones who had the sense to go and live in Delaware and become Americans.'

'Whatever your private motives, they have no bearing, as long as they don't colour your operational judgement,' Renard said quietly. 'I just want to get the job done.'

'Good. But you will see, and I will teach you, that in this situation it's not possible to separate professional from personal motivation. How could it be? Russia is Russia – and here no one makes those kinds of distinctions. You understand nothing about Russia unless you understand the implications of that.'

Renard told her he had a few private feelings too, after his last visit to Varta.

Next morning Renard awoke from a profound sleep of more than ten hours. The house was quiet; it was late and the occupants had gone about their chores. He shaved in freezing water from the ewer on the table and went to find Zidra Latsis. She was sitting in the refectory, working at papers. She offered to go to the deserted kitchen and prepare an omelette for Renard, and then watched him eat. 'Do you like to ski?' she asked. 'It's not the Alps of course; but there's some beautiful cross-country here. We could talk while we go.'

When Renard asked, 'Where is Father Pyotr? Shouldn't we wait here?' she only laughed.

'This is Russia, everything takes a little longer. Even the apocalypse will happen *mañana*.'

Renard knew it was true. Anything could happen. (The left-luggage depot could be closed for 'Sanitary Day'. What if one was a passenger en route for, say, Arkhangelsk, and when you came for your luggage it was 'Sanitary Day'?) Apocalypse could wait while they went skiing for a spell.

They found skis and even ski suits, which looked as though they were paratroop issue, in a small tack-room by the kitchen. Zidra also found a pair of Tento 16×40 binoculars and took them as well. It was another glorious morning, the snow brilliant and crystalline, the air temperature minus fifteen.

They set off and pushed through the gate on the northern perimeter of the stackyard. Renard led the way to begin with, moving effortlessly over the snow. They headed north. The ski trails soon ran in sociable pairs; the going was easy and in any case they were in no hurry. They ran smoothly side-by-side, and the woods watched them in silence. She told him of another settling of accounts between the Latsis and the Sakharinov clans when her grandfather was sent by Stalin to rebuild the new Soviet Latvia after the war.

'The *polizei* leaders were shot and their families went to Siberia, among them the Sakharin family,' she told Renard. 'They were Latvians of three generations standing, but they originated from the Carpathians. They were among the most vicious torturers and killers in the German auxiliaries. It seems to be genetic, like music in the Bach family. The Sakharins tended to be inventive plotters, ruthless killers and expert thieves. Alfredo and Sergei were among those despatched. Their mother died en route, and in 1950 they ended up in an orphanage in Varta. My grandfather had sent them. They knew it.'

Zidra spoke so quietly that Renard had to push forward to hear.

'In time they Russified the family name; changing it to "Sakharinov". It still sounds strange to a Russian ear, of course. They became loyal supporters of the system. But that happened later. The story of the Sakharinov brothers is horrific but typical of the fate of many dispossessed people in Soviet Russia. What was not typical was the brothers themselves – they and their family traditions. Alfredo spent his childhood in an orphanage whose very name spelt disgrace: *Orphanage for the Children of Enemies of the People*. It was a specially designed hell, but that's where he began his climb to power. The orphans were neglected, of course,' Zidra avoided emotion. 'Those who were not killed off by tuberculosis became the playthings of their guardians.

'By the time Alfredo left at the age of eighteen, he had become unchallenged ruler at the orphanage. His form of justice was summary, ruthless and effective. Many of his fellows were, like him, the gifted children of the socially dispossessed. They formed a clan, intensely loyal and protective towards its members, united in secret hostility to the system and to the adult world they would one day inherit. And as no mercy and no shred of principle had ever been shown them, so they

125

would be pitiless in the pursuit of power, respecting only one ideal: blind loyalty to the group, unquestioning obedience to its leader.'

'And the leader was Alfredo Sakharinov.'

'Indeed. By the time he got to be Chairman of Varta Soviet he was obviously headed for greater things, but he'd made many enemies and had plenty of scores to settle.'

'Including your family.'

'Including my family, certainly. But it wasn't so easy to touch *us*. My father also had a successful career and he finished up as a KGB commissar. For a long time he was untouchable for Sakharinov. We knew too much. He didn't dare attack us. But he knew how to play a waiting game.'

'And today?'

'If he wins, my life isn't worth spit.'

Zidra suddenly flashed ahead, and Renard watched her go without trying to catch her. She had the poise and fluid movement of a born skier.

She waited for him behind a rocky bluff studded with icicles made incandescent in the low sun. He asked where she had learnt to ski. In the Caucasus, she told him, 'where there are fabulous ski slopes, absolutely unknown in the West'.

'I'm afraid some of us had to make do with the French Alps.' He gave her a lopsided grin.

'Tell me about *yourself*, Douglas. About your family.'

'My family? Which do you want, the legend or the truth?'

She laughed. 'Can you remember the difference?'

'Just about. My grandfather was a French Canadian. Got sick of the Union Jack and all that Queen-and-Empire hypocrisy which the Canadian establishment so indulges; went south and settled in Omaha. Married the daughter of a Russian immigrant.'

'Ah! I was wondering where you got your Russian from. People never speak it as well as you unless it's in the family.'

'Yes. I was close to my grandmother; my mother died in childbirth when I was three. So this good Russian woman raised me. I think there was Cossack blood in her. Her family were merchants; they left Russia after the Revolution.'

'So we're from two sides of a mirror, you and I. My family stayed, yours left. It could easily have been the other way round.'

'But in that case, would we have met?'

Zidra laughed. 'I don't know. I'm quite a Romantic. I probably would have ended up a spy whichever side of the line I hailed from!'

'Whereas if I'd been born Soviet, maybe I'd have snuckered down and been a good, quiet bureaucrat,' countered Renard.

'No, I think you'd have been the same wherever you came from.' Slewing round an outcrop, her skis crackling in the dry snow, she asked him if he was married.

'Yes. But my wife died a few years ago.'

She looked in his eyes. 'It's still very fresh, isn't it?'

'Inevitably. She was badly burnt in an accident. She suffered a lot before she died.' He pursed his lips. 'They discovered in hospital that she was in the early stages of pregnancy. She probably knew; I think she wanted to surprise me. She certainly succeeded.' Renard paused to draw breath for a slight gradient. 'I've never talked about it.'

Zidra adjusted her bob cap and waited.

'In another six months she would have delivered the baby. Would have been a boy according to the placental biopsy. Poor Lisa, she fought like hell. The worst of it was that I couldn't even touch her, not anywhere. She was just one entire wound.' Renard made for the sweeping glade ahead with an ironic snort. 'People keep trying to kill *me*, but I don't let them! Sometimes it's not because I don't want to die, but because I'm buggered if I'll let someone else say when. Funny, isn't it? Maybe I've become invulnerable because I have nothing to lose.'

As he spoke, Renard pushed into the thick, dark woodland that lay beyond the glade. Zidra was not far behind and the forest closed inscrutably around them. For a while there was no sound but the swishing of skis. The woods began to thin, sunlight weaving through the trees like threads in a brocade. They came out of the wood and into the meadowland beyond it.

Zidra twisted to a sudden stop, then crouched, pointing with her ski stick to the left. 'There! See it!' she whispered. 'Thirty metres. A Siberian hare.'

The hare was in its winter white, almost indiscernible against the snow.

'I brought some vodka,' she said. 'We can eat, if you can hunt.'

'That was foresight.' Renard had already pulled out and fired the silenced automatic. The hare subsided in a bloody smear on the snow.

They collected the hare and went on to a small hut which Zidra had been inspecting through the binoculars. It was little more than a wooden bothy, made of rough-cut pine logs tied at the corners. Inside, the equipment consisted of a broken stool and a rough pine table placed on the bare earth floor. Sweet-smelling hay was heaped in one corner. There were bundles of kindling and logs for the fire.

Zidra said: 'Light a fire; I'll dress the hare.'

Previous guests had left an enamelled, fire-blackened stove pot. When the fire was going, Renard collected snow to boil. Zidra made herself busy in the lean-to behind the bothy. He went to see, pushing the blackened door on its rusted hinges. It was a tiny Russian *banya* – the bath-house that was the ceremonial heart of the place. Wooden buckets for dousing were placed around a heavy iron stove. *Veniki* – bunches of birch twigs tied roughly together, for scourging – were hung from the ceiling.

Zidra had the kindling in the *banya* stove blazing and when Renard looked incredulous she told him that the *banya* was the point of skiing, wasn't it? 'Don't tell me you've never done this before?'

'Never like this.' He grinned at her. 'Do we have time?'

'Of course. Father Pyotr will wait. The President has postponed the opening of the Duma. It means we have a few days more to prepare.' She paused and said, 'The *banya* is a sacred thing for a Russian, but I don't want to impose on you.'

'Well, of course not. I like the sauna.'

'A *banya* is not a sauna.'

'I know that too.'

Renard left her, went outside to look at a view sweet enough to lick with your tongue. The gold-foiled domes of two churches shone like stars a few kilometres distant. The river unwound through the valley into a blue conjunction of earth and sky. It was a vast, bountiful Russian landscape.

Zidra cleaned the hare and Renard drew the fire in the *banya*. When the thermometer over the furnace registered +120°C he closed the draught door and waited. She did not come. Then he swept the wooden floor again, put more wood on the fire and wondered how long a hare takes to cook. In the end he threw the broom down and went to find out.

Zidra was standing outside the bothy. She looked angry, told him she hated obsessing about people. 'It's a distraction, as if I am following you around in my head. I really blame you for it.'

Renard was speechless. '*You* are obsessing?' He watched mist form from her breath. 'You blame me? That's crazy. What about *me*, then?'

'I'll tell you what about you.' She turned on him. 'You collect people like an entomologist collects butterflies. It's unforgivable.'

Renard laughed in her face. 'Do you know how crazy that is?'

They stared at one another. Then they kissed. Gently, to begin with. Then frantically. Embraced, breathed in one another, clung on, while a collusive silence spread over the place, while snow slid from the warmed eaves of the bothy, shadows crept off the spinney and the sun faded.

'You terrified me,' Renard told her. 'My knees were knocking.'

'And mine.'

They sweated in the *banya*, scourging themselves with *veniki* that filled the air with the scent of birch sap. They went outside and deluged one another with snow, then sweated in the *banya* again.

Then they made love, first in the *banya* and then, in a delirium, under the hay.

Afterwards, Renard traced the line of her nose, just visible in the fading firelight, kissed her lips, throat, breast.

They remembered the stew, still warm by the fire, and ate hare and drank vodka. Then they made love once more, and then again. When they slept, this time she was the first to wake. She threw more wood on the fire but the place was growing cold, and soon Renard stirred too.

She kissed him and told him again that she was in love. He told her she was glorious, a woman to die for.

She inspected him with her great green eyes. 'Listen to me, Renard. This isn't a chance encounter, the kind of thing we've both seen happen in these kind of circumstances. I don't feel like that – don't want to feel like that.'

'I know,' he said.

He stroked her cheek, and laid her down and ran fingers through the great fan of golden hair spread over the hay, kissing her throat, closing his eyes for a moment. She put a finger to his lips and kissed him again, and again they made love.

They found their way back to the orphanage by moonlight. Father Pyotr's car was already there, and light glowed behind the refectory curtain.

'Wait here,' Renard told Zidra when they were at the gate. He slipped off his skis and walked quietly round to the side of the house, standing by the refectory window, listening.

'OK,' he called softly. 'Let's go in. The good father is waiting.'

When she joined him by the door, she was trembling.

In the refectory, Father Pyotr was entertaining Mother Vera to the second or third bottle of *Kagor*. The children were watching Popeye videos somewhere. Renard and Zidra entered in a flurry of cold air, rosy cheeks and flashing eyes. The priest shouted: 'Close the door! Close the door!' and called to Mother Vera to bring more *Kagor* and serve supper.

Pyotr had come back from Moscow with sensational news he told them: 'Sakharinov is having difficulties with his caucus in the Duma.

They have gone into secret conclave. He wants to seize power, but they're afraid. Perhaps all will end well, and we'll muddle through, Russian-style, without the disaster we feared!'

Zidra said: 'That's because they don't know anything about Molniya, and nor can he tell them, of course. So he must demonstrate it. Things are moving to a head.'

'That's hardly sensational, what you've told us,' complained Renard.

'Ah, but just wait a moment, Mr Renard. There is more. I met Claud Perkins,' Father Pyotr told them, 'and I had the pleasure of seeing something like emotion cross his face when he heard the news that Renard lived and was free – *and* had the metacodes. I've never seen the little man work so fast. That part was fine, but unfortunately it took a day to organize the operation at the Remex offices. Kavtoradze was out of town, the cracksman they found was drunk in bed with his girlfriend and took four hours to sober up; and so it went on.'

But the plan worked out with Renard had gone like clockwork. In and out of the *osobniak* in six minutes. Only one follower – because, yes, there had been someone watching in a car in the street outside.

'Not a good sign,' Renard said.

'But not a surprise, either. You have to know Alfredo Sakharinov,' Zidra said.

They lost the follower, Father Pyotr explained next. The only departure from the plan was that he'd decided not to leave the new equipment from Remex's office, and from the left-luggage depot, at the Sobor safe house. He had brought it all with him.

'And there's one big surprise amongst all the papers which Travkin gave you, Mr Renard. Something we thought had been lost together with Ivars. It will be an important weapon for us now.'

He produced one of the piles of Geological Survey reports bound with blue ribbon, and opened it. 'This is one you didn't have time to look at. But maybe it wouldn't have meant anything even if you had.'

Hidden amongst the papers were two black-and-white photographs. They'd been taken in a sauna and showed two men wrapped in white sheets, steaming themselves and evidently in conversation.

Zidra seized the pictures. 'My God! It's the Zamok meetings – so Ivars kept something from the wreckage . . .' She looked stunned. 'So that's your news. You like to tease us, don't you, Pyotr?' She gave him an angry look.

'I saved the best till the end, that's all,' he said, his rotund, florid face beaming with pride.

'What wreckage? What meeting?' Renard demanded.

'What Father Pyotr says turns everything upside down. It means Ivars won after all,' Zidra said in a whisper by way of answer. 'Look.' She showed the pictures to Renard. 'Do you know who these men are?'

Renard scrutinized them. 'Hard to see in this light. But the one on the left does look like Dmitry Zamok.'

'It is Dmitry Zamok. And the man next to him is none other than Sergei Sakharinov.' She riffled through the pages which had fallen from the packet. 'Jesus, it's not even been encrypted,' she muttered.

'Exactly!' Father Pyotr was beaming. 'Word for word: how they plan to betray Alfredo and take power themselves. It's the transcript of the tape. We spent a long time penetrating Zamok's inner circle, Mr Renard. Six months ago we began to understand what was afoot. We were not alone – the President's KGB staff were also watching Zamok's every move, and soon picked up what was going on. But they had no hard evidence. Zamok was too careful, he screened everything through his own security apparatus. Only Ivars found the way in. But then Medved came on the scene and—'

'Medved indeed!' Zidra interrupted. 'He was on to Sergei Sakharinov's growing treason – because it was exactly his job to keep an eye on the President's KGB.' Her voice was dark, the way Renard had never heard it. 'That was the normal state of affairs,' she said slowly. 'Tit for tat between the KGB centres in Moscow and Varta. Medved's job was to look out for Sergei, make sure he didn't embarrass his brother with any more scandals. But he couldn't find much hard evidence. Probably he tried to warn Sergei not to trust Zamok, but that didn't stop Sergei plotting: he was just put on his guard.

'Or maybe Sergei just bought Medved, or compromised him somehow. Who knows? Maybe Medved does have the dirt on Sergei, and not just strong suspicions, but perhaps he's keeping it as his insurance policy, against the day when Alfredo becomes supreme ruler.'

Father Pyotr stepped in. 'Whatever the reason, Medved didn't divulge it to Alfredo Sakharinov. But—' Father Pyotr shook the pile of papers in his hand, 'I've read this, and this is enough. If this material reaches Alfredo Sakharinov, it's the end for Sergei.'

Zidra had been looking feverishly through the papers. 'Everything is here. *Everything!*' She put the pile down on the table but didn't take her hands from it. 'We thought we'd said goodbye to this, Douglas.' Her eyes were shining now when she spoke. 'We lost one of our people whom we'd infiltrated into Zamok's gang. They made him talk.' The radiance left her gaze. 'Poor Valery. After Medved had finished with him, they returned him to us. We got a message to pick him up like so much lost baggage, from some waste ground at Vnukovo airport. He was still alive, and all he could do was to beg us to finish him off. And he was right. We had to do it – Ivars shot him.'

'Poor Ivars,' Father Pyotr said. 'It was a terrible thing to have to do to a friend. Some day someone will settle accounts with Medved – in this life or the next.'

'Before they returned Valery to us – and as long as I live I hope I never have to hear such screams again – they pulled everything out of him, everything. That was a terrible blow to Sobor – and the beginning of the end for Ivars. For the first time Medved realized who was behind Sobor – the Latsis family. He still didn't know that Ivars was actually in Varta, mining the very ground under the Sakharinovs. Valery never knew about the Shadrin cover. But what he'd told Medved was enough. Ivars knew then that time was running out for him. All the connections were made: the traitor in Washington had given them Shadrin, and now they were about to learn that Shadrin was none other than Ivars Latsis.'

'They made Valery talk, but not quickly enough,' Father Pyotr said. 'We had time to clean up the operation. We saved the tape and the transcripts. But it was Ivars who had custody of them, and when he was lost, so was this precious evidence. That was the worst thing – it made his death so pointless.'

'Does Sergei know Ivars had kept back copies of the transcripts?' Renard asked.

'I'm coming to that and this is what's really sensational—' began the priest.

But Renard was still thinking aloud, 'The transcripts might be useful, but they aren't strong enough by themselves.'

'Well, I've been trying to tell you the whole story for the past five minutes,' Father Pyotr said.

'*What? What?*' They both pounced on him.

'I found a note in the papers – in our Sobor code. There is a copy of the tape, and I know where it is.' He grinned triumphantly. 'The most obvious place, of course. Ivars left it in a Sobor safe house in Moscow – the one I mentioned to you.'

Zidra said: 'I suddenly have new hope. Ivars didn't fail at all, and he left us a precious weapon.'

'The crisis in the Duma is worsening, there are already signs of a split between Sakharinov and the Nationalists. So the Lord has given us the instrument of vengeance at just the right moment.'

'How do you plan to use this tape and pictures?' Renard wanted to know.

It was Zidra who answered. 'We can break Sergei Sakharinov with them. He's mortally afraid of his brother, and rightly so. Look at this—' she shuffled the papers. '—here he talks quite openly to Zamok about his feelings, and they discuss different scenarios for taking power. Listen to this: Sergei is speaking: "Apart from Alfredo, only I will be able to fire the weapon. There are keys to it, like the keys that control our missiles." So the fool has already blabbed about the existence of Molniya to Zamok. That'd be enough by itself to cost him his head.'

'Probably what Sergei planned was to use his relationship with Zamok to broker a deal,' Renard said. 'He wanted to create a ruling triumvirate for Russia as an alternative to exclusive rule by his brother.'

While he spoke, Zidra went on shuffling the pages. 'Listen. He goes on: "We will engineer a profound crisis at the centre. What I propose is really very simple. My brother will be in Moscow – the bastard will try to pull all the levers with his own hands, of course. Which means I will have to go to Molniya – it's in the Arctic region, in Semiransk—" Christ, he's blabby!' Zidra interrupted herself, '"—while I'm there, that'll be the time for you to strike. You must present him with your ultimatum. He will certainly call me at the Molniya base, and that's when I'll tell him: there has to be a deal with the Nationalists. We must go forward together."

'Zamok then asks him when all this is going to happen. Within three months, Sergei tells him.'

'Very interesting,' Renard said. 'It directly confirms what we thought – Alfredo Sakharinov will use the crisis in parliament to strike, and he definitely plans to use Molniya. He wants to paralyse the West, then force it into submission, at the same moment when he takes power in Russia.'

'Sakharinov and Zamok are tactical allies. They need each other up to and including the moment one of them grabs power,' Zidra said. 'But there can only be one Tsar. If Sakharinov wins he'll turn on Zamok immediately. There'll be no games, no deals. And Zamok likewise; if he comes out on top in the next few days, he will sooner or later have to destroy Sakharinov. He owes him too much; he'll settle the debt with blood. That was obvious to both Zamok and Alfredo Sakharinov. Only Sergei was too stupid not to see it. Alfredo is strong, but he's not a charismatic leader like Zamok. He has no hope of bringing the masses on to the streets. He needs Zamok to do that; Zamok will deliver the popular support which is necessary for Sakharinov to exercise absolute power. But then he will entrench himself behind a whole new KGB state. He won't need Zamok, and neither will Zamok need the Sakharinovs if he wins out. Sergei thought he would hold the balance of power, but in fact he is just the meat in the sandwich.'

'But Zamok's popular support is the ace in his hand,' Father Pyotr amplified. 'It'd be very dangerous for Sakharinov to openly go against him. Even so, Sakharinov isn't like those German industrialists who supported Hitler and then found that once the genie was out of the bottle they couldn't put it back. Sakharinov will form his first government literally over Zamok's dead body.'

'If Molniya were used,' Renard added, 'it seems to me that this material by itself would almost be enough to brand both the Sakharinovs as international war criminals.'

'Indeed it would. There seems no limit to Sergei's imbecilism, does there?'

Zidra smiled ruefully. 'He's a very typical product of the Russian bureaucracy, in fact. The kind who have destroyed this country.'

'Well, we need to find him, and before he finds us.'

'Through Zamok: that's the way. He's the easiest to reach. He's in the parliament, he's accessible. He will lead us to Sergei.'

'We have to offer him something,' Renard said. 'Only the US government can do that. A safe passage out, defection, a new life, an island in the sun. And to organize anything like that we'll need some help. In fact, we need Claud Perkins.'

'We'll do it – tomorrow.' Father Pyotr, yawning, looked weary but pleased. When Mother Vera returned from supervising lights-out he took her on his knee. 'Human frailty,' he mumbled sheepishly to Renard. 'Life is short, and the Lord forgives.'

Zidra and Renard said their farewells and left. That night they lay together, on the narrow cot in Renard's room. Outside, a hard moon buffed the land till it gleamed like old silver. They made love and slept coiled around each other. In a dream he heard her say that they would be together, and he agreed. To the end.

When Renard opened his eyes in the morning she was standing with her back to him, looking out through the little sunlit windows, her knuckles pressed on the sill, one knee resting on the wicker chair so that the pale-lemon sole of her foot was visible.

She came to him and kneeled over the bed, legs astride him.

He said: 'You look different.'

'That's because in the night I lost my loneliness.'

He kissed her mouth and her breasts and then they curled up under the heavy quilt for a while longer and made love again, fiercely, without gentleness, seizing and opening and entering and devouring, as though daylight and the thought of duty had made them frantic.

Soon after while they were dressing Renard told her he was going to ask Father Pyotr to marry them, and dared her to object. 'I want to be the first member of the Company to have the knot tied by a full KGB colonel.'

No objection was voiced.

Downstairs, it was back to business. Renard pulled the laptop from its canvas sack and installed the encrypted floppy disk which contained the command files he needed to plug into the X.25-protocol packet switching circuits from any telephone in the world. From then on he could communicate with Washington. Finally he connected the portable hand scanner he'd placed in the holdall together with the laptop and baby printer. He tried scanning in the rows and columns of figures on the rolls of A3 paper which were the Molniya codes.

The results were not a success. The scanner's optical character-recognition software was supposed to learn from its mistakes when it wrongly interpreted a letter or digit. But the codes were smudged carbons on creased and crumpled paper, and the scanner couldn't pick the numbers up; there were hundreds of errors. To correct them would require two people, one to proofread and one to enter the corrections from the keyboard. It would take two or three days to arrive at the faultless result which was necessary.

Zidra peered at the screen. 'We'll have no time to fix all that. You'll have to give me the codes; I'll do as we decided. The fall-back. I'll see to it now.'

'The *fall-back*? I thought that was a joke over a glass of vodka. Are you serious? It'll take all day – maybe two.'

'It's your choice. But I think it's necessary to make a copy, to have a backup.'

'OK then. In the meantime I'll try out the Magnavox, and we'll see whether anything still works up there—' Renard pointed skywards, '—after all the magnetic storms of the past few weeks.'

Zidra commandeered the classroom and organized the orphans to copy out the Molniya codes. Renard shook his head and left to set up the Magnavox.

The equipment came in two medium-sized aluminium suitcases, each weighing around twenty kilos. It offered the user truly global communications. The Magnavox had telephone and fax lines, and a telex link. It was simple to set up; the parabolic antenna unfurled like an umbrella. It only took a compass bearing to orient the antenna at one of the two available Inmarsat satellites. Once the satellite linked the Magnavox to a ground station such as Goonhilly Down in the UK, numbers could be dialled up anywhere in the world on the normal public telephone system.

Renard tried first to connect to the satellite in geostationary orbit over the Indian Ocean. It was impossible to lock on to it.

'Can't wind the gismo up,' he told Father Pyotr, who was pacing up and down in an attitude of prayer. Instead he reoriented the antenna and tried to lock on to the Inmarsat satellite hovering 20,000 miles over the Pacific Ocean. Father Pyotr couldn't bear the tension and left for the garden.

'Either the Magnavox is faulty or the whole Inmarsat system is down,' Renard told Zidra who had joined him, briefly. 'I'm sure about the Magnavox; it's reliable and I installed it myself before I came here. So Inmarsat is down – that's because of the testing of Molniya's EMP generator. That'll have catastrophic consequences for the world's maritime communications, apart from anything else.'

'We'll take the originals to Claud today,' urged Zidra, 'and he'll get them to Washington; so they'll get the stuff one way or another. The copies will be stored here. You've played your part, Douglas. You couldn't have done more. But the fact is that civil aviation has been thrown into total chaos as well. Father Pyotr checked yesterday with Moscow air-traffic control. There'll be no more flights to the US for at least three days.'

She watched him play with the keyboard: runes scrolled over the LCD screen and suddenly Renard said, 'I'm there! We've got it!'

The next stage was to prepare the metacodes in the form of a fax. Mother Vera recruited one of her teachers and worked with the orphans for six hours, copying, recopying, checking against the originals. Then everything was checked, double- and triple-checked by Zidra, Renard and Father Pyotr. The result was a pile of 195 sheets of A4. These had to be scanned into the PC – which took Renard another three hours. He then had to encrypt the fax datastream: another thirty-two minutes.

'How will we reward the children?' Zidra asked.

'Hell, I'll bring them Arnie Schwarzenegger here in person!' Renard laughed. 'Only in Russia,' he said, 'could the fate of the world depend upon the handwriting skills of a bunch of kids sitting in a godforsaken orphanage in the back of beyond.'

'Not *god*forsaken, Douglas,' Zidra corrected. 'Forsaken by the world, perhaps.'

At 2.30 in the morning the Magnavox was switched on again. This time the log-on routines worked at once. In less than two minutes Renard was dialling a fax number in Washington. The transmission began at once. It took two hours and 52 minutes to complete. Next morning, when Paul Gregory arrived at his desk at Langley he would find a 198-page fax waiting for him, consisting of a letter from Renard and 195 pages of crabbed juvenile handwriting. The Molniya metacodes.

Renard picked the bundle of pages up and held them close to his chest like a trophy, but Zidra took them from him, laid them aside, and led him up the stairs. 'They'll be safe for an hour or two,' she told him. She took his hand to her lips and kissed it. 'You were in pain today; I saw it.' She reached her arms around his neck and kissed his lips. 'I see everything,' she said.

CHAPTER 10

They set off for Moscow before seven. It was still dark outside when they left the orphanage. Mother Vera and little Maria came to say good-bye. Maria solemnly produced two giant Antonovka apples, one each for Renard and Zidra. Renard had been befriended by her on his kitchen forays and now he swept the shivering girl into his arms and kissed her. 'I'll be back,' he promised.

He had changed into a loud check suit brought from his office by Father Pyotr. *The archetypal Houston joint-venturer*, Zidra had dubbed him. It might have been better to avoid an American identity, Renard had thought. But the others were sure this was right. Where they were going it would not look out of place.

The car swept south. They talked about Russia, where nothing had changed according to Father Pyotr, despite the collapse of the old order.

'You're wrong,' Zidra said. 'There are a great many differences, but I'll give you one key example. People used to say that the Soviet Union was a lawless state. But now ordinary Russians feel abandoned by the law. For each one of them, it's sink or swim alone in a black ocean. The only chance of survival is to be poor and inconspicuous. And if you become the victim of a crime, God help you if you're stupid enough to complain to the police whose real paymasters are the criminals themselves. That's the sort of decay I'm talking about. And I'll tell you when it began: not in Stalin's time, but in 1984, with the assassination of Yuri Andropov. He was the General Secretary of the Communist Party and the most powerful man in Soviet Russia; and he was shot down by the wife of his own Interior Minister *at a Kremlin reception for all the country's rulers to see*. Murdered, because he wanted to do something about the cancer of corruption! The world was told he died of kidney disease – a lie which the West connived at for its own reasons. And after that, no one ever again dared challenge the power of the Soviet mafia – not Gorbachev, not Yeltsin, none of them. The shooting of Andropov was the beginning of today's lawlessness, because the country's chief policeman openly proclaimed himself a criminal who could organize any crime with impunity, even the murder of the head of state *in public*.'

'And Stalin's times were *better*?' Renard queried.

'Ask almost any Russian the answer to that, and see what they say,' Zidra told him.

By mid-afternoon they had arrived at the Sovietskaya Hotel, a once-fashionable monument to Stalinist architecture in downtown Moscow. Renard was booked in – 'for one night, while we arrange something else,' Father Pyotr had promised.

'Why not a safe house?' Renard asked.

'Anonymity,' was Zidra's answer. 'We only have one safe house left that we're sure of, and it's not equipped to stay there.'

She then suddenly announced that she would have to spend thirty minutes meeting some Georgian crony. Disarmingly, she poured Renard a tumbler of Black Label and left.

Renard decided to have a bath while he waited for her to come back. That took forty minutes. While he dressed he watched the news on television. It began with advertisements by Russian enterprises for such desirable consumer items as fork-lift trucks, meat-processing machinery and heavy industrial chemicals, followed by advertisements for Western products such as Plainsman cigarettes, 'the smoking of which brings you closer to America'; authentic American chewing gum; American-style furniture made in Finland; American-style furniture made in Kiev. And finally a sequence of advertisements for food products such as: 'Minsk No. 3 Egg Factory offers you world-standard eggs' – pictures of hens in batteries laying eggs on conveyor belts.

The main news showed the deputies arriving for the Duma session. The Russian Nationalists, who were in the majority, had demanded that Government ministers, and in particular Minister Plenipotentiary Alfredo Sakharinov, act decisively to overcome Russia's crisis. Dmitry Zamok, their leader, was shown at a rally, denouncing the 'Western Finance conspiracy against the Russian people' and demanding that all non-Russian citizens be required to register at their local police stations, 'to help stamp out speculation, corruption and the destruction of the nation's moral strength.'

Then there was a talking-heads interview with him. 'We are not opposed to Germany. There must be a strong state in central Europe,' he told the interviewer, a pretty blonde of about twenty-two. 'But Russia must also be a strong state, let them not forget that. Must be; *will* be. We are not going to become some kind of historical backwater, a third-world hinterland for German business to roam freely in.' Zamok's voice began to rise. 'Cheap labour, cheap raw materials, a dumping ground for toxic wastes, for their surplus production, for the poor quality goods they insult us with, the leavings of Europe?' He had started to screech. The girl nodded timidly. 'That is *not* going to be our future. No! Let there be unity, let us be allies, great Germany and great Russia. But *we* are not going to be slaves.'

By now Zamok was frothing, his right hand sawing the air, as if the girl in front of him was personally responsible for the cataclysm which had overtaken Russia. '*They* want a weak Russia, but Russia defeated the Mongol hordes and the Teutons, Russia buried Hitler and saved Europe. That Russia will arise anew.'

Finally Zamok turned to the practicalities: he would stamp out crime by reopening labour-and-reeducation camps, and by the summary execution of miscreants. 'Bribery? Simple. Corrupt bureaucrats will be summarily shot. The government has failed to defend Russian interests abroad. It is a government of infamy, peopled by criminals whose only goal is to plunder Russia and make their get-away.'

The next news item reported that Alfredo Sakharinov's office had issued a statement reaffirming support for the President, and declaring that if the crisis continued unabated, decisive measures would be required. Sakharinov, it said, supported good relations with all of Russia's neighbours and with the West.

There were food riots reported in some Urals cities, then protests and riots over job losses in St Petersburg and Moscow. In St Petersburg the management of the newly privatized Putilov concern had dismissed half the workforce – 15,000 workers – who were now trying to burn down the works in reprisal.

And there'd been more freak magnetic storms over Europe and parts of Central Asia, which had downed two civilian airliners over Europe: one of which had crashed in a Paris suburb, the other over the Austrian Alps. An airliner had also crashed in Kazakhstan. The storms had brought air transport to a standstill over the whole of Europe and chaos to global telecommunications systems. Two communication satellite systems had been totally disrupted and even landline and fibre-optic pathways were affected.

Watching it all, and on his own, Renard's thoughts raced. What was it Bob Hill had said to Duncan, that last day in Washington? About Zamok and Sakharinov. *The victimization of Russia is their theme tune: they both talk about the bleeding frontiers, just like Hitler did.*

Someone had said 'Bunkum'. But for once Bob Hill defended Admiral Duncan. *If Germany and Russia had been allies in either of the last two World Wars they would have won. Look at the situation today, when fascist movements of one kind or another are important forces in Italy and Germany, and are near to taking power in Russia.*

Renard switched off the television and looked at his watch. Zidra had been gone more than an hour. He took out the heavy silenced automatic and broke it down and cleaned it, checking the ammunition clips, then returned it to his shoulder holster. He went to the bathroom and inspected his face; the bruises had gone and the scar over his temple was fading.

Back in the lounge, he poured out a large Scotch, drank it, poured another and checked his watch. Two hours had passed. Outside in the corridor he heard a shuffling sound; he strained to listen. The shuffling receded, amid drunken laughter and words exchanged in what sounded like the Azeri language. Renard picked up the hotel guide and checked for the number of his floor lady, dialled it and complained about the drunks in the passage. In less than a minute he heard her shouting at them down the passage. So they were not hotel KGB. Or else the performance tonight was extra special.

Overhead the party which had been warming up for the past hour was now in full swing. Through the massive walls and floors of the Sovietskaya he could hear loud music and shrill female laughter. A rhythmic thumping began, signalling a new stage.

Two and a half hours. He went to the double windows which gave on to a tiny balcony and threw them open. It was snowing. Renard's room was on the fifth floor and the only way of escape would be to swing down to the balcony beneath, which in all probability would be no escape at all since that exit route would certainly be covered.

He closed the windows, wondering again why he had not insisted on staying at the safe house, when he heard a scratching at the door from the corridor. Renard was there in two strides, gun in hand. He opened the door and Zidra stalked in, radiant, scented, perfect. She pounced on Renard, kissed the anger off his face and walked through the bedroom, throwing her coat on a chair.

'You are cold,' he followed her and chafed her frozen hands and kissed her cheeks.

'I need a drink. Did you miss me?'

Renard gestured, 'A little. I thought of calling the militia, you know, just to tell them I'd lost you.' He put the gun down on a sideboard and picked up the whisky bottle. 'Then I decided not to bother and drank Scotch instead.'

'Everything is done,' she said. 'Pyotr's been calling around like crazy. The arrangements are made.'

'Good. Then there's nothing more to do but wait.'

She kissed him very gently on the lips. 'That's not the main news. Which is that we're to meet Sergei Sakharinov. As we decided. All or nothing, now.'

Renard nodded slowly. 'I'm impressed; Sobor is working.'

'You ain't seen nothing yet.' She uncoiled the long student-style scarf around her neck and the reason for her absence was clear. 'I went to our safe house where I keep some clothes. What do you think?'

She twirled, and Renard inspected her. She was wearing a plain calf-length dress made of amber-coloured botany wool. It clung to her all over. Around her neck was a single string of pearls. On her feet were amber-coloured patent stilettos. She carried a small amber handbag.

Zidra kicked off the shoes, walked across the room on her toes, like a dancer, and stood on his. They kissed and he mumbled: 'Where the hell *were* you?' into the warmth under the coils of hair on the nape of her neck. 'I love you and I've just spent two hours and thirty-eight minutes learning what *going crazy* over someone means.'

She laughed, whispered in his ear: 'We're secure here. We have friends in the hotel security. And there's a good restaurant at the Sovietskaya. We've arranged a private room, so we won't be disturbed.'

Renard said OK, went to the bathroom to wash his hands. He could see her in the vanity mirror; her back was to him. She was rolling up the hem of her dress to adjust a suspender on her sheer white stocking.

'Perhaps we'll have room service send up dinner,' Renard said. 'Then we can—'

'—You're kidding! This is an authentic Russian hotel, so there's no room service. We need to go now or the restaurant will be closed. Your slave is famished. Come on!'

'OK, as you say.'

As they were leaving, she told him not to worry. 'We're anonymous here; and we won't be mixing with anyone.'

They arrived at the lift which was old-fashioned, Soviet-made, with doors modelled on the entrance to a Pharaoh's tomb. They ground open. The two drunk Azeris had come from nowhere and pushed in too. One of them made faces at Renard and winked at Zidra. 'Come to *my* room,' he whispered. 'All Yanks are impotent. I read an article about it. They put hormones in the water. Number 404.'

Zidra emulsified him in Azeri just before the lift opened on the crowded entrance to the restaurant.

The hotel restaurant had the intimacy of a railway station. The head waiter, a bullet-shaped man called Arkady Ivanovich, Arkasha to his friends, received twenty dollars from Zidra. At which point, he remembered that they were friends. He clapped his hands, and minions came running.

Arkasha had the well-fed appearance and wily eyes of a Venetian courtier. His raven black hair was battened to his scalp with Macassar oil. His overgrown brows beetled to the bridge of his nose and it seemed to Renard that he used lotion on them as well. He bowed, and waved Renard and Zidra through the main hall to a private room. He convoyed them like a cruiser through his restaurant, making signals to his staff on the way. A small oak-panelled room awaited them and they watched while waiters raced to set the table with Bohemia lead crystal and gold-plated knives and forks which reminded Renard of a story about a legendary great-uncle who had bought a canteen of the stuff from the Sears Roebuck catalogue in about 1895 . . .

Zidra nestled in the red velour of a pompous carver chair and Renard watched her steal two of the spoons for luck, while the dishes piled on the table: red Kamchatka caviar and Kamchatka crab with good Russian mayonnaise; black Astrakhan osetrina caviar – 'Grade Nine, the best in the world,' Arkasha said – with its pungent, salty aroma; *blini* and sour cream; crunchy Niyezhinsky cucumbers and blood red tomatoes graced with fronds of fresh dill; *Essentuki* water, and *Byelii Ayist* cognac. Zidra tickled Renard's ankles with her stockinged feet, scrutinized the bottle and told him that *Byelii Ayist* nowadays existed only in dreams.

Arkasha beamed and the team of waiters disappeared. Renard poured *Byelii Ayist* and they drank to each other. Renard told her what place its honey scent and smoky aftertaste reminded him of and how he envied the haemoglobin cells which visited there 62,000 times a day from the inside.

'You are a monster!'

'You are the future Mrs Renard.'

He ate caviar, watched her eat a cucumber and gave up on the caviar. Arkasha's team returned and swept away the uneaten *zakuski*, which had been fetched to their table from the remotest corners of the former Soviet Union. Wild mushroom juliennes followed; they were tasted and abandoned. Strong chicken broth accompanied by small glazed sweet cabbage pies was produced. She nibbled a pie. He ate one and felt sick. Their soup congealed.

They were in love but they knew very little about each other. So they talked about her schooldays. She had worn pigtails and a brown smock, with the crimson kerchief of the Young Pioneers round her neck. The smock had to have new lace cuffs and collars stitched to it each week. At the start of each term she went with her mother to buy a new set of each from a shop opposite the Latviya Hotel in Riga. Afterwards they had ice cream with bilberries and went on the tram to the Riga planetarium. When the Soviet Union sent a rocket to Venus the planetarium put on a special show, and she had learnt that the Planet of Love has the atmosphere of a public lavatory.

Her classmates elected her brigade leader and she had to wear a little enamel badge pinned to her smock with Lenin's head in a sunburst. One International Women's Day a boy called Andrei gave her flowers. Later, Andrei went to live in Paris where his father worked in the Consular Department of the Soviet Embassy. Later still, Andrei came back when his father was expelled for undiplomatic activities. Now Andrei too was a diplomat, but he still sent Zidra cards every 8th March.

Renard gloomily stabbed a remaining cucumber and Zidra scrutinized his curly hair and his brown eyes, and deliquesced in the heat of his gaze. She told him his damaged face was the only face she loved, together with the delicious paranoia of its absurd owner.

When Arkasha came with chicken *tabak* and Golden Ring champagne, Renard suddenly found his appetite and ate both portions, then they finished the *Byelii Ayist* with Turkish coffee and left.

The party in the room above theirs was over. Quiet reigned. They went to bed; it was midnight of the 19th November.

In the thick of the night Renard awoke. A door had opened, somewhere. He swung out of bed, but a hand clamped across his mouth and a torch flashed on. It was Father Pyotr, one fat finger pressed to his lips.

Renard switched on the bedside lamp and woke Zidra. He motioned Father Pyotr into the other room and grabbed the clothes scattered over an easy chair. While Renard struggled into his suit, Father Pyotr peered round the thick velour of the curtains through the window which overlooked the Leningradskii Chaussee many floors below. Light flickered up – headlights – three sets; Renard went to the bedroom and beckoned Zidra. With no word spoken, Father Pyotr opened the door to the corridor and they left at once. It was 5.30 on the morning of 20th November.

Father Pyotr led them through a fire exit on to a flight of narrow concrete steps.

'They'll come for us through the main entrance,' he said. 'I saw three cars arrive. Our only chance is to leave by the east-wing where they won't be waiting in any numbers. All the internal doors between the two

144

wings are locked at night and there's always someone on duty on each floor. So it has to be this way – over the roof. That's what they *won't* be expecting and it may save us.'

He led the way up three flights of stairs, stopping by a small service access. The door to the access was less than a metre square and little used: Renard couldn't force it open wider than forty-five degrees. The panic-stricken clergyman, muttering 'Jesus and all the saints, save me,' had to be pulled through the tiny gap. He recovered in the narrow corridor, less than a metre wide, formed by the space between the roof and the inner walls, answering Renard's questions while they went.

'They know that you're here. They found out only in the last ninety minutes, and I was tipped off less than an hour ago.'

'How come? What happened?'

'Microphones in your private suite at the restaurant. Nothing new in that of course. The innovation is the use of computerized voice-print matching.'

'And what about our cover? Is that blown too?'

'No. You made a call from your room to the *dezhurnaya* on your floor. She sits five metres away, but the call was routed through the local exchange – a common system in Soviet-era hotels. From where Sakharinov's new computers picked it up. So although they know you're here, they only know what the hotel says: that you're with some oilmen from Houston.'

Renard grinned. 'The old ways were the best. Microphones. Charmless spooks with seedy manners and bad breath sharing your breakfast table. Now those guys are all on welfare.'

'The old ways still exist, don't worry. Nothing much has changed in our brave new Russia. Now the Moscow rumour mill is working overtime and that's a bad sign. Someone is stirring the Kremlin *bouillon*. There are all sorts of stories going round the ministries and embassies. The President will be assassinated before the Duma opens; the President is planning a provocation so he can suspend the Duma if it's hostile . . . God knows what's actually going on, but something is. One more thing. The President has been informed of your presence, Mr Renard. I got word through the Patriarchate's office at Sergeev Posad last night. He wants to meet you. Unofficially. Invisibly. But today.'

'Why me, Father Pyotr?'

'It's at the request of your own President. I'd say it's a sign of mutual desperation. You're authoritative; you can tell the Russian President what Molniya is, if he doesn't know, and explain why the US and its allies will have to take action if Alfredo Sakharinov isn't stopped *now*.

145

It's a last attempt to solve the problem informally – to avoid a diplomatic break-down. The only justification for involving you in this way is because the alternatives involve hostilities breaking out between the USA and Russia.'

'Let him use Loken,' Renard said at once. 'My mission is Molniya. If he wants Western moral support, Ambassador Loken can provide that.'

'No, they can't use the US Ambassador. I'm sorry to point out the obvious to you, but that immediately puts things on a different level. The Russian President must be seen to deal with Sakharinov himself, and not at the behest of the US. I spent half a day with the Patriarch discussing the matter. He is a worried man. More than that – frightened. He doesn't want the Church to become more involved. That's not his style. But he is alarmed, like your government, by the political paralysis in the Russian regime. He wants our President to confront the situation – to expose Alfredo Sakharinov and try to win back some of the political ground he has lost. The President isn't completely isolated; he still has supporters, including some among the Kremlin garrison, many of whom will lose their positions now that the Varta takeover has begun.'

'We must help the man, Renard,' Zidra said. 'You represent what may be our last chance. That's why we need a change of plan. We must go to Sergeev Posad this morning, to meet the Patriarch today; he will arrange safe conduct to the President's office.'

'How? Our cover is blown and —'

'*Your* presence – Renard's presence – is known. But they don't know what roof you're under.'

'They'll be looking for anyone who tries to visit the Kremlin today. So they'll soon find me, won't they?'

'Douglas,' appealed Zidra, 'how can we refuse to meet the President of Russia? Think for a minute. We can still deal with Sergei Sakharinov.'

'I began to arrange that yesterday,' Father Pyotr said. 'I need one more day, that's all. But everything helps. You can show the transcripts of his talks with Zamok to the President, for instance. It'll be like putting a bomb under the Sakharinovs, and will destroy any alliance between the Varta camp and the Nationalists.'

Renard was angry, but had to agree to a rethink. 'I'm here on a covert mission and even the goddamn President of the goddamn country has got me in his diary, and invites me to have a discussion about the political situation! My mission was to go to Kalegut then make contact with the USS *Nashville* – and hit the Molniya base. *That's* what I'm here for. But—'

'Mr Renard, you should also know that Itar-Tass announced overnight

146

that a foreign submarine, thought to be American, has "got into difficulties" in Arctic waters. It doesn't surprise me. Molniya is well defended. I don't think your mission *ever* had a chance. How could your commandos hope to overwhelm a garrison of forty thousand, then dive through the ice and blow up Molniya? I mean we're only talking about a gigantic steel-and-titanium structure that's rooted to the seabed and that's the size of two *Queen Marys*.'

Zidra spoke up again. 'In any case, your mission *is* completed; you've sent the metacodes to Washington. Now you can call Washington – call your own President – from the Kremlin. And we can start to prove the danger of Molniya, to reveal the nature of the plot against the President and the Russian people.'

'I agree, Douglas. What choice do we have? If we think the President stands to be murdered by his political opponents, then surely we must take any chance of warning him.'

Renard reluctantly conceded, 'OK, I'll think it over, damnit. But first let's get out of here.'

They proceeded along the corridor which was lit along its sixty metres by a few dim inspection lights. They had to scramble under overhanging steel beams, across a bare concrete floor which was meshed with cables and pipes. At the far end they came to a double-locked door. Renard forced a broken spar on to the bolt to lever it open. 'Destroying Molniya is the main thing,' he muttered to Father Pyotr. 'Presidents come and go, but Molniya is a strategic fact which needs to be dealt with *whoever* is in power here.'

'Agreed. Now, please, Mr Renard – the door.'

Renard savagely twisted the beam, and the lock crashed apart. The doorway led on to the roof of the hotel, leaving them to crawl out on to a duckboard which led to the edge. The roof rose up on either side so that they were hemmed into a narrow passage. Renard and the priest reached the end together. There was just room for them to kneel side by side on the narrow, ice-covered ledge which looked out on the void engulfing the street below. A raw night breeze swept over them.

Zidra came up behind them, and said at once: 'I can't do this. I suffer from vertigo. I'll get stuck halfway – you'd better leave me here, I'll find another way down.'

The priest was panting, either from fear or from exertion. 'There's no alternative,' he whispered. 'We need to get out of here, and this is the way. Just follow me *quickly*.' And he crawled forward.

'Pyotr, wait,' Renard ordered. 'Let me go first.' He pulled the priest back into the narrow entryway.

'OK, you lead; let Zidra follow and I'll come after. Perhaps it's best,' he said. 'Go left once you're on the ledge; after twenty metres or so there's another entry similar to this; use it.'

Renard turned to Zidra. 'Follow me as close as you can and don't look down; you won't fall, I promise.'

There was pure animal fear in her eyes – but she nodded, and gripped his hand once in affirmation. Renard pushed out on to the ledge; it was less than 300 centimetres wide, convex and covered in ice. He inched his way forward, leaning as far into the roof as possible and going on all fours for most of the way, his fingers digging into the freezing ice. He could hear Zidra shuffling behind, her breathing shallow with fear. And he could hear voices from ground level.

He froze.

'What is it?' Zidra hissed.

'Just wait a minute. Pyotr, you OK?'

'Yes.'

'They look like friends of yours?' He pointed a half metre forward.

Cars were just visible below, lights on and engines running. Black Volgas.

'Definitely not; better get a move on, Renard,' the priest urged.

Before he'd finished speaking, figures sprang from the Volgas at a run, four going into the main hotel entrance, as Father Pyotr had said they would, and three more scattering around its perimeter, one of them heading for the east-wing entrance.

Renard had pulled forward on to the outer ledge in response, when a stifled cry came from behind, followed by the crack of a giant icicle, two metres long. Zidra had dislodged it from a buttress, sending it crashing into the street below. One of the observers in the forecourt flashed a light up, then down to where the shards of ice lay and turned away.

Renard's party scrabbled forward over the ice-filled gully until Father Pyotr slipped, his left leg disappearing over the edge, arms flailing as he grabbed at the metal lip secured to the base of the roof. But the jagged metal sliced into the palm of his hand and Renard had to lunge forward to catch his other hand, finally swinging the priest back up to his own level. They all three lay panting for a few seconds in the corner of the ledge and the roof, then set off again, crawling face down towards a catwalk leading to the next inspection gantry.

In a few minutes more they were back in the building. Father Pyotr, still gasping for breath, frightened and angry, vented his feelings on Renard. 'This unnecessary episode is entirely because you gave yourself away yesterday evening,' he told him.

Renard made as if to retort but the priest had already set off down the corridor, leading the way through another hatchway which opened on to a stairwell and a lift to the eastern exit.

Zidra and Father Pyotr left the lift on the first floor and walked down to ground level. Renard waited for half a minute, then pressed the button. The lift sank down and almost at once its heavy doors slid open. He walked straight out into the centre of the hotel's grand entrance hall. It was deserted, lit dimly by the light from the few functioning bulbs in one gigantic, dusty chandelier.

A blue-capped doorman was sleeping at his desk by the entrance doors, which were locked and chained together through the handles. No one had come through that way; if anyone was waiting, they were still outside.

Renard shook the doorman. As he had done a million times before, the man stumbled over to the chains and unlocked them without so much as a glance at the irate guest who wanted to leave early. As the doors swung open, Zidra and Father Pyotr joined their fellow runaway. He led them in a crouching run out into the car park.

'Where's your car?' Renard whispered.

'Right outside. It's clean; we can use it.' Father Pyotr led the way to the white Volvo 940 estate parked close by.

The priest started the engine and the car nosed slowly forwards, prompting a figure to come running across the forecourt.

'Run him down!' Renard hissed, grabbing the wheel as the car shot forward so that it crashed sideways into the human obstacle. The car then skidded to a halt and Renard leapt out, running to the crumpled body, dragging it behind a parked car, at the same time ordering the priest to stay where he was in the driver's seat. But Father Pyotr had already lunged from the car and begun shouting hysterically. Renard raced over and for a moment the two were locked in struggle.

'Forget it,' Renard instructed. 'He's dead, believe me.'

From the courtyard opposite came the sound of men running and, next thing, they could be seen as they raced over, torches flashing. Zidra had swung out of the back of the Volvo and grabbed the priest from behind. Together with Renard, she pushed him into the car and Renard hurled himself into the driver's seat. The Volvo shot out into Leningradskii Chaussee.

'It'll take them a minute or two to get mobile,' Zidra was shouting. 'Make a U turn and head back into the city. We need to get clear of the Leningradskii before we pass any GAI posts.'

149

'I know a way, don't worry,' the priest said hoarsely. 'I'm sorry for what happened – it's just that—'

'*Tell me the way, Pyotr!*' Renard roared.

'Turn off into that alley,' Father Pyotr said immediately.

Renard skidded into it, doused the lights and let the Volvo crawl slowly forward in first gear. In the mirror he saw two of the black Volgas scream down the Leningradskii Chaussee. 'I hope you're not planning to take us far,' he told the priest. 'Or I think we'll need a change of car.'

'OK, don't worry.' The fat priest, doubled up almost to the floor in pain, was still struggling to catch his breath. 'We're here,' he told Renard in a hoarse whisper as they pulled down another gloomy alley-way, stopping outside a ground-floor apartment in a Stalin-era apartment block. 'This is it, the Sobor safe house. I'll let you in, then garage the car.'

The place was empty except for a few broken chairs, and some tea chests and cardboard boxes used for storage. It was a flat belonging to the Moscow Satirical Theatre Company and had been used to put up troupes from the provinces. Now it was just a store for props – sublet to a theatrical agency which was actually a Sobor front.

Father Pyotr returned from garaging the Volvo. 'No one around, don't worry,' he said in answer to Renard's questioning look. 'I need to find some priestly clothes for you. Zidra, put the samovar on, please. Let's drink tea.'

Zidra went over to the priest. 'Father Pyotr, are you OK?'

'Yes. I will be.'

'There was no choice.'

'I know that.'

'Help me find Renard a change of clothes.'

'I'll do it, Zidra. Really. Go make tea.' He smiled wanly at her.

She went to the kitchen and left him rummaging. He came back with a monk's habit which was more or less Renard's size.

'I think it must have been used to dress some production of *Boris Godunov*. It's quite well made; try it.'

Renard clambered into the outfit. 'Is this really how they are? Ye gods!'

When Zidra came back in the room she had already changed into her lay-sister outfit: dowdy black lace-up shoes, heavy tweed jacket and ruched blouse, a bouffant raven-black wig and cobble-stone glasses. She paced slowly around Renard, nodding.

The priest looked at them quizzically. 'A lot hangs on this disguise.'

150

'We need to give the reverend father a name,' suggested Zidra. 'How about Sergei – like Tolstoy's naughty priest.'

'Who he?' Renard asked.

'Zidra is teasing you, Mr Renard. In Tolstoy's story, a very ascetic nobleman struggles against his carnal desire by becoming a monk. But, just as before, he continues to be tormented by the attentions of beautiful women. It seems even the vow of celibacy cannot save him.'

'Tolstoy wanted to show that nothing was stronger than sexual feeling,' Zidra said. She was standing in front of Renard, straightening his black clerical bib. 'Not even religious devotion. Poor Sergei takes an axe and chops his own finger off, but it doesn't take his mind off his temptress.' She smiled sweetly at him. 'You wouldn't do that, would you, Mr Renard?' she said softly. 'It was useless anyway; in the end the noble cleric runs off with the lady.' She scrutinized her handiwork. 'No,' she said with sudden decision. 'Sergei won't do as a name for you. You're too sinful. I think something simple and Anglo-Saxon . . . Father John for example.'

'OK, but God save me from meeting any real clerics.'

'They won't talk shop if you do. Better forget Russian, anyway. I'm your interpreter and you're Father John Bernard from an American religious community, don't forget. The Houston Orthodox community. Is there really such a thing?'

'Actually, yes, but in reality it's a—'

He didn't finish; Father Pyotr called them over to a locked door. 'I want to show you this, then we must leave at once.' He opened it and beckoned Renard. Inside was a mass of equipment: a file server and back-up. 'It's the digital overlay units and the Nokia base station. Your embassy people installed it all.'

The walls were lined with thin sheets of pink plastic. 'This room is absolutely insulated against electromagnetic emissions. Nothing gets in or out. The pink wall covering is actually Soviet-made. It was designed to shield Soviet ICBMs against President Reagan's X-ray lasers. It's vinyl, impregnated with certain rare earth metals. Fifteen times more impervious to radiation than twenty millimetres of lead sheet, and it's paper thin. That's what Soviet science was up to in the Star Wars epoch. The physicists who developed it at a cost of a hundred million dollars now run a joint venture supplying dentists and hospital radiographers with X-ray proof aprons. That's how the West bankrupted the Soviet Union.'

While Pyotr spoke he opened the massive door of an old Soviet-made safe. 'The two hundred and fifty thousand dollars from the Remex offices.' He handed the money to Renard.

'Keep it here,' Renard told him. 'I can't think of anywhere safer.'

'Something else, too.' The priest held up a microcassette. 'The Sakharinov-Zamok tape. Do we take it?'

'Yes.' Renard pocketed the tape.

It was almost 6.30 in the morning when they left the flat. Moscow's rush hour had started – earlier than usual because of the effects of the massive security operation in the city centre.

They had to pass through the chaos. Preparations for the convocation of the State Duma were evident everywhere, and mostly they showed the apprehensiveness of the Russian government for whom each new exercise in democracy had come to seem a landmark in the falling-apart of their country. Queues of traffic crawled past checkpoints as vehicles were searched by GAI men who were unusually aggressive even by their own unique standards. At the Vernadsky Street checkpoint a machine gun poked in at Father Pyotr who was in the driving seat. A GAI man, face livid from vodka and the bitter cold, ordered the priest out. Two further GAI men proceeded to question him. One of them went to a patrol car and spoke to an officer inside, passing him the documents which Father Pyotr had produced. In a moment he came back and waved the priest away.

In a few minutes the priest returned to his companions. '*Provokatsiya*, they told me,' he said as they set off again. '*Diversiya*.' He spat the words. 'Our GAI men earn a hundred dollars a month. Obviously it's not enough, but that fact needn't make them the most corrupt police force on earth. They obey no law but that of the highest bidder. There's not one amongst them who isn't for sale; if such a one *was* found the others would kill him the same day. They don't serve the people; they work for racketeers and gangsters. Perhaps that's as it should be: in Moscow, the gangs are the most efficient government we've got. In fact, they *are* the government! They've divided up the city, and they control everything: not just drugs and prostitution and racketeering. They control the retail trade; so the food supply for ten million people is in the hands of these gangs. Through extortion and their monopoly control of trade – the real reason for most of our hyperinflation, by the way – they've plundered the people's wealth. The result is that a river of gold flows upwards, from the street racketeers to the big *papas* who control whole districts – and from there it flows to the mayor's office. There isn't a single public official of any rank in Moscow city government who isn't a rouble billionaire; the mayor is a dollar millionaire who has sold off Moscow's buildings to buy himself real estate in the Côte d'Azur.'

Zidra added her voice. 'And the Papa of all the gangsters sits in the government and is at the President's right hand. That is our Russia today: a home to the world's criminals, where everything is for sale; where the national wealth is stolen and sent abroad; where our children are kidnapped from the streets in broad daylight to be purchased by childless Westerners if they're lucky, or by transplant clinics if they're not.'

CHAPTER 11

It took an hour to pass over Kuznetskii Bridge and reach Tverskaya Street via the Manezh Square – a distance of a kilometre or less. The entire area around the Kremlin was closed to traffic, as it had been for a long time now, a decision which produced constant traffic chaos in the city centre and underlined the authorities' fear of a possible rising in the narrow streets around the seat of government. Now the traffic had seized up in a brawling, snarling gridlock. It moved only when way was made for the chauffeur-driven Cadillacs and Lincoln super-stretch limousines which swept government officials and other servants of the people about their business.

For days past, Duma deputies had been arriving in Moscow in a steady stream. By tradition they stayed at the huge Friendship Hotel, adjacent to the White House, scene of the rising led by Vice President Rutskoi in October 1993. The hotel and adjacent cafés, bistros and bars formed a seething cauldron of meetings, rallies and caucuses. Everywhere, the fascists and their Communist allies were on the march. Posters bearing the dour face of Zamok, leader of the fascist Russia First party, covered the walls of downtown Moscow. A kind of fever gripped the capital, as the government split into factions and rumours spread of an imminent coup by those at the heart of state. Things were moving to a climax. Ready for a strongman to appear, to rally the people and to save the nation.

The people themselves stood on the sidelines and watched and waited.

In another forty minutes Father Pyotr's Volvo was free of the city and speeding down the six-lane Murmansk highway, past the grinding streams of ancient trucks spewing out muddy snow from their uncovered wheels. After an hour they turned off the German-built freeway and on to a deserted country road. They passed through forests and giant ploughed fields. Occasionally there were settlements – tumble-down cottages with hearths that seeped smoke into the cold air, set among tiny orchards riveted by ice into the desolate landscape.

Renard gazed out at the blank sheet that was Russia, while Zidra and the priest discussed events in the capital. His gloom deepened. Sometimes it seemed to him that even Zidra, her professionalism a mask on a life steeped in blood feuds, was also part of the desolation.

At least Renard could say of himself that he was engaged in something which more or less bore upon such things as orderly relations between nations, upon preserving a certain framework of mutuality, of common expectations, which was the premise for life to go on and for people to live out their time quietly pursuing wealth and happiness. Nothing was ever perfect in a human world and every social institution was a proper subject for scrutiny, but if anyone wanted to know why for all that, and for all its disfiguring shortcomings, America was still the House on the Hill, or why England was still the pole of European civilization – they only had to try to make a life for themselves and their families somewhere in Russia. Then they would find out.

Renard knew what he was fighting for, and any 'more or less' factor became a categorical imperative when he was faced with the need to extirpate the likes of Alfredo Sakharinov. But where did it coincide with what Zidra knew? Yet when he looked at her he knew that if he lived here another six months, he too would be more interested in settling scores than in organizing free elections.

The previous night while they'd made love and she had lain with her back to him, he had placed his hands around her neck, so that his fingers and thumbs easily touched. Thus he had surrounded and taken literally into his hands the nexus that joined her clever head with her clever body. The thought of that one act was still somehow as intoxicating as anything he'd ever known.

'We'll be in Sergeev Posad in twenty minutes,' Father Pyotr interrupted Renard's reverie. While he spoke the car phone began to ring. It was someone from the Patriarchate. His face grew sombre as he listened.

'Not good news,' he told the other two. 'You won't be meeting Patriarch Fyodor, unfortunately, but someone very close to him instead – the dean of the theological seminary at Sergeev Posad.'

'Who is he?'

'His name is *Vladika* Dmitry.' Father Pyotr looked angrily ahead. His fat knuckles clenched the steering wheel. '*Vladika* means "bishop". He's the Patriarch's *éminence grise*, in fact. I guessed this might happen, but had hoped not . . . *Vladika* Dmitry's people are everywhere now, and it's difficult to get through him to the Patriarch.'

'What's his line?'

'A proponent of reform. Self-advertising.' Father Pyotr sighed. '*Vladika* Dmitry wants to remake the Russian Church; he wants more of a Reformation than just reforms.'

With this latest development on their minds, the delegation from the Orthodox community in Spring Falls, Texas arrived at Sergeev Posad – the glorious heart of Russian Orthodoxy with its multitude of gleaming gold domes, its blue and white cathedrals and its vast hoard of icons and other treasures. They stopped by an archway set in the high battlemented wall. Heavy wooden doors studded with bolts and laced with iron were set in the arch. But when two uniformed gatemen raced from a watchpost, and Father Pyotr showed a pass, the gates swung soundlessly open. The Volvo slipped through and Renard swung round and looked behind. Above the white painted arch, on the inside, was the painted image of a frowning saint, the halo gold, the right hand raised with the grotesquely elongated first and second fingers extended, offering the benediction. Above the image was an inscription in gold lettering. The letters were in the Old Slavonic alphabet and Renard had no time to decipher them.

'The Seminary,' Father Pyotr announced as the Volvo came to a halt by a large two-storeyed building in the classic Russian white stucco and ochre style. Three men in clerical robes were waiting by the entrance. Renard heard the priest mutter, 'My God, it's the *Vladika* himself.'

'Good,' Zidra said. 'It means they take us seriously.'

'We'll soon see.' Father Pyotr opened the door and got out. 'Come on, let's meet them. Remember, you're on an informal mission from your government. They'll treat you as a visiting dignitary.'

Vladika Dmitry was flanked by two subordinates, both athletic young men in their late twenties. Like the *Vladika*, their long black clerical robes were immaculate, tailored from imported worsted and not the usual local cotton. Their unsmiling eyes alternated between watchfulness and boredom. Renard looked them over and told the *Vladika* his boys were in good physical shape.

'I encourage a proper Christian attitude to the body, which is the temple of the Holy Spirit,' Dmitry replied. A wiry, slight man in his late thirties, five feet eight inches tall, *Vladika* Dmitry's presence shone like an ominous beacon. What he lacked in physical bulk he made up for in the magnetism of his will. His black, glittering eyes radiated a kind of malevolent curiosity as if a strong thirst for knowledge had learnt to satisfy itself by possessing its subjects, by bending all to its will.

Now he focused his attention wholly on the American guest whose next appointment was with the Russian President at the Kremlin, at the behest of Patriarch Fyodor and with the blessing of the American Government. The *Vladika* did not hide his contempt for the portly Father Pyotr and for Zidra all he had was pure annoyance. He spoke enough

English, lucidly expressed if with a limited vocabulary, not to need her services as he showed them round his seminary. 'This building is a representation of my system, which is spreading throughout Russia,' he told Renard. 'Sergeev Posad is the heart of Russian Orthodoxy.'

'I have cherished the dream of visiting here,' Renard said politely.

'Perhaps you know that the Bolsheviks renamed the town after one of their own, the atheist Zagorski. That's how they insulted the Church! Now this beautiful place is restored to the memory of Saint Sergei, who lived here as a hermit, sharing the forest wilderness with the birds and wild creatures. I hope and believe that the Church will return to the simple spirituality of those early times.' The *Vladika*'s small black eyes glittered. 'We play our part. We have made a start on cleansing the filth of corruption. But only when Holy Russia is once more a theocratic state, will she again be a leader amongst the nations.'

'I have no interest in politics, *Vladika*,' Renard told him. 'I came to Orthodoxy to escape all that.'

'Then you made a mistake. We must also be of this world, my son. And while I do not believe we have much to learn from the West, there are some examples we should copy. I think of St Ignatius Loyola, the founder of the Society of Jesus, as one.'

'You surprise me greatly, *Vladika*. I was baptized into Catholicism, and a more inappropriate apostle for the renewal of Orthodoxy than the founder of the Jesuits I cannot imagine. When I was a child my teachers were Jesuits, and they were much more impressed by an incendiary vision of Hell than by the pursuit of grace. I had thought that the Orthodox way was more kindly and tolerant.'

'Of course, we seek grace first and above all. Our music, our liturgy, show that the God of vengeance is not a Russian God – alas, revenge is too everyday an experience to need the invoking of the Almighty. Unfortunately in our times we need to scourge our flock, not humour them,' the *Vladika* said. They had entered a sparsely furnished refectory and while an austere lunch was served *Vladika* Dmitry explained to Renard that he sought to make Orthodoxy become something more: a militant Church capable of bestowing discipline and leadership as well as blessings.

'This movement of spiritual renewal is a sign of our times,' he told Renard. 'And it's indicative of how deeply our reforms are now scouring Russian society and the Russian soul to the very depths. Without spiritual reform, what chance is there of a normal, civilized society emerging here? We'll be swallowed up in a swamp of criminality, because our people simply don't know right from wrong; their souls are utterly perverted and corrupted; they too must be scourged and cleansed . . .'

After lunch they went to his Foundation, some kilometres distant, and saw the spiritual and physical training centres where *Vladika* Dmitry tried to produce a new generation of strong, disciplined and stern religious leaders, men who could form the sinews of a new Russia. The atmosphere was military. Young men drilled in the classrooms and the gymnasium.

'Take back to your President, your people, these signs of hope,' *Vladika* Dmitry willed Renard. 'I have a mission and my brothers will fulfil it with me; it's the Lord's work, and nothing can stop us. Throughout history, the Church has required all, everything, from its followers. Only if we risk all, risk the most precious of all, do we show our faith.'

Renard asked about the planned meeting with the Patriarch. *Vladika* Dmitry explained that they would not need such a meeting. The audience with the President of Russia was already arranged, through his own office. And it was already time to go. He then told Renard that their lives were linked. In the future he would provide him with a personal *dukhovnik* – a spiritual adviser. More to the point, he would also lend his Zil limousine and two young priests to escort them back to Moscow. The Volvo with Father Pyotr would follow behind. He gave Renard a souvenir of his visit: a well-fashioned leather document case embossed in gilt with the twin-barred Orthodox cross. 'There are some papers inside – including my report to the President on reforms in the Church. You'll have time to read them on the way.'

They made their farewells and left. 'Damn that costive monk,' Renard heard Father Pyotr mutter as he walked off alone to the Volvo.

The armour-plated Zil rumbled away from Sergeev Posad. The two silent and unsmiling clerics sent as escort, Fathers Anton and Ivan, sat bolt upright on the dickey-seats, each with hands neatly clasped in his lap, each with a small black gladstone bag placed by the right foot. Renard stared at them. They ignored him.

After a while Renard said to Zidra in English: 'What does Father Anton think about the Sakharinov family? Are they strong men or just crooks? Tell him, we hear so many things . . .'

When this was translated, there was a long silence. Then Father Anton said: 'Characters and people can change, can develop, for the better or for the worse. The development can be so great that it removes all traces of its own origins. But it still cannot be other than its origins. Thus, in one sense a person's fate is predetermined, but in another it still has to be made. The Sakharinov family are an example of this.'

158

Anton looked as though he were reciting for a test.

'Ask him what has been effaced in the origins of the Sakharinovs.'

'The Sakharinov brothers are great national leaders,' the glassy-eyed father told Renard. 'That was not always so. Many years ago, when they were young men, younger even than Father Ivan and myself, there was a notorious episode.'

The other priest looked sharply at him, then away, focusing on some distant object with a basilisk stare. Father Anton had begun to perspire; he mopped his face with a black silk handkerchief.

'Sergei and Alfredo Sakharinov were both leaders on the Komsomol National Executive Committee when there were allegations of misconduct.' The young priest stalled, giving Renard a pleading look.

'What misconduct?' Renard demanded.

'It was said that Sergei had assaulted a girl. Unfortunately she was the daughter of a leading Politburo member, his name was Annenkov. Sergei denied it. The girl was not attractive.'

Unexpectedly, Father Ivan leaned forward and spoke, his tongue darting like a lizard's. 'When Annenkov challenged him about it, Sergei laughed it off. He told Annenkov that he would derive no pleasure from entertaining his daughter however much she asked for it.' A smile dry as death passed over Father Ivan's face.

'What happened afterwards?'

'What happened? Annenkov swore to have the Sakharinovs expelled from the Komsomol. If he'd succeeded, the matter would never have rested there. It would've ended only when he'd put them in prison or in a camp. The Sakharinov name would have been dust and ashes.' Ivan smoothed his immaculate habit. 'The Sakharinovs had plenty of supporters, of course, favours they could call in. Everyone knew that. But the people were frightened. Annenkov was a secretary of the Party Control Commission. He was untouchable. That's what was assumed.' The father gave Renard a close look and smiled his crooked smile.

Renard began to recall, 'I remember something of this: it happened at least twenty years ago. But Annenkov died of a heart attack, it seems to me?'

Anton, who had visibly relaxed the moment his colleague started to speak, said, 'Father John, you are very well informed about our history. But Annenkov didn't die from a heart attack. He was as strong as a bull. Alfredo Sakharinov went to Annenkov's dacha, supposedly to apologize, and there he shot and killed him.'

'What do you think, Father John?' Ivan asked Renard. 'Was he right to do it? Alfredo Sakharinov was defending his family interest, wasn't

159

he? "When a strong man armed keepeth his palace, his goods are in peace." Do you agree with St Luke?'

Before Renard could reply, Father Anton did so. 'Holy Russia. That is our Zion. And if the Lord wants Russia to be strong, then Sakharinov will be His instrument.'

'Russia has bleeding frontiers,' Ivan said, leaning forward and tapping Renard's knee, his blanched tongue licking spittle from his thin moustaches. 'The Chinese are at our borders. Think about it. Russia had already had three hundred years of Mongol slavery. But we kept the Golden Horde out of Europe. We saved civilization. Were we wrong?'

The Zil was by now entering the Moscow city boundaries, speeding along the crown of the highway, headlights blazing at oncoming vehicles and at the GAI men saluting and waving them through every intersection. Renard unzipped the leather case which the *Vladika* had presented to him. Inside was a single wad of photocopied pages, stapled in the top left-hand corner. 'Our Vision of the Future' it was entitled. Renard slid it back in the case which he zipped shut.

'I'll read it later,' he explained to Father Ivan with a wry smile.

They swept past the Lubyanka, circled down Nicolskii Street, past GUM and over the cobbles on Red Square. More GAI men swung their white batons and the Zil entered the archway which leads into the Kremlin grounds.

The Volvo carrying Father Pyotr was nowhere in sight; twice, Renard had peered through the grubby curtains on the Zil's rear window. The first time, when they were chasing down Tverskaya Street, the white Volvo had been in view and he had glimpsed the fat priest's strained face as he struggled to keep up. Then two intersections later, he had gone; the centre lane down which the Zil was moving being completely empty as far back as Renard could see. It was as if a giant hand had snatched the Volvo away.

The Zil circled to a halt inside the Kremlin grounds, at the foot of a wide stone staircase leading up to a palatial ochre-and-white building. A plain-clothes Ministry of Security man met them there. He inspected the documents which the priests handed over, shook hands with Renard, and waved the party through the first guard post, manned by soldiers of the Alpha Division Presidential guard. At the top of the staircase, more greatcoated soldiers armed with Kalashnikovs paced the glossy parquet. Their commander, motionless under an unsmiling portrait of the President, saluted the Ministry of Security guide who swept past with Renard's party.

They arrived next at a pair of heavy oak doors, open and leading into

160

a great entrance hall. A young soldier sat at a small desk in the corner by the doors. A blue-epauletted colleague clicked the heels of his mirror-bright jackboots and saluted. Again, no words were spoken, the young soldier merely noting their arrival in a leather-bound *grosse-buch*.

They were taken to a cloakroom and invited to remove their hats and overcoats. No one had asked to see any identification documents other than the letter from Patriarch Fyodor which Father Anton produced. No one searched them.

They were led back into the main hall and then another plain-clothes officer appeared, introducing himself in English as, 'Colonel Orlov, Mikhail Lvovich. Presidential aide.' Orlov looked curiously at Renard and as he ushered the visitors down the corridor he took up station next to the American. The remainder of the party fell into step behind, Zidra with a black-habited figure on each side of her.

'It's unusual for the President to meet someone in your position, especially at a time of such intense political activity,' Orlov said, speaking in a confidential whisper. 'You're either very lucky or very important.'

'Just lucky I guess; I'm surely conscious of the honour.'

Orlov proceeded down a long, high-walled corridor, along which small tables were placed at ten-metre intervals, each equipped with a telephone, a table lamp and a saluting boy soldier. They entered a lift and were taken to the seventh floor. The KGB man then turned left out of the lift and led the party forward. Occasionally a door opened on an office interior: hushed voices, phones ringing.

'This is a very private meeting,' Orlov told Renard. 'It's not on the official list for today, and no passes were issued by the Kremlin *kommandatura*. Very strange. A sign of the times, I suppose. Nothing is as it should be.'

'I'm not sure I follow.'

Orlov now looked cryptic. 'Oh, just that I didn't expect you, that's all. But then, I didn't expect to be here myself.' He laughed. 'I've got compassionate leave – my wife's had a baby.'

Renard smiled at him and offered his congratulations, adding, 'Well, why *are* you here?'

'Because my friend, the deputy Commandant of the guard, called me last night and asked me to come in. There's been an unexpected change of routines – an altered duty roster, and I have to sign hundreds of forms and God knows what else. We have a new Defence Minister and he wants his own Varta men brought in.' Orlov sighed. 'It's all a damn nuisance.'

'A new Defence Minister?'

'General Medved. Just been promoted from Colonel, and a week later is made Minister.' Orlov was shaking his head, speaking now in a whisper. 'Don't know what's going on in this damn country any more.'

Renard had stopped so suddenly that Father Ivan just behind nearly crashed into him. Orlov took him by the elbow at once, flashed him a worried look and said: 'Forget it, Reverend, it's not your problem. The President is waiting for you; don't waste time listening to me go on about our domestic affairs.'

But Renard looked suddenly pale, and Zidra came up to say, 'Are you all right, Father John?'

He turned to face her, 'Guess it was something I ate yesterday, miss. I'm thinking that I could use something for stomach ache. Perhaps you could go downstairs and find something for me?'

She searched his eyes. *Something is wrong*, she read.

'You can't not meet the President now, however ill you are,' Orlov intervened. 'Wait here; I'll be back in a moment.' He marched up the corridor, knocking on a door twenty feet away.

Renard had locked eyes with Zidra. He shook his head in an infinitesimal gesture, then indicated with his gaze the two priests standing nearby. 'I don't believe I want any Russian medicine,' he said in his best Texan drawl. 'I should prefer if you went back to the hotel and saw the pharmacist. Maybe it's infectious. I wouldn't want you to catch anything.'

She shook her head, slowly. 'If it is, I already have. But you're right, Father John. There are a lot of unpleasant microbes around just now. We need to be careful with your poor unaccustomed American stomach. But I'll look after you.'

Orlov had returned, proffering a glass of water and two small yellow pills on a saucer.

Renard gingerly took the pills. 'What do they do?'

'Immobilize the lower colon,' Orlov announced loudly as Renard was given little choice but to swallow them. 'Take them and it's a case of *no pasaran*! For a couple of hours anyway.'

Father Ivan laughed. 'Now I understand what *La Pasionara* meant by not living on our knees.'

They set off again. The corridors grew wider, the carpet underfoot thicker. The walls were hung with portraits of eminent statesmen and aristocrats, all pre-revolutionary. Some of the paintings were too small to cover the squares of dust left by the pictures they replaced. 'What happened?' Zidra asked Orlov, pointing to one blank space that had been left bare. 'Disgraced socialist realism, consigned to the cellars?'

'Not at all. Certainly, the portraits of party leaders and the paintings

162

of collective farms and steelworks were removed when the Soviet Union collapsed.' Orlov was speaking in Russian so that Renard did not understand. 'But they weren't stored in the basement, they were smuggled abroad and mostly sold to wealthy collectors. Socialist realism is quite a fashion in the West nowadays, so they say. Our former Vice President started the craze a few years back when he organized an exhibition in Venezuela.' He grinned at her. 'You see how inventive our businessmen are. It's not just icons we export; everything in the new Russia has a value.' He leant over and whispered something in her ear, then winked conspiratorially at the two monks. Zidra stiffened and glanced over at Renard, but said nothing.

They walked further and now the guards' tables also bore small vases with flowers: carnations, roses, fragrant lilies. Rounding a final corner and entering a long gallery at the far end of which a group of soldiers in paratroop uniforms were milling about, they could hear voices raised in anger.

'Wait here,' Orlov commanded, and marched off in double-time to where the soldiers stood.

Renard smiled at the two priests and motioned Zidra over to where he stood, a few metres apart. 'What the fuck's going on?' he whispered. 'The whole thing stinks. This is provocation, I can feel it. They want to arrest me and create some kind of scandal. We need to abort.'

'Yes. Orlov says so. *Trust him*; he wants to help.' She mouthed the words, but her eyes were wide with fear. She glanced at the monks, who were watching them intently. '*He's not with them.*'

They heard shouts from the soldiers and three ran towards them, chasing Orlov. A door flew open, Orlov and the others disappeared behind it, and an officer appeared and walked towards the visitors. The officer, a captain, dressed in combat fatigues, smiled, asked which was the American.

Father Ivan pointed at Renard. The captain saluted and in broken English introduced himself as Captain Smirnov, apologizing for what had just happened.

'You can speak Russian,' Zidra told him. 'I'll translate.'

'Ah, thank you very much, *gospozha*,' he said with obvious relief. 'Please tell the father that he must not be concerned; there's been a change of guard and a general increase in security, that's all. Colonel Orlov has been relieved of his duties.' He grimaced. 'For incompetence.'

'He's not the only incompetent,' Renard told him. 'For one thing, no one's even bothered to search us; yet here we are, supposed to be meeting your President.'

'You will be meeting the President. And you will be searched – at the next checkpoint.'

Smirnov looked frightened; beads of sweat stood on his forehead. His eyes darted to the room where Orlov had been taken. He hurried them to the checkpoint, where the search they were given was perfunctory. The troops looked ill at ease and unsure of themselves, nervously fingering the butts of their submachine guns. Captain Smirnov led them to a lift with just enough room inside for the five of them. The control panel had only two buttons – up, and down. Smirnov pressed 'Up'. The lift was hot, stifling, and Renard felt his stomach start to yaw, whether from fear or from the effects of colonic remedies he could not say.

They exited the lift to face a barricade in the form of an enormous gilded Alexander II table. Behind it was the reception area to the private Kremlin offices of the President of Russia.

There were no more toy soldiers. A plain-clothes officer stood by the table with four hard-eyed paratroopers armed with machine guns. Renard watched one of them heft his gun. The magazine was loaded. He glanced behind; the lift had descended to collect Smirnov's detachment. They wore bullet-proof jackets.

Renard felt suffocated. Close to retching, he ran a finger round the collar of his clerical jacket.

Smirnov stood talking with Father Ivan behind Father Anton, who stood facing Renard and Zidra, staring fixedly at them. For the first time Renard noticed a peculiarity of the monk's habit; the skirts were divided like culottes underneath the black outer coat. Father Anton was big, but his bulk was all muscle; he moved with a feline grace. Renard had knelt to fumble at his shoelace, glancing at Zidra, who was following every move. As he stood up again, he gasped out loud and spun round, the leather document case spinning out from under his arm across to where Father Anton stood. Father Ivan swung about just as the other monk put down his own gladstone bag in order to pick up the case. In one and a half strides Renard was there, catapulting himself across the divide and cannoning into Anton who straightened up at once.

'Thanks,' Renard said, grinning. 'I stumbled.' He took back the document case and in the same movement handed to Father Anton his gladstone bag. The look on the monk's face told the whole story, even if the weight and feel of the bag and its contents had not.

'Are you all right?' Zidra fussed, dusting off Renard's habit, straightening it.

'I think so,' he said, leaning forward and whispering two words in her

164

ear even while Father Ivan shouted at the guard to open the reception doors.

'We'll go in at once,' Father Ivan ordered.

The paratroopers stiffened as Captain Smirnov motioned them to group up; they formed a half circle around Renard, Zidra and the two monks. There was no way back, and Renard pushed through the enormous pair of gilded doors confronting them. Above them a sign proclaimed in gilded letters 'Reception. President of the Russian Federation. Administrator: A. I. Fyodorova'. They had arrived, and Renard knew for sure that something far worse than provocation was about to happen.

They entered the Presidential reception, a grandiose office with four or five enormous baroque desks housing computer screens. Behind the largest desk sat a woman in her late fifties, with red hair done up in a beehive; and behind her was another pair of large double doors, above them a sign which read simply 'Office of the President, Russian Federation'.

She rose as they entered, Zidra first, followed by Renard and the two monks. With a startled look on her face, she reached across and pressed a button. But as the monks began pushing past her towards the President's inner office, she tried to protest.

Now Renard made his own move, slamming a knee into Father Ivan's groin. Renard was tall and heavy, and the blow should have brought the monk crashing to the ground. But the man was iron, shouldering Renard aside like wheat in a field, ripping the Heckler and Koch silenced submachine gun from the gladstone bag and lunging forward all, in one movement. It was Zidra who stopped him with a heavy glass paperweight which smashed into the bridge of his nose. Father Ivan sprawled forward and on to the Heckler and Koch; there was no time to pry him loose from it, because the paratroopers were now piling in, whilst Father Anton had already leapt over the body and was crashing into the President's office, Zidra racing after him.

Renard felt he was under water, Zidra and the priest already just a blur of motion on the surface. He tried to drop-kick Captain Smirnov but something battered into him so violently from behind that he found himself diving into the Presidential office just after Zidra.

It was over before it began, and he knew it. He had time to raise one arm in a mute protest at the only warning he heard, the clicking that is emitted by a silenced Heckler and Koch. A crash and a stifled scream followed.

Only then did Renard register what was before him: a mahogany desk,

165

with a long conference table extending from it across the length of the high-walled room. Two men were standing by the table. One of them had looked round in surprise: tall, strong and distinguished-looking with his shock of steel-grey hair. It was the Russian President. The other was shorter, dark-haired.

The President began to speak, but Renard saw Father Anton aim and in the same moment Zidra threw herself across the room, her dumpy jacket making her arms thump like the wings of an ungainly bird. The first hail of bullets meant for the President instead struck Zidra in the back and threw her crashing into the desk. And even as the blood spurted from her body, the second slew of bullets raked the President from crutch to sternum, smashing his torso open.

The firing continued as the President crashed back over his desk and then an alarm bell clanged, right in the room, making even the gunmen suddenly start, until the bell was silenced by another burst of automatic. A picture crashed from the wall behind the President's desk – it was a portrait of the Empress Catherine.

Something had struck Renard on the back of the head and he stumbled forward. Strong hands wrenched up his arms from behind, viced them together in handcuffs. His ears were filled with roaring, his mouth with blood, but he willed himself to turn round. He saw Alfredo Sakharinov; then two others: the first was certainly the brother, Sergei Sakharinov. Beside him, also holding a Heckler and Koch, was someone in steel-rimmed glasses: it was Medved. He smiled at Renard.

'*General* Medved, late of Varta KGB,' Alfredo Sakharinov was saying, the voice polite, almost shy, reverberating in Renard's head. He spoke as matter of factly as if he were updating a friend on another's career moves: 'As of now the General has been promoted, and he's to become the Commandant of the Presidential bodyguard.'

Renard was powerless to do anything except glare at Sakharinov.

Sakharinov went on: 'You've met, of course. What a pity he was too late to save the former President. But at least we have the assassin – Mr Renard? You have created a *Grand Guignol* for us today.'

He too was smiling.

There was a sudden choking, then the sound of blood plopping on the deep carpet. The air smelt bad – acrid with spilt blood, the stench of spent ammunition, gunsmoke. Somewhere a klaxon was blaring. From far away, Renard heard voices crying, shouting. Somewhere else he knew the sun was shining. The sun is always shining, somewhere.

The rag doll that had been Zidra slipped a little from the desk on which she had been slumped, then fell suddenly to the floor. Renard edged to her, but Alfredo Sakharinov motioned to someone behind him. There was a crashing blow to the side of his head. Darkness.

CHAPTER 12

'What were you doing when the President was killed?'
'Watching CNN.'
Lots of people would be saying that to their children twenty years
down the line – so Father Pyotr supposed. If there were any children.

In every reception room outside the office of every boss in Russia
there's a television set. The more grand the office, the bigger the TV. A
giant *Rubin*, the colours invariably out of phase so that human faces
leach green around the edges. Or a *Temp*, with its shoebox-size transformer buzzing like a swarm of angry bees on the floor beside it, prone
to burst into flames. Dusty, ignored, but always switched on. Today they
would all be tuned to CNN – except for the sets in the front offices of
government departments which would be switched patriotically to a
Russian channel. It wouldn't matter which because they'd all be showing
Swan Lake.

It occurred to Father Pyotr, sitting in the Sobor safe flat in Mayakovskii
Square, that Russians ought to be allergic to Tchaikovsky, the broadcast
harbinger of wars and coups d'état. The portly priest sighed, settled
deeper in the one rickety armchair the room boasted and continued
watching CNN. Like its presenters, whose tired voices would stitch
history together during the coming days, he was waiting. The difference
was that CNN and the world did not know what they were waiting for,
but Father Pyotr did. First he just had to make it happen.

By his side was a tin of cashew nuts and a half litre of *Absolut* vodka.
The bottle was almost empty but he would not be drinking any more. He
knew the necessary dose. Enough to fortify. Enough to brave out the
day. Enough to go through a meeting with Claud Perkins and a battle
with Langley, the results of which would decide the fates of Renard and
Zidra Latsis, and much else besides.

. . . more on that story breaking in Moscow, someone in Houston was
saying. *An assassination attempt has been reported on the life of the
Russian President. Details are sketchy, but there are reports of gunfire
from within the Presidential complex in the Kremlin earlier today. If true,
that would make this the sixth known assassination attempt on the*

President during the past three years . . . we'll be updating that story as . . .

. . . in the last half hour all Russian broadcast media have abandoned scheduled programmes and begun to broadcast solemn music . . .

. . . the assassin is rumoured to be an American citizen who killed the President for private reasons. Don Gilson in Moscow, do you have any more on that?

As Don Gilson began to speak there came a loud knocking at the front door of the flat. Father Pyotr rose to his feet and tiptoed to the door, waiting. After five seconds the same sequence of knocks was repeated. He slid back the bolts and opened the door. A small man in old clothes and with a very dirty face pushed in. The man was carrying a heavy canvas bag stained with black oil. He dumped the bag on the ground; it was full of steel pipes. Father Pyotr shut and bolted the door and they shook hands. 'Let me change before anything else,' the little man said. His breath stank of very cheap cologne, the kind which pervades Moscow's metro in the early rush-hour. His trousers reeked of urine. The combination was devastating.

'This is the last time we do this; it's too dangerous,' the newcomer spoke again, using the perfectly modulated brand of English which New England lawyers deploy. 'I had the devil's own job to get out today. MVD and watchers everywhere. The Garden Ring is crawling with the sods and the queue outside the consulate's visa department is two-thirds KGB this morning.' His voice was bird-like but querulous, as if KGB watchers came in the same nuisance category as unruly neighbours.

'That's no surprise, Claud. What else do you expect?' Father Pyotr watched the man peel off several layers of clothes and roll them into a large black binliner. The priest took it to an empty tea chest and dumped it, together with the bag of tools. Then he went to an ancient wardrobe, one of whose doors was missing, and took an overnight bag from it, handing it to his visitor – who was now naked except for black silk socks held up by red suspenders. This was Claud Perkins, an obscure officer in the US Embassy consular department – thought by Russian Counter-Intelligence to be a minor and generally sidelined CIA man – in fact the most important Western Intelligence officer in Moscow.

Perkins took the overnight bag, went to the bathroom and started the shower. Father Pyotr went back into the big empty lounge and sat down again.

Don Gilson had said whatever he wanted to say about the identity of the assassin and the picture cut from a Houston community studio to a windswept Red Square. Another Moscow reporter invited viewers to witness the police presence as the camera panned across the rows of heavily armed troops, behind which stood armoured personnel carriers and trucks. There was, she said, still no confirmed information about whether the killer was a loner or part of a plot. Moscow had been rife for weeks with rumours of plot and counter-plot; but then Moscow was always rife with rumour when big political setpieces began, like the opening of a controversy laden parliament . . .

Father Pyotr retrieved the nuts, ate some, and waited. After a while Perkins reappeared wearing check trousers, a black dog-tooth jacket, a check shirt and a yellow polka-dot bow tie. There were black patent pumps on his tiny feet. Instead of *Krasnaya Moskva* cologne he now smelt faintly of Armani. Pince-nez were pinioned to his sallow and somewhat pronounced nose; a brown cord attached them to his lapel buttonhole. He took them off and polished them with a silk handkerchief in a matching polka-dot design which he pulled from his top pocket. They'd already left red marks on the bridge of his nose which he rubbed as if they irritated him. In fact he cloaked himself in irritation as small people sometimes do.

The priest offered to make tea, but Perkins refused this with a petulant wave. 'How did you avoid arrest?' he asked, his eyes on CNN.

'They didn't want me. I wasn't even allowed to take the car into the Kremlin grounds. I left and came here to wait for the others. I've been here the whole time.'

'You shouldn't have called me.'

'Why not? If neither of them's dead, I want to get them out.'

Claud smiled incredulously. *'You want to get them out?'* The smile was acrid. 'Only in boxes, I fear.'

. . . A month-long State of Emergency has been declared in Moscow today, CNN was saying. *The man who will take the place of the murdered President, Minister Plenipotentiary Alfredo Sakharinov, is expected to appear before the opening session of the Duma tomorrow to be sworn in as the country's new President . . .*

. . . In a further development, Itar-Tass has revealed the identity of the alleged assassin. He is thirty-eight-year-old Douglas Renard, an American citizen. Renard is said to have an accomplice, a twenty-eight-year-old woman named by Moscow police as Zidra Latsis. The woman, a citizen of the Baltic republic of Latvia, was reportedly wounded in the shoot-out in the President's offices and is now in hospital. Her condition is not known. There are no other known accomplices. The Latvian Government has put out a statement deploring the killing of the President and one of

his chief advisers, Mikhail Ivanov. The Latvian ambassador in Moscow has been called to the Russian Foreign Ministry, it is not known why . . .

'So, they've pinned it on Renard. Sakharinov has won. A masterstroke! If an American did it,' Claud mused, 'no Russians are to blame. So now no one will have a reason not to support the new President and rally to the flag.'

A blurry black and white mug-shot of Renard appeared on the screen. *Douglas Renard, the alleged assassin, is said to be a member of a Texan Orthodox Church congregation, the voice-over said. There is no word as to the motivation behind the killing, or how Renard came to be in the President's office.*

. . . The Government of the United States, in common with other Western governments, issued a statement earlier, expressing its outrage at the assassination of the Russian President.

The US statement went on to express the heartfelt condolences of the US President and his family for the family of the murdered President and for the Russian people. 'There are no words to express our sorrow and that of the American people and all mankind for the outrage that has occurred,' the statement said. 'In this dark hour the United States will make every effort to support and assist the government being formed by incoming President Sakharinov.'

There has been no comment forthcoming from the US State Department about allegations that the killer was an American citizen. A spokesman for the State Department, Mr Henry Washington, said it was too early to make a judgement and that the US has yet to receive official word on the matter from the Russians. Mr Washington went on to say that the US authorities were aware of the democratic credentials of the President's likely successor, Mr Sakharinov, and were satisfied that the reform process in Russia would be in safe hands . . .

'*Yet to receive official word!*' Claud's smile set like a lesion. '*Any* word. No one in the Russian Foreign Ministry is even answering our Ambassador Loken's calls. There's a wall of silence. They didn't even tell us what had happened: we only heard that the Russian President had been murdered when CNN asked the Embassy to comment on a statement about the killings put out by Itar-Tass, for Christ's sake. The President of the United States himself tried to put a call through to Alfredo Sakharinov early this morning. The swine refused to speak to him.'

In other news from Russia, the Russian Defence Ministry announced that a foreign submarine, thought to belong to a Nato power, had gotten into difficulties while under the polar ice-cap. The submarine, thought by the Russians to belong to the US Navy, made a distress call but has since disappeared. The Navy Department confirmed that the nuclear-attack submarine USS Nashville *had been on a routine patrol in polar waters, but was not thought to be involved.*

'Bingo! They've fucked us absolutely.' Claud sat down in the chair vacated by Father Pyotr who'd got up to switch off the TV.

The priest pulled over the only other chair the room boasted. 'If that's to be believed, they are alive, but Zidra's wounded.' He looked at Perkins. 'I expect them to be taken to Lefortovo, which is the logical choice of prison anyway, and where they have a hospital and can treat her.' He leaned forward and touched Claud's right knee, which was fastidiously crossed over the left. 'I have friends at Lefortovo,' he said. 'In the prison, and in the hospital too.'

'*Former* friends by now, I should say. Russia is sliding back under the ice, Petrusha my friend. If you stay here you'll go under with it. I can help you leave. Maybe. But not more than that. You and I are working to different agendas now.'

'Why? I don't see why.'

Claud rubbed the red marks on his nose. 'I have to leave here in half an hour. Frankly, I came only because you were the last person to be with Renard. I must tell you, Father Pyotr, that I'm not interested in hearing any more of your Sobor loony tunes. I grant – we all do – that something *was* achieved. You told us about the existence of Molniya. But there's a debit side, isn't there? I don't have to catalogue the things which have gone wrong; it's enough to point to this mess to see how *not* to run an operation. So now I'm interested only in covering the damage already done. To that end we are working on a legend. "We", meaning Langley *and* Foggy Bottom. Imagine that – things have gotten so serious we're cooperating with State. And we want the legend to relate to at least some of the facts. That's where you can help. As for rescuing Renard – forget it. I don't even want to be in a room where I hear that kind of crap being spoken.'

The priest looked at the floor, then again at Claud. 'In that case I also don't have much time for this meeting, I'm afraid; so let's get on with it. What legend? How can I help, assuming I agree to?'

'Depends. On what happens next. What the Russians do. But there are two stories. One variant is that Douglas Renard was a loner, he was out in the cold too long, and he went off the rails. That's if we get faced with something conclusive about his CIA status. There is another variant which we prefer. You had him disguised as a priest. We can go along with that. As a matter of fact we have a legend like that in his files which just needs dusting off. If we can make that fly, it would get Uncle Sam off a hook. Maybe we can use you.'

'How? I don't follow—'

'We can smuggle you out and then put you in front of cameras back home. You will simply confirm the story. Renard came to you with bona fides from an ex-pat Russian Orthodox community. You didn't know he was stark raving mad, so you helped him. There is such a community in Texas as a matter of fact. We started it as a front, many years ago. The surprise was just how many Texans discovered that in their hearts they'd always wanted to be Orthodox Christians. That community really took off. They have a big congregation now, and they send trainee priests to some seminary right in Moscow.'

Father Pyotr groaned. 'I know them,' he said. 'I thought they were upfront! I was delighted that somewhere in the world a Russian Orthodox congregation existed in which half the clergy weren't secret policemen. I had no idea that . . .'

'—that we do the same things with religion that you do?' Claud's face was unreadable. 'Such naïveté is not merely inexcusable. In your case, it can only be deliberate. OK, on with it. That's Option One as of now. But in either case, one fact is clear: we disown Renard, we have to. More than that. We have to cover all the bases. You know what *that* means. You may not like it, nor do I. But you know the way these things work. So does Douglas. He knows what we'll be thinking about now – and he wouldn't expect anything else. He's a pro.'

Father Pyotr pursed his lips as if he'd just tasted vinegar when he was expecting to find communion wine. 'I'm not sure I'm following you,' he said, following perfectly well.

'Loose ends, Petrusha. They have to be tied. *Now*. This is going to be like the Bay of Pigs, the Iran hostages and Contragate – put together and remixed with the Cuban missile crisis. Damage limitation; that's *our* priority. Not stopping Sakharinov from holding the West to ransom with his goddamn secret weapon. The boys with the big toys in the Pentagon will have to deal with Molniya now, if they can. And damage limitation means not leaving matters where they stand with Renard. You and I both know that if they have their mitts on Douglas for more than a month or so, then he'll soon be singing from their hymn-sheet. Then we'd get some ultra-embarrassing court-room confessions. That's the way it goes; you know it. Renard doesn't want that. He'd be better off dead and he'd say so himself.'

'So what you're saying is that you want my help in this too – to organize the murder of Douglas Renard?'

Perkins gazed stonily at him. 'Yes,' he said. 'Call a spade a spade, if you like. And we have to get to the girl, of course, but she's secondary. Either we kill them ourselves or we get him to commit suicide.' His tone was almost prim.

Father Pyotr didn't hedge, 'That's a completely bizarre option. Impossible to contemplate.'

'It's not an option. It's *the* option. If we're going to do anything, then it has to be that.' Perkins' eyes narrowed. '*You* are also a problem. I can hardly just leave you running around. Can I?'

'You mean you are threatening *me*?' The priest looked coldly at Perkins. 'I think that, as a physicist friend of mine might put it, there's a lack of isomorphic fit between your mind and reality. In any case, you don't need my help to fix Renard. You'll get a consular visit; I'm sure they'll play everything by the book just to score points.'

'That may not happen for weeks – and by then the Russkies'll have reprogrammed him. That would rather defeat the object.'

'Mr Perkins, I am not going to organize the death of Mr Renard. Forget it. But I can tell you this – I believe it *is* possible to help him escape.' His voice rose when he saw Perkins' intransigent face. 'More than that – we can make a counter-blow against Alfredo Sakharinov, one which will seriously damage him, perhaps even destroy him. And we may just be able to destroy Molniya into the bargain.' Perkins' look at last flickered into interest, despite himself. 'There are risks, of course,' the priest went on. 'But as far as I can see, your side has nothing better to offer. Even your submarine is lost. You can't touch Molniya without our help. And if you don't do that, then World War Three will be fought and lost in a few hours. And very soon at that, as you know. So, I think you ought to listen to what I have to say before you decide it's *loony tunes*.'

The priest pressed on: 'Sobor is not finished. There's still one possibility left. One card we can play. With your help. With substantial support from Langley.' He stood up. 'I should like you to follow me into the adjoining room. It's bug-proof, I'll stake my life on it.'

Perkins followed on into what had once been a small bedroom, not more than three metres by three. Once inside, he closed the door and they found space to sit amongst the humming machinery, the file servers and transceivers. The priest was going to say his piece.

'We do have one ace in our hand,' Pyotr began. 'There's someone very close to Alfredo Sakharinov, someone extremely powerful, who is compromised and whom we can use. I have the evidence of their betrayal, and I will show it to you. If you're convinced by it, then I want

174

you to help me persuade Langley to take a chance on us. But time's short, and we need to be up and running right now.'

'Get real on me, Petrusha. Who's the traitor you've uncovered?'

'*Sergei Sakharinov.*'

Claud hunched his chin on his knees and enveloped them gnomically in his arms. 'Not very original. But I'm listening so it better be convincing,' he said.

'I'm going to play you a tape. It's a recording of a conversation between Sakharinov and Dmitry Zamok.'

Sounds like mice scratching under a skirting board tinkled out of the microcassette machine. Claud leant forward to hear, and as the vast betrayal unfolded a small smile panned across the sallow face. When it was over he gave a low whistle: 'They're all quite stupid really, aren't they? That's what most impresses. Not the depth of the stupidity, but its existence at such proximity to power.'

'Well?'

'Well, Father Pyotr—' Claud's eyes glittered with suppressed excitement and he all but rubbed his hands together. 'I see we'll need to sit here for a while longer and make a few calls. Can you still connect to Langley on that thing?' He pointed to the machinery opposite him.

'After a fashion,' Father Pyotr told him. 'But before we do, there's one other detail you should know. Renard had a copy of this tape with him when he went to see the President. He meant to play it for him. Medved's men must have searched Renard after his arrest. My guess is that it's with General Medved.'

'Jesus! Then the shit's due to hit the fan *today*.'

'Exactly.'

'What will Medved do with it? Tell his boss immediately, or try to use it some way, perhaps to blackmail Sergei?' Claud thought aloud.

'There's no way Medved can try to play with it; he'll have to tell Alfredo. It's just too big,' mulled the priest.

'It's a mega-catastrophe for Alfredo. Having to arrest his own brother for treason, when he's just promoted him to Prime Minister.'

'Sergei Sakharinov's a dead man. Unless we warn him. And if we do that, he'll have no choice but to help us . . .'

'I've been in this town for a long while, Petrusha. I've acquired some of your bad habits. So let's begin, but begin properly.'

Father Pyotr understood and went for the vodka bottle.

It was going to be a long day. They would have to discuss matters with Langley. It would take several eternities even if all the kit worked as it should. It never did. Father Pyotr had become something of an expert

175

on the glitches which seemed to find their way into the shiny icon-studded software Langley supplied. There would be the usual delays; then – after the comms program had been started, abandoned and restarted several times, by which time Langley's receivers would be in the full throes of automated paranoia – the tiny encrypted messages would begin to crawl uninterrupted over the C-Sat's creaking 14,400 baud link. After this the CIA would fall into sphinx-like silence while it digested everything Sobor was telling it. Then after *that*, the final decision would lie with the US President.

Would they pay or not? How much was Sergei Sakharinov worth? One million? Ten? A hundred? And how to tickle him up out of the bed of the stream, how to play him, hook him, land him, in the short time left? Then – if they did all that – if they established that he could be bought off on the idea of defection, of a future spent in some Caribbean nirvana reflecting on his sacrifice for democracy, how in fact were they going to get Sergei Sakharinov out of Russia? Which begged the even knottier question of how to get Renard and Zidra out. Father Pyotr knew the prison commandant at Lefortovo. He was an old, familiar bribee. But purchasing his help to spring the alleged assassins of the President might not be possible at any price.

And what of Molniya?

Claud said, and Father Pyotr agreed, that if they did manage to spring Renard he would head straight for Semiransk, come what may. Renard was a stickler for duty. He had accepted the mission, and he would go on to the end. 'Blow the fucker up.' That's what he had told Father Pyotr he meant to do to Molniya. Only a bullet or an order from a superior officer would stop him.

Then why not combine everything? suggested the priest. 'Get them out of Lefortovo. Fly them to Kalegut somehow.'

'God knows how,' Claud said. 'And then what?'

'I already know how,' Father Pyotr smirked. 'And after that they can meet Sergei Sakharinov *there*, at the Molniya base. We know from our source that when the Molniya thing is turned on, one of the Sakharinovs has to be there. They don't trust anyone else and Alfredo Sakharinov will be busy at the Duma, taking power, so it will be little brother.'

Sergei Sakharinov would help them incapacitate the thing. Then they'd leave. That was the way.

When the two of them had worked that strategy out and killed another half litre of *Absolut*, Langley came back on the line and said, *Yes, agreed*. The gist of their agreement was $50 million for Sergei Sakhari-

176

nov. Another submarine under the Arctic. Plenty of aircraft – you name it. Just do it.

'Well, all we have to do now is contact Sergei,' Perkins hinted.

That was when Father Pyotr put his call through to Sergei Sakharinov. It took a while, even with the CIA-supplied gimmick – an ordinary cellphone, tweaked and reprogrammed – which let him hack into the *Iskra* governmental communications network. He found Sergei through the system's operator while he was being driven from the Kremlin to his offices in Staraya Ploschad, and gave him the good news about the Zamok tape which even then was probably being played back to his brother by General Medved. After that it took Sergei Sakharinov about eight seconds to agree to meet.

'How are your patients?' Dr Zarbayev asked his colleague, the eminent surgeon Dr Fillipov, when they met that evening on the threshold of the small outbuilding which housed the medics' *banya* in the grounds of Lefortovo Hospital.

Dr Fillipov said, 'Healthier than yours, that's for sure.' Both men laughed; they had entered the building's tiny hallway and were taking off their heavy winter coats and boots in the confined space allowed. 'My God, it's cold; must be twenty below in Moscow.'

'At least! I hope the stove's hot for us. I ordered it this morning, so it should be.'

Beyond the hall a pine door led into a small lounge. This was not one of those pretentious modern *banyas* where pink marble and gilded plumbing had replaced old wood and a proper freezing plunge-bath; but it was one of the best in Moscow.

The lounge wasn't large, and homely rather than elegant. But it was well appointed, with wood-burning samovars, which were hissing and clicking comfortably; deep leather couches, and in the centre, a solid, old-fashioned trestle table. That day the table was especially well laid with the traditional *banya* fare: cod livers, salted herrings and mounds of fresh, hot mashed potato; ice-cold vodka, beer, salad, plenty of fruit and *pirozhki* pies.

After inspecting the food, both men stripped and went next door to the showers, where there was also a solid, big old massage table. Beyond the showers was the plunge room; the small pool was full of crystal-clear icy water. And beyond that was the *banya* itself. It had been properly and thoroughly heated. The air temperature inside was 115°C. The wooden walls were probably nearer 140°C; enough to ensure the *banya* stayed at a proper temperature throughout the ensuing ritual; but not so hot as to damage the wood itself.

'Excellent,' Dr Fillipov said. 'Let us begin.'

The doctors sat for nearly twenty minutes in the dry heat before either of them reached a limit which made the plunge necessary. Then they both took it, and at once returned to the *banya*. After repeating this process four times within ten minutes or less, Fillipov sought his colleague's permission to throw on to the rock-filled stove ladles of water from a bucket in which fragrant birch *veniki* had been steeped. Super-heated steam exploded into the *banya*. They bore it for a minute, two minutes, then left for the plunge – and after that, wrapping fresh white sheets toga-like around themselves, went to the lounge, to rest, to eat and drink a little. It was nine o'clock. Dr Zarbayev turned on the television, where almost all the items were connected with the assassination of the Russian President.

Itar-Tass had announced that all foreigners resident in Moscow, as well as all residents of other Russian cities staying in Moscow, were instructed to report to their nearest militia station within the next forty-eight hours.

All leave was cancelled in the Russian Armed Services.

By government decree a day of national mourning was declared for the President's funeral. Until then his body would lie in state for four days in the House of Unions. Unusually, the coffin would remain closed, a decision necessitated by the disfiguring nature of the wounds which had ended the President's life.

It was announced that President-in-waiting Alfredo Sakharinov would that same evening receive Patriarch Fyodor of the Russian Orthodox Church. The Office of the Patriarch had issued a statement calling for an investigation concerning the alleged religious links of the arrested assassins. The Patriarch stated that he warmly supported the various initiatives taken by President-in-waiting Sakharinov.

But it was the item on the preliminary report of the MVD investigators that startled the two watching doctors. It stated that the President's death was the result of two bullets fired by a single gun.

Dr Fillipov turned off the set. 'Well?'

'They're lying. Bastards!'

'I know; I also saw the body. But you carried out the post mortem, so—'

'The President died instantly,' Dr Zarbayev said at once. His face was pale with anger, and fear. 'There's no problem about that. Any one of the eight bullets which entered the body would have been enough. The bullets were fired from several guns – at least three, to judge from the pathways through the body. So the assassin wasn't alone.'

In the silence that followed, Fillipov looked intently at his colleague, then spooned some olives on to his plate before he spoke again. 'You've filed the report?'

'No. It's in my desk.'

'What are you going to do?'

'I don't know. Only *I* was present at the post mortem, with one assistant. Only *you* have seen the bodies apart from that. Plus the MVD, of course.'

'Plus the Sakharinov brothers and General Medved.'

'Exactly.'

It was left to Fillipov to state the awful truth: 'Even if you rewrite the report to reflect the official story, it won't save you.'

'I know.' Zarbayev looked helpless, panic growing in his eyes.

'Let's think it through a bit. What about the other post mortems? On the President's aide, and his secretary?'

'I can't be sure, but it seems to me that Comrade Ivanov's end was not quite so sudden.'

'Why do you think so?'

'In the first place, his hands and forearms were covered in blood, presumably because he presented them to the stomach wounds – which wouldn't have killed at once. I reckon he was conscious to the end. What's more, he was struck first by a volley of four shells, in a diagonal line traced across the chest and lower abdomen—' he traced a line from lower left to upper right across his own torso.

'Secondly, one bullet entered the body at a different angle – through the throat *here* and exiting through the spinal column *here*, so that the angle of entry was at least sixty degrees to the horizontal.'

'Meaning?'

'Meaning, I guess, that he was on his knees, when someone approached him *like this*—' Zarbayev stood over Fillipov and pointed a finger down in the direction he wanted to indicate – 'and delivered the *coup de grâce* at close range. That would also account for the burn marks associated with that entry wound, and the much larger size of the entry wound.'

'So the killer—'

'—the *killers*.'

'Indeed. The killers aimed first for the main target, the President, and finished off the aide standing by him only afterwards. What about the woman, the redhead?'

179

'She was seen off by a single shot through the head. It was done in the outer room, as they were going through to the President.'

'Strange.'

'Why? She tried to stop them, so they shot her.'

'You don't find that strange? They were with two monks or friars as well, remember. And no one tried to stop them except a secretary. You're telling me that's how top-level security works?'

'Well, OK, let's reconstruct it. They'd arranged to be received by the President, through the intercession of the Patriarchate—'

'No one's admitting that. Even his own ministers could hardly meet the President, Patriarch or no. Especially just now, before the Duma.'

Fillipov said, 'I guess you're right. But God knows; this is Russia. Anything can happen.'

'So the sequence of events is this: the American and the woman arrive with two priestly escorts from Zagorsk. They walk unimpeded to the President's suite, and not a single security officer or guard tries to stop them. Then, they find it necessary to shoot the secretary outside the President's door. Why? Because she's the first person to ask what they're doing? What happens next? Do the priests do anything, I mean, raise an alarm, shout, run, scream? No; they allow the assassin to walk over the dead woman, into the President's office, where they shoot him too. No – *the official story has stood the truth on its head. It was the priests who killed him.*'

'Well, what about the woman? Was she involved?'

'She was shot herself. I spent an hour with her today, and I can tell you that I started to believe her more than our own government.'

'Just how seriously wounded is she?'

'Not very. She was wearing a *kevlar* jacket – so she was obviously prepared for something. She was hit four times. Three bullets were deflected by the jacket; one bullet passed through the underarm, just nicking a vein. She lost some blood, but she's OK. She was lucky. But how did it happen? Look—'

Fillipov drew a sketch on a cigarette packet back. 'Here's the President's office; I got this description from the detective who came to interview the woman today. The doorway faces a long table, and the President and his aide were standing at the table, backs to the door. All the bullets impacted their bodies from the front, right?' Zarbayev nodded assent. 'So they'd turned to see what was going on, who was entering. Now the woman was hit *in the back*. Why?' Fillipov answered his own question: 'Very simple. She ran across the room trying to cover the

President with her own body. That's what she told me, and now I'm sure of it.'

'You weren't supervised when you visited her?'

'There were guards and a colonel with us. They tried to shut her up. In the end I had to sedate her. But they heard as well.'

'I'd say you are definitely in the same shtuck as me.'

Dr Fillipov poured two small glasses of vodka. 'Indeed. I haven't forgotten what happened to Stalin's doctors . . . The fact is that the Sakharinovs murdered our President and they will also murder anyone who knows it.'

Zarbayev was the first to break the silence which followed this remark. 'Things are not quite as they were in Stalin's time. *We* can't be told what to say, or frog-marched off to a firing squad.'

'On the other hand, Sakharinov cannot avoid involving us, unfortunately. He's trapped by *glasnost* and CNN like everybody else. Until he brings the Iron Curtain down again, anyway.'

'Too right. He won't go for us now while we're in the public eye, but won't let us live long knowing what we know.'

'I think I've had enough *banya* for tonight,' Fillipov said decisively. 'I'm going to get dressed.'

'Me too. And I'll tell you something else; that report stays in my desk. At first they'll just be keeping a close eye on us, at least until after the funeral. That gives us a few days. But if we don't use that time, then you're right – our own funerals won't be far behind. It means we have to get away from Moscow. *Now.* And I think I know how.'

'How?' Fillipov asked the obvious question.

'Ask the Americans to help. The man accused is one of theirs, after all, and we can prove his innocence.'

'What about the American, by the way?'

'I was asked – or ordered – to visit his cell at Lefortovo today. We had to straitjacket him. He seems completely deranged. Got no sense out of him at all.'

'So he's no help to anyone. And we can't just stroll round to the US Embassy. Even if we got in, we'd have to spend the rest of our lives there.'

Fillipov looked Zarbayev in the eye, assessed him and said, 'Let me trust you, my friend. That Latvian girl. Although she was screaming hysterically, it was all an act to throw the guards. While I was giving her an injection she gripped me by the lapels and reached up to me. Very calmly she whispered a number. I called it this afternoon from a payphone – got a recorded message telling me to put the phone down and wait. It rang back again in less than a minute. Someone gave me an address in Artillery Street. They told me to go there tomorrow carrying carnations. There was no other discussion. What do you think?'

'I think you showed unusual courage,' Zarbayev said, reaching out to clasp the other doctor's shoulder. 'I also think it's interesting that she thought she could trust you.'

'Yes, but do I go? We must be under surveillance by now . . .'

'What's the address?'

'It's a church. Novoyavlenskaya.'

'It's a public place. That gives cover for anyone trying to make contact. I say you should go. *Go.*'

CHAPTER 13

Zidra is dead.

Renard stared at the cell wall for hours, only ever thinking that one thought. *Zidra is dead.* The three words aborted any other concern. If he willed them away, they crawled back like broken fingers from the cracked and peeling whitewash to taunt him.

Then came delirious sleep . . . followed by a period of restless dreams that gradually began to make sense and signalled Renard's return to the rational world.

On awaking, he registered the fact that his back pocket had been relieved of its contents by Medved. So . . . the microcassette would deliver. He imagined Alfredo Sakharinov's reaction when fawning Medved showed the sound of Sergei's treason. There was sharp pleasure in the thought, so he crushed it out. Vengeance called, but his mission was to correct, not to requite. Retribution made one complicit, scarcely better than the malefactor. No; not even justice could be the motive. Only correction. For the sake of Zidra, and of his lost Lisa, there must now be a cleansing, a lustration of the Russian soil.

And he had time to plan. They would not break Douglas Renard in days or even weeks; they would have to be patient. Renard laughed his dry laugh, knowing they were already gasping to keep up with the events that were sweeping Russia over the edge. He looked up at the little camera high on the wall and showed his teeth.

Something had now begun that could slide the country into civil war and, thanks to Renard, the fault-line would slice straight through the Sakharinov camp. Good! Brother against brother – the most murderous scenario of all, played out through history from the Roman Empire onwards. He exulted at the vision, envisaged the abyss.

Kevlar-lined, he reminded himself. She had never told him, but he'd guessed. Theoretically, therefore, Zidra might still be alive. He rigorously excluded the possibility, because that was how they'd break him – by giving him hope. The pain generator. Like the first false hopes that had racked him when Lisa died. For one blinding moment he was back in the flower-filled ward, where her scorched life had slipped through his fingers all on a fine Saturday afternoon. He had not noticed the precise moment when she'd ceased to be, had missed it and then panicked.

This time it was different, he would not be boarding that old roller coaster again. A man who has no hope is without fear. That is what makes him dangerous.

It seemed to Renard that Sakharinov would not move against his brother at once; he would need time to organize and to check loyalties. An open split would drive Sergei immediately into Zamok's hands and force the crisis into the open. Then the country would divide, and after it the armed forces. To avoid that and the catastrophe of civil war meant preparing a surgical strike against Zamok's Nationalists. That would take a few days at least, and only then could Sergei Sakharinov be dealt with, no doubt summarily. That was the window of opportunity for Renard. They would try to break him and he knew they would use Zidra – *Zidra!* – to do it. And he also knew he would make them fail, make them give him a last chance to strike back.

He saw the scenario in two parts: Medved would have to come and talk with him, to find out how much the Americans knew and whether they were in contact with Sergei. Equally, Renard was sure that Sobor would try to find Sergei Sakharinov, to warn him and to solicit his help.

Sergei or Medved? Which card would show its face first?

Renard leered up at the camera. What could they do to him? He waited for interrogation. He wanted it now and when they were slow in coming for him he punched the wall till the whitewash stained red. That was the beginning: his startled guards called for help, then he was restrained and forcibly sedated. It took four of them to get the straitjacket on, one of whom nearly had an ear bitten off.

Let the game begin. This time he was going to win. Renard clenched and unclenched his teeth and when he roared, the sound penetrated the vile deeps of Lefortovo and many people heard it.

He was the star player, and laughing inside. Never had Renard been so lucid, ready. He was the centre; they would come to him and he would destroy them; he was sure of it. Because now the words were all around, stabbing at him. *Zidra is dead*, they echoed like an angelus. Fear of losing her need not hold him back.

But it was a waiting game that his captors had in mind. Very well then, he waited. His cell was small and he watched the trellis of feeble sunlight that spilled from the high window creeping inch by inch over the flagstones. Watched until it stalled in a corner. The light stagnated there for twenty minutes and then slid up to the wooden cot.

Over Renard's head, the malevolent little eye watched and recorded everything; the spasms of anger, the hours spent frozen, immobilized. And Medved and his advisers, who knew so much about a victim's pain, shared their conclusions.

Had he been told anything? Did the American know the girl was alive? Was it possible that this legendary spy had allowed himself to become sexually involved? How could the theory be tested? This wildness he displayed came as a surprise to them. He had behaved with icy control in Varta, and they were keen to learn why he had changed. Of course it was Medved who figured it out, and worked out how to use it. It was easy: one had only to look at the girl.

They had looked at the girl. Had had her stripped and looked more closely. Had asked the simple question: were they ever alone together? Zidra and Renard? If so, when and for how long?

They looked at the answers and drew the obvious conclusion.

The following morning the Lefortovo Commandant paid a cell visit. He looked sympathetically at Renard, told him at once that Zidra was not dead. Wounded, maybe soon to die. But not yet dead.

Renard showed no emotion.

Would he like to see her? Maybe comfort her?

Would he care to co-operate just a little with the authorities, for her sake? To be realistic, there could be no clemency for an assassin. But it could be different for her. Why not take that step? His own side had publicly and privately disowned him, he owed them nothing, he owed no one. But a girl, love – of course, that was different. He was a man himself, he could understand that. *She* was worth it. He had seen her. God forbid she should rot in a place like Lefortovo and become a prison plaything.

Renard had sat very still and listened to this, and a lot more besides.

What was the price? he'd asked at last.

A very small thing, indeed, considering that the President was dead and nothing was to be gained by too much raking over the coals of who did it or why; Russia was divided enough already. Let him play his small but important part, now; let him take responsibility. Shoulder the whole burden himself, like a man should. Let the girl not suffer.

Renard was glacial. *OK, then, but what about the guarantees?*

No guarantees. But Commandant Glazunov explained what they had in mind.

He could play the fool; pretend to be a religious fanatic who had acted for private motives. That would let his own side off the hook. The whole thing would be recorded in the presence of a US official. And then – why, then there would be two options. A trial, followed by what he knew must follow. Or they could make it easy for him. They could even let his own side help him do it. And after all, what was the alternative? His life was already over.

Renard agreed easily enough that there was probably no alternative. But he wanted to talk through the details. With whom on the American side, and when, would the interview be made? What access would he have *now* to certain necessities? Including writing paper and a razor which worked, for God's sake.

Elsewhere in Lefortovo, Medved watched the whole performance.

'He is brilliant,' he said to an aide. 'Quite brilliant!'

'Does he believe Glazunov, though?'

'Oh, certainly. We've forced his hand, and all in less than twenty-four hours.' Medved smirked while he polished his glasses. 'One of my more signal achievements, I think.'

In truth he had never worked so hard, never crammed so much into one day, starting with the revelation of the tapes – which he'd taken to Alfredo as soon as he'd heard enough. And even if the Kremlin had been Pompeii there could not have been more volcanic fall-out afterwards. Medved had seen the *khozyain* in most of his moods, but never one like that before. It had taken a while to restore the calm necessary to take decisions. They had agreed in principle how to finish with Sergei and with Zamok, but the details remained to be developed. Most importantly for Medved, he had lived through this drama with his chief; it was a new bond between them, which promised well for the future.

On this note he went to his quarters to think through the problem of holding Sergei in check while steps were taken against the Duma. In his opinion Sergei Sakharinov had made everything easy for them, played right into their hands, at the same time revealing both his cretinism and his links with the enemy. Sergei had come openly to them to try to arrange a meeting between US officials and Renard in Lefortovo. That's when he and his chief had acted blindingly fast, had worked out a scenario and said yes, they would make a deal. Renard would certainly understand from where the approach had come; the Americans would make that clear to him and Medved intended to play along, would even help them pass a few secret messages to Renard. He wanted the captive to believe absolutely that his allies outside were continuing to work for him and that there was a real chance that the woman at least would be freed, somehow. In exchange for that, he believed Renard would play his part.

The meeting between Renard and Glazunov was the first step and it had been a spectacular success. Now it was up to the Americans to carry on. Medved did not neglect to warn his own people to turn a blind eye to almost any breach of security that might result.

The meeting between Renard and his American colleague was set for the next day, the third since the killing of the President. Even in that time, the tectonic effects of the killing were gathering momentum. The forces which had destroyed Renard and Zidra Latsis were sweeping to triumphant power in Russia. The opening of the Duma session, postponed after the assassination of the President, was to take place in another three days. It would be the coronation of Alfredo Sakharinov.

Renard's guards visited him the next morning. 'You'll get a visitor today,' the deputy commandant who accompanied them told him. 'Someone from your Embassy, just to see that we're looking after you nicely. That's how civilized we are in Russia nowadays. You murder our President, and we respect your human rights.'

Renard glowered at the man, then was led manacled out of his cell and through the dismal labyrinth that was Lefortovo. Its gaunt ensemble of buildings had seen its share of human drama, of despair and euphoria. The creation of Peter the Great, it included not only the prison, but also Russia's most famous hospital – as well as an asylum, Lefortovo Church, and a morgue. Standing in a corner of Lefortovo Square, this building was unobtrusive but imposing in its own way. It had formed the first brief resting place for some of Russia's greatest sons – her poets, statesmen and scientists – when they passed away. A whole democracy of death had passed through its doors: prisoners from the jail, the bodies of inmates from the asylum, aristocrats who could not survive treatment in the Lefortovo Hospital.

It was to this same morgue that the bodies of the slaughtered Russian President and his close aide Mikhail Ivanov were brought to lie in state, after Dr Zarbayev had carried out the autopsies on them.

The small cortege which brought the bodies was accompanied by Sergei Sakharinov, the Prime Minister, and General Medved, Defence Minister of the Russian Federation. They went from the morgue to the prison where they were received by prison commandant Yuri Glazunov. A ranking officer in the Russian army, Glazunov was pleased by recent events which promised him new powers, new promotion.

Glazunov led his distinguished guests into an office adjoining his own. Inside, two uniformed technicians sat before a table bearing two video recorders and three monitors. Both men rose to salute the newcomers. Medved had already passed some hours here; it was sufficient for him to nod curtly in response. They were his assistants.

Sergei Sakharinov didn't acknowledge them at all and slumped down on the nearest armchair. He looked under strain and depressed. Medved stood in front of the monitors. One showed Zidra Latsis' cell. She was pacing up and down its narrow length, one arm in a sling, her prison haircut – they had almost shaved her head – revealing a certain angularity of the neck and head, no longer softened by a mass of blonde hair.

'Close in on her,' Medved ordered one of the operators. The camera zoomed in on Zidra's face, which showed no sign of emotion. But she must have heard the solenoids clicking because she glanced up at the camera, once. Her green eyes met Medved's and he stiffened involuntarily. She was something feral, an unpredictable, caged animal.

'It is as they said – as I thought,' he said very softly, as if to himself. 'She will repay study. And the other?'

The second monitor showed Renard sitting motionless in a chair. 'This is an interview room. He's waiting for his visitor to arrive.'

'Show me his face.'

The camera closed in. Renard's expression also betrayed no emotion, but this was blankness of a different kind. The gaze was staring, and a small tic was evident under a damaged left eye.

'He's quite a survivor, that one,' Medved said. 'He showed remarkable fortitude in Varta. Willpower – and the benefits of rigorous training, of a discipline fostered over many years. A remarkable man.'

'He seems to have gone insane, sir,' the second of the two officers said. 'He's been in a straitjacket most of the time since you were last here. He almost bit the ear off one poor sod. The doctors recommend not restraining him while he meets the American, but we're keeping a double guard there just in case he repeats yesterday's performance.'

Medved looked satisfied at this news and turned to Sergei Sakharinov, 'Prime Minister, the Americans are just as anxious as ourselves to be rid of this Renard. That's why we've agreed to the meeting today. So that he can hear from his own side that his position is hopeless. In twenty-four hours, I think I can promise you that Renard will be dead by his own hand.'

'The visitor has arrived, sir,' one of the technicians announced.

The monitor in the interview room now showed the door closing behind Claud Perkins. Two guards had entered with him; they stood with their backs to the door while Perkins sat down to face Renard across a small deal table.

'I know that man,' Medved said. 'Perkins – Claud Perkins. A junior consular official, he's an unimportant CIA man on his last foreign tour before retirement.'

'If only we all had your photographic memory for faces, General,' Glazunov fawned.

'Can we hear them?' Sakharinov asked. He had started when he saw Perkins, knocking his plastic coffee cup to the floor. He rose to his feet and crossed the room, staring at the monitor.

Glazunov turned up the volume, and Sergei Sakharinov listened intently to the sounds coming out of the tinny speaker. Medved motioned to the second of the two technicians: 'Misha, this is your part. Translate for the Prime Minister.'

'Have a tape sent to me in any case, Medved. I want the Russian transcript with it. Today.'

'Of course.'

In the interview room, Claud was introducing himself. He gave Renard a card which simply said, 'Claud Perkins, US Embassy Consular Department'.

'We never met,' he said flatly. His eyes were hunting Renard's.

'No, we didn't,' Renard agreed.

Claud relaxed imperceptibly. 'May I sit down?'

'As you wish.'

'Mr Renard, I've been permitted to visit with you, to check how you're being treated and to see if there's anything you need.'

'Who sent you?'

'I told you, I was given permission. It's my job – looking after the interests of US citizens who find themselves in your position.'

'*In my position?*' Renard's laugh was brittle. 'And what exactly do you suppose that to be?'

Claud Perkins took off the pince-nez he wore and rubbed at the bridge of his nose.

'First time here, pal?' Renard asked him.

'Yes, it's the first time I've visited an inmate here. However I have been to these premises before: with a party of colleagues. We were invited by a United Nations Associations Human Rights Commission, right here in Russia. Just six months ago. The facilities are acceptable, despite the age of the building. But let's come straight to the point, Mr Renard. I'm allowed only twenty minutes with you.'

He pointed to the camera on the wall. 'We live in a transparent world, Mr Renard, do we not? Our lives are not our own. Even presidents and prime ministers can be surprised sometimes by the truth of this.'

Renard leaned forward and said conspiratorially: 'There's a camera in my cell, no privacy.' He leered at Claud. 'I can't even take a crap.'

The pince-nez were returned to base.

'Hell, I'm not joking. I kinda have a problem in that department.'

'Wait a moment, please.' Claud took out a small notebook and opened it, carefully furling out a fresh page of primrose-coloured paper. '*Constipation, surveillance*,' he muttered, tracing out the words in a tiny hand. 'Mr Renard, I am unable to arrange for an Embassy physician to visit, unfortunately. But do you require any proprietary medicines?' He leaned across the table and whispered: 'Do you *understand* what you have done, Mr Renard?'

'I did as the Lord commanded, buddy. I scotched the Antichrist. It had to be.'

A tiny smile burrowed into the creases on each side of Claud's sallow face. '*Antichrist*,' he scratched.

'And now my task is over. Others will carry on where I leave off.'

'Others?'

'The godly. I hope you are among them.'

'I see. Mr Renard, I want to explain your position to you.'

'Man, I understand that already. I killed the President of Russia. I did the Lord's work.'

'I am talking about the secular powers, Mr Renard. And if they find that you and your accomplice – I mean this Latsis woman—'

Renard raised his eyes to meet Claud's. 'She must be released,' he said calmly. 'What I did, I did alone.'

Claud answered. 'Well, there are perhaps extenuating circumstances in her case. Your obvious guilt places you differently. You must know the sequel?'

Renard picked up Claud Perkins' official card, inspected it minutely. At last he leaned across the table and said very quietly: 'You ever look at demographic charts? You know, population statistics? They tell you about the health of the nation. And I'll tell you, sir, this Russian nation is not healthy. There should be one hundred million more Russians than there are. That's what demography proves. *One hundred million unborn souls*. Think about it. And you know why?'

Renard rubbed his forefinger up the side of his nose, and gave Claud a heavy look.

'One word, one hand, man. *Onanism*. They're all at it. All of 'em. I hear them! Even the guards. The whole damn male half of the nation; what d'you think about that?'

Claud snapped the notebook shut.

'Is there anything you require, Mr Renard? Writing materials for example. I need to emphasize to you the finality of what will happen to you.'

'Pal, if that there woman is freed I don't mind what happens to me.'

'*Mr Renard*, you are going to be tried, found guilty and probably executed. And on my information, very quickly at that.'

'What's the alternative?'

'Only you can decide.' Saying this, Perkins pushed a small package wrapped in brown paper across the table. 'I've cleared this with the Commandant,' he explained. 'Here're some disposable blades, soap, good American toilet tissue. And some American chewing gum.' He leaned across and whispered: '*Special* gum. You understand me, Mr Renard?'

Renard took the package and held it up to the light, turning it over. He looked gratefully at Perkins. 'I think I do, sir, and I'm obliged to you. You've given me comfort.'

Claud Perkins stood up. The meeting was over. 'I'll be back in two days, Mr Renard. But believe me, I hope your troubles will soon be ended.'

Renard offered his hand. 'Maybe we'll meet again. Maybe not.'

Claud beamed. 'Goodbye, Mr Renard. I'm glad to have been of some service.'

Elsewhere, Sergei Sakharinov turned away from the monitor he'd been watching and told Commandant Glazunov he required a word in private. As they were leaving, Medved approached him and told him he would take the opportunity to begin interrogating the girl. Sergei Sakharinov nodded. 'Don't be in a hurry,' he said. 'Take your time and get results, General Medved. Not like last time in Varta.'

As soon as they were alone, Sakharinov told the commandant he had an important matter to discuss. 'What I'm about to tell you is for your ears only, Glazunov. Not to be shared with anyone, *including* Medved. Understood?'

Glazunov nodded dumbly.

'I can't go into details – obviously. Matters of high national importance are at stake. You're privileged to be party even to that much.'

Glazunov straightened up. He was an old intriguer who sensed the approach of one of those windfalls which can transform a life.

'Major promotion will be yours if the task I give you now is carried out conscientiously.' The carrot in place, Sakharinov placed himself on an old leather chesterfield, motioning the donkey to sit in the armchair opposite.

191

Glazunov duly sat, mesmerized. Sakharinov crossed his knees, the knife-edge creases in his Cerrutti suit perfectly draped, so that his whole body looked like one coiled spring, from the angular, narrow face, to the Gucci-clad feet pinioned together for security.

Sergei Sakharinov had always had trouble with eye contact. He was physically smaller – more vulnerable – than his brother. Where Alfredo had the weight to bear down on others, challenging, forcing them into submission, Sergei had to rely on his ability to disconcert and frighten for opposite reasons. His power was insidious, borrowed like a coat. But for all that he was elusive, invisible, he left animal traces – the bloody smears of broken lives. This was how he scent-marked.

Now, when his life depended on it, Sergei Sakharinov found the strength to dominate. He gave Glazunov his task, and an astonished Glazunov accepted it. At the end of their talk, Glazunov, cheered by the thought of imminent promotion, offered to open a bottle of cognac and Sergei agreed. He hated the stuff; it dulled the senses, and he preferred cocaine. But he understood the predilections of the Russian officer corps.

In another part of Lefortovo, Medved was also pleased; and more than just that. Renard was broken, would be dead within two days, and the Americans were conniving at his downfall. Things had worked out well. He had the girl in his pocket and he had managed to turn the wild strength of the American back on its owner. Plus, there was the fact that in less than twenty-four hours Sergei would be arrested for treason. This would be the signal for a general move against all forces opposed to Alfredo Sakharinov. The Duma would be closed, its deputies dispersed. The West would support Alfredo, whatever his crimes, because they feared Zamok more. Dmitry Zamok would be annihilated.

The Varta divisions Medved had been quietly transferring to Moscow were ready to move. And *he* would start to harvest the benefits. Beginning with Zidra Latsis. She was a real discovery! This beautiful woman, the last of a line of bitter enemies of the Sakharinovs . . . He would plan her limited future with all the finesse of which he, uniquely, was capable. It would be a feast of the senses, one he would share with his grateful Sakharinov master.

He had already enjoyed contemplating her for half an hour through the one-way glass pane installed high in the wall of her cell, first sending the governor away. His small black eyes had hunted her as she paced the room – she was a caged tigress. Medved had shown no emotion, but a speck of saliva appeared in the corner of his mouth. His pulse rate marginally increased.

In a long career, this would be his finest destruction of a fellow creature. He would take his time. He needed to assess her full spectrum, both psychological and physiological. He would not keep her here, of course; there would be several disorienting moves before he finally located her in his own workshop. He always worked on the principle that it was necessary to *know* his subjects in order to complete their destruction. To gorge oneself on the slow unbinding of every nerve, knot and sinew required observation and periods of calm discussion aimed at securing the subject's collusion in their own destruction. Only in the cultivation of this awareness was there any hope of artistry, of an aesthetic consummation. Without that, one might just as well be demolishing a wall. The torturer seeks in his subject someone who will come to regard his executioner as a friend destined to release him; then the triumph of the torturer is complete, then is the time to strike.

Professionally, Medved modelled himself on his great predecessor, Lavrentii Beria – Stalin's executioner. Beria favoured those torments induced by the subject's enforced observation of the suffering inflicted on his loved ones. But this, though effective, holds little interest for the torturer. Medved preferred a one-on-one relationship with the victim where nothing more was at stake than his own pleasure, as in this case.

His technique would take her through each gradation of pain, with no form of self-abuse and humiliation left untested. It would require two or three days, perhaps more, before her life was finally surrendered to him. And then he would possess her, making her *his* for ever, his through *metousiosis*, through the transubstantiation of her body and blood into his own.

It would be an epic.

CHAPTER 14

In the early afternoon of 24th November a warder making his rounds noted an unusual smell emanating from Renard's cell. He called the control room; nothing untoward could be observed on the monitor. Nonetheless, two members of the Presidential Alpha battalion were sent to open the cell door. They immediately noticed the strong aroma of bitter almonds. The smell was intense around Renard's head. His lips were blue, there was no sign of breathing and his eyes were open, staring fixedly at the ceiling. The warder pressed the alarm buzzer and in less than ten minutes Doctor Zarbayev arrived from the Lefortovo Hospital, checked for vital signs and pronounced Renard dead.

'Obviously death was the result of self-inflicted cyanide poisoning, and I should say he's been dead for an hour at least,' he told the hovering Commandant.

Glazunov's response was immediate. 'Very well; then have the body removed to the morgue. Place a guard inside the mortuary and in the chapel as well. I want Zarbayev to carry out the post mortem today.'

Renard's body was placed on a trolley and covered with a white sheet, then rolled through the four guardpoints which lay beneath his cell and the side entrance of the prison nearest the morgue. Two guards pushed the trolley; Zarbayev went in front, together with a third guard, who was given the keys to open up. The trolley was taken through the modest front entrance of the morgue, across the parquet floor to a heavy metal door beyond which lay the mortuary. 'Do we put him in a fridge?' someone enquired.

'Don't be a fool; the autopsy will be in an hour. There's nothing worse than cutting up chilled cadavers. I get chilblains.' With this, Zarbayev left.

Two of the guards remained. One sat in the room with Renard's body, the other beyond the locked door in the hallway to the chapel of rest.

After thirty minutes there was a knock at that door. 'Seryozha? I've brought tea. Open up.'

The guard inside opened the door. 'Christ, but it's cold in here! Thanks,' he said to his colleague, taking the tea gratefully.

'I've had a call; Doc's changed his plan and the autopsy won't be until this afternoon, so we can relax a bit.' The guard from the hall sat down. 'Here, I've got the cards. Let's play a few hands.'

They sat down and played a desultory hand.

'What the hell's that noise?' the newcomer asked. There was a snapping sound which came from the direction of the mortician's table, followed by a rustling of cloth and then a long sucking noise.

'Nasty, isn't it? But don't take any notice. It's just rigor mortis. The body stiffening. Ignore it. Doc said not to look; it's full of cyanide.'

The other man was obviously unnerved; his eyes constantly slid in the direction of the trolley which bore Renard's body.

'Concentrate; you already owe me a packet from last night.'

'OK, OK.' The visiting guard picked up his hand, looked at it. But a waft of cold air bit on his neck. 'Jesus, it's cold in here! Gives me the creeps.' He snapped a card down on the table.

'I'll see you, baby,' the other said and snapped down three cards.

His partner made no reply, his hand froze and the cards scattered over the floor.

'What the hell's the matter with you?'

But the guard's face was a study in terror, nostrils dilated in fear, eyes glaring fixedly at something just over his colleague's shoulder. He spoke but no words emerged. Hearing a very familiar click, his partner spun round: in front of him stood the corpse. It was naked; a terrible smile was pinned on the blue lips.

Renard swung up the guard's carbine and snapped off the safety catch. 'Hi, hope I didn't frighten you guys? Sit quite still, gentlemen, please. For a corpse I'm nervous, and my trigger finger's itchy.'

The guards sat still.

'You're right, it is cold in here,' Renard said conversationally. 'I could use some clothes.' He looked the guards over. 'You'll do,' he said to the taller of the two.

He told the other to lie full length on the tiled floor, hands behind his head. Neither showed a desire to argue. The first guard stripped and Renard ordered him to lie on the trolley. He soon found some masking tape in a drawer, and a bottle of chloroform, which he put to good use. Then he ordered the other to get undressed as well.

'What's your name?' Renard asked him.

'Borzov. Vladimir. I'm a corporal,' he volunteered. He was shivering violently, more in fright than because of the cold.

'Good for you. Tell me, does the Commandant or his deputy know you?'

'We've only been drafted here a few days ago,' confessed the corporal, not knowing whether he was saying the right thing or not. 'We're . . . we're the squad that provides the fresh blood for transfusions.'

'So you're based in the hospital? Not the prison?'

'Yes.'

'What time do you go off duty?'

'Not till this evening, eight o'clock.'

'Old stiff on the trolley, does the Commandant know him?'

'No; I told you, we're new.'

'Right, on the slab with you; face down, please.'

'What – I mean what are you going to do?'

'Kill you, if you don't.'

Renard chloroformed and trussed him like his pal, tying him on the slab located to one side of the mortuary. By now his own head was spinning and he was desperate to get into the outside air.

First he checked the guards' guns carefully; they were loaded. He claimed the corporal's machine pistol and then explored the mortuary. In the corner was a heavy porcelain sink, above it a mirror. He washed his face and gargled his mouth free of ball-point ink and the foul taste of bitter almonds.

Fillipov, who would that day pay a visit to the left-luggage office at Three Stations Square, and leave $50,000 richer, had advised him not to be active for the first hours. He had concealed inside Renard's person a hypodermic containing 5ml of a mixture of dilute curare and bufotenine, the paralytic venom of the Bufo alvarius toad, warning Renard that the mixture potentiated the effects of each separate agent, so that he should inject himself while already sitting down. He had not elaborated. Had the American realized the dangers? The slightest miscalculation about dosage rates in relation to body weight would result in paralysis of the basic life functions, and death. But he was sure the risk *had* been understood. The Renard man was brave. Phenomenally brave – or foolhardy to the point of madness.

Right now Renard was as weak as a kitten, bathed in cold sweat, deathly pale and afflicted with hallucinatory double vision. Yet there was no choice but to go on. Zidra was alive, and he would free her. Now. And then he would begin.

For the second time they had tried to finish with him, and for the second time they had failed. This time they would pay. And someone else would pay as well – the traitor in Washington.

196

The uniform fitted, down to the shiny boots. Finally he put on the blue-rimmed khaki cap. His hair had been close-shaven on the first day at Lefortovo. He pulled the gleaming peak low over his nose, and inspected the result.

His chloroformed companions were elite guards from the Tamanskii Division, the Moscow garrison. Renard was a dozen years too old in the face, but it would have to do. The main thing would be surprise. Lefortovo had the reputation of being an unbreakable prison, but it was old and had been disused for some years until recent events had brought several waves of new high-level occupants. It was a maze of labyrinthine corridors, alleys and entrance ways. Security depended on heavy forged locks and the paranoia of individual guards more than it did upon modern electronic systems. More than that: this was still the Russia of more-or-less unquestioning obedience to superiors, in the army at least.

Renard found a clipboard in a cupboard by the mortician's desk, which he tucked importantly under his arm. He took the heavy bunch of keys from the table where the guards had played cards, and left the Lefortovo morgue, locking it behind him. He checked his watch. It was 16.15. He marched across the square to the main entrance of the prison. The prison officer behind the glass sliding window was slow, so he rapped it smartly.

'OK, OK! I'm coming!' the man grumbled. He slid open the window. 'What is it?'

'Corporal Vladimir Borzov. From the morgue. Doctor's arrived. I have a document for the Commandant to sign.'

'The Commandant? He won't see you. Show me the document.'

'Call him now or you'll be on report in ten minutes.'

The prison officer gave him a sullen look. 'What name?'

'Corporal Vladimir Borzov,' Renard repeated.

The officer dialled a two-digit number, saying: 'Where are you from? Where'd you get the accent?'

Renard made no answer.

'Masha? That you? It's Kolya. Someone here for the Commandant. From the doc. He has a form to sign.' He listened then said to Renard: 'What form?'

'A release. For performing an autopsy. The American's body. It must be released to the hospital.'

The prison officer repeated these words, then listened and said: 'OK, OK. I'll do it. You're to go up,' he said to Renard.

'Where?'

'Don't you know?' The prison officer looked immediately mistrustful.

197

'Of course I fucking don't know, you old cunt. *Tell me the way.*'

'OK, OK, no need for that. Follow me.'

A catch released on the turnstile by the window and Renard entered the prison. The guard led him over to a small lattice-gated lift. 'Third floor, on the left. You can't miss it.'

Renard crashed the gates closed and the lift whined into life. At the third floor he left the lift and walked down the ill-lit corridor until he came to a sign announcing the offices of 'Commandant Yu. P. Glazunov'. He marched in. There were two doors leading from the empty reception area: one was the office of the Deputy Commandant and to the right, covered in quilted leather plush, was the imposing entrance to the Commandant's quarters. Renard opened its double doors without knocking, and found the Commandant alone.

He rose to his feet as Renard entered, his face immediately turning livid with anger. 'Where's that damn adjutant?' he said, then with surprise, 'You weren't supposed to come in here.'

'That a fact?' Renard went over to the desk and pushed the Commandant hard so that he sat abruptly on his chair again. He unslung the machine pistol and slipped off the safety catch. Then he put the muzzle under the Commandant's nose.

Commandant Glazunov glared, but didn't move. He said: 'Ah! *Myatezh!*'

'Listen to me, pal. I don't trust you. Surprised? Don't be. And this is not *mutiny* because I'm an American citizen and I just like cross-dressing, that's all. I also have a strong urge to kill you, because I'm getting tired of all the uniforms around and I think one less would be a benefit to mankind. Keep your hands on the desk.'

'Why have you come *here*?' Glazunov repeated. 'You should go to the cells—'

'We'll go together. Any attitude from you and you're dead. *Comprenez?*'

A long moment passed in silence. The Commandant's eyes flicked once to the left and once to the right and came back to rest on the muzzle which Renard shoved into his gums. 'Yes, I understand,' he whispered.

Renard pointed to a framed plan hanging from the wall by Glazunov's desk. 'That the prison?'

'Yes.'

He moved the gun into Glazunov's stomach. 'Show me where you bastards are keeping her. And show me the exit route. *Now.*'

*

While Renard was resurrecting himself in Lefortovo, Sergei Sakharinov was en route for the Russian parliament building – the Duma – where he had urgent business with Dmitry Zamok. His visit was in breach of protocol, for the Prime Minister was answerable to the President, not to parliament. But his reason for visiting would not wait.

As the *Chaika* limousine with its police outriders swept down the Moskva embankment and on to the squat former Gosplan building which housed the parliament, he braced himself for the deluge of Duma deputies, reporters and bystanders that would greet him on his arrival.

The Duma was home to the controversy, infighting and political intrigue in which the new Russia was being forged. Although it had been granted few powers in Russia's first post-Communist constitution, it had turned out to be the country's centre of political gravity. It was a place where advisers, pundits, hangers-on, agitators and media folk mingled with harassed and hurried Duma deputies. Here the remnants of the pro-Western reform parties, the *democratia* which most Russians seem to prefer calling *deremocratia* – *shitocracy* – argued themselves into extinction whilst the pendulum swung to the right and the Russian Nationalists readied for office. In the Duma, Dmitry Zamok, the firebrand Nationalist leader, was undisputed king. His party was in the majority and his politics held sway.

For Zamok the Duma was relevant only as a springboard to the Presidency. It was to Zamok's offices that Sergei Sakharinov was now hurried by his bodyguards. The division bell had just sounded and the deputies were hurrying from the chamber. The arrival of the Prime Minister of Russia had been announced and Sergei was expected to appear at the rostrum of the chamber. But instead he made straight for Zamok's offices – the best guarded in the Duma, perhaps anywhere in the Russian state.

This day the guard was doubled and armed Nationalist soldiers wearing Cossack uniforms, and with the double-headed iron eagle of the Cossack Union pinned to their chests, lined the outer corridors. *Osnaz* elite troops in plain clothes mingled inside with the aides, courtiers and colleagues of the Nationalist leader. Sakharinov swept through them all and was shown immediately into Zamok's private quarters – which were modest, consisting of little more than a small sparsely furnished salon, with several adjoining rooms for his secretaries and personal guards.

Zamok rose to greet Sakharinov and the two men shook hands. Sergei immediately went over to a window and glared silently at the view of the River Moskva and the vast skeletal hulk of the Ukraina Hotel, waiting until his two security men had swept the suite for recording devices. Only then did he utter the first words of greeting to Zamok, who smiled back in sardonic silence.

'Well, what now?' were Sergei Sakharinov's first words when the technicians had finished and left.

'You trust *them*?' Zamok said, motioning with his head to the door through which the security men had exited.

'I don't even trust myself any more.' The half-smile on Sakharinov's face could have been etched in acid. 'I have only one chance now, and that's you, unfortunately.' He shrugged, and the shrug looked like a shiver. 'Anyway, everything's arranged. The American will be released today or tomorrow morning at the latest. Now it's time for your part of the bargain.'

Zamok waved Sakharinov towards one of the two sofas forming an L-shape by a small coffee table in the centre of the room.

'Well, let's be civilized and talk in comfort,' he said. 'If everything is happening as we decided, then there's no reason for anxiety. And you know *I* have nothing to hide or be afraid of.' The tone was mocking Sakharinov, just on the edge of giving offence. 'I'm taking the constitutional route, as always. I don't need to plot palace coups like you *apparatchiki* who have no friends among the people. I'm sure enough of mass support, without any extra-legal manoeuvres. All of this is just to help you, my friend. Not more than that. Mistakes like extra-legality I leave to your brother, unlike me he's a former Communist and therefore has no experience of any other way.'

Sergei Sakharinov sat bolt upright on the sofa, waiting. Dmitry Zamok on the other hand, who was a large, heavily built man in his late forties, teetering on the edge of being overweight, slouched back comfortably, the jacket of his ill-fitting suit bulging over his stomach.

'Don't patronize me, Dmitry. You have no less at stake than I. And if your hands are not quite as dirty, I'm sure that's only lack of opportunity. I've looked at some of the bums you keep around here. A more psychotic, power-crazed bunch I've never seen. You've got your budding Himmlers and Goebbels itching to write a few bloody footnotes in history.'

Zamok laughed. 'You're a poet! That's why you are so unhappy, Seryozha. You're always out of your depth, but not stupid enough to understand the fact.'

An aide crept into the room bearing coffee and cognac. Zamok waited till he'd left before continuing. 'Let's come to the point, Seryozha,' he said in his low, gravelly voice, the result of constant talk, exhortation and reiteration. 'You want out; the Americans have offered you something. That's fine as far as it goes. But what worries me is the small matter of the missing tape.'

He watched Sergei blench. 'You didn't want to bother me with that? Oh, how very kind. But Seryozha, I am your final friend, you shouldn't keep secrets from me.'

'Who told you?' Sergei gasped.

'Never mind who. I invite you to consider the position your indiscretions have put me in. I don't want to start a war with your brother. I want to win peacefully. But as long as you are here, we're both in danger. You came here openly; it was a serious mistake. Now your brother will conclude that we're about to march on the Kremlin, and may do something foolish himself. This isn't politics, Sergei. It's just a mess!' Zamok was pale with anger. 'You've jeopardized everything. Now we have to bring forward all our plans to have any hope of succeeding. And you must leave, immediately.'

'Leave for where?'

'The United States, obviously. You must perform your civic duty and tell the world who really finished off our late lamented President. Apart from my obvious duty as a democrat, I have a personal interest. Since I plan to be President for a long time myself, I want this unfortunate episode not to form a precedent.'

He lifted the cognac to his lips and swallowed. 'Your health, Seryozha. And don't think I needed things to happen this way. I repeat that I planned to come into office legally, constitutionally. But now it's here, I will certainly take this opportunity, if only to block your brother's criminal schemes. Your announcement that he organized the murder of the President must be made today. There's a continuity studio downstairs you can use. CNN are waiting – they don't know for what, as yet. And Russian television.'

'I understand everything, Dimichka. But we must deal with the loose ends. It's fortunate that the procurator is your pal and could arrange things at Lefortovo. But now let's be clear what happens next. First of all – Medved. He must be arrested immediately, as soon as my announcement is made. That's in your own interest too.'

'I'm aware of that. So are my Cossacks, so don't worry. And, as agreed, I'll cover for you – you fled the country to protect yourself from your brother. Once he's arrested, you'll be free to return, with honour, if you wish. Alternatively, I don't mind if you stay over there. Probably I'll make you Governor of Alaska, after it's been returned to us.'

'Thanks, but I think I'd prefer California.'

'You're weak, Sergei. That's your problem. There's no one holding you to ransom. You're free to do what you want. So what if your brother does find the tape? I don't give a damn. He and his kind have the political permanence of mayflies. He's a technocrat, a functionary, that's all. He's grown too powerful and we'll shorten him by a head. Nothing can save him, because Russia doesn't need him any more. Can *he* restore Russia's place in the world, can *he* make Russia great again? Of course not. But—' He leaned forward over the table, 'I say I *will* do that for Russia! Our borders will extend from the Arctic to Germany in the West, and to the Indian Ocean in the South. I will use new weapons like the elipsons and Molniya – but only when we're ready and not before. Does your brother say that? No, he does not. I say I'll rebuild the army. Does your brother agree? Does he *want* to protect our country? No, he does not. It's only bureaucrats who can't wait, and you know why?' Zamok stood up. 'Because your feet aren't planted on good Russian earth.' He marched on the spot a few times. 'You live in a world of palace intrigue. That's why your brother wants to use Molniya *next week*, like a firecracker at a salute, just to celebrate the day he takes power.' He spat on the carpet and the gravelly voice went lower. 'Alfredo Sakharinov represents everything that has perverted great Russia. He is a political prostitute, who will use even so precious a thing as *Molniya* for mere personal advantage – it is a crime so cheap that—' Zamok crashed a fist on to the table, 'I'll tell you Sergei, when we've finished with him you won't even know where to find his carcass.' He went to the picture window, swept an arm over the panorama of Moscow, and seemed to be stifling a sob.

Sakharinov watched fascinated. The man was pure theatre, his delivery, his timing was perfect. Even his emotional incoherence was staged.

Zamok knew when to repeat key phrases and when to pause for effect, to exhale slowly as he did now . . . 'To use the Russian people . . . in this way – it is simply obscene, and I never will permit it. Never!'

Zamok returned to the sofa and sat down again, giving Sakharinov a telltale glance full of an actor's curiosity. Sergei had seen the performance many times, and it grew ever more hypnotic. Zamok called himself the bell which the masses pealed: his style was to study his listeners, to pick up their secret fears, hopes, loves and hates, and to announce them, amplify them, glorify them. So that when the people repeated his slogans, it was their own desires which they proclaimed. And the programme was simple enough: *We shall never forgive the West for trampling on Russia! Russia will be great and her empire will flow out over Europe and Asia. We shall build a new order!*

'Alfredo Sakharinov represents everything rotten and that's why I'll *crush* him.' Zamok ground his right fist into his left palm. 'In the name of our Great Russia!'

Sergei agreed without hesitation, exulting in the betrayal of his own brother because family, principle, *anything* could be betrayed in the service of the Motherland.

Refuelled by more cognac, Zamok introduced a change of mood, saying, 'So the American will be released – then what?'

'His circle will get him out of Russia – with CIA help. He will tell his story. And . . .' Sakharinov paused, uncertain how to phrase the betrayal of Alfredo which they had discussed often enough before.

'And you will be on the plane with him,' Zamok said matter of factly. 'That's logical. Then everything will happen within the next twenty-four hours. You will fly to where, first?'

'London,' Sergei Sakharinov said in a whisper. 'That's what I agreed with the American, Perkins.'

'And then Washington?'

'Immediately afterwards. I would go there first but every hour is precious – as we decided.'

'Of course – your life is worth nothing as long as Alfredo is free. But don't worry. Your brother will be arrested in the same hour you leave Russia. Your sacrifice for Russia will be greatly honoured, Sergei. You have put country before family. There is, however, one thing we've not discussed – I mean, Molniya. I don't have the metacodes; you have not offered them. Very strange. My people tell me the weapon has been programmed to recognize commands emanating only from you or your brother. That's an awkwardness we need to solve, is it not?'

Sakharinov started to speak then changed his mind.

'If you give the metacodes to the CIA, perhaps you will undermine the weapon. How can I allow that?' Zamok came over to where Sergei sat and placed one bear-like arm around him. 'How is it that you did not tell me these small details, Seryozha?' he said reproachfully.

'Because that's what they are – details. Not problems – just technical questions. I'll make sure your people get what you need before—'

'Well, that's not enough, if my information is correct. You will have to go there yourself.'

'What, to Semiransk? Impossible, I can't do that!' Sergei Sakharinov laughed, shrilly. 'You're asking me to commit suicide. My brother will never allow me near the place, now. No, it's out of the question.'

'Nevertheless, you *will* have to go. Inconvenient, isn't it? But I see no other option. You can take a long-range Ilyushin and you can refuel at

203

Semiransk airbase.' He glowered down at Sakharinov. 'Don't be afraid; I'll send my Cossacks with you.'

'Your Cossacks?' Sakharinov's lips shrivelled in scorn. 'Do you suppose they can conquer Molniya for you?'

'Don't worry, Sergei. Semiransk is mine – I mean the base. And not only the base. I'll tell you a small secret. The Molniya commander, Admiral Essen, is a party member. A *long-time* member. Surprised?'

Sakharinov obviously was; he couldn't hide a rueful smile. So much for Medved's much-vaunted security arrangements.

'The Molniya weapon is *already* under my control, and you would never be allowed to use it without my agreement.' Zamok grinned triumphantly. 'You see, your dear brother is not omnipotent. So when you arrive there you'll be amongst friends. Admiral Essen is another Nakhimov, a good Russian man. So from him you'll get everything you need. You just have to follow his advice. You will hand over the base to his personal control.'

Sakharinov was defeated. 'If you insist, then so be it. But if you're wrong, I'm a dead man. Maybe you know and maybe you don't, but there's a parallel Molniya command centre right here in Moscow, in the Defence Ministry. Essen has been stalling the commissioning of it, but my brother is determined. He may succeed, and if he does that will be the end for you, Dmitry.'

Zamok smiled and said nothing.

'OK, I see you think you have all the answers, but a hell of a lot can still go wrong in practice. If I go to Semiransk, then I'll be separated from the American; I'll still be in Russian airspace when he escapes from Lefortovo and all hell will break loose once that happens—'

'Certainly; and General Medved will be very busy, if we still haven't caught up with him. Good. But all irrelevant to my plan, which I expect you to fulfil. And don't worry about the American. He'll go with you.'

There was nothing more Sergei Sakharinov could say, no feasible way to object. He was in Zamok's hands now that the endgame approached and the players had begun to reveal themselves.

As Sergei rose to leave it was in the knowledge that Alfredo was sacrificed; the Rubicon was crossed; the decision irreversible. He felt light-headed, empty. But when he shook Zamok's hand in farewell he acknowledged him, without shame or resistance, as his leader.

CHAPTER 15

'I don't agree to do this,' Glazunov whispered stubbornly. 'I took an oath and I—'

'You're a hypocritical son of a bitch.' Renard leant over the man. 'But I understand your problem, and here's how I'll help make a hero of you.'

A small display case stood behind Glazunov's desk. Its shelves held various dusty trophies and unremembered military *objets trouvés*. Renard smashed the glass door and took out a large, old-fashioned commando knife, the kind with a rubber handle and a bowie blade.

'Where'd you get this?' Renard asked him.

'Vietnam.'

Renard took the knife and tested the edge. Blunt and rusty. He threw his pistol on a chair and in the same movement took Glazunov by the collar, kicked his legs from under him and shoved him down on to his own desk, so that his face was resting on a very inky blotter, his hand trapped in Renard's own. The bowie knife went through the flesh of this hand with the crunch a butcher's knife makes going through a pork chop, plunged into the wood beneath and stayed there.

Renard let go and turned back for his gun. Glazunov raised himself half upright and stood looking at the skewered hand, at the blood that was beginning to trickle through his fingers and into the blotter. His head slowly turned to Renard. He spoke stupidly, 'I think I'm going to be sick.'

'Sit down then. Don't worry, you'll live. Like I said, you'll be a hero even.' Renard put the plan of the prison on the desk in front of him. 'So now you can help me. The sooner I understand the way out, the sooner you won't have a knife in your hand, brother. OK?'

The Commandant nodded, and Renard took a cheap plastic ball-point from the desk-set mounted on a plinth of red jasper. The irrelevant thought occurred to Renard that such a large piece of good quality jasper ware would be worth a month's salary back home. In the old Soviet Russia no one had known the value of anything. He thrust the pen in the Commandant's good hand.

'Show me the way out,' he ordered.

The man's gaze kept lurching off the plan on to the pinned hand and his voice came and went, but finally Renard was satisfied he knew the route. By then the ink-stained blotter had gone the same red-brown colour as the jasper desk-set.

Renard pulled out the knife, whereupon Glazunov groaned and collapsed in his chair. As he did so, there came a loud knocking at his office door, which was thrown open unceremoniously. It was an adjutant who walked in – a young carbine-bearing soldier aged about twenty, pompous-looking and carrying a large file of papers with a self-absorbed air. He absently saluted Renard and marched over to the Commandant's desk. Renard made as if to salute him back and struck the adjutant behind the ear with the butt of his gun. He collapsed in a soundless heap on the carpet.

'Stand up and walk into the middle of the room,' Renard told the Commandant. 'Good. Now, listen while I give you your instructions.'

Fifteen minutes later, Commandant Yuri Petrovich Glazunov left his office, followed at the regulation distance by a very smart guards corporal who very correctly wore his carbine slung across his chest. They took the lift, exiting in the basement where Glazunov gave orders to a startled individual at the first guardpoint. The Commandant's left hand remained in his trouser pocket the whole time – even when saluted by subordinates. Like this they marched to the second checkpoint. Renard looked over the guard while Glazunov spoke to him. He coughed and Glazunov immediately ordered the guard to accompany them as they marched down a long corridor.

At last they stopped before a door which the guard opened. The Commandant was the first to step through. The guard followed and as he did so, Renard arm-locked him and dragged him into the cell. They both fell heavily, and it was Glazunov who struck the guard a fierce blow on the forehead.

'Hello!' Zidra greeted Renard. 'I'd given you up.'

'Sorry. I was deadly delayed.'

'I understand, darling. It's a grave situation.'

Renard turned to look at her. She was standing by the small bed, looking very pale, with her left arm in a small sling. He wanted to cry. 'I see they gave you a prison haircut, too,' he said.

'Yes. It was this bastard's idea.' She nodded towards the Commandant, who was kneeling by the guard. 'I'm glad he's earning his money now.'

'It's regulations,' he mumbled. Renard told him to shut up.

'Well, having short hair helps the disguise,' he told Zidra. 'How bad is the arm? Do you think you can get the guard's uniform on? I selected him myself. I think he's fresh.'

'Ugh! I *hope* so.'

There was urgency in Renard's eyes now. 'We need to be in a hell of a hurry, Zidra. I don't know how long we've got, but not long.'

Zidra took off the sling and stretched out her arm. 'OK, I'll manage.' She began scrambling out of her prison clothes, pulling on the unconscious guard's jacket and breeches in less than three minutes.

'The jackboots are five sizes too big.'

Renard tore a sheet into strips. 'Wind them round your feet. Puttees, they're called. First World War soldiers used to wear them.'

She finished and Renard said: 'OK, let me look at you.' He adjusted the angle of her cap so that the peak almost concealed her eyes. 'That's how they do it. You look down your nose at the world.'

Her eyes were cool and untroubled. She was ready – armed and every inch an unsmiling young guardsman.

'OK?' He looked at his watch; 16:47, thirty-two minutes since he'd left the morgue.

Anything could have happened, including a silent alarm. However, Renard reminded himself that silent alarms weren't the Russian style. Checkpoints were, but he had plans for those. That's why he'd taken Glazunov along. It was what might happen afterwards which worried him.

Renard stopped at the threshold of the cell and said to the Commandant: 'I'll kill you if this is a trap. You know that. But not otherwise. You'll be free as soon as we are.'

Glazunov glowered fearfully at him.

'OK, let's go! Keep your hand out of sight.'

There were four checkpoints along the corridors and landings which led to the main block. Three were not manned. Glazunov had emptied the place of guards, as Sakharinov had instructed. The fourth checkpoint was manned by troops from the Tamanskii division who wore the same uniform as Zidra and Renard. Glazunov waited till they saluted and used the same password as he had on the way down to the basement. '*Byelarus.*' The guards waved the trio through; Zidra going in front of Glazunov, Renard on his right, the machine pistol aimed to shoot if the need arose. In two minutes they were out of the cell block, in another minute and a half they were at the main entrance. The old gateman looked surprised, but opened the turnstile – Zidra was the first to go through. Then she turned to face the Commandant behind. The Commandant nodded to the gatekeeper, the brake clicked on the turnstile and Glazunov pressed through. Renard watched him through the bars, two metres high, and waited for the gatekeeper to press the brake again.

Nothing happened for several seconds. Renard slowly looked round at the old man, who was crooking his finger at Renard, motioning him over to the little gatehouse window.

'What do you want?' Renard was brusque.

'You're new, aren't you?'

'So what of it? Open the gate.'

'You look like that American. I've seen his photo on TV. Did you know that? That you look like the American?'

'Open the door, you old fool.'

The brake clicked and Renard pushed through. 'No, I didn't know that,' he said.

He was out.

The Commandant's *Chaika* limousine was waiting, engine running. Renard climbed in the front with the driver; Zidra sat on the dickey seat facing the Commandant in the saloon. She told him to show her the wound he was clutching. The hand was swollen to double size, his sleeve soaked in blood, but the bleeding had almost stopped. 'You'll be all right,' she told him. 'Don't worry.'

In the front, the driver nodded at the gatekeeper by the main entrance to Lefortovo prison. The huge ornamented gates swung free and the *Chaika* turned into the road. The heavy car ponderously moved away and the engine, expiring on a diet of 76-octane gasoline, emitted a burst of backfires.

'Go by the embankment,' Renard told the driver, who showed little inclination to argue. 'New traffic rules around the Kremlin,' he explained. 'It'll be quicker this way.'

'They change the rules every five minutes,' the driver grumbled. 'Even in Stalin's time it was never like this. What they've done in central Moscow, God alone knows.'

The car swung down by the slip road that led from the bridge over the Yauza down to the embankment's one-way traffic flow and towards the city centre. As they crawled down the slip road a siren began to wail.

'Prison alarm,' the driver grunted. 'Means an escape.'

'Stop under the bridge; I need to check with the Commandant.'

'OK.'

The limousine pulled up on the rough ground under the first arch of the bridge. There was little traffic, but less than twenty metres away two or three boys were huddled around a brazier. They were running their small business of washing cars, using water drawn through ice-holes cut in the Yauza.

Renard said: 'Give me the keys, I need to put a parcel in the boot.'

The driver, more irritated than made suspicious by all the unusual requests, complained, 'What parcel? I should've done it already—'

Renard's straight left caught the chauffeur on the chin and he crumpled over the wheel. The horn let out a long blast as Renard pulled him over and down. The boys at the car wash looked round in surprise.

Renard snatched the keys from the ignition, swung out of the front and entered the saloon.

'What's going on?' he shouted at Glazunov.

'I don't know.' The Russian hostage looked bewildered. 'Maybe one of the guards gave the alarm; it wasn't planned.'

Through the archway the boys at the car-wash were numb with cold, but they were taking notice, the way street urchins do. A helicopter suddenly clattered overhead, wheeled and came back to hover nearby.

'I've got a wife—' the Commandant was gasping.

'You want me to finish you off, then?' Renard asked. He grabbed him by the belt and thrust him, groaning, into the *Chaika*'s vast boot. Renard dragged the driver to the back of the car and dumped him in the boot as well. But one of the urchins, who had detached himself from the brazier and begun wandering across, broke into a run as he heard the Commandant's scream of pain. Renard was back in the car in a second, fighting the key into the ancient ignition lock; the engine ground slowly round but the boy was at the side window by the time it fired.

'*You got cigarettes? West? Marlboro?*' the kid shouted above the noise of helicopter rotors, peering in at Renard. Then he ran to the front of the car, checking the licence plates; it was a state car, sure enough, and not the property of some local gang. Renard watched him in the mirror as they pulled away, flagging down a blue-and-white militia car.

Zidra slid open the partition window and quietly told Renard to drive back up the slip road and over the bridge. They crossed into Bolshoi Pochtovaya Street, heading into Baumanskii district – one of Moscow's oldest industrial areas. The helicopter ascended a few hundred metres for a better view, but suddenly a militia car came careering towards them, strobe lights flashing. Renard swung into the narrow alley between some tall, tree-lined residential blocks to watch the militia car scream past.

'Not in the plan,' he said.

'No; but we don't have much further to go; a couple of blocks and we should be met.'

'Well, we need to change transport first.'

The big car slipped and slid on the ice, then ground slowly down the alley towards a pair of high steel gates which blocked access. Renard stopped the car by the gates and got out. As he did so, a militia car crawled past the entry, also heading down Bolshoi Pochtovaya Street. It skidded to a halt, reversed a few metres into the entry, and stopped. 'Jesus, they're looking the wrong way,' Renard realized, running for the gates. There were no markings, no sign of what lay beyond. On the wall by the left-hand gate a small metal box housed an entry phone, which he pressed. No response.

The militia vehicle had turned on its blue and red warning strobes; suddenly two more militia cars shot past the alley at speed, heading back towards Lefortovo, sirens and lights working. At this the original militia car slewed out into Bolshoi Pochtovaya Street and sped after them.

'Yes?' a voice pronounced in Renard's ear.

'Special delivery.'

'Who? What?'

An over-zealous *Revisionii Commissiya* worker making an inventory had evidently noted the existence of the cast-aluminium entry phone bolted to the gatepost. A small sign had been typed and duly pasted to the phone. It read, 'Moscow RBL Typographical Kombinat No. 3/3645. 1985.'

'I have some papers – a manuscript,' Renard shouted. 'From the Central Bank.'

The helicopter had moved away for a minute, perhaps losing them under the tall trees lining the alley, but now it swept overhead again.

'*Manuscript?*'

'Special print order. For your General Director.'

'Wait a minute.'

The steel doors suddenly began to slide open; Renard was already back in the car gunning the engine. He pulled the *Chaika* inside the compound; in front were several blue and grey three-tonne *Gaz* lorries, a loading bay, men working. He stopped behind a small gatehouse.

'*Not there!*' the gatekeeper was shouting through his window.

Renard ran to the gatehouse, pounding on the door, and a thickset man in his early fifties, much the worse for drink, opened up and delivered a volley of abuse. Renard punched him in the solar plexus, hoping he wasn't too drunk to notice. When the watchman obligingly sank to the floor, Renard helped himself to his thick blue cotton jacket, ripped off his belt and also took an old overcoat hanging by the door. Dousing the gatehouse lights, he left.

Outside, a forklift truck was raising a roll of newsprint from the back of a *Gaz*. Some men were loading another truck with bales of printed paper. The *Gaz* was the kind which has an aluminium shell on the back, so as to make a van out of the standard truck. Next to it stood another; its engine came to life and the truck began to reverse slowly from the loading bay. As the *Gaz* came lumbering across the compound, its headlights flashing, Zidra leaned from the window. 'I borrowed this!'

'Then let's go. Can you drive, with that arm?'

'I'll manage. Get in.'

'Where to?' Renard asked. 'We'll have to dump this in five minutes.'

'I know. But the loading crew are all drunk. It's near the end of their working day. They won't notice they're one truck down straightaway.' She looked at him, and laughed. 'Come on, it's a start. Freedom!'

The truck lumbered down the alley, but before they reached the entry into Bolshoi Pochtovaya, Zidra swung the wheel hard to the right; they lurched into a rutted drive which ran between two residential blocks. The truck crawled down the drive a few metres before emerging into a small square which was bounded on all sides by apartment blocks. It was already dusk. The place was silent, empty except for one or two passers-by hurrying home, made oblivious by the cold. Zidra steered to the far corner of the square, and out down another narrow entrance. They emerged into a road which ran parallel to Bolshoi Pochtovaya Street. The road was narrow, quiet.

Zidra said: 'This is Friedrich Engels Street. We can get down to Baumanskii market from here, and from there we can head out.'

As she spoke, a militia car roared past and slewed to a halt in front of them.

'Shit!'

'Look under the sun visor; drivers always leave the papers there.'

'I don't have a passport.'

'You're from the Typographical Kombinat; making an urgent delivery to the Baumanskii District Administration.'

Zidra took the papers and clambered from the cab. Even in the half-light the military boots she had on were clearly visible. Renard snapped the safety catch off the machine pistol and left the truck, working his way round to the side of the police car opposite where Zidra was talking to the two officers. Both militia men had left their car; one was carrying a submachine gun as if he meant it. Renard's first shot hit him in the neck. He slumped forward, crashing into his partner, dragging him down and out of Renard's line of fire. Suddenly there was a second shot, the characteristic plop of a silenced weapon. Renard raced around the car; Zidra was already tucking the gun back in her belt.

'Get them in the back of the truck,' she ordered.

Renard looked around; the street was completely deserted, but there

211

were any number of potential witnesses in the apartment blocks all around. Nevertheless he opened the rear doors of the truck and levered the bodies of the militia men inside. Zidra opened the coat of one and peeled out the walkie talkie he carried. Then they slammed the doors and raced back to the militia Moskvich.

'Now what?' Renard asked as he took over the driving seat and gunned the engine.

'Head down towards Baumanskii market as planned.'

A woman's voice was squawking on the radio, giving a stream of instructions to every militia car and GAI post in central Moscow. Roadblocks were being set up on every major route within a five-kilometre radius of Lefortovo. Baumanskii district was the focus: there were confirmed reports that the prison Commandant's hijacked car had been seen heading towards the district centre. Troops were in the process of cordoning off the area; no one was being allowed through the checkpoints which were being set up at every road, metro entrance and tramway route, except on production of the identity documents which Russians must carry by law.

'The trouble is, the militia is not sleeping as usual,' Zidra said. 'And they must have drafted in tens of thousands of troops after the President was killed.'

The Moskvich slithered down the ice and snow of Friedrich Engels Street towards the big circular building which housed Baumanskii market.

'Stop there,' Zidra said, pointing to a row of public telephones. She peered through the window, but whoever she was looking for wasn't there. 'We'll have to carry on,' she told him.

They set off again, listening to the stream of orders and announcements which came through the stolen walkie-talkie. Troops and police had been despatched on to suburban commuter trains, it told them. No long-distance trains were to leave Moscow without scrutiny of passenger lists and a physical check of every carriage.

All Moscow airports were closed until further notice.

Then a different voice: male, announcing itself as 'Colonel-General Streltsin', informing the Moscow Municipal Militia that until further notice they were placed under the direct control of the Moscow garrison command. Operations were being co-ordinated by the Ministry of Defence. All units were hereby ordered to respond to any orders given by ranking army officers attached to garrison units. All officers were ordered to shoot to kill if the state criminals, Latsis and Renard, made any attempt to resist arrest. The Minister of Defence, General Medved, would be making a public statement on the matter shortly.

This flow of general information was scattered through a stream of detailed orders issued to individual officers and patrol cars by the Baumanskii militia command.

There'd been no mention of events at the Moscow Red Banner of Labour Typographical Kombinat No. 3. But there was a request, repeated several times: 'Ivanov, Drozhkin, where are you? Unit 36?'

Zidra pointed at the number painted in red on the reinforcement bar welded across their dashboard. 'Number 36.'

Renard pressed the transmit button. 'Yeah, Drozhkin.'

'Drozhkin, where are you?'

'On the embankment. Stuck in traffic.'

'The embankment? Why there? You should be in Bolshoi Pochtovaya.'

Renard didn't answer.

'Let's go, Douglas. We'll find our own way to Pervomaiskii.'

'What's in Pervomaiskii?'

'A way out. And a restaurant I know. Georgian cuisine.'

'You planning a last supper?'

Zidra laughed. 'These are friends. They've already helped us.'

A militia car raced past them in the opposite direction, siren and lights going. Behind it two army trucks carrying troops churned through the snow.

Renard fumbled around the switchboard and found what he was looking for. He switched on the red and blue strobe lights.

Zidra pointed: 'Go right here.'

Renard cut between two lumbering trams and heard a tram warning bell clatter as the driver frantically braked to avoid him; he thrust the car into the busy highway, narrowly missing an oncoming Mercedes, then accelerating away.

'Who's organized our escape?'

'Pyotr – and Claud Perkins, of course.'

'I hope the good father is all right.'

'We'll soon find out.'

A GAI man waved his white baton at them. At the same moment the announcer warned that Unit 36 might have been stolen.

'Let's worry about us first,' Zidra said. 'Turn left here, on to Pervomaiskii.'

The central lane on Pervomaiskii Chaussee had been cleared, as the militia announcer had said. They passed one roadblock with no difficulty, sirens and lights going. The GAI men who waved them through were evidently behind events.

Renard took the car a kilometre northwards and then Zidra directed him down a maze of entries and alleys. At last they turned into a gated entrance; a sign over a wooden door announced 'Restaurant Esherri'.

Renard looked unimpressed. '*This* is it?'

Zidra said: 'One, we have no choice. Two, yes these are Georgians but they won't betray us.'

She disappeared into the restaurant, asking him to wait. And when she appeared a few minutes later, she was with a tall, strongly built Georgian with exceptionally long forearms and massive hands. Renard guessed he was in his early forties. He was bald and had a typically Georgian nose – big, fleshy, hooked.

'Douglas, this is a friend. Tomas Kavtoradze.'

The man grinned and shook Renard's hand. 'Any friend of Zidra Latsis is welcome here,' he said. 'Come in.'

Kavtoradze led them into the kitchen. The restaurant beyond was hectic and industrious Georgian waiters wearing high boots, bandoliers and blue sashes shouted orders to and fro. As well as the kitchen staff two or three strong silent types with hard eyes were standing around. They wore identical blue blazers emblazoned with the logo of the 1993 Whitbread Round the World yacht race and they were all armed.

Kavtoradze led them through a dark passageway and upstairs into a small, over-furnished sitting room. Another Georgian was stretched on the sofa, watching a football match on a huge colour television which stood in the corner, dominating the room.

When he saw Zidra, the man jumped to his feet with a startled look. He bowed to her, and his face went pale, but he didn't speak.

Kavtoradze said, 'Sergo, fetch wine. And some *chacha*.' The Georgian stood up and left without a word.

Kavtoradze was grinning at Zidra. 'He's a good boy – he organized that break-in for you the other week.'

'The Remex break-in?' Renard asked.

'The same. Caused us quite a headache – some guy followed our cracksman around for a day afterwards. We sent him back home to Sukhumi and guess what – they started looking for him there, as well. Then I began to understand how hot you are these days, Zidra.'

'What happened?'

'Nothing. We sent him to Capri for a holiday. Don't worry. Just tell me what's going on. We were waiting for you at Baumanskii, but all hell broke loose.'

'Someone gave the alarm too soon. Unfortunately we killed two militia men.'

Their host gestured to the sofa, inviting them to sit and placing himself on a high-backed chair facing them. 'That's not so good. But sit down, relax. Take it easy. You'll be OK here.' He looked them both over, a quizzical expression on his face. Renard, sweating and short of breath, looked in worse shape than Zidra, who sat very pale and still. 'Take it easy,' he ordered them. 'It's not the first time. They won't find you unless you led them here.'

'Don't think so,' Renard said.

'Well, we need to be in even more of a hurry now,' Zidra pressed. 'Where's Father Pyotr?'

'At the flat in Mayakovskii. He won't be able to come here before you leave. He's organizing something big, with your American friend. But the good news is that the plane is ready, Zidra, as you asked. I knew you'd turn up, so I prepared.'

'Thank you, Tomas.'

He grinned at her. 'I heard a rumour that you really were at the Kremlin. So who in fact killed our beloved President?'

'Alfredo Sakharinov. His men.'

'I guessed as much. It's his style. For once, I approve!' Tomas spat accurately into a glass ashtray overflowing with spent *papirosi*.

'Tomas, I'm sorry about the militia car. It's hot, you need to get rid of it.'

'Don't worry. Sergo will see to it.' The Georgian gestured dismissively, then looked at Renard. 'This restaurant is named after another one which is set amongst the most beautiful ravines and mountains of the Abkhazian part of Georgia,' Kavtoradze told Renard. 'In *that* Esherri, the sky was our roof and the stars were our candles; our dinner tables were carved from living trees. No European will ever go there. Not even a *nelegali* – a spy like you.'

There was a sudden knock at the door at this point, and a young Georgian girl carrying a tray appeared. She set it down and poured drinks. Tomas said a few words in Georgian to her, and she left.

'I guess you're both hungry so we'll eat a little.' He waved one huge forearm at the room. 'This is more private than the restaurant.' He then became more businesslike in tone. 'Zidra, just tell me what you need.'

'The plane must have a range of at least two thousand kilometres, I'd guess.'

'No problem.'

'Tomas is a pilot,' Zidra explained to Renard. 'He owns an air transport company, based in Georgia. But you keep planes in Moscow – don't you Tomas?'

215

'We have a small Yak cargo plane at an airfield south of Moscow. And we own an AN-24—'

Renard groaned.

'Don't insult him about his beloved *Anushka*,' laughed Zidra. 'Since we don't have any alternatives. Tomas, this isn't just for us,' she said to Kavtoradze. 'This is geopolitics. Big stuff. What's more—' she indicated Renard '—he has saved my life. He's one of *us*.'

'Ah! In that case, *Amerikanets*, you will be a brother!' Kavtoradze offered his hand; it swallowed Renard's.

'And listen: he's got clout with the US Government. We're playing for high stakes, Tomas. If we win it could affect everything and everybody; your homeland included.'

This was met with a grin. 'I believe you, Zidra! Let's get down to specifics. What else do you need?'

'Who will fly the plane?'

'Me,' said Tomas. 'And we'll take Sergo.'

'When can we leave?'

'That's a bit tricky. There've been problems with Russian air-traffic control recently; we've been grounded every day for a week – normally we fly at least twice weekly to Tbilisi. There's talk of a ban on civil aviation in the Moscow region until further notice. Magnetic storms, or something. Been clobbering the radar.'

Zidra looked at Renard. 'We can't wait,' Renard said. 'Where is your plane? I mean the AN-24?'

'We lease space from a military airport south of Moscow; about forty kilometres from Domodedovo civil airport. But where do we fly to? I need to know now.'

'Kalegut in northern Siberia. That's the provincial capital of Semiranski-Nanai to be precise.'

Tomas looked surprised. 'I was told by Father Pyotr you'd be leaving the country – heading south.'

Renard ignored this and said, 'How good is your navigation? Can you fly blind, with no radio location?'

'If necessary. Where we fly in the Caucasus, survival often means flying blind – there are plenty of people with itchy fingers on the triggers of heat-seeking missiles, just waiting to down planes which have hyperactive electronics advertising their presence.'

While Tomas was speaking, Sergo had appeared. He spoke to him in rapid Georgian, motioning at Renard and Zidra. Tomas listened in silence and then gave a stream of orders. Sergo asked a few questions and quickly left.

'We'll get rid of that car tonight. It really *is* hot.' The Georgian smiled at Renard. 'Your pin-ups will be in every militia station in the land by tomorrow. But don't worry. You won't be the first to kill a few cops and get away with it.' He spat in the ashtray again.

Despite their predicament, it was Renard's turn to smile when he saw the Georgian girl return laden with aromatic *lavash* bread and *khachipuri* dough fried with *suluguni* cheese. After that she brought *chiburiki* pies stuffed with ground mutton, and fresh cucumber and tomato salad, followed by bowls of flash-fried liver and of *tsatsivi* – chicken cooked in its own weight of garlic, and served with nut sauce. They ate everything, and there was even a sense of festivity.

'Remember Mashka?' Zidra asked Tomas.

'The bear. Of course! I like to think that the old girl is still guarding the place, as ever.'

Renard recalled the sign he'd noticed over the restaurant's door, depicting a black dancing bear, and asked for the story.

'She lived in the restaurant,' Zidra said. 'She used to sit by the front door and welcome the guests, almost all of whom were GRU people vacationing from Moscow or from their stations abroad. Mostly they were spies – *nelegali* – working undercover in senior posts in NATO governments. They always got drunk and they made an alcoholic of poor Mashka. She drank two or three litres of vodka every night and then she danced with the guests.'

'You had to avoid her in the mornings,' Tomas said. 'Talk about a bear with a sore head. She used to chase the women around the kitchens.' He laughed and then took Zidra's hands to kiss them.

While the girl was clearing the dishes, Zidra eyed her up. They were similar sizes and Zidra asked her to help with a change of clothes. They left the room together and Tomas poured more *chacha*. He explained about his own Abkhazian part of Georgia, and about how civil war had germinated among generations of Georgians and Abkhazians who had previously lived in peace, his great arms windmilling the story, his thick lips beneath the hawk-like nose arcing contemptuously downwards when he got to the apostate architects of the new Russia.

The girl came back and poured red wine. 'This is *Fanchkara*,' Kavto-radze told him. 'Stalin's favourite. It comes from Abkhazia.' The wine was thick and aromatic like a good Madeira.

Renard never found out what he didn't know, because at that moment Zidra appeared in the room. She had showered and changed and now she was wearing a wildly impractical cocktail dress which had been given to her by the little Georgian girl. It seemed to consist of no more than a

217

square of black silk buttoned at the front, with a red sash over the right shoulder to hold it up. Its two gilt buttons had been located with precision by a designer who knew too much and thought too much about the anatomy of women.

Renard saw immediately that Zidra was enjoying re-entry into the normal world where a woman can revel in the effect she has on men. She turned slowly through 360 degress and they watched her in silence. Then she burst out laughing. 'I don't know whether to sit or to stand in the damn thing. I feel like an exhibit.'

'Probably the safest thing is if you sit and we stand,' Renard said. Both men continued sitting.

Zidra laughed some more, and it was pure release. 'Whatever I do the result is more pornography that couture. But that's all the poor creature seems to own. That's your doing, Tomas.' She perched on the edge of the sofa. 'She's a charming girl; she found a plaster to go on my arm.' She showed them an arm as white as bone china before it is glazed. Then she folded the arm in her lap amid a short but deep silence. Zidra smiled. 'You were talking about the old times, Tomas, I bet?'

Tomas was reassuring. 'Don't worry. Everything will work. Pyotr is supposed to come here this evening with another person, I don't know who. But I need to leave you for a while to make certain arrangements. You can rest here; I'll send Tamara with some bedding; this sofa turns down into a divan. It's the best hospitality I can show you.'

'Tomas, please be careful. We must succeed. What you do now will be for all of us, for Russia – and for Georgia.'

He kissed her hands. 'Mostly, it's for you,' he said.

As soon as Tomas had gone, Renard voiced a doubt. 'I believe in Tomas Kavtoradze implicitly. But I'm not sure about Sergo. It might be better not to hang around here.'

'Don't worry about Sergo; I'll vouch for him. They're brothers by the way. In any case, what's the alternative? Even setting foot in the street is dangerous. Let's rest while we can, my beloved Renard. I'm exhausted.'

He looked sidelong at her and sighed. They were alone at last. 'How much exhausted?'

'Completely.' She smiled radiantly and didn't look tired at all. 'Do you like my prison hairdo?' she asked provocatively. 'I think it's quite gamine actually.'

Renard told her it was and pressed the palm of his hand to hers, which was dry and hot. He wanted to find the right words, but he imagined the wiseheads back at the ranch saying, *The poor lad has gone to bush. Like*

*in the nursery tale, they fixed him up with a beautiful blonde KGB colonel
and now he drools about love.*

Instead it was Zidra who whispered, 'I feel as though my life is hanging
by a thread – if I should lose this connection with you, then I would lose
the life which I've only just found.'

She was perched very stiff and upright on the sofa but he felt her
tremble. He pulled her down off the sofa, seized her mouth in his and
bit until they tasted blood. The little black frock came off and she arced
into him as his fingertip traced fire the length of her silken spine. Now
the whole warm, white, magical, shimmering parcel of flesh was in his
hands, which knew what to do and did it without being told.

CHAPTER 16

At three o'clock that morning the lights in Alfredo Sakharinov's Kremlin offices were still burning. They were burning in the Defence Ministry, and in the Ministries of Security and of the Interior.

The lights were also on in the Duma where a seething mass of party workers, couriers, officers in uniform and political leaders pushed and shoved through the Cossack guards outside Dmitry Zamok's ninth-floor offices. Some wit had pinned a sheet of paper by the door. On it was pencilled the word 'Smolny' – the name of the St Petersburg ladies' academy from where Vladimir Lenin had organized the Bolshevik Revolution in October 1917.

Order of a kind still reigned in the Kremlin. For one whole hour Alfredo Sakharinov had received Vadim Medved; had made him stand to attention on the brim of a gigantic blue Azeri rug, which Sakharinov crossed and crisscrossed while fulminating . . .

The failure of security at Lefortovo was a disaster: a political, public relations, diplomatic and personal catastrophe which must be reversed *now*, *today, without fail* because otherwise they were all dead, starting with Medved.

Only Medved's promptness in reporting Sergei Sakharinov's betrayal to Alfredo had saved him; temporarily, because it implicated Alfredo in the security lapses, the over-confidence and the botched planning which had allowed the Americans and their Baltic quislings to spirit Renard and Latsis away.

No one, *no one* ever escaped from Lefortovo so it was also a humiliation in the eyes of history and the new President would personally mangle Medved in his own goddamn machinery when this was over unless the situation was retrieved. And for starters that meant finding where the hell was that deranged, cocaine-eating brother of his? True, Glazunov had been taken and shot earlier that night, but that left plenty more bullets waiting for a target.

Secondly, Alfredo had spoken to Essen who assured him that the Moscow command module for Molniya would be at least sixty per cent operational by that very evening. This appeared to mean that Sakharinov could sit in a cubicle in the cellars of the Kremlin holding a kind of dead-man's-handle, like they use on the Metro, while Essen switched the damn thing on and off and, it was to be hoped, switched the United States on and off at the same time.

So that was something, *if* you could believe Essen. Or was everything still to play for?

Medved explained that the Duma was surrounded, and that was more difficult than surrounding the White House in 1993 had been. The main phone lines were down, the power would be off later that morning. And Zamok was effectively under house-arrest, Medved added. Why, he could be brought to the Kremlin in irons if necessary. Medved took off his steel-rimmed glasses and polished them with the end of his tie. *However*, as for Sergei, there was a problem.

The gist of it was that their own plant in Zamok's entourage was reporting that the duplicitous Sergei had left for Semiransk, presumably to try to seize control of Molniya on the spot. Since no one had ever informed Sergei of the electronic gamesmanship which had severed his interface with the AlphaScan control mechanism, the danger was not immediate, but—

Alfredo exploded at this news. *But that's just like saying that the danger from a bullet already in the air isn't immediate because it's yet to penetrate one's skull. The danger is immediate and so must be the response. Essen is a traitor, almost certainly; only our own Varta guards are reliable, and then only if they are personally under our command.*

Medved responded that this was exactly what was intended; a Sukhoi was waiting to fly him east as soon as this interview was concluded. And the Varta guards were already on the spot, having reinforced and infiltrated the Semiransk garrison to the point where any opposition had been swamped. And yes, Essen was a known quantity.

Alfredo wanted Medved there *yesterday* to take control. Only strong deeds impressed Russians, and weakness lost their support immediately. The news of the escapes from Lefortovo couldn't be suppressed, and might be making the BBC news at any moment.

Medved said he just wished Renard and the Latsis female *would* approach a journalist, because then they would be arrested at once. But no one knew where they were. Only – he hesitated to say it, but there was the possibility that the American was also heading for Semiransk. Heading for Molniya.

Then get yourself on that plane! Report to me constantly!

But the imperative was unnecessary, and Alfredo Sakharinov found himself addressing a clean pair of heels.

The last guests left the restaurant of the dancing bear at about the same time Medved left the Kremlin and hurried by helicopter to an airbase south of Moscow. The kitchen had closed long before; when Renard went to fetch tea at one a.m. the place was in darkness. When he returned he put a chair under the door handle and sat with Zidra, and without planning to they had begun again and somehow made love on the tiny couch. Afterwards they fell asleep in a naked embrace. No one came to disturb them and when they both woke together it was because a car engine had started somewhere. Renard quietly dressed and went to look in the courtyard. It was empty – the stolen militia Moskvich had disappeared. He went back upstairs and waited. Still no one visited them upstairs. Father Pyotr had not arrived. Renard doused the light and sat down to wait. Zidra was sleeping deeply on the divan.

Eventually a vehicle approached and stopped outside. He looked through the darkened window; it was a Kamaz truck. Two men climbed out – he recognized neither. They disappeared into the gate leading to the courtyard. Renard checked his watch: 5:10 a.m. After a few minutes they backed the truck into the entrance way and he heard the sound of the stolen militia car being run up ramps. The Kamaz left at once; Renard watched it crawl up the street – and watched the lights come on in a car parked fifty metres lower down. As the Kamaz passed the car, it swung out behind and followed it out of sight.

By six the first snow ploughs had begun trundling down the street. A concierge swept his threshold, his aluminium shovel noisily scratching at old ice. Daylight struggled through a leaden sky, and a weary Renard drifted into sleep.

He was woken by the sound of voices downstairs; he swung upright and leapt to his feet. The door had already opened, the light came on. It was Sergo. He swept triumphantly into the room; Renard saw elation in his dark eyes.

'We need to go, *Amerikanets*,' he said. 'Wake the lady up. The plane is waiting.'

'You took the Moskvich – the militia car?'

'Of course.'

'There were watchers; I saw them follow it.' He noted Sergo's change of expression and went on. 'They weren't yours then? The car was a Volga, light-coloured I think.'

Sergo went without a word to the phone and began dialling. Renard's eyes met those of Zidra who was now well awake. 'It must be Zamok's people, keeping an eye out for us.'

'Maybe. I hope so.'

Sergo was speaking rapidly in Georgian to someone; he put the phone down and the elation in his eyes had died. 'Now we need to change our plans a little,' he said, buttoning up his quilted jacket and pulling a woollen hat proclaiming 'Sovietski Sport' down over his ears. 'You must wait here; I need to organize another truck. I'll be gone ten-fifteen minutes.' He left the room, his boots pounding down the wooden stairs.

'I don't like it,' Renard told Zidra.

'I agree, but the main thing is that they didn't call to collect us. It's just a matter of tradecraft now, that's all. We'll get away from Moscow, don't worry.'

'How did they find us? That's what interests me.'

'Not difficult. Maybe Kavtoradze's gang is penetrated – plenty of waiters saw us arrive. Forget it,' she said with iron certainty. 'I'm sure Tomas will do as he promised.'

She squeezed his hands and stood back from him to speak again when a shattering explosion blasted in from the street below, and Renard flung himself over her in blind response. There was a short burst of small-arms fire from somewhere and then an eternity of silence. Zidra coughed quietly and he felt her move underneath him. They began to hear shouts, men running, a sudden volley of shots from the street. Then, again, silence. 'You don't need to flatten me, darling,' Zidra said quietly. 'I'm available.'

'Where in hell did I find you?' Renard gave a low whistle, pulling her up. 'Come on! We need to check out.'

From below they could hear shouts, now coming from inside the building. Someone called Sergo Kavtoradze's name and feet ran up the stairs. It was Sergo himself who crashed through the door. 'OK, OK!' he shouted. 'Let's go,' and he pushed Renard to the door. 'Everything is OK, don't worry.'

They followed him out, soon tumbling into the courtyard. A blue three-tonne *Gaz* truck was parked where the stolen militia car had been, its engine running. Sergo thrust a carrier bag into Renard's hands and as the rear doors of the truck swung open he pushed his charges in. The doors slammed shut at once and the truck slammed into reverse, wheels spinning on the rutted ice until they caught and the truck shot back into the street, swung violently round and accelerated away.

The *Gaz* was refrigerated, with two rails in the centre running its length. Beef quarters and sides of lamb hung in ranks; frozen haunches were piled four and five deep at the front. Renard grabbed hold of Zidra as they lurched away, and they both ended up on a side of frozen lamb lying on the floor. A thermometer above Renard's head showed minus fifteen degrees.

Zidra, shivering with cold, was still wearing the inadequate black cocktail number, but the carrier bag which Sergo had given Renard held more practical women's clothes – supplied by the same Georgian girl. Jeans, sweater, warm boots. Zidra changed in the pale light which came through the translucent plastic roof of the truck, and the silk dress was discarded amongst the bloodstained sawdust on the floor of the truck.

Renard slid open the window into the driver's cab and asked Sergo what had happened.

'Small local difficulty. Someone saw you arrive in that stolen militia car. Some heroes from the neighbourhood militia station decided to win medals by storming the restaurant without calling for help. Very obliging of them, otherwise we'd have had two guards divisions on our necks. Unfortunately someone let off a hand grenade. Big mistake.' Sergo lit a cigarette and grinned at them. He had gold teeth and smiled like a coffin-handle. 'This truck is untraceable, for sure. We'll get free of Moscow, no problem.'

'Medved's people will be on the scent now, so we'll just have to chance it. Tell me, Sergo, where is Father Pyotr?'

'You'll be meeting him. Don't fret.' Sergo turned to look back for a second. 'Sorry about the truck,' he said apologetically: 'It's the best we could do. If we get stopped you'll have to hide behind the meat.'

Renard and Zidra moved from the lamb and found a more spacious side of frozen beef to sit on, hugging their knees for warmth. Moscow's rush hour had scarcely begun, but progress was slow. Many drivers had simply abandoned their cars in the chaos of the previous evening, and the streets were littered with vehicles half-covered by overnight snow-falls. Sergo told them how two months before a GAI patrol had found the frozen bodies of three teenage girls hanging from the meat-hooks of a butcher's van, and for weeks afterwards he'd been stopped at every other GAI post. But now things had gone quiet, he said. Instead the militia were looking for a new set of entrepreneurs who had been selling shrink-wrapped joints of meat door-to-door in central Moscow; only the meat had been found to come not from some European aid scheme, but from a hospital mortuary.

After an hour the truck stopped and Sergo threw open the rear doors.

'You can come out,' he said cheerfully. 'Come and sit in the cab for a bit; there won't be any more GAI checkpoints where we're going.'

224

They had stopped on a snow-covered track running through fields. The country was flat for miles in every direction. There were no signs of habitation. The air felt warm after the freezing cold of the van: Zidra stamped her feet and swung her arms to get warm.

Renard said: 'Where are we?'

'We have another ten kilometres still to go. This track runs through former Defence Ministry territory; it goes as far as the site of an old quarry, now disused. Very few people know the path from there; it's the back door to the airfield.'

They duly climbed into the cab. The *Gaz* bumped its way through the heavily rutted track; twice it bogged down in deep drifts. Renard warmed himself digging them out. In another hour they crawled up to the foot of a slight elevation – it was little more than a knoll. Beyond it the ground fell sharply away and in front of them lay the enormous pit which was all that remained of the quarry. To either side lay encircling arms of birch and pine forest. On the far edge they could dimly see through the morning haze the red runway lights of an airstrip. But Renard saw no way across.

The quarry had been excavated by corkscrewing with graders through the contours of the soil to get at whatever valuable mineral had once been deposited there. A vast pit remained, 2 kilometres wide at the top and half that at the bottom, circumvented by a narrow ledge which spiralled its way 200 metres down around the edge. The ledge was almost indiscernible; it had crumbled and eroded over time, and was now partially obliterated by the snow which had drifted over it.

Sergo pointed to show where a path had been cut from the lip of the quarry to meet the ledge.

Sergo clambered back in the cab and started the engine. At first there was little to indicate that they had entered the quarry. Then the path began to descend steeply and the ground rose sharply to their left. Suddenly, a sheer drop appeared on the right, where the ground fell vertically away before it levelled out again on the next lower circle of the spiral. The ledge was less than a metre wider than the truck's axle-width. The side mirror, which was bolted on struts to the door, was suddenly smashed away by a rocky outcrop, and at the same moment the front wheels slithered on ice over to the crumbling edge. The engine stalled and Sergo and Renard had to leap out to dig the front wheels clear of the drifted snow.

After thirty minutes the truck was free again and they set off. At last the *Gaz* reached the far side of the quarry, from where the path to the top of the pit slashed upwards through the snow. Sergo abruptly pulled up and jumped from the cab. They could hear him cursing. Renard and Zidra got out and joined him.

'Look,' he said, pointing to the way ahead. 'We're completely blocked.'

The path which led sharply up to the lip of the quarry rose in front of them – but there was no way to reach it. The entire surface of the ledge had crumbled away. Nothing remained but a heap of spoil, lying below on the next twist of the spiral. A gap of ten metres lay between them and their access from the pit.

Sergo said, 'We have to go back.'

Renard objected, 'We would lose half a day finding our way back to the airport. There's no time.'

'If we climbed out, how far is it from the quarry to the airfield perimeter? How far will we have to walk to get to the plane?' Zidra asked Sergo.

'It's a kilometre at least. But that's not the point. People walking around the perimeter are noticeable, a *Gaz* bringing supplies is not. There's a small militia squad at the airfield; they'd be almost sure to come and pick us up once we were seen from the control tower.'

Renard was scouting the way ahead. 'We'll leave the *Gaz*, we can't go back in it anyway; there's nowhere to turn. But there are enough handholds to climb out; let's go.' Sergo went back to the truck and returned with a coil of nylon rope; he threw one end to Renard, who had already reached a narrow foothold above their heads. 'Quickly, Zidra; it's past midday already. Wind the rope around your waist and I'll pull you up.'

As he pulled her up they heard the chopping sound of an approaching helicopter, and suddenly an Mi-8 swung over the quarry and hovered above them, whipping up small volcanoes of snow all around.

'Don't worry, it's ours!' Sergo shouted above the din, once he had seen the face of the pilot.

So they all three applied themselves to the climb after this, but it took another thirty minutes to reach the beginnings of the path, thirty minutes more before they clambered out of the quarry. The helicopter did not return.

'Some short cut!' Zidra said.

The runway lay to their left; to the right, a kilometre distant, was a hangar and other airfield buildings, and a row of aircraft. Sergo set off down the perimeter road. They walked for ten minutes, then Renard saw a vehicle leaving the hangar.

'Someone's coming,' he told Sergo, digging for the Makarov revolver

Tomas Kavtoradze had given him the previous evening. But as the car – it was a beige Mercedes – approached, Sergo announced that it was Tomas himself who had come out to meet them.

The Mercedes slewed to a stop and Tomas emerged. He didn't waste words in greetings. 'I sent the chopper to check the quarry – I guessed what would happen if you came that way, so I was keeping a lookout for you. Let's go; we're short of time and you're being followed.'

They climbed in and as he drove them to the hangar, Tomas explained, 'Father Pyotr is waiting in the plane, with some other guy from your outfit, Zidra. But like I told you, we've got a problem with restricted air-traffic movements in the Moscow region. What with all the hoo-ha, they've now gone and imposed a complete ban until tomorrow. Like with every Russian rule, there's an exception, of course, but today the exception cost me fifteen thousand in dollars. What that did was, it got me permission from the air ministry to take medical supplies to Tbilisi this morning. But we have to take off right away; my departure slot finished thirty minutes ago, and I guess you know the regulations; after so long on the tarmac, I won't be allowed to fly unless I can find fresh aircrew.'

They raced to the hardstand on which was parked an AN-24 painted in Georgian colours and marked 'Air Tiflis'. One of the two turboprop engines was ticking over, to provide power and heat for the plane. They boarded at once, and Tomas scrambled forward with Sergo. He fired the remaining engines at once, desperate to get free of Moscow's air defence command, which was the first of Medved's tripwires. If he could at least do that, there was some chance he could disappear; certainly civilian air-traffic control would be easy to lose. After a flurry of conversation with the control tower, the plane lumbered on to the runway and began to taxi. In a few minutes they were airborne, the roar of the turboprops eliminating conversation on the flight deck.

Zidra and Renard went aft as soon as they boarded. Father Pyotr was waiting for them in the saloon. With him was someone else: Sasha Vernov, the taxi driver from Domodedovo airport. Renard and he shook hands at once. 'How's your sister?' Renard said.

'Kicked me out,' Sasha said and laughed.

It was their first meeting with Father Pyotr since the murder of the Russian President more than a week earlier and it was Zidra the priest went to first; touching her cropped head and embracing her warmly, as the Anushka rumbled uncertainly over the pitted concrete. Renard took his hand but the priest embraced him too, and kissed him three times on the cheeks. 'You did a phenomenal job to spring us from Lefortovo,'

Renard began. 'You and Claud both. And I hear that's not all you've pulled off.'

'Indeed not.' The priest could barely contain his delight at meeting them again; his round face quivered with it. 'And you can scarcely imagine what an unholy alliance has been helping us – truly it is the Lord's work. But when you have such friends as Dmitry Zamok and Sergei Sakharinov, anything is possible.'

Renard put it another way, 'Ah, "My enemy's enemy . . ." and all that.'

'But when the time comes and Zamok no longer needs us to help him dump Alfredo Sakharinov, then we'd better watch out,' warned the priest.

'Let's make sure that we see that moment before they do. But right now we still need all the help we can get, however tainted. Someone came for us today at the restaurant and I think they may come after this plane too.'

'Medved's people, yes,' said Pyotr. 'But a very interesting situation has arisen: Sergei Sakharinov has disappeared. He's not at the Duma – and nobody knows exactly where he is. There's been no word yet from the Kremlin, but the Tamansky guards have been called into the centre of Moscow. By whom, is another matter.'

'So they are looking for Sergei as well. Good. And they won't expect us to be going north. They don't assume that we are completely mad, fortunately. But you are right. Medved is following you and they certainly will be glued to their radars now. But Tomas will lose them: that is what he excels at.'

'So, Father Pyotr, where the hell *is* Sergei Sakharinov?' Renard asked.

'The question of questions. Claud and I met him the day before yesterday: the most frightening day of my life, bar none. We saw him at his dacha in the Lenin Hills. And I made a discovery – there's a whole private metro system which runs from the Kremlin to Stalin's *dachnaya*. We met in a disused tunnel. Sakharinov was even more frightened than us; shaking with fear and didn't try to hide the fact. He simply pounced on poor Claud, lifted him by the lapels and shook him like a dog shakes a rabbit.' They had walked right down the saloon now, which had been decorated by some previous maniac owner in pink vinyl wallpaper with a rosebud design. 'We think he's flown to Semiransk,' Father Pyotr continued. 'I don't know why; it wasn't the plan at all. But we weren't supposed to be going either. This is the result of your fatal determination to do things your own way, Mr Renard! The plan Claud and I concocted

228

was to fly us all to England, today. What will happen now is a mystery to me.'

'That was the plan you discussed with Sergei Sakharinov when you met him?'

'Yes, it was. At first he tried to frighten us. He succeeded with me! I didn't think I would see another dawn, whether we gave him the incriminating tape of his meetings with Dmitry Zamok or not. But Mr Perkins is made of different stuff.'

Zidra took the priest's hand and squeezed it. 'Don't be coquettish,' she scolded him. 'We know who you are, and what you are by now.'

'Thank you, dear. I've been feeling guilty, actually – what with you inside Lefortovo. Claud made Sergei understand that the US knows too much by now, and that we have the Molniya metacodes *and* the tape of him and Zamok. After that, the discussion changed. He stopped blustering and started worrying about whether he'd still be around to see his next birthday. So we got down to details. Sergei will go to America and be given the chance to tell the world the truth about the President's murder. And he'll get a staggeringly large pension too.'

The Anushka had lumbered aloft and the demented howling of its twin turboprops abated. Father Pyotr led Renard and Zidra past a small office next to the saloon, which was equipped with two pink telephones and a heavy East German typewriter. Next to it was a small bar and galley. Sasha was already working the galley. As they passed Renard stuck his head in and greeted the driver, 'Still fixing breakfasts, Sasha? And here's me thinking you'd been making yourself useful.'

'You bet! I'm a new man – you brought me luck, *gospodin* Renard.'

'Hell, I was worried about you. What happened when I hightailed out of the flat?'

'I decided discretion was the best part of valour, so I left the same way you did, and I'd just about worked my way round to the front of the block when those hooligans from 38 Petrovka turned up. They were about one minute going into your place and five seconds coming out. After that I decided to go and hole up at my sister's place for a while.'

'That the same sister who nearly killed Zidra Latsis?'

Sasha looked surprised. 'Stories change in the telling, don't they? Yeah, Sonia was a bit mouthy, waving a knife and cursing. But we stopped *gospozha* Latsis from throwing her down the well.' He grinned sheepishly at Renard. 'Never mind. Thanks again, boss.'

'I'm glad you're here.'

'And glad I'm fixing breakfast?' He'd already poured *chacha* for Father Pyotr and Zidra, but now gave a glass to Renard and took one for himself. 'Excuse me for saying this, but she's as beautiful as they told me, your *gospozha* Latsis. She's amazing!'

'Yes, she is, Sasha.'

'Usually Latvian women are bigger built than Russians, bigger bones, but she—' Sasha made a circling movement with his hands. 'Well, OK, I'll fix breakfast.'

'Do that thing,' said Renard, tossing back the *chacha*.

In the saloon itself were placed six wide armchairs, covered with matching rosebud chintz. The three of them sat down facing each other, Zidra's eyes wandering over the decor. 'Jesus – is Tomas responsible for this colour scheme?'

Father Pyotr laughed. 'This plane used to belong to the general who was commander of Soviet rocket forces in the Moscow region,' he told them. 'I had the whole story from Tomas. He was a real old bureaucrat, a "servant of the people". So it has everything except a sauna. You should see the bedroom! It comes complete with double bed and en-suite bathroom with pink acrylic shower.'

'I'll do more than see it; I want to crash out,' Zidra said. 'So let's finish this discussion, dear friends.'

'You enrolled Sasha, then?' Renard asked Father Pyotr.

'Yes. And he's proving useful.'

'Aren't you showing a big slice of trust?' Renard asked.

'We didn't have much choice in the circumstances. Nor did he. Anyway, I trust in the Lord and leave the rest to luck.'

'He's naturally loyal, so I believe you did the right thing. But you were describing your meeting with Sergei Sakharinov . . .'

Father Pyotr resumed, 'I think he regards himself as a dead man already, but on the whole he'd prefer to die at the hands of the CIA rather than his own people's.'

'He's right!' Zidra said. 'And if that Alfredo doesn't get him, then I surely will.'

Father Pyotr said, 'Yet he continues to insist that he didn't kill your brother.'

Renard intervened, 'But what can he be going to the Molniya base for? That's what I don't follow.'

'It's all connected with Dmitry Zamok's plans,' Father Pyotr looked serious. 'Zamok understands that Molniya is the key to everything. He expects to come to power in the next few days, not after the next Presidential elections as he'd thought. So he wants to use Sergei one last time, to consolidate his control over Molniya. Apart from his brother Alfredo, only Sergei Sakharinov has authorization to use the weapon.

My guess is that Zamok wants him to hand it over to his own people, and that probably has to be done on the spot, in the Molniya base itself.'

'And of course, if he refused to go, it could trigger Zamok into realizing that Sergei has betrayed him as well, that we know everything and have the metacodes,' Renard said. He turned to Zidra. 'When we get to Kalegut, somehow we have to find your brother's source. I see no other way of getting close to Molniya.'

'We certainly shall meet the Molniya source: I've been speaking to them for the past two days,' Father Pyotr said. 'For now, I suggest you both rest a little. I'd be very interested to hear about your time in Lefortovo, but I'm suppressing my curiosity.'

Sasha appeared and offered them drinks and breakfast. They ate some cold *khachipuri* and drank brandy.

'How long to Kalegut?' Zidra went upfront and asked Sergo, taking him and Tomas a glass of tea each.

'Four hours at least; we'll have to make a big sweep south before we can disappear off their radar screens. So you have time to get some kip.'

She then went aft to inspect the berths, which were appropriate, as Renard said, to a flying brothel. She sat on the double bed and peered out through a porthole. They were immersed in snow-sodden cloud; nothing to see. She took her shoes off and began to get undressed. Renard came in to sit on the bed and watch her. When she peeled out of her sweater her warmth and scent flowed round him like a surrender, but her smile was formed from pure fatigue. Yet she inclined to him and embraced him, and the noise of the world fell suddenly from them. He kissed the back of her neck as she pulled her arms about him and gripped him tightly, like a child hungry for warmth.

He kissed her and told her that he belonged to her, and it was only when she fell asleep that he left her and went forward.

At 2,000 metres Tomas turned on to the southerly bearing marked on the flight plan previously agreed with Moscow air-traffic control. He continued southwards for an hour before suddenly taking the plane down to hedge-top level. Moscow controllers, who had little other traffic to distract them, noticed his disappearance at once. Tomas told them to get a new valve for their radar; he was proceeding normally at the agreed height and bearing.

'There's an air corridor between Moscow and Ekaterinburg regions which we can try to slip through; if they notice us we'll just have to play dumb and press on. I've switched off the IFF; it'll look as though this clapped-out plane has lost its electronics, which happens all the time anyway.'

231

'Let me know when you want to be relieved,' Renard said.

'Not for an hour, anyway. But stay and talk; Sergo, be hospitable – go and tell that barman to bring some brandy. Tell me, *Amerikanets*, what do you plan to do when you get to Kalegut? How do you plan to deal with Molniya?'

Renard leered at the Georgian. 'Blow it up. If I can.'

Tomas nodded silently. Then Sasha came in to pour cognac and said gravely that it was a pity Molniya wasn't a Georgian submarine.

Tomas asked why and then immediately shouted 'No! Don't tell me!'

'Then it would be easy to sink it,' Sasha said anyway.

Renard played his part, grinning, 'How do you sink a Georgian submarine, Sasha?'

Sasha: 'Simple. You send a diver down to tap on the hatch.'

'Crazy Russian fool,' Kavtoradze mumbled.

'OK, Sasha, what's the difference between Georgian cognac exported to Russia and cognac sold in Georgia?' Sergo asked.

'The label has five stars instead of three printed on it.'

'No, fool, the export bottle has "open other end" stamped in Russian across the bottom.'

'Funny ha ha. But I'll tell you a true story about Georgian cognac. One day Gorbachev took Helmut Kohl to his old stamping ground in Stavropol to discuss the sale of East Germany. The negotiations were a success and that night they went out drinking together. Unfortunately all the restaurant could provide was cognac. Next morning Gorbachev wakes up feeling very refreshed however, and he goes to the bathroom to wash. He looks in the mirror but to his horror he sees that the famous trademark has disappeared! So he rushes out in the corridor and slapping himself on the forehead he says to the KGB man on guard, "My birthmark has gone!"

'"What did you expect, Mikhail Sergeevich?" the man says. "In the Kremlin you are drinking Stolichnaya, but all we've got in Stavropol is Georgian stain remover."'

Amidst the groans Sergo Kavtoradze spoke, 'It's certainly true that cognac isn't what it used to be. Things were better under Brezhnev.'

'Really?' Renard asked.

'Sure. Think of what he did for the people.'

'Like what?'

'The advances of science for one,' Sergo said. 'One day Brezhnev is driving his American sports car when suddenly he's overtaken by a chicken. He accelerates to two hundred kilometres an hour, but he still can't catch the chicken. At last it runs off down an alley. Brezhnev stops the car and beckons to a man in a white coat standing nearby. "How come that chicken runs so fast?" he says.

'"It's a product of Soviet genetic engineering," the scientist answers, "and it's the world's fastest chicken."

'"And what does it taste like?" Brezhnev asks. "We don't know," the scientist answers. "We haven't managed to catch one yet."'

'But Brezhnev read everything from cue cards,' Sasha said. 'Everyone knows that. Once he received Mrs Thatcher at the Kremlin. "Good morning, Mrs Gandhi," he says, "I am pleased to welcome you to the Soviet Union."

'An aide whispers in his ear. "But that's Mrs Thatcher."

'"I know it's Mrs Thatcher," says Leonid Ilyich. "But here it is written *Mrs Gandhi.*"'

Father Pyotr took his turn, 'Well, at least Brezhnev was religious. One Easter Friday he was strolling down the corridors of the Central Committee. "Christ is Risen!" a passing functionary said in greeting. "Thank you," Brezhnev answered and walked on. Another bureaucrat passed and he also announced, "Comrade General Secretary! Christ is Risen!"

'"Thank you," Brezhnev said, "but the fact was already reported to me."'

'Quit telling Brezhnev jokes or leave the plane!' Tomas said, pushing everyone but Renard away.

'Lenin, Stalin and Trotsky were shipwrecked on a desert island,' Father Pyotr began to groans as the three of them went down the passage to the saloon. 'And they had one bottle of vodka between them . . .'

The cabin door swung shut and Tomas immediately said: '*Amerikanets*, we don't have much time and I want to tell you a different kind of story.'

They drank more chacha and Tomas told Renard what had happened a few years before, when a couple of Abkhazians had tried to pull protection money from Sergo. 'He refused to pay, of course. Later, when the mafia took over City Hall and put their men in the top jobs in the Moscow police force, no one had any more illusions. But in those days gangsters were not yet in control in Moscow. So a big *papa* – the notorious mafia leader Joe Kaban – got angry with Sergo. Kaban, nicknamed "the Musician" because he'd once played bassoon in the orchestra of the Moscow Circus, was famous for his vanity, and even had an associate scalped for a chance remark about the extravagant wig he wore to cover his premature baldness. An example had to be made. So one day Sergo's pregnant wife was abducted in the street. A couple of days later they sent him a video. That was just for their trouble; the Kavtoradzes had already agreed to pay.

'Then two Abkhazians arrived at the restaurant. They carried a canvas sports bag; inside was Sergo's baby son. Unfortunately, they explained, his wife could not remain among the living. But they were sorry to part with the lad and they even left feeding instructions.

'Time passed. The restaurant paid its dues, and then Sergo contacted the Musician. Would *Papa* like to become the child's godparent? The Musician was a big man by now, but he agreed. There was a celebration in the Savoy Hotel, in the company of prominent friends, officials from the city government (Kaban was the closest friend of the mayor of Moscow; together, in the heroic days after the fall of the Soviet Union, they had planned the "privatization" of municipal real estate, with the help of prominent western law firms). The evening was a success; the Musician was shown an exquisite Russian blonde and he took her that night to his ranch south of Moscow.

'Next morning the blonde had disappeared, the fountains played red and the Musician's exsanguinated body was in the lake. It was said that his wig was used to stuff the saddle on a circus camel. After that the gang was rolled on, *nakatila*: eight Abkhazians died – the remainder went home to the Caucasus. No one bothered the restaurant again. The mayor of Moscow didn't even attend his friend's funeral; he was too busy organizing his next political campaign: to be elected President of Russia.

'Maybe you don't know it, but Zidra's grandfather was the architect of Soviet espionage in Europe after the war. He was a genius amongst spies, and he taught her and Ivars both. Ivars was also a great man. I feel his loss. But what I'm saying is that Zidra is *unique*.'

When Renard said that was his good fortune, Tomas laughed and sent him aft.

Renard went to the cabin at the rear of the plane and had to prise open the bolt on the door, sliding the blade of his knife in a crack which from the look of it had been forced before. It slid to again, behind him. Zidra was asleep in the double berth, one naked arm lying on the pink satin pillow, the palm of the hand upwards, the fingers slightly curled. She seemed not to be breathing, the only vital sign a small pulse visible in her throat. But her cheeks glowed. Renard kissed her forehead and throat, and pulled the covers down to look at her. His lips brushed her belly and breasts, but when she stirred he covered her again and sat watching. She was the original of Rublev's *Madonna* and stillness shrouded her. There was a Russian word that described the feeling: *Sobornost*. Communion.

234

Now the past was done, but for the one matter which they would finish together, and then his debt to Lisa was settled.

Renard bent to kiss the almond-pale eyes, left Zidra and went forward to relieve Tomas.

At 6.10 that evening the Anushka entered the airspace of the Semiransk-Nanai Autonomous Region – according to Tomas' dead reckoning. Moscow's air-traffic controllers had lost interest in them long before. As Tomas explained, this was not the first time. Any complaints about pilot negligence would be squared up later with a suitable bribe. They were less than forty minutes' flying time from Kalegut airport – and they were not expected. Renard roused Zidra, who sat up in the bed rubbing her eyes. And as she did so there was a shattering noise from the starboard side of the plane – a crackle which sounded like gunfire followed by two sharp explosions.

'Get dressed!' Renard shouted and raced to the flight deck.

Sergo was shouting something in Georgian; Tomas had to fight the plane on to a stable path. 'Look there!' he shouted to Renard.

Through the windscreen were the red and green lights and flashing strobes of another plane, which bobbed and darted and suddenly disappeared, streaking ahead into the cloud cover 1,000 metres above.

'Mig-29!' Tomas shouted. 'There are two of the fuckers. Came from nowhere. He was trying to tell me to follow him down, firing warning shots across my nose, but the stupid incompetent bastard's drilled my wing tip.'

Suddenly the second Mig appeared in front, waggling its wings.

'Here we go again! He wants me to follow him . . .'

'Where?'

'Looks like due east. They're being *very* serious about it; but due east takes us south of Kalegut.'

'They're taking us to the base at Semiransk,' Renard said. 'We need to decide. Maybe it's for the best.'

'*Decide*? What does that mean?' The look he gave Renard would have curdled milk. 'I want to die with my boots off, *Amerikanets*, not in deep-frozen fragments on the goddamn polar ice.'

'How far are we from Kalegut?'

Now the other Mig-29 had reappeared, flying close alongside; the pilot was visible in the half-light of his own instrumentation, his gloved hand pointing downwards and to the left, where he wanted the Anushka to follow.

'Five – ten minutes flying time, not more.'

'Ask him what he wants.'

'I've been trying. They don't respond.' Tomas opened a channel and tried again. 'Who are you? Identify yourselves. Why the hell have you fired on me?'

This time the answer was immediate. 'You have no IFF beacon. You have no right to be in this airspace. We're entitled to shoot you down.'

'You've already shot me, you stupid bastard! Do you know who I am?'

For answer the Mig on the starboard side fired tracer shells a few metres over the nose of the Anushka.

Kavtoradze said, 'Jesus, maybe I will just follow him. He's not joking!'

'Ask him why you can't put down at Kalegut. Tell him you've lost a fuel line and an engine is about to blow.'

Tomas repeated Renard's words. The answer was immediate: 'Follow me at once or we shoot you down. You have no permission to land at Kalegut.'

Renard nodded agreement to Tomas, who told the mike, 'OK, will co-operate. I have engine trouble but will try to gain height above cloud cover.'

Renard asked him, 'Is there a parachute on the plane?'

'No.'

'OK, we'll jump anyway.' He tried to reassure the startled Tomas. 'We do this all the time, back home, you know. At rodeos. Try to aim for a snow drift, when you come down out of the clouds. How slow can you go?'

'Sixty knots, maybe fifty-five, but at this height I can stall her in a split-second if I make a mistake. Are you crazy, *Amerikanets*?'

'It's been done before. Find some soft snow.'

Father Pyotr was horror-struck when given the news, but Renard squeezed his forearm. 'No need for you to do this, Father,' he told him. 'They're not looking for you. I think it's safe for you to stay on the plane.'

'As you say,' the priest shouted above the gathering roar of the engines. 'God alone knows. But I think I'll be OK.'

Renard ran aft. Zidra was already dressed. 'We'll have to jump, and there's no chute. Otherwise we'll be taken at Semiransk base, and this time they'll shoot first and discuss it afterwards. I've told Father Pyotr to stay.'

'Of course. He's not the one they want. But we have to try it. Let's go!'

Renard was already heading for the rear exit door. He started working on the release handles.

Sergo came back, and handed him a small package containing flares. 'Very lights,' he explained. 'And take this.' He gave Renard a pocket compass; Tomas had marked a bearing on it with a felt-tip pen.

'Thanks.'

Zidra grasped Father Pyotr by the wrist, shouting to be heard above the howling which grew with each twist of the door-release handles. 'When you get down, contact Fillipov direct. Ask him to help officially. There's no alternative now. There's nothing left for Sobor after this anyway!'

The priest nodded. 'Agreed!' He was gripping her upper arms from behind as though to prevent her from falling, but the handles had already spun free and as the rear door fell open their ears were filled with the roaring of sudden decompression. Then the landing ladder sank down out of the fuselage. They could see nothing – the Anushka was still in and out of cloud.

'The cloud base is two thousand, eight hundred metres,' Sergo was shouting behind them. 'Tomas will take her down as low as he dares. If it looks like snow and not rocks down below, then jump! And good luck!'

The aircraft plunged back into swirling cloud and just as suddenly was free of it; the plane was surging down, skidding through the Arctic air. Tomas had just radioed the Mig pilots that he was losing power and height, as a result of damage sustained by their gunfire. The ground rushed up, and in seconds Zidra and Renard were staring at the snow-covered contours of a steep hill flashing underneath.

The voice of Tomas suddenly crackled over the intercom: *'I'll tell you when to go. It looks like deep snow, good luck to you both. Airspeed one hundred and twenty knots, height one hundred and thirty metres—'*

They were crouched over the open doorway, the frosting below made the ground look like a wedding cake racing past. The loudspeaker hissed for them again, *'There's tree cover approaching, so get ready – airspeed seventy, sixty, fifty knots – this is the best I can do – forty knots – twenty-five metres – twenty metres – go when I say – ten metres—'*

The snow sucked up from the ground now swirled through the door. There was a howling inferno from the raging engines, and from the roaring blast of frozen air which gnashed at the bucking tail of the plane. The Anushka slowed to a near-stall, its engines screaming defiance of gravity; and then the intercom crackled again: *'Now! Jump! Jump!'*

Renard gripped Zidra round the waist, and suddenly they were falling into silence: 'Brace your knees!' he had time to call, when a giant hand

237

smacked him in the midriff and he was drowning in the snow that tore at his face like sandpaper.

The roaring in his head died and disappeared. Then Renard could hear no sound at all other than the rasping of his own breathing and the thumping of his heart. His left leg had buckled under him, and his knee was in agony. He rolled over gasping with pain, his mouth instantly filling with snow. He threshed his arms and sank deeper into suffocating snow. He was beginning to panic when suddenly he heard Zidra's laughter – a musical chuckle, very close – just above his head.

Then the snow was swept off him.

'You're alive? Nothing broken?'

She was standing over him, shining a small flashlight at him, herself thigh-deep in whiteness.

'It would be easier just to be arrested and shot,' he grumbled.

She laughed. 'This was *your* idea, my leader.' She helped him up, and dusted the snow off his coat. 'Tomas Kavtoradze is a genius. He threw us out on a slope; it couldn't have been better planned. And I think this is the River Astur below us; with any luck we'll be able to walk easily on the ice.'

'I can hardly walk at all,' Renard said ruefully.

'Come on, get up; I'll help you, lord and master. Lean on me.'

They stumbled down the slope; in places the snow was three metres deep, and its depth, which had saved them, made it completely impassable without skis. But the river was a different matter: the same gales which had piled drifts everywhere else had scoured its icy surface almost free of snow.

Renard took out the compass. The course of the river was close to the direction they needed; Tomas had done a good job.

'During the Second World War, our Soviet airmen were specially trained in making jumps without parachutes. I heard lots of stories about it from my grandparents when I was a child, but I never expected to do it myself.'

Renard answered dourly, 'I just hope Kavtoradze gets down OK.'

'Don't worry about him. He'll get down, and when he does he'll buy his way out of trouble. After all, we're not there to embarrass him. And the hold of that plane is stuffed with goodies. Georgians never miss a chance to trade, do they?'

'Could they have seen us jump?'

'Unlikely. I landed more or less on my feet; I saw the Anushka hightailing it back into the clouds, but there was no sign of the Migs.

Tomas came down like a stone, and they lost him for a few seconds. It was enough.'

'We're still a long way from Kalegut – about five kilometres as the crow flies. If we have to divert from the river, we'll never get through this snow. And it's hellishly cold – what do you suppose the temperature is?'

'Quite warm for the time of year, I should say. Not more than twenty below.'

'Well, we'll die if we have to stay out in it much longer. Thank God it's not a blizzard.'

Zidra's musical laugh which stirred Renard even in his desolation was answered from over the river by a low growl which erupted into a blood-freezing snarl.

They both squatted, nostrils flaring, straining to see past the blackened clumps of frozen reeds sticking through the river ice. 'What the hell?'

'It's a white wolf. Be quiet!'

Impenetrable white silence. Then Zidra suddenly relaxed. 'OK, it's not interested in us.' She leaned over and kissed him and they walked on in silence for a while. 'Don't worry,' she told him at last. 'I'll look after you.'

'Fine, but who's looking after you? And by the way, who's "Fillipov"? You mentioned his name to Pyotr before we jumped.'

'You don't miss much do you?' she whispered. 'Fillipov – Dr Yuri Andreevich Fillipov – is the Chief of the Semiransk Geological Survey team. And he is—'

'Don't tell me.' Renard looked at her knowingly. 'It's him – Fillipov! *He* is the Molniya source.'

'Yes.'

'The man who gave us the Molniya secret. And maybe a double, a traitor.'

'Not very likely, knowing him the way I do. But there is circumstantial evidence, I admit. Something happened to Ivars which we still don't understand. Maybe now we'll find out. Every infamy is possible in this world, I suppose.' When Renard looked pained at this, Zidra continued: 'But what lies between *us* comes from somewhere else. If *that* was betrayed, I wouldn't want to continue this life at all.'

'Thank you for that. The mystery is only that you surrendered yourself to someone like me—'

'Don't be silly, I love you.' She turned and her jacket crackled with frost when she touched him. 'It isn't just the cold that makes me shiver

239

like this,' she said. 'I'm glad to be here with you. I'm glad to be anywhere with you.'

He laughed. 'In fact, the mystery is *you*. The mystery of your endless white beauty. Do you know what fractals are? Your body is a fractal space occupied by beauty. How could such a thing as you come into being, in this miserable existence?'

She laughed. 'Even if I was the ice maiden in the fairy tale, doomed to melt when I give myself to a mortal, it wouldn't happen here, would it? Too bloody cold!'

They plodded on through the sticky, exhausting snow whose deceptively smooth surface concealed dips and hollows so that every few steps they would stumble or plunge in up to their thighs. Behind them as they walked, and receding now, they heard the wolf howl again. Nothing answered. A gibbous, baleful moon hung over a shrunken world.

CHAPTER 17

In three hours they had made poor progress, not more than two kilometres along the frozen River Astur. Then Zidra saw lights moving ahead, heard the sound of engines: 'Sounds like ski-bobs,' she said to Renard. They moved closer to the river bank, where clumps of bushes blackened the gloom, offering some scanty cover.

The lights weaved and bobbed along the river; there were three ski-bobs.

'It must be Fillipov,' Zidra decided. 'Anyone else would have sent a helicopter.'

Renard pulled out the Very gun.

'Wait here. And don't fire that thing yet,' Zidra said this and was gone, racing to the centre of the frozen river. As the ski-bobs rounded the next bend, she flashed her light. It was enough. The lead vehicle stopped at once, the other two pulling up behind.

Renard watched her meeting the driver. The two of them talked for what seemed a long while. Eventually, though, they started walking back to where Renard stood.

Zidra perfomed the introductions. 'I don't think you've met. Douglas, this is Dr Fillipov. Yuri Andreevich, meet Douglas Renard.'

Fillipov shook hands with Renard and they all walked downriver where Fillipov introduced the other two ski-bob drivers. 'This is Lieutenant-Colonel Sasonov, the head of Semiransk KGB. And my deputy, Ivan Renkulov.'

It was almost impossible to see their faces in the gloom.

'Zidra, you will come with me,' announced Fillipov. 'Ivashka, take Mr Renard with you. Let's go!'

They mounted the ski-bobs and set off back downriver, turning off in a short while. The ski-bobs were Russian-made; their two-stroke engines buzzing like chainsaws, but they went willingly enough. In ten minutes or less Renard, peering over Renkulov's shoulder, saw the first dim lights of a settlement. 'Kalegut, the capital of Semiransk,' Renkulov shouted over his shoulder. 'And the backside of Russia.'

The ski-bobs zipped down an ill-lit street which was flanked on either side by low slab-sided buildings, mostly residential, and not laid out in any kind of order. They came to a halt by a two-storey building, larger than the others and surrounded by a low fence.

The building was a primitive structure made of tied logs. Snow had drifted up to the first-floor windows, and elsewhere Arctic blizzards had formed a ramp of snow up to the roof line. From somewhere on high came a loud snorting noise followed by an angry roar.

Fillipov shouted: 'Silence, Igor! Go to sleep!' and the roaring died away. Fillipov explained to Zidra: 'We've been adopted by a half-tame polar bear, and he likes to sleep on our roof. I haven't the heart to shoot him.'

Stamping snow off their feet, they entered a small wooden threshold, over which a naked bulb glimmered, feebly illuminating a mauve plastic sign bearing the state insignia of the Russian Soviet Federative Socialist Republic. There was the familiar five-pointed star – symbol of the solidarity of the proletariat of five continents – over the hammer and sickle signifying the union of peasantry and workers and set in the wheat sheaves of socialist plenty. Gold letters spelt: 'RSFSR. Semiransk Geological Survey. The Pearl. House of Recreation and Study.'

Sasonov helped them off with their coats and led them through into a large, low-ceilinged room. One end of the room was furnished with simple wooden tables and chairs. On the left was a bar, also of wood, crudely lacquered with cheap varnish so soft that a thumbnail could scratch it. Two landscapes of the polar north hung lopsidedly over the bar, beside which was placed a small karaoke machine, the gift of some passing Korean oilmen. Narwhal and reindeer bone carvings portrayed scenes from Nanai life: fishing, hunting, the wooing of bashful girls. A one-metre high doll was placed on a ledge on the wall. Crudely fashioned of wood and reindeer skin, it had the slanted eyes, broad smile and rosy cheeks of a Nanai woman. Branches of rowan and holly, studded with scarlet berries, were placed around it. A freshly-killed white hare lay before the image.

'That is *Bayanai*,' Sasonov said. 'The Nanai goddess of the hunt.'

A television set was switched on: it showed the nine o'clock Moscow news, with pictures of Alfredo Sakharinov in his office, receiving delegates in preparation for the Duma session the next day.

At the far end of the room was a big open fireplace, with a roaring log fire. Fillipov led them to it and sat them down. 'We have no food to offer you, Zidra,' he apologized. 'Just a little bread and caviar. The kitchen is closed.'

'Of course, I understand, Yuri Andreevich. We're more in need of sleep anyway.'

'Then let's just exchange the main news; we'll talk later. You'll have a few hours of rest tonight, at any rate. But I must tell you that the situation is very serious. Kavtoradze has been arrested – he was forced down at Semiransk airbase. Fortunately I know the base commander – General Ivanov. We're old friends as a matter of fact, and he owes me a favour or two. He called me at Kavtoradze's insistence.'

'Ivanov must know that we're here then – otherwise how did you find us?'

'No, he doesn't know – not for sure, anyway. But he suspects. I asked Ivanov to send a helicopter for me, and I went to the base and met him. He was almost hysterical – someone in Moscow certainly warned him to expect you, and General Medved is due to arrive from Varta any time – with two thousand of his own troops.'

Renard raised his eyebrows at this.

'We were followed, we think by Zamok's people, from the moment we escaped from Lefortovo. But they didn't touch us and they even helped us to lose some local MVD people yesterday. Zamok wants me to escape together with Sergei. That's how he plans to expose and destroy Alfredo Sakharinov.'

'In that case Zamok also sent Sergei to Semiransk. Obviously he thinks that with Sergei's help he stands a chance of somehow wresting control of Molniya from that brother of his,' Zidra added.

'He may be right to think so,' Fillipov said. 'Because if Zamok warned Ivanov, then it means Ivanov is also Zamok's man and a traitor to Alfredo Sakharinov's cause. So Zamok's already got control of the Semiransk base, to some degree at least. We'll just see what happens when Medved arrives.

'Ivanov may well have been expecting Mr Renard to climb out of Kavtoradze's plane when it put down at Semiransk base, but he couldn't say as much to me openly. He may have assumed that you parachuted out. So he'll be half expecting you. Anyway he won't keep Kavtoradze, although he wouldn't release him to me either. He's obviously waiting for new orders from someone, and I guess that can only be Dmitry Zamok.'

'Even so,' said Renard, 'we can't assume that Alfredo Sakharinov is a spent force. I don't believe that for a second.'

'At any rate, you'll be safe here for tonight. Tomorrow we'll have to decide a number of things. One thing's for sure – if Zamok *has* been helping you, it's only because you're a pawn in his game with Alfredo

Sakharinov. If he sees you getting near to Molniya, he'll turn his forces against you. He wants to inherit Molniya when he comes to power, no mistake.'

Carrying a tray with vodka, bread and a plate piled high with black osetrina caviar, Sasonov joined the group. He handed the glasses round and Fillipov toasted them. 'We expected you a long time ago, Mr Renard. At last you have arrived! Not without certain adventures.'

'Yuri Andreevich, although I don't relish the memory of Varta jail, if I'd not had those *adventures* I would never have met Zidra Latsis.'

'Well said, young man.' Fillipov was big, bigger even than Tomas Kavtoradze. Standing by the fire with his great legs planted like trees, he overshadowed Sasonov, like a chieftain in an ancient land full, as Siberians say, with the riches which fell from God's frozen hand when He first flew over it.

'I was arrested the moment I arrived in Varta last September,' Renard told him. 'I came at the urgent request of Ivars Latsis, but my cover was blown – I still don't know by who.'

Fillipov laughed grimly. 'Do you think it was me who betrayed you? That I'm playing a double game? Of course I am! But the traitor is someone on your own side, someone high up in your government.' He looked steadily at Renard. 'I've learnt how to survive in a hard school. When I was younger than you are now, I once did the same foolish thing you did today. I'd been delayed for four weeks in Khanti-Mansyssk by bad weather. A biplane served the route in those days – I remember it was heated by a wood-burning stove and the chimney stuck out through the fuselage. Well, at last we got permission to fly – and we came all the way to Semiransk, where it turned out to be snowing harder than ever. The pilot circled a few times but refused to land – so I jumped anyway.'

'I heard something about it,' Renard said.

Fillipov seemed pleased – although it was hard to detect emotion in his glacial features. 'In those days we imagined we were Stalin's falcons, flying over Siberia and dreaming vast dreams. I thought I was invulnerable, immortal. Well, I'm not. I broke a leg and nearly died of the cold. It was a lesson. You were lucky today. You should look after Zidra better.'

Renard smiled and asked Fillipov when they had first become aware of Molniya.

'Our activities against Molniya began very early on, when I and one or two others first began to understand what was planned for our beloved polar North. We didn't mean to betray the country; we had no political interests. No, our naïve idea was that some things are just too important

244

to be left to the military and their scientists. We wanted to warn the Party – imagine our colossal stupidity! We only succeeded in alerting Alfredo Sakharinov to what was going on in his own territory. It gave him a brilliant idea, the results of which we are unfortunately beginning to see.'

Renard said: 'Stalin said that a secret shared with one person is no secret. Why did Alfredo Sakharinov spare *you*? Why were you allowed to continue?'

'Mr Renard, I'm not a young man, I learnt a few tricks along the way. But you'll see why Alfredo Sakharinov let us continue – although the answer's obvious when you start to see matters from his perspective.

'Later, after the deaths – or murders – of two members of our group, we went completely underground. Latsis organized Father Pyotr's group; its only function was to support our work and in particular to develop contacts with the West. Of course, Latsis wasn't with us from the beginning. There were three of us: besides myself, there was Sasonov here, and Mikhail Leshkin, who is the Survey's Chief Oceanographer. He's waiting for us next door, so you'll meet him, Mr Renard. We three constitute the Molniya source.

'The irony of my position is that the very first person I complained about Molniya to was – Alfredo Sakharinov. From that time onwards we remained bound to him, one way or another. It's difficult to explain to a foreigner like you – but this strange mixing of people and institutions was the secret nature of the Soviet Union. Western "experts" cannot really understand, because they've not had the misfortune to live through the moral compromises that such a life forces you into.

'Using Ivars Latsis' circle we made contact with Paul Gregory in Washington. Almost immediately, we realized that your services are quite penetrated, as you probably know. Then a miracle – or so it seemed to us – took place. I was suddenly called to Varta for a meeting with Alfredo Sakharinov. I imagined the worst. This was a little over two years ago. Not long afterwards, Sakharinov was taken to Moscow and began his meteoric rise to power. But at this time he was still the boss of Varta Region.

'When we met, Sakharinov came straight to the point: there'd been a leak and the CIA had learnt something about Molniya. He was obviously very concerned, and talked a lot about damage limitation. But, as the conversation went on, I began to realize that damage limitation was only his secondary consideration. In reality, he'd come to see some possible advantages: if the Americans knew *something* – enough to worry them, but not enough to make them capable of reacting – then he was well

245

placed to play the situation. In fact, this was the beginning of a whole new stage in Alfredo's career. From this time forward, Molniya became more important to him than ever; it meshed in with his grand design. One can't help but be impressed by the man; he means to take power in Russia, and to use that power to rebuild the country as a military and economic superpower. Of course he has his rivals, notably Dmitry Zamok. But no one to compare with himself. And Molniya gave him a chance to move on beyond the petty politics of bribing Western business-men and of buying, compromising and corrupting Western civil servants and political leaders. Now he started to think really big.

'Maybe Sakharinov really believed that I had got frightened off the whole business, and had nothing to do with any leaks to Washington. Who knows? I considered our organization was watertight and I knew that the Latsis family were old-time enemies of the Sakharinovs; nobody else in Russia could have taken them on, in fact.

'It made no difference. Alfredo Sakharinov had decided to use me, and I decided to be used. I could see no other way of surviving and of staying near the centre of events. Besides it became ever clearer that Molniya was something really special. Of course, in Soviet times, the whole Arctic region was full of missile and submarine bases. But never before had it been the epicentre of our entire war machine. Molniya turns the whole region into the world's most dangerous war zone. Alfredo Sakharinov is betting on the environmental instability of the region, and on the reluctance of the West to risk causing international calamity by, for example, bombing Molniya. That's what I call brinkmanship with a difference. And the consequences could be catastrophic for the entire planet.

'So Alfredo Sakharinov offered to include me in Molniya – and I accepted. At that point he said this to me: *I have a man in Washington. He's close to the Secretary of State; I want you to work with him. Feed the Americans information – about Molniya. Your information will always be first, and it will be impeccable. Soon they'll believe you more than anybody.*

'Well, I was certainly at the centre once again, and the more time went on, the more my own growing knowledge served to protect our circle.'

Zidra said, 'It didn't protect Ivars.'

'Or me,' Renard added. 'And I'd rather like to know the name of Sakharinov's man in Washington.'

'By a curious coincidence that's also his name – *Washington*. Henry Washington. He's an under-secretary at the State Department. Do you know him?'

246

'Yes, I do.' He smiled bleakly. 'Thank you, Dr Fillipov.'

'We took many risks, but we were treading a tightrope. What destroyed Ivars Latsis was the fact that Langley insisted on sending you, Mr Renard. Your mission was compromised from the start. Sakharinov knew you were no petroleum consultant. Your cover – Remex Offshore Limited – was almost amateurish. It just shows in what unjustified contempt Western Intelligence now holds its Russian counterparts. You'd all forgotten: it wasn't the KGB which collapsed. It was the Party – a different thing altogether. Something else was revealed at the same time: just how deeply Sakharinov has penetrated the CIA. That's easily explained. Your guard was down – the Cold War was over. And Sakharinov plays with far larger resources than the KGB ever could. The KGB could run to a million or so on an Intelligence operation; Sakharinov can spend billions if he wants to. Is that understood on your side of the fence? If it is, I suspect it's understood mostly by those people who've already been beneficiaries of Sakharinov's largesse, and therefore have no interest in talking about the matter. Well, let us refresh ourselves a little. Sasonov—'

'I know. Pour.'

'Ironically, what saved the day was the fact Latsis had managed to win a high-ranking Varta KGB man, someone of no worth in fact—'

'Travkin,' Renard said.

'Exactly. Colonel Travkin. A very unlikely candidate – an unscrupulous bribe-taker and coward. But that was the special genius of Ivars Latsis. Sometimes he made people behave out of character.'

'I met Travkin; I formed exactly that impression of him. I was very surprised later to find that he didn't betray me when he had the chance. And I think he paid the price.'

'He was killed, yes. He had it in his power to save Latsis, but did nothing till it was too late; Latsis was already en route to the last, fatal meeting when Travkin warned him what was likely to happen. Latsis was the bravest man I ever knew. Without him, there'd be no hope of stopping Molniya, or of preventing Russia from being thrown into the abyss.'

'What I still don't understand,' Renard pointed out, 'is why a rescue party came for me – or for Latsis, whichever it was.'

'My theory is that it was just an afterthought – nothing more than that. On such small wheels does history sometimes turn. Sakharinov Junior got the idea that just dumping Latsis' body – I'm sorry, Zidra, but this is how it was – that leaving the body in the forest was something done in anger, to be regretted later. It left the trail cold, and it occurred to him that at least they should make some kind of forensic autopsy to find out whatever they could from fingerprints and so on. As you see, Sergei Sakharinov is no Einstein of the espionage world. He gave the command and thought no more about it.

'Then a week or so later he heard – quite by chance – that Shadrin was alive and being treated in Varta Geological Hospital. Nobody had told him! Probably such things can happen only in Russia. In fact Travkin was the only person who was informed at the time. He had a good idea how important the information was, but he wanted to play with it for that very reason. The situation was that Renard was supposedly dead, and Shadrin still alive – much like the original plan. Travkin was delighted. He'd received the metacodes from Latsis, and now fallen right into his hands like an apple from a tree was the very American who could make the deal with him.

'We couldn't understand what had happened. On the one hand we knew from Travkin that Latsis was dead. And on the other we had no reason to suppose that Douglas Renard was alive – that a man like Medved had failed such an elementary task. And we had to know – what had become of the metacodes carried by Latsis?'

Fillipov smiled at Renard. 'You are a clever spy – for an American. It was hard to track you down. We got to you in your Moscow flat just before Sakharinov did. Am I right?'

Renard's smile was rueful. 'Indeed you are. You gave me just a few minutes' warning; Father Pyotr called, and for some reason I listened to him.'

Fillipov sighed. 'What worried us greatly was that we soon understood Travkin had begun a double game. Evidently he decided to play with the mistaken identity. He worked out the significance of the Molniya metacodes and he knew their price – millions if he decided to sell to the Americans. So he made up his mind to use you to smuggle this highly valuable material out of Varta, then to meet up with you in Moscow and reveal the exact nature of this precious cargo. But events were starting to spin from his control. Once Sergei Sakharinov found out you were in hospital he sent some of his *rebyata* to collect you. And of course, he did so without bothering to inform the highly expendable Travkin. The plan went wrong – you are a professional.'

When Fillipov smiled at him, for the first time Renard felt something akin to warmth in this obelisk of a man.

'You defended yourself and one of the attackers was killed. When Travkin arrived that night, and again the next morning, he still had no idea that those attackers were Sergei's men. His main thought by then was to get Douglas Renard on a plane out of Varta as quick as possible. When he did that, of course, he signed his own death warrant.'

'But I was told that it was General Medved who had me trailed to Moscow,' Renard said.

'It wasn't. It was all Travkin's initiative. Once again, Mr Renard, you were too efficient. The people he sent lost you twice. And then Travkin did begin to panic. One mistake followed another – first he let you go to Moscow *with the metacodes*. Fantastic folly, in fact. Then he made the mistake which cost him his life: he actually *told* Medved what had happened. Not his role in it of course. Just his suspicion that the man in Varta hospital was actually you, Mr Renard.'

Zidra said, 'But why did Travkin give the codes to Renard in the first place? He could have made his own deal with the Americans.'

'Travkin was junior. He was absolutely out of his depth. And he was irresolute, of course. It's one thing to be sure of something in theory; another to stake your life on it. What if he got to Moscow and had no luck with the Americans, for whatever reason? Or worse – he might have been trapped approaching them. That was highly probable, given the degree of penetration by Sakharinov's KGB boys at the American Embassy. Like many a fool, Travkin overestimated himself and underestimated the people he tried to deal with. He decided to use our Mr Renard as a cover, and only show up himself at a later stage – when he could see that his commodity was truly saleable, but before Renard himself could sell it.'

Sasonov had been listening, and now said: 'Sergei Sakharinov was still chasing the man he thought was Ivars Latsis, of course. A surreal situation arose – I don't know if you're aware even now, Mr Renard, of just how many fragments of our once-monolithic KGB have been getting in each other's way chasing after you. Sergei was beside himself by this time. He expected to be arrested and hauled in front of his brother by the hour. He's a wilful, unruly type. That's probably the reason why they may fail – Sergei is his brother's Achilles heel. When he heard that the person incarnating Shadrin was not Latsis after all, but you, he relaxed a little. He thought at last that his secret was safe – as if the Zamok tape had died with Ivars.'

'In fact, that was the worst moment in the Sakharinov camp for everyone except Sergei,' Fillipov continued. 'They'd lost the metacodes and got nothing in return. There was a hell of a row between Medved and Sergei Sakharinov. I'm told that Sakharinov pulled a gun on Medved. I doubt if they're on speaking terms even now, these conquerors of Russia.

'Matters only got worse when Medved started work on Travkin. The moment Medved pulled from him the fact that the person in Varta Geological Hospital wasn't even Shadrin, he understood that Travkin must've been involved. He arrested him and Travkin was so mistreated that he died under interrogation.'

By now Sasonov had circulated the vodka for the second time, and they drank to wildernesses without people.

'I came to the polar north more than thirty years ago,' Fillipov volunteered. 'We all grew to love this strange land. Which is why we hate the Sakharinovs and what they stand for, the whole great gang of them. They mean death for the Arctic, but you can't finish with them in a day.'

'You have to understand something of our lives here,' Sasonov said. 'When I first came, there was no one and nothing in Semiransk peninsula except for the native Nanai and their reindeer. Now there are nearly ten thousand staff employed by the Survey – you can't move a step in Semiransk without us. Unless, of course, you're the military. They came after us. The Survey never worried about how we lived as long as we pumped out the black gold. Actually, the first geologists had to live like natives, and there was lots of intermarriage. My own father was a geologist, and my mother the first daughter of a wealthy Nanai hunter.'

'Yes,' Fillipov said, 'we were sent here to carry out the Five Year Plan, with no idea what we were letting ourselves in for. In those days, we believed in the Party without question. But whatever good we did, we also did much damage. And we changed the Arctic North for ever. We were taught to think of this beautiful wilderness as just another economic opportunity. We saw only empty tundra, waiting to be sown with mine and mill. We didn't know any better.'

Sasonov took over, 'Local people say that Yuri Andreevich is the Father of Semiransk. Probably that's why he blames himself too much. Maybe no one here was to blame for what happened – maybe it was your America, constantly frightening us with atom bombs when we'd just been devastated by Hitler's war. But the mess the Soviet army made was even worse. The Arctic became a death zone, full of nuclear weapons and missiles and submarine bases.'

A table had been set in the hall but seeing that their discussion was continuing, a Nanai serving woman had brought them a few dishes of bread accompanied by rare white caviar. They ate a little, but first Sasonov poured citrus-flavoured *Limonnaya* vodka.

'Utterly to be recommended,' their host said, holding his glass to the light. The vodka was cloudy, viscous pale yellow.

'I drink to Zidra Latsis,' Sasonov interrupted, 'to her serene beauty.'
They stood and drank to her and then to the Nanai.

'No one else can do what they do,' Sasonov said. 'The Nanai put to
sea in canoes made of reindeer hide, Mr Renard, and hunt the narwhal
amid the ice-floes during the white nights. They live in a world so cold
that removing gloves is sufficient to risk death from freezing. They
survive, with their dog teams and reindeer herds, when our machinery
simply packs up.'

Fillipov hailed them, too, 'The Nanai people are the soul of Semiransk.
You can do nothing here without them. Look at the fools from Sibinternefte. We told them not to lay their oil pipelines across the reindeer
trails. They laughed at us! Our fools knew better; they wanted to save
money, so they planted six pipelines seven hundred kilometres long,
down the centre of the peninsula. They did it over the permafrost, in
winter. The following summer the permafrost melted and the pipelines
sank into the marsh. It was a catastrophe which will take decades to heal.
And they destroyed our reindeer herding grounds to boot.'

'What's happened inland is bad enough. What's been done to the
ocean is ten times, a hundred times worse,' Sasonov said. 'Our Arctic
seas have always been full of life. From the red starfish crawling along
the sea bottom, to the perfectly formed aster blooms floating on the
surface. But now we've got that *monstrosity*, sitting like a tumour on the
seabed. And nothing is certain any more.'

'You mean Molniya?'

'Of course!' Sasonov and Fillipov answered in unison.

'I know what you've come here to do, Mr Renard,' Fillipov said next.
'You're unlikely to succeed, but you could easily destroy us in the process
of trying. You represent such a powerful country, but you have come
here alone; you will seek our help and no doubt we shall give it. I hope
you know the cost of that help, because we shall be paying it long after
you are safely back on your own soil. I wonder if outcomes like that ever
occur to you, when you're rushing around having adventures and saving
the world from Russia?'

Zidra intervened diplomatically, 'Yuri, you were right when you said
we should rest. I'm whacked. Do you have a bed for me?'

Fillipov's irritation vanished as quickly as it had begun, and he at once
asked Sasonov to show them to their room.

'It looks like heaven,' Zidra said, on seeing the guestroom.

She closed the door and they went inside. Renard began to speak but
she took his hand and, shaking her head, pointed a finger at the ceiling.

'Not here,' she whispered. She stood up to him and kissed him and

251

told him softly that the thought of him ran through her like something intoxicating, and that she never wanted that to end. They undressed and crawled shivering with cold and tiredness into the narrow bed, where they fell asleep instantly in each other's arms and slept for over twelve hours. No one disturbed them and the endless polar night was silent except for the occasional grumbling and thrashing of Igor the half-wild polar bear, in his lair on the roof.

It was after six that evening when Sasonov knocked on their door to tell them their friends had arrived.

They dressed hurriedly and went downstairs. Sasonov met them at the foot of the stairs and led them down an ill-lit corridor to Fillipov's office.

Fillipov rose from his desk to greet them, motioning them to a small conference table.

'I hope you had a good rest,' he said. 'General Ivanov sent your colleagues here an hour ago. I have invited some other guests to meet you, and we will join them shortly. But first, please . . .'

He gestured and they sat round the table, Fillipov and Sasonov opposite Zidra and Renard.

Fillipov looked gloomy and also angry, and the reason why soon became apparent. 'Mr Renard, you have managed to put us in a very difficult position. General Ivanov came in the same helicopter as your friends and I have conferred with him. Medved still hasn't arrived, but that's because he's preparing a massive stroke, to ensure control of both Semiransk and the Molniya base. Ivanov realizes that you and Zidra are here, and is protecting you for now because he's Zamok's man, but that situation can't last. When Medved does arrive here, nothing can save us.' There was a weighty pause before he added, 'Perhaps the safest option is to leave at once. I can suggest nothing better.'

'What about Sergei Sakharinov?' said Renard. 'If we leave, he's supposed to go with us.'

'Then Alfredo Sakharinov will be destroyed, and we'll get Dmitry Zamok for a leader, which the world will find just as dangerous.'

'Well, Yuri Andreevich, there's only one real answer,' proclaimed Zidra. 'We need to destroy Molniya. Somehow.'

Sasonov and Fillipov exchanged looks, then Sasonov said: 'There may be a way to do that, or at least to immobilize the weapon temporarily. But you're talking long shot.'

'Tell us.'

'Let him think on it first while you meet our other guests,' Fillipov prevaricated. 'We won't move against Molniya without their help. And that's something they won't give automatically.' As he spoke, he led

252

them out of his office and back to the main communal area of The Pearl. They entered the hall where a waiting group of people included Tomas Kavtoradze and Father Pyotr. Tomas crossed the room in three giant strides, sweeping up Zidra and embracing Renard in his bear-like arms.

'I picked a good spot for you to jump, eh?' He stood back and looked at them both. 'No damage done, then. But you've the luck of the devil, both of you!'

Renard saluted him, 'The luck was your Anushka. Your ground speed must have been less than thirty knots. Thank you, Tomas – it was a brave thing.'

Kavtoradze swept them across the room, 'Nothing to it,' he said. 'My Anushka will fly backwards if I need it to. Now, come over to the fire, and get warm.'

'What happened to both of *you*?' Zidra asked. 'And where are Sasha and Sergo?'

Father Pyotr laughed. 'They're mounting a joint guard on our Anushka and its precious cargo of vodka, cognac and *Fanchkara* in case of military predators.'

'We put down at Semiransk airbase, no problem,' Tomas said. 'There was quite a welcome committee; they are *very* nervous. But I persuaded Ivanov that we had some urgent medicines to deliver to Yuri Andreevich here—' he nodded at Fillipov. 'Ivanov lent me a helicopter for the journey.' He grinned. 'That's an enormous base, at Semiransk. And there is a lot of activity; helicopters landing and taking off; a lot of troop movement. Something big is going on, all right.'

Renard found himself standing in front of a woman who could have been and perhaps was the model for *Bayanai*, the Nanai goddess of the hunt whose image he'd seen hanging further down the entrance hall the day before.

'This is Yekaterina Yelfimovna Prokhorova,' Fillipov introduced her. 'She's a director of the biggest reindeer collective farm in Semiransk, the *Komintern*. They had a board meeting today and the chairman decided she should stay and meet you.'

Katya Prokhorova was in her early thirties – the prime of life. She had Nanai cheekbones, black hair scraped against her head, a face that seemed set in a smile. An enamel badge on her lapel announced that she was a member of the Kalegut Municipal Council. Beneath it was another badge, which Renard recognized as the Order of Lenin.

Fillipov put the hand of the Nanai goddess in his. 'Katya is a dear friend.' Then he indicated the man who had previously been talking with Tomas Kavtoradze, 'And this is Mikhail Leshkin – our oceanographer.

He's the only man in our circle who has actually been inside Molniya and who knows something of its layout.'

Leshkin bowed to the newcomers. He was the blond-haired, blue-eyed type of Russian, young, strong, honest-looking. Renard shook his hand.

'We're waiting for one other person, but we'll start anyhow – he must be delayed,' Fillipov said as he led them to a long table where women in Nanai dress filled glasses. While they ladled out portions, Renard said to Father Pyotr, 'I never did hear the end of your story, by the way . . . About Lenin and the bottle of vodka?'

'Ah! That! Lenin, Stalin and Trotsky are on a desert island,' Father Pyotr said at once. 'And there's no corkscrew. Lenin places the bottle in the sand and stares intently at it for a while, until Trotsky says, "Why are you doing that, Vladimir Ilyich?" So Lenin says, "I'm opening the bottle by means of an act of the Revolutionary will."

'"Pure voluntarism," Trotsky says. "That'll never work. What you've got to do is to *imagine a corkscrew.*"

'"Rubbish!" says Stalin, who jumps up and grabs the bottle in his good hand—'

'This is *yushka*,' Fillipov interrupted in a loud voice. 'Fish soup, Nanai-style. We should drink to it, friends.'

'Good for your sex life,' Tomas said, winking at the Nanai women. He made a toast in praise of good fish soup.

Renard shook his head, succumbing to the feeling of unreality which had been growing since jumping from the plane. Sitting next to him, Katya laughed and said, 'Here, try this product of our polar nature.' She heaped caviar on to his plate. It came from beluga caught in the mouth of the Ob; the grains were huge, soft and separate. 'At least this is pure,' she told him, 'but we have so much pollution, nothing is as it was.'

It was delicious, the best he'd ever tasted, Renard told her.

She looked seriously at him. 'I have no children, because I never got married. But I have three sisters, who've produced eight kids between them. They live much further south, in the oil-producing regions. One was born without eyes, ears or nose. He lived for five months. Three others were born disfigured in some way. Another of my nieces is in Varta General Hospital just now, dying of leukaemia.

'Our people are dying, our wildlife is poisoned. The whole of the Arctic North is dying. I see it every day. I think the Nanai are already doomed. But enough is enough; now we are going to *do* something. And you, Mr Renard, arrived like the warrior in the fairy tale, to help us.'

'Well, that's some fairy tale, but I hope you're right,' Renard told her.

'And I do understand your environmental problems. Unfortunately they're not unique to the Arctic.'

Renard looked round the table at the force which would soon take on the pride of the Russian armed services. The discussion had moved several bottles on from toasts in praise of boiled fish soup and, thus fortified, the team were considering whether the concept of private property can exist under socialism. Renard tried to catch Father Pyotr's eye. The priest had drifted in and out of the conversation and now stared fixedly at a point behind Renard's shoulder, one immobile hand clutching a full glass of *Limonnaya*. Renard leaned over and said: 'So what *did* Stalin do next, then?'

Father Pyotr gazed dreamily at him. 'Stalin?' he enquired. 'When?'

'With the one bottle of vodka.'

'Ah! And the railway train.'

'What railway train? They were on a desert island, and—'

'No, no, not at all.' The priest replaced his glass as carefully as if it were a Fabergé egg and pointed a stubby finger at Renard. 'Lenin, Stalin and Brezhnev are sitting in a railway train when it stops unexpectedly.'

'Trotsky. Not Brezhnev. *Trotsky*.'

The priest looked puzzled. 'No, the way I heard, it was Brezhnev. The conductor comes and tells them that the engine has broken down. Lenin wants to disembark all the passengers, and have them push the train to start it. So everyone gets off and tries to push, but it's no good . . .'

Renard leant forward to hear, but the priest did not speak again. He was catatonic.

Sasonov's voice piped up: '*I'll* tell you what happened. Then Stalin says, "I know what to do, Ilyich," and he disappears to the front of the train. They hear the sound of a shot and after a while Stalin returns looking very satisfied. "What have you done?" Lenin asks. "Shot the driver, obviously," Stalin says. He sits down and they wait but still the train doesn't start.

'"Now what?" Lenin says.

'"I know!" Brezhnev says. He goes to the window and closes the curtains. Then he sits down and opens a bottle of vodka. "Let us *pretend* the train is moving."'

CHAPTER 18

Mikhail Leshkin shoved a pencil across a point on the Soviet Admiralty chart he had spread on the table. It showed a corner of the Semiransk peninsula.

It was early next morning, before dawn – if day could ever really be said to break the polar night.

'Here where I've pencilled a cross: this is Molniya. The site of the base is on the intersection of two submarine contour lines. Molniya is lying in a trough; to the south is the shelf which forms the bed of the Bay of Ukotsk. In places it's very shallow: twenty to fifty metres. To the north, the sea floor rises again slightly, reaches the incline here—'

Leshkin pencilled a line.

'—and then falls away sharply.'

'Tell me about the crew,' Renard said.

'Molniya has a permanent crew of four hundred and fifty; they're almost all officers formerly of the Soviet submarine service.'

'*All* officers?' Renard asked.

'There are no true ratings on Molniya. The lowest rank is a naval lieutenant; on Molniya that would class as a rating, no higher. If and when you get to board Molniya you should remember this: *nothing and no one will be what they seem.*'

Fillipov clarified, 'Molniya also has a detachment of marines: one hundred and twenty men, all drawn from elite units. It's highly self-supporting, generating all its energy, oxygen and fresh water. It's powered by a two thousand megawatt nuclear generator, an astonishing feat of downsizing by the Urals engine fabricators.'

Renard said, 'But that still doesn't seem like much power for a device like Molniya. EMP radiation of the intensity required would need the equivalent of H-bomb explosions. So where's the power coming from?'

'Well, Molniya's energy release is channelled along certain directions and in certain wavelengths. Molniya waves can traverse the earth, they can even be held stationary, like a panther silently waiting. No energy is used until the selected target is struck. The operator can cause Molniya

256

to blanket out incoming missiles: or to black out whole cities on the other side of the earth. It *is* a truly terrifying blackmail weapon.'

'How do the metacodes fit in?'

'They control Molniya's operational parameters. The heart of the system is the four Cray supercomputers in two parallel systems, one for backup, which are located in the Molniya installation. They're probably the world's first Cray computers to be fully operational on the Arctic seabed. I've no doubt that the manufacturer would be delighted to hear of this success! And the whole Molniya system has massive built-in redundancy; like the human body, there's mostly two of everything. No expense was spared to safeguard the weapon.

'Molniya needs massive processing power, because it depends upon the successful interpretation of meteorological data. This kind of data requires phenomenal number-crunching power. Without it, Molniya would still work. But it would be a wild, uncontrolled beast. The problem has always been to control and direct the EMP pulse-radiation it generates. It's taken a lot of trial and error to get this right.

'Incidentally, the whole nuclear-winter scenario was a by-product of this research. In the 1980s Soviet scientists were spending a great deal of time on the generation of functional meteorological models, which could accurately predict weather patterns. It was all done for Molniya. Nobody before had tried to produce a model of the world's weather in the aftermath of a nuclear war. But in the course of research to find out how better to deploy the Molniya weapon, they discovered what the worst consequence of nuclear war would really be: something even surpassing the long-term effects of radioactive fall-out on the biosphere. Namely a "nuclear winter" of permanent darkness; meaning cold, hunger and death. That changed everyone's thoughts about the idea of nuclear war.'

'So there was at least one beneficial by-product of the Molniya research,' said Zidra.

'You could say that. But it didn't deter Alfredo Sakharinov; on the contrary, it encouraged his mad schemes. The more unreal and suicidal nuclear war came to seem, the more invulnerable and potent Molniya seemed. As an alternative to nuclear war, it's superb: there are no explosions, there's no fall-out, and, of course, no nuclear winter. It gives its possessor the power to switch the lights on and off at will, and that's about all. But it's enough for any side that has a monopoly on the weapon.'

Renard then asked how the security systems worked and learnt that for practical purposes Molniya was tamper-proof. And too well defended to succumb to torpedo attack.

'Then how do we destroy the damn thing?' Renard asked. 'What's this mysterious "long shot" option that was mentioned last night?'

'Yes, tell us, Mikhail,' Zidra said.

'Well . . . it boils down to the fact that the EMP waves are propagated using an array of remote transmitters, which are attached to submarine buoys and spread out in a pattern over the seabed. Theoretically, it is possible to *reverse* the action of the Molniya generator. Energy would be drained out of the Arctic waters and focused back on to Molniya. The Barents Sea might freeze; I'm not sure what would happen to Molniya itself, though. It might blow up, or there might be a meltdown which could boil off the Arctic. Or perhaps ignite the gas reservoirs under Semiransk peninsula.'

'That wouldn't help much!'

'*Or* . . .'

'Go on, this is better than the movies.'

'Or the reversal of Molniya's polarity might freeze the seas locally, but not in a way which produces normal ice. The effect might be allotropic; you'd end up with molten ice, which could be very cold indeed – 160, 170 or more, degrees below freezing. But the ice would flow, it would remain semi-liquid. If the effect was very localized, you'd end up with a virtual chain-reaction, but in reverse; energy would be continuously drained from the surrounding ocean, but ice would flow around Molniya and cool it down sufficiently to prevent a catastrophe. The allotropic ice might in turn recirculate sufficient energy to the water to create some form of stabilized lower temperature range. There would be a feed-back loop which would perpetuate itself, at least until someone switched Molniya off. Except that if the control centre was flooded, it might be impossible to switch it off. Picture a vessel entombed in a bed of constantly circulating molten ice, through which access would be impossible.'

Leshkin studied Renard's face. 'Just speculation,' he added.

'Speculate some more.'

'Well, it might be possible to reverse such a negative chain-reaction, if the crew had not lost control. In that case, the whole process would continue until aborted by a catastrophic failure of the Molniya systems.'

'Then what?' Zidra asked.

'Then the feedback loop would break; the surrounding ice might undergo a further allotropic change and instantly solidify. This would leave the vessel encased in tens, hundreds of millions of tons of supercold ice which might take months or years to disperse.'

'Of course, no one knows if this is what would really happen,' Renard objected. 'You're talking of initiating a meltdown, with the possibility of *unpredictable* secondary consequences being triggered within the Arctic environment.'

'Or nothing at all might happen?'

'Or nothing at all might happen. Indeed.'

Zidra found her voice and told them they needed to move on. 'You have your own link with the CIA. How does it work? By direct transmission?'

Fillipov answered that one. 'We were supplied with a special low-power short-wave transmitter. I believe the messages are relayed from a listening post in western China.'

Renard said, 'It seems a bit back-to-front, doing it that way. We need to contact Paul Gregory direct.' He checked his watch; it was five past three in the morning, local time. 'In just sixteen hours, that's three o'clock Moscow time, seven in the evening in Semiransk, Alfredo Sakharinov will be on his feet announcing his new programme for the salvation of Russia, blaming the West for all Russia's woes. He'll say the CIA assassinated the Russian President, and he'll announce the existence of Molniya. And at exactly the same time, just to show he's not kidding, Molniya will be demonstrated to the world . . . *Like hell it will.*'

Zidra said, 'Yuri Andreevich, the time has come. Let us now make the final decisions.'

It was already past nine in the morning when they finished their preparations.

Zidra and Renard put their coats on and went outside for some fresh air. The sky had cleared and Renard said he wanted to see the polar night.

'Come with me,' said Fillipov, leading them to the end of the street where, facing east, a vast glittering snowscape opened out before them. And over it a huge moon poured its pale light.

They watched in silence as a coral pink line was pencilled on to the horizon.

Zidra turned to Renard, 'You see, even in the polar night, there is a dawn. But there's no day. When the moon sets, it grows dark again.'

The pink deepened to a scarlet which inflamed the stubby trees and the steel-grey rocky outcrops which broke up the vast, empty land. But in a few minutes the reds began to leach away again, melding into a pink-grey twilight, which deepened as the moon sank and disappeared.

They retraced their steps to The Pearl. The two Nanai serving women had anticipated them and a breakfast was prepared.

As they were finishing, Sasonov came in, his face red with cold. He dumped a military kit bag on the floor.

'I've done it; everything is here.' He indicated the bag. 'But do I have news for you! Ivanov was dead tricky. Evidently he's been sheltering Sergei Sakharinov at the Semiransk base. Now I understand why he was so nervous yesterday. At the very time when Kavtoradze appeared, Ivanov was rounding up all Medved's men at the base. This morning there was a hell of a shoot-out, and at least half the base is now in the hands of Medved's troops. Medved himself has landed, and troop transports are flying in thousands of men . . .'

Renard looked shell-shocked. 'So where's Sergei now?'

'Gone to Molniya! He's probably already aboard.'

'But whoever controls Molniya will win Russia. If Sergei's there—' Renard suddenly sounded short of breath.

'Yes but it depends on whether the Molniya systems will respond to him or not.'

'Well, which outcome is better?' Zidra asked. 'We can't leave it in the hands of either Zamok's gang or of Alfredo Sakharinov.' She, too, spoke tersely.

'We have to get to Maly Utinsk, coastal support base for Molniya.'

'There must be planes at Kalegut airstrip?' Zidra asked.

'They'll shoot us down,' Sasonov said.

'We have to get to Maly Utinsk,' Renard repeated. 'There's no alternative.' He read aloud the message on the slip of listing paper Sasonov had just given him. It was the answer from Paul Gregory to the signals they'd sent on an American radio set in the early hours: *Herewith the recycled numbers. Nashville is down and out. You are on your own. Try to hack your way into the system – or something. Good luck. We have no other recourse but you. Our fingers are crossed. Paul.* Mikhail Leshkin had worked with Sasonov through the night: they had succeeded in downloading the Molniya subroutines prepared in Langley. With the note had come a read-write CD.

'I don't know if it will work, of course,' Leshkin said. 'But I do know how to load it – assuming we can get anywhere near the Molniya control centre – and can then persuade Sergei Sakharinov to press the button which will accept only his fingerprint.'

'And if we hacked our way in, as Gregory suggests?'

'Forget it. The Molniya system defences are impregnable. Long before I found any passwords, they'd have a truckload of troops knocking on my door. And we'd all be living or dying in Alfredo's brave new world.'

260

'And if we do manage to load the disk? Is there any way out of Molniya?'

'You mean, how do we escape before it turns into an iceberg? I've been thinking about that. I don't see how we can all leave, that's if any of us is still alive by then. Someone will have to stay; more than one person.'

'OK, we'll cross that bridge when we come to it.' Renard turned to Sasonov. 'Are your Nanai friends ready?'

Sasonov smiled. From his bag he took a small box and presented it to Renard. 'It's a token of friendship,' he said.

Renard opened the box. Inside it was an ivory carving, depicting Nanai fishermen canoeing through stormy seas.

'Come; they're waiting for us. We knew it would be this way – one day.' He slapped Renard on the shoulder, and raising his voice, exhorted everyone present: 'Let's go! There's not much time.'

Outside The Pearl a Latvian-made RAF microbus was waiting, engine running. Leshkin would go with Sasonov, Zidra and Renard. Fillipov would stay behind. 'I'll slow you down,' he had said. 'You don't need any passengers.'

Renard still wondered about Fillipov, and which masters he truly served. But if he was a traitor, then so was Sasonov; so were all of them, and he and Zidra were already dead in that case . . .

As the *Rafik* lurched through the rutted road out of Kalegut, Sasonov spread his chart over the microbus's small table.

'You see here, where I've pencilled in the extent of the ice-cover.' His stubby finger described an arc over the map. 'The Gulf Stream keeps a narrow strip of coastal waters ice-free most of the year, but within the Bay of Ukotsk the sea is completely frozen over from November to March. The small naval facility in Maly Utinsk is unmarked on the chart, of course. A concrete jetty and enclosed harbour has been constructed – a very simple affair, as you'll soon see. From there, the channel has been dredged so that lighters can go in and out.'

'How is the channel kept ice free?' Renard asked, but just then there was a beeping sound, and Sasonov pulled a walkie-talkie from his rucksack. The conversation was in the Nanai language; when it was finished he said: 'We're in luck! Sergei Sakharinov is late as well; his party still hasn't left Semiransk base. But we've a long way to go – it'll take at least three hours to get there.'

Once clear of Kalegut the way improved. They passed through a vast and desolate landscape and there were few road markers, but the driver, a cheerful Nanai with teeth like piano keys, never hesitated and never needed to consult a map. They continued for nearly two hours until a squelching sound from the rear and a sudden lurch indicated that a wheel had been punctured. The driver and Leshkin had to leap from the *Rafik*. Their jack worked despite the cold, but when they began unbolting the wheel, first one and then another bolt simply sheared off.

'It's the cold,' Leshkin said. 'It makes the steel brittle.'

It was minus 40 outside; they had travelled over 100 kilometres north of the Arctic Circle. The grey twilight of Kalegut had deepened into deep violet. The sky was cloudless, the air still. 'Not good,' Sasonov said. 'The weather is turning.'

The driver took a gasoline-soaked cloth and lit it under the wheel. In five more minutes the wheel was changed. 'We were in too much of a hurry,' Sasonov said. 'But don't worry; there are three more bolts.'

They set off again, and Sasonov began talking urgently on the walkie-talkie, reporting back to his companions, 'Medved's left Semiransk by helicopter. He'll be at the Maly Utinsk port in an hour. From there he'll be taken by boat to meet the submarine which will convey him to Molniya.'

'Why don't they fly out and land on the ice?'

'We don't know; probably the ice is unsafe after all their recent activity. At any rate, it greatly simplifies matters for us.'

The *Rafik* ground on through the Arctic night, more slowly than before.

Sasonov said to Renard, 'You were asking about ice clearance. First of all, the traffic is constant, and all these vessels are double-hulled, ice-class ships. Secondly, there's an icebreaker. The channel runs to a rendezvous-point out in the bay, where the water's deep enough for the Delta-class boats to come in for supplies and personnel. That's how the system works.'

'We've monitored all that traffic over time, of course,' Renard said. 'But it didn't help us locate Molniya.'

'No. Molniya is nearly fifty kilometres away from the pick-up point. That would give your surveillance people a lot of seabed to cover. But you must admit, our Soviet science was clever! We managed to hide two hulls the size of ocean liners on the seabed and you didn't notice!'

Renard leaned over Zidra who was facing the window and watched the yellow stars which danced low over the horizon. As the stars danced closer and turned into lights, he sat up, his hands propping Zidra – who was asleep – holding her between the crook of her arms and the soft warmth of her breast.

'Zidra, wake up,' he whispered urgently as the *Rafik* suddenly jerked to a halt. Sasonov was shouting and jabbing them both. Outside black shapes crystallized from the murk of the polar night – one, two, three or more pairs of lights that circled the *Rafik* and disappeared then reappeared.

Then their side door crashed open and Renard heard voices, and the whinny of animals, the bark of dogs.

'Quickly! Let's go! General Medved's at Maly Utinsk already – there's no time to delay!'

They tumbled out, found teams of reindeer right in front of them, steaming despite the intense cold, hitched to sleighs. Katya Prokhorova embraced Renard and Zidra.

'This is the only way to get to where we're going,' she told them.

They bundled on board and Katya threw them piles of skins and leapt up, seizing the reins and whistling to the animals, her eyes shining.

'Today we'll settle some old scores!' she cried.

Renard looked around and saw other sleighs, as many as ten or twelve, some drawn by dog teams, others by reindeer. Silhouettes solidified from within the gloom and he briefly saw the pale, strong face of a Nanai man in the light of a yellow lamp. There were perhaps fifty people, or more; amidst shouts and halloos they all mounted their sleighs and suddenly the whole convoy moved off, a skein of dancing lights and jingling brass bells.

'They are called *Valdai* bells, Mr Renard,' Kayta cried to him. 'No others make such a glorious sound. Whenever I have to go away, I hear them in my dreams.'

The reindeer cantered through the snow and the hiss of the runners filled the air. Renard sat back and gazed up at the indigo sky studded with diamonds like a jeweller's cushion, and experienced a pure delight. The sleigh swerved and spun and raced through the frozen tundra.

After nearly an hour of running in this way, the convoy slowed and the drivers had to pick their way through a land of spiky boulders, treacherous drifts and great shards of ice.

'We're near the bay,' Sasonov, who was sitting directly behind Renard, said in his ear. 'We'll go out on to the ice – it isn't safe but we have no choice.'

The convoy of sleds slowed still more and they slithered and slewed down a short slope, at the bottom of which lay the vast sheet of ice which was the Bay of Ukotsk. There was still no moon but the stars were brilliant and they could see the dim shapes of great shafts of ice, upreared like giant crystals through the frozen surface of the Bay.

After twenty minutes of cautious progress, they saw more lights, which resolved into hurricane lamps. They stopped. A challenge whispered hoarsely across the ice – then ten or fifteen men emerged from within the ice field. Sasonov embraced two of them and there was an exchange of hurried whispers.

Sasonov said: 'These are my brothers. They have done as we asked. But we must hurry; Medved's boats have already left the port at Maly Utinsk. You can see their lights – look!'

A necklace of navigation lights bobbed on the distant water.

'What the fuck's he planning?' Renard whispered. 'How many troops can he hope to get on one small submarine?'

'He'll try to create a beachhead on Molniya and ferry down his reserves.'

'Is he in the lead boat or what?'

Sasonov, face bright from the cold, was straining to see through his night-glasses. 'Almost certainly. It makes no difference, anyway, because that's the boat we'll take.' He spoke ominously.

They looked at each other. The moment had come. They parted with Katya, shook hands silently and set off towards the lights. Soon they could hear the sucking, slopping sound of open water, and the ice underfoot began to crack like a whip. Then they could see water; oily, black, viscid. A way had been cut through the ice, no more than ten metres across; it ran like a black ribbon, back towards the shore, and out into the Arctic.

Sasonov gripped Renard's shoulder. 'The submarine is waiting five kilometres out; that's the nearest it can approach – the bay is so shallow. We're going to create a small diversion behind the lighter; but first you and I must take a canoe ride.' He pointed and for the first time, Renard saw the indistinct shapes of several boats, very near but so low in the water that the surface of the ice-sheet was a metre above them.

Zidra said to Renard, 'Just don't try to go without me. I'll shoot you.'

Renard exclaimed and told Sasonov, 'Find a place for Zidra Latsis, or I'm a dead man.'

Sasonov gave them an inscrutable smile. He was excited, like an animal which has scented spoor. But his movements showed something else: a stillness which went beyond all emotion. He pointed at Zidra and said, 'She's too good for you, American! I ought to take her myself.'

Zidra and Renard clambered into the nearest boat; it was little more than a coracle made of reindeer skins and whalebone. A Nanai oarsman aided Sasonov into a neighbouring vessel in which Mikhail Leshkin was already installed. The instant they were all aboard, the crews wrenched their mooring pins out of the ice and dug their paddles into the foaming water.

Renard held Zidra's hand. It trembled violently. 'It's the cold, that's all,' she said. 'Though I'm not saying I wouldn't dearly love to know what the hell we're supposed to do next.' As she spoke, they began to hear the regular beat of a ship's propeller and the thump of marine diesels running at low speed.

'Keep the floppy dry, that's all,' Renard said.

'Don't worry; it's in a safe place – next to my . . .'

Her words died to silence as they saw the silhouette of a boat inching down on them. Immediately a vast sheet of flame erupted on the waterway behind them. The fire swept backwards in a ribbon of fierce orange and red, racing hundreds of metres towards the doomed string of boats behind.

In front of the inferno the boat which was carrying General Medved to his rendezvous with the submarine lunged ahead. They could hear its engines scream in frenzy as it struggled free of the flames. And starkly silhouetted in those flames they saw figures running on the bridge. This boat bore down on them, its engines straining to carry it out of reach of the engulfing flames, its searchlight carving a white slice out of the Arctic gloom. The little coracle tossed and plunged in the wash of its bow-wave.

CHAPTER 19

The lighter continued to surge down on the canoes, its propellers thrashing wildly. The bowman in Renard's boat stood up and as the wall of water crashed around them, throwing them back on the ice-shelf, his body flexed and moved with the action. Renard saw him throw their anchor-line upwards, saw it crash down on the lighter's deck rail. He also had a momentary glimpse of the lighter's bridge: the men were leaping from the companion ways and running aft, and he could see their forms against the crimson backdrop. Behind them the waterway was a sheet of fire, seemingly born out of the teeth of ice which studded the bay in jagged clumps on either side.

As the anchor-line tautened, the canoe leapt forward and tons of black, freezing water crashed down on them. The rope held, and the canoe leapt up like a salmon on a line. The Nanai fisherman in the rear of the canoe swung up, catapulting across the side and up over the lighter's deck rail; then he was reaching down to help Renard and Zidra up.

Zidra missed the guide-rail when she stood up, and collapsed, doubled up, her head out of the canoe and under the water streaming past. The bowman reached for her, his body like a sine-wave that flowed in mathematic unity with the motion of the coracle, the passing sea, the surging lighter. He leaned back over Renard and, grabbing the hood of the reindeer-skin coat Zidra was wearing, pulled her head and shoulders from the roaring sea. She reared up, gagging and spluttering, and the Nanai boatman on the lighter heaved her over the deck rails. She disappeared from view and Renard leapt up after her, but as he did so the canoe disappeared beneath him, sucked down in the backwash of the lighter.

He, too, missed the deck-rail, the canoe danced away from under him, and he crashed down into the water. Hands grasped his hair, gripped his head under the chin, and he saw propellers churning inches from his feet. Then, miraculously, his head came clear of the water, but there was not enough air left in the world to fill his lungs at that moment. Other hands grabbed him and, kicking like a new-born foal, he floundered down on to the deck of the lighter. Then Sasonov and Leshkin were there, their faces next to Renard's, Sasonov's black expressionless eyes interrogating his.

'The wheelman – *Go!*' Renard gasped, rolling over to his feet. Men were flashing past him – five, ten or more – he hadn't even seen their canoes, but there they were. He saw Zidra's face for a second, then the air was shattered by shots: two large-bore shotguns, a rattle of small-arms fire, and the sudden scream of dying men.

Hands grabbed him, helped him up. Nanai hands. They led him aft, and he was half dragged, half pushed up the steps to the wheelhouse. He stumbled through the door, and it was Sasonov, beaming for once, who pushed him down into the wheelman's revolving chair.

'You got a little damp,' Sasonov was saying. 'Better give me that coat – quickly!' Someone pulled the sodden reindeer skin coat off his back, and waved a bottle of *Sibirskaya* in front of him at just the right moment. He grabbed it and drank, feeling the fire race through him.

'Thanks! Sorry to be a burden to you guys.' He coughed and the taste of seawater filled his throat.

Zidra, who had just finished dragging on a new pair of heavy uniform trousers taken from one of Medved's guard, came over and kissed him, and helped him into a thick serge greatcoat. 'Now you are Captain,' she said. 'Which is as it should be. When you're ready, you can meet your guests. The survivors, anyway.'

Behind the lighter, the sheet of fire from 1500 gallons of gas condensate, laboriously dragged over the ice in 200-litre drums by Nanai men, and spread over the waterway, was burning itself out. The lighter's engines were cut to dead slow. Now it was inching through the ice. They saw from the bridge the searchlights of a helicopter, then another, which had been sent from the base.

Sasonov took a revolver to the chief officer's head who yelled into the ship-to-shore that they had accidentally dumped fuel overboard and it had ignited. The Maly Utinsk base commander told them to heave-to and wait for the helicopters, but Sasonov shook his head: they had to get to Molniya as soon as possible. Outside, the two helicopters circled around then suddenly left, heading back for Maly Utinsk.

'Who's dead and who's alive?' Renard asked Sasonov.

'There are fifteen of them left below decks. But there are more than fifty of us onboard now; so everything's under control.' His eyes were glittering.

'Dare I ask,' Renard said: 'Is Medved here?'

'He's in a master cabin below, with some of his officers.' Sasonov grinned. 'They've barricaded themselves in. We can just pop a grenade down a ventilator if you like.'

'No. We need the answers to some questions, Sasonov. We've no idea what's behind us *or* in front. Let's talk to the bastard.' He looked at Zidra. 'Let me meet him alone. Anything could happen. There's no need for him to know that you're here.'

The great green eyes shrouded for a moment, she shrugged infinitesimally and turned away. Renard snuggled into the officer's greatcoat she'd just given him and went below with Sasonov.

At the foot of the steps a narrow corridor led to a wooden door. Two more doors were on either side, only one of them open. Renard slipped on the blood pooling on the bottom step; a Nanai had been wounded and they had dragged him into the open cabin.

The corridor was full of Nanai men, shouting at each other and at Medved's men behind the locked door.

'Make them shut up and get in there,' Renard told Sasonov, pointing to the open cabin.

Sasonov began pushing and shoving at his men, ordering them to be quiet, levering them into the cabin.

'What's going on out there?' a voice called from behind the closed door, which had already been raked with machine-gun bullets from the inside. 'No tricks, or we'll sink this tub and take you with us, sonofbitch aborigines!'

Renard noted that the surface facing Medved's cabin was a thick steel bulkhead. If the barricaded men fired through the door again, the bullets would ricochet everywhere. In fact, the attackers were hardly less vulnerable than the defenders, and Medved could sortie out at any moment. That would be Renard's choice in the General's shoes.

'Get all your men upstairs,' Renard said loudly to Sasonov. 'If anyone but me comes up there, drop a grenade down; don't wait. Got that?'

Sasonov nodded. One by one his men filtered out of the cabin, leaving only Renard and the wounded Nanai who could not be moved.

Now Renard called out to Medved, softly at first. 'Come close to the door,' he said. 'Don't wet your pants, we're not going to kill you, unless you do anything stupid.'

There was silence, then he heard Medved laughing. 'So, it's you. *Amerikanets!* A real little Scarlet Pimpernel, aren't you? But you shouldn't have chanced your arm here. There's nowhere for you to go now, unless you plan to live among the polar bears. It's dead-end time. You should just go back to your nice America, and leave us alone.'

'You're going to be a bit dead-ended yourself, Vadim,' Renard said. 'If you don't co-operate. Whichever way you like it.'

Medved's laugh was gentle, schoolmasterly. 'There you are wrong, Mr Renard,' he whispered. 'You should show more respect. That's why you got into so many difficulties.' He began to sound plaintive. 'Think who I am, and think who you are, and be a little less foolish. You cannot possibly beat us, an anachronism like you.'

Renard was silent. Unfortunately he needed Medved alive in order to board Molniya. He could hear massed movement and whispering through the door. They were going to break out, Renard felt it.

'Where's your bitch? *I enjoyed having her,*' Medved now hissed. '*I think she enjoyed it too, in the end.*' From behind the door Medved made an obscene sucking noise. '*I made her do it, American. She liked that. She took it all in. Did she tell you?*' The sucking grew louder. '*I guess she didn't. She was afraid you'd be angry. But you were too busy running here and there when you should've been looking after her, weren't you?*'

Renard's eyes narrowed to slits. Nothing existed but the door and Medved's hissing drivel. The clattering engine, the shouts of the Nanai overhead, the viscous water slushing by the hull – all disappeared.

'Don't waste my time, Medved. I want you outta there now.'

'You left your Lisa, too – didn't you? Left her to die,' the voice whispered. 'You are *very* irresponsible, Douglas.'

The Makarov made a lot of noise. The bullets went high, at least six inches over Medved's head, so Renard hoped. The cumbersome handgun with its solid butt felt good in his hand.

Now the voice was rattled. 'I could develop a dislike for you, Renard,' it said angrily.

'Shut the fuck up, Medved! I'm going to count to three and then that door will be open and you'll be standing behind it, all of you, hands in the air. Otherwise you're gonna get grenades on your heads.' He shouted up the stairwell. '*Sasonov! Pull the pins!*'

Sasonov shouted 'OK!' back.

As Renard strained to hear behind it, suddenly the door was thrown open.

Renard called up to Sasonov again, who came at a run with five of his men and disarmed Medved and the four officers with him. They tied the General by his hands to a narrow central post in the cabin, and Renard ordered everyone but Sasonov out. The other officers were locked in the next-door cabin.

Renard stood in front of Medved and for the first time realized how short the man was – not more than five feet five inches, and of slender build. Medved looked up at him through wire-rimmed glasses, which were almost flat and reflected the light.

'Now what, now that you're the commander of the expedition?' he asked Renard. 'Ah! You've brought your plaything.'

Zidra had entered. 'I should do something to you only I don't want to stain my clothing,' she told him levelly. Even she was slightly taller than Medved, Renard noticed.

During this confrontation the lighter's double-skinned hull had begun scraping the ice as it crept forward through the gloom. But now there was silence. One of Sasonov's men came below and whispered something to him.

'We're in open water,' Sasonov announced. 'And the *Alexei Tolstoi* is hove-to and waiting for us. That's the Molniya support ship.'

Renard told him to send word back to the bridge to signal the captain of the *Alexei Tolstoi* to await further instructions before sending a boat across. He and Sasonov went on deck, leaving two men to guard Medved. Leshkin and Zidra joined them on the bridge, staring across at the other ship, which was dead in the water not fifty metres off.

Renard turned to Sasonov. 'Who told them to come over?' A tender had already pushed away and was coming towards them, the noise of its engine clearly audible through Arctic air as thick as custard. 'You'd better get your men organized.'

'No one told them, but don't worry, Mr Renard. We know what to do.'

The submarine's shore boat arrived and from along the deck came the sounds of ropes being cast, a greeting exchanged. A naval lieutenant appeared on the bridge, saluted Renard who happened to be wearing a senior officer's greatcoat, and said: 'Lieutenant Lebedev, sir. From the submarine *Alexei Tolstoi*.' He looked around curiously. 'We saw the fire; what's going on?'

Renard saluted him wearily. 'If you mean the fire allegedly caused by the negligence of Maly Utinsk personnel, we don't require assistance, as you see. But I suspect sabotage, and that concerns me far more. Your task now, Lebedev, is to ferry the Minister of Defence across to your vessel, under the command of Colonel Sasonov. Clear?'

'Yes, sir.' The lieutenant saluted again.

Some two hours later as Vadim Medved, the Russian Defence Minister, stepped gingerly on to the cowling around the *Alexei Tolstoi*'s floodlit conning tower, the strains of the Russian national anthem suddenly blared from a bullhorn. Captain Serov, the commander of the *Alexei*

Tolstoi, welcomed Medved and his aides aboard. As he had already welcomed Leshkin, Sasonov and all his men – including Zidra – on the three previous trips made by the lighter's tender.

'Forget the formalities,' one of Medved's officers told Captain Serov. 'Take us to your quarters. Now.'

Serov nodded and led the way. The officer introduced himself as General Melnikov, from Alfredo Sakharinov's personal staff. 'When do we reach the Molniya base?' he asked as they went down a gangway to Serov's cramped, dimly lit cabin.

'Within a couple of hours,' the captain replied.

As the others entered the captain's cabin, Melnikov motioned for the door to be closed behind them, leaving him alone in the passageway with Serov. 'You took the Prime Minister to Molniya earlier today?' he asked.

'Of course, yes, sir.'

'Under whose orders?'

Serov looked surprised. 'I was detailed by Maly Utinsk – is there a problem?'

'Have you heard nothing about events at Semiransk today?'

Serov shifted uncomfortably. 'There's been some talk, sir. But I've been on duty for thirty-six hours and I'm out of date.'

'The fact is that General Medved has been brought here under arrest. He's a state criminal, wanted for crimes committed against both private citizens and state bodies. He's a rapist, a mass killer, and worst of all – a traitor. I arrested him an hour ago for conspiring to assassinate the Russian President at the behest of the CIA.'

Serov was shocked. 'I was under the impression that General Medved was the most trusted co-worker of the new President—'

'So were we all,' Melnikov said. 'This sort of episode demonstrates the need for vigilance and more vigilance, Serov.'

'Yes, sir. But I shall need to verify—'

'You will. You must connect with the Prime Minister immediately. Today, Medved initiated insurrection at Semiransk, where order still hasn't been restored. Now we need to ensure that the same thing doesn't happen within Molniya itself. That would be a catastrophe. This can be the hour of our triumph – at last – over the Americans. But only if we stop Medved. I hope we can rely on you, Serov.'

'Absolutely, sir.'

'I do not doubt the loyalty of the Molniya base commander, Admiral Essen. However, let's take no chances. You, Serov, must now place yourself under my direct command. Give the order to take this boat

271

down to the Molniya base. But first of all – please connect me with Molniya.'

Serov, looking dazed, led the way to the communications room where he went to a keyboard on his desk and punched buttons. After a few seconds the pale, spotty face of a midshipman who had forgotten the meaning of sunlight appeared on a flat screen hung on one wall. '*Dispatcher*,' the boy said in bored tones. Serov ordered him to connect them with Sergei Sakharinov.

'He's in Admiral Essen's quarters,' the midshipman answered. 'Who wishes to speak with the Prime Minister, sir?'

'General Melnikov; the commander of his personal guard.'

'Admiral Essen is on the line, sir,' the dispatcher told him after a few moments. His voice was suddenly fearful. The screen cleared and then showed the face of a solid, middle-aged officer with admiral's epaulettes.

'That you, Serov?' Admiral Essen said. 'Who've you got there? The Prime Minister doesn't know any General Melnikov.'

Renard stood next to Serov so the admiral could see him. 'I am Melnikov, Nikolai Andreevich. Please tell the Prime Minister I have a tape for him from Ivars Shadrin.'

Sergei Sakharinov appeared at once. '*You!*' he hissed.

'I want a private talk. Ask Admiral Essen to leave, but first please confirm to Captain Serov here that you are expecting me.'

The screen went blank again for a few seconds, then Sergei reappeared. 'Serov? I wish to talk to, er, General Melnikov.'

Serov nodded to Renard. 'I'll be on the bridge,' he told him and left.

'I have General Medved with me,' Renard told Sakharinov.

'Are you crazy?'

'I'm giving you advance notice, your excellency, that's all. Please be sure to have us properly met when this boat docks. I bring new orders for you from our chief.'

Sergei Sakharinov's mouth opened and then snapped shut.

'You have a role to play, Sergei,' Renard said. 'You know what it is.'

This time, Sakharinov smirked back. 'We'll see about that. I shall be waiting for you.'

Renard laughed, shortly. 'Your brother trusts you – to be yourself. That's why he sent you here; to guarantee the integrity of Molniya. Only you can do that.'

Sakharinov gave a vicious look. 'You have to guarantee me,' he whispered. 'From *her*, I mean. I know these Balts.'

Renard snorted. '*I'm* your only guarantee.' And the screen went blank.

Renard went back to the bridge. 'Serov,' he said to the captain, 'you understand the significance of what I've told you, I hope.'

'I do, sir.'

'There must be no leakage. We're at a critical moment in the nation's fortunes. Talk of treason in high places can destroy morale. Can I rely on you?'

'Absolutely.'

'Now, where are we? Can you show me?'

Serov led Renard across to the command centre and flicked the screen to a display of the *Alexei Tolstoi*'s position relative to Molniya. In one corner a digital clock was counting down. The display showed two hours and 58 minutes.

'That's the countdown to A-Hour, the first attack-wave which will be on the eastern seaboard of the United States,' Serov told Renard.

The graphic displays showed Molniya's outlines in skeletal form – the two cigar-shaped hulls webbed together with a lattice of tubes, each hull with its various ports and docking bays. A cursor slowly traversed the screen towards Molniya.

'That's us?'

'Yes. You can see how big Molniya is by comparison. It's the size of two *Queen Marys*. Enormous.'

'How the devil did Russia accomplish such a thing? What a feat of engineering.'

'Molniya is basically two all-titanium *Typhoon*-class hulls; they were brought here separately and joined *in situ*. It is an astonishing achievement, sir; in my opinion, only the Russian defence industry can do such things.'

A second screen showed the view from a camera on the bow of the submarine. At first nothing could be seen but the grey wedge of the bow searchlights cutting into the gloom of the Arctic Ocean. Then, eventually, a necklace of points of light began to separate out, and then a second necklace. The huge bulk of Molniya solidified from the surrounding waters, its vast twin hulls illuminated on all sides with sodium flares.

'Christ! Makes it a bit noticeable, doesn't it?' Renard asked.

'That was General Medved's decision, sir. Perhaps now I understand why.'

A docking bay swam into view, its great ports swinging apart as they approached, like a giant mouth opening.

'Like Jonah and the whale,' Renard observed. 'I suppose everyone says that the first time they see it.'

'Only the more religious among us, sir.'

The buzz of routine commands given and repeated grew louder, as the crew of the *Alexei Tolstoi* talked their boat into the cavernous maw of Molniya's entry port. A series of deafening clangs resonated through the hull as she scraped through the entry and bumped the sides of the internal dock.

Sasonov came to Serov's quarters to tell Renard in a whisper that the augmented guard was ready. There were now more than sixty of them, with only two tasks. Get Sergei Sakharinov to the Molniya command centre alive. And secure Medved.

Captain Serov returned to the bridge to oversee the final docking procedure. The entry doors groaned and clanged shut behind the *Alexei Tolstoi*. Arctic water stormed out of the hold under pressure and in minutes the port was empty. The hull of the submarine clanked against the side of the chamber while the docking crew secured the boat. There was a hiss of air as hatches opened and the party made ready to board Molniya. As they clambered down from the submarine, Medved winced visibly and hunched deeper into his greatcoat when Sasonov's men supported him off the submarine.

The adjutant, sent by Admiral Essen to meet them, led them through the massive doors of the airlock, which were forged of titanium and designed to withstand the colossal pressures in the depths of the Arctic Ocean. Beyond the doors, he turned to the left and placed his palm over the sensor on the doors of a lift. They were swept four floors up into the base, coming out into an area guarded by marines. Double doors sliced apart and they marched into Admiral Essen's vast quarters, sumptuously over-decorated with heavy leather-bound furniture, aspidistras on mahogany stands and large oil paintings depicting naval battles in the age of sail.

'Medved will be punished for his treason,' Sergei was saying to the Admiral as they came in. 'I just hope his views haven't affected morale at this base as they did at Semiransk.'

'They have not,' Essen said, his voice trembling with anger. 'But you certainly told me a strange tale today.'

Both men turned to greet the newcomers. Renard saluted the Prime Minister and the Admiral, and immediately requested a private talk with the Prime Minister, which Sergei Sakharinov acceded to with a nod. Admiral Essen and his adjutant left them to it.

Having watched Sakharinov motion with his eyes to the ceiling, Renard led him over to the corner of the room where he'd noticed a water cooler standing beside a large *Oka* refrigerator. He opened the door, leaving a small space for them to crouch in.

'What's the guarantee?' Sakharinov began in a fierce whisper.

Renard gave it to him straight. 'You'll be protected, given political asylum and preserved from any harassment. You know perfectly well that it's not in our interests to renege on our pledges. I'll see that no ancient feuds follow you to the States. But now, I *have* to know how Molniya works.'

Sergei shook his head hopelessly. 'Every thirty minutes,' he mumbled, 'I have to be there.'

'What?'

'I have to put my head in the helmet-thing. Stupid, isn't it? But that was the best they could devise. Then my brother suddenly appears in front of me – we're in the same room.' His hands clenched till the colour leached from the knuckles. 'As if he's sitting in my own head.' His head slewed from side to side. 'God, how I hate that helmet!'

'So the machine's fail-safe system checks whether you're physically present, while the weapon is operating?'

'Yes. Every thirty bloody minutes.' He said it like a refrain, giving the feel of being in thrall to something oppressive, something that had come to rule his life.

'What happens if you're caught short or something? Does Molniya just abort its operations?'

Sakharinov grinned. 'Is Armageddon delayed while I go to the toilet? No, it's not like that. It's not like bombs going off. More gradual. You close down cities, sort of in waves. It takes time.'

'And your brother appears?'

'Yes. Suddenly. It's always a shock. I think it's because he's watching everything, so he chooses the moment. Dialogue is possible, but he can't control Molniya from Moscow. Not yet. So he just haunts the controller instead.' He grimaced.

'Why?'

'To check that everything's done according to his orders. There's no one else he can trust. Only me.

'Zamok's people have got control of Semiransk – for now. We'll see what tomorrow brings. I guess that my brother's mobilizing the army wherever he can. Tonight, either he or Zamok will win. Or,' he hesitated, '. . . a civil war will begin in Russia.'

'Maybe it has begun.'

'Well, of course it has. But the winner will be whoever gets control of Molniya. That's why Medved came rushing over to it. Of course he needs me – you all need *me*, don't you? Both my brother and Zamok will only keep me alive until I've given over control of Molniya to someone else. And that's why I need you, unfortunately.'

'Let's finish this business while we have time, Sergei.'

The two men stood up and returned to the Admiral's state quarters.

Zidra was now standing inside, having boarded with Sasonov's forces, holding Medved from behind. She pushed him until he stood in front of Sergei Sakharinov, hands tied behind his back, face livid with fear. 'They are planning to shoot me,' he whispered. 'You can't permit this. I'm still Minister of Defence.'

'Stop whining, Medved,' Zidra told him. 'Be a man, face facts.'

Medved's eyes opened wide. 'You see how they speak to me! This woman openly tells me I'm a dead man.' He began to hiss incoherently.

Sakharinov was unresponsive so Medved turned to Admiral Essen. 'Is this reasonable, Admiral? Have them untie me, at least.' He groaned aloud. 'Where is the dignity of the Russian armed forces, when such things are possible?'

The Admiral went puce. 'Sir, I cannot accept the necessity for this,' he said to Sergei Sakharinov. 'What possible grounds can there be for this treatment of someone accused, but not yet judged, and who occupies such a high position? What are we coming to?' Without waiting for an answer he stepped forward and, pulling a Swiss army knife from his pocket, cut off the nylon twine round Medved's wrists.

Medved thanked the Admiral. 'I see not all of Russia has lost its senses. But Admiral, there is something I must say to you alone. I cannot speak in front of these people.' He stopped in horror when Zidra stepped towards him, then whispered, '*She is going to kill me! Save me, Admiral!*'

Essen stepped between them and said in perfect seriousness, 'Please, Madam, do not intimidate General Medved.'

'Look,' Renard said at once. 'The fact is that events in the past two days have unhinged him completely. He's convinced, for example, that I'm an American spy. You can't allow him to have any contact with your personnel in this condition. I suggest he remains here under guard.'

Medved grew frantic. '*Do not leave me with these people!*' he implored Admiral Essen.

'Shut it, Medved!' Sergei Sakharinov snapped, speaking for the first time in his presence. 'You are a traitor, and the inevitable punishment awaits you. Admiral, see that the outer doors are guarded and let's be going.'

'Very well.' Admiral Essen gestured to two of Sasonov's men who pushed Medved forward and led him away towards an inner cabinet that could be locked.

'Sergei! You'll pay, you'll pay!' they heard him shout as the door slid to behind him.

'The General is convinced that I'm organizing a campaign against my brother,' Sergei Sakharinov told the Admiral.

'Ye Gods! Thank the Lord I'm safe down here at the bottom of the Arctic!' came the response.

'Essen, I want to introduce you to Mikhail Leshkin and his female colleague. They are programmers who have recently completed a study of parallel processing with Cray computers. They will install the new targeting instructions.' Sergei was at his most gracious.

'Ah! We were expecting you. You've come to help interface the new Moscow AlphaScan centre? Alfredo Sakharinov warned me to expect someone.' He indicated the big green digital display on the wall behind his desk. It showed fifty-four minutes. 'As you see, Prime Minister, the countdown to Alpha-Hour is proceeding and if software changes are to be made they must be made now.'

'In that case I suggest you have someone take Leshkin and his aide to the operational centre. They need to begin. And please send the commander of my personal guard, Colonel Sasonov, to me at once.'

Essen duly rang for an adjutant to take Leshkin and Zidra to meet the Molniya programmers. When Sasonov arrived with five of his number, Renard looked a question at him; he nodded affirmatively. It meant that the *Alexei Tolstoi* was secured. With the help of Captain Serov he had placed his men at key points between the docking bays, and the heart of the Molniya complex where the operations centres were located. Once he'd established this crucial fact, Renard made a show of conferring with him over staff matters, and then let Sasonov go back to the bowels of Molniya.

Meanwhile Sergei Sakharinov had switched on the television set placed in a wall unit near Admiral Essen's desk. The scenes in the Kremlin as Alfredo Sakharinov prepared to make his historic broadcast to the nation were being shown. The picture cut to the Duma and an interviewer asked a senior aide of Dmitry Zamok to comment on the apparent absence from Moscow of the Prime Minister, Sergei Sakharinov, and the rumours of troop movements near the Duma building.

She was told, 'The Nationalists led by Dmitry Zamok do not believe that Alfredo Sakharinov has any right to assume the Russian Presidency. We want new elections, and in the meantime the country should be ruled by the Duma. We believe that the Prime Minister shares this view.'

Recollecting the requirements of protocol, Admiral Essen offered refreshments to his guests. 'We shall have to put the countdown on hold in any case,' he told Sakharinov, 'until the new targets are programmed into the system, which may take time.' He sent an orderly to fetch drinks and sandwiches.

Sakharinov had switched from Channel One, the official Russian network, to CNN. It too was showing scenes from the Russian Duma. The announcer, his words simultaneously translated into Russian, was reporting on feverish speculation about an imminent anti-Sakharinov coup – which it was rumoured would sweep Dmitry Zamok into power. Admiral Essen looked curiously at Sakharinov's expression, waiting for a cue to guide his own response. But Sakharinov was expressionless.

A big monitor hung on the wall by the table. As if the mounting drama in the Duma held no interest for him, Sakharinov switched off the television and asked Admiral Essen to interpret the data displayed on the monitor.

'It repeats the status screens in the command centre,' Essen said. He clicked some buttons on a remote controller and a succession of status reports flashed up. 'These show various readiness states. The clock in the top right-hand corner shows the countdown.'

He pointed a laser remote controller at the screen. The icon it touched zoomed out into a giant world map, across which cloud formations and the movement of various weather fronts were superimposed.

'Current global meteorological data,' he explained. 'Conditions are extremely favourable for the execution of the attack plan. Everything is going like clockwork,' the Admiral was rubbing his hands.

'Can you show more detail? Of what will happen at A-Hour?'

For answer the Admiral touched the screen again. The display changed to a map of the Western hemisphere.

'It will be the most devastating surprise attack in the history of warfare. Devastating not in terms of physical destruction, of course – that will be minimal. From our enemies' point of view, Molniya will look like a visitation by a superior civilization. It's the fifth horseman of the apocalypse. The West will be our plaything – helpless, paralysed. It's going to make Hitler's attack on Russia in 1941 look like a nursery game. Three successive strokes will overwhelm the Western heartlands completely. The war will be over in twenty-four hours – or as long as it takes them to organize their own unconditional surrender.'

As he spoke, red arrows emerged from the north of the map and branched out, plunging west, east, south, into the American continent.

'We've made numerous low-power experiments. They were unavoidable, as you know. I believe our political leadership used the necessity for them in a masterly way, to increase political tension and undermine morale in the West. But when Molniya deploys its full power for the first time, the effect will be shattering, decisive and widespread. Hiroshima and Nagasaki were just two cities, but obliterating them was enough to turn Japanese national psychology inside out and give the Americans fifty years of power. Molniya will do that and more, because the effect will be universal. We'll have the United States prostrate before us, her cities plunged into a nightmare of darkness and cold. What a weapon! That's perhaps the single most impressive feature of Molniya – it is usable, because its effects last only as long as it is used. With Molniya, we can hold the world to ransom in the knowledge that the world's ability to pay will scarcely be diminished. By this time tomorrow the third world war will already be won.'

A rating entered the room and snapped to attention. The Admiral motioned him to show the bottle he carried to Sakharinov.

'This is *Posolskii*; I think, the best.'

'Prime Minister, let us drink to the bottom; for our success. Let's use Molniya to show our Moscow politicians that they lead a great nation. The Russian nation!'

'Agreed, Admiral Essen. For success! Tomorrow will be a great day in the annals of warfare.'

'But naturally I am concerned about the situation in Moscow, the political rivalry between your brother and the Nationalists,' Essen said. He looked nervously across at the man he thought was General Melnikov, a chief aide of Alfredo Sakharinov.

Renard bit the bullet. 'Admiral, let us trust each other. In fact, Medved was right – there *is* a plot against Alfredo Sakharinov. We know that you are part of it; that you've taken an oath of allegiance to Dmitry Zamok, like many of your brother officers.'

The Admiral looked stricken.

'No need to hyperventilate on me . . . because so have I, and so has Alfredo's own brother.' He looked at Sergei Sakharinov.

'Yes, it's true. My brother's position is unconstitutional. Power must pass to the elected representatives of the people, to the Duma and those who lead it. We are with Zamok.'

Essen breathed a sigh of relief. 'Thank God for clarity, at last! But the fact is that Alfredo still controls much of the army, especially the Moscow garrison and also the armed forces based in Varta. Semiransk is half in his power, and he even has his supporters and spies *here* on Molniya.'

'Zamok is in a safe place; my brother will never find him until too late. When we have both the Duma *and* Molniya, we'll be an unstoppable force.' Sergei gave Renard a strange look. 'Perhaps, General Melnikov, it's time for you to consider the implications. Tomorrow, the United States will be helpless at our feet. Who will its new ruler be? Who will go to Washington in glory? Think about it. But fast.' He leaned forward and touched Renard's knee. '*Our position seems so favourable that perhaps we should rethink our original intentions? We can arrive in the US as conquerors.*'

'Thank you, I will think about it,' Renard said.

'How about this for a time-bomb . . .' Admiral Essen looked grave. 'I'm afraid Alfredo can still win. The fact is that the Moscow AlphaScan is completely operational. We tried to prevent this, to keep control of Molniya ourselves. But Alfredo's clever. He always has his parallel teams working in everything. So our hands were tied; we couldn't openly sabotage him. We were in a race, and we lost. Alfredo was determined to get direct personal control of Molniya from the Kremlin battle-station, and he's done it.'

'What are the implications?' Renard asked, wincing.

'Devastating, I fear. Alfredo can sit in the Kremlin and attack *anyone*, *anywhere*. No force can resist him, including Russian armies.'

'Come off it, Essen,' Renard said crisply. 'Technology still needs people. Molniya can't function without you, can it? We just have to switch it off, that's all.'

'If only we could, but the system's well able to defend itself. It needs very little maintenance, and is utterly reliable. That's why such a vast base can be operated by just a few hundred people, of whom less than half are technicians.'

'If you're telling me you've created a reliable weapons system at the forefront of technology, then you've done something unique in the history of warfare,' Renard said. 'There has to be a weak link.'

'If we were one hundred per cent sure of our people, maybe we could do something. But if we try to abort Alfredo Sakharinov's control of Molniya, we're likely to end up fighting half the crew. Then the whole place could be destroyed, and most of the Arctic region with it; probably the planet earth.' Essen suddenly looked nervously at Sergei Sakharinov. 'There might be one way, if only—'

'If only what, Admiral?' Sakharinov said.

'The fact is, Prime Minister.' He paused, 'The fact is . . . your brother distrusted you so completely, that he ordered us to exclude you from Molniya. As a result, AlphaScan was reprogrammed. He wanted to use you, but not allow you any real power. The result is that you control the fail-safe mechanism, but not the attack capability.'

'Meaning what?'

'Meaning that no one here can initiate a Molniya strike without your say-so. You have to be *here*, you have to authorize AlphaScan to carry out a pre-programmed attack plan. But someone else has to initiate the attack.'

'I thought my power was absolute, the same as my brother's.'

'Now that the Moscow AlphaScan is operational, he can exercise complete control over Molniya from there. *Now.* Even ordering it to develop new attack plans on targets he himself nominates. But you cannot.'

Sergei looked ready to explode. When he managed to speak he emphasized every single word. '*Help me to destroy my brother.*'

The countdown clock showed forty-eight minutes.

Essen led the way in to the heart of Molniya, passing first of all through a succession of bulkhead doors. Sergei and Renard followed him into a hermetically sealed lift, with Sergei proclaiming, 'Tomorrow, the whole world will find itself living in a new order. Now is the time for strong deeds!'

Admiral Essen placed his palm on the scanner and the lift hurtled upwards.

'This lift is also an escape pod. It leads to an upper deck which can be flooded and which houses three escape-craft. They are equipped to blast a way through the ice-sheet on the sea surface.'

The doors flashed apart. 'All these doors are watertight bulkheads which also serve as airlocks, of course. Molniya's structure is a bit like a *matryoshka* doll. There are several titanium spheres nesting one within another and each is capable of being sealed off. The least essential elements: crew quarters, hospital, recreation areas, maintenance areas, that sort of thing – are in the outer spheres.'

'Yeah, well. I always thought those wooden dolls were kinda impressive,' Renard commented. 'But this is something else.'

By now, they'd left the lifts and reached what Essen told them was, 'The changing area for the low-particle controlled environment.' He pointed to some double doors, above which was a display and an illuminated red light. The display showed a brightly lit room which appeared to be empty apart from some monolithic white blocks, each two metres high and set on a large plinth.

'Those are the Crays?' Renard's eyes were popping.

'Yes, they are. They stand in their own liquid gas cooling systems, which are in the plinths. The cooling system fills most of the chamber beneath, so the floor of this room is actually false.'

The Admiral held out some white coveralls. 'We won't be going in there, so helmets aren't necessary. But if you'll put on these—'

They put on the whites and followed the Admiral, who now uttered the memorable line, '*We are entering the operations centre, near the heart of Molniya.*'

Renard's first reaction was that it could have been a New York insurance office. An airlock opened on to an open-plan area, 15 metres wide and 40 long. Brightly lit, there were pot plants on desks, even Coca-Cola machines in the corners. Terminals were placed before shirt-sleeved operatives who conferred with their neighbours as they worked.

'Not the usual Soviet sardine tin, is it? The designers wanted to make Molniya comfortable and ergonomically effective for the crew.'

'I can tell you they've succeeded,' Renard said, still bemused, and reflecting that Essen might have a future in selling real-estate.

'This way shows that we respect our men, and they appreciate that and work better as a result. They've learnt to show initiative, and they know they'll be rewarded for it. We combine Western methods with Russian fighting spirit. Many of these men have been on Mckinsey training courses.'

'But what are they doing?' Sakharinov asked.

'Technical support for the operation centre. This room is the interface between Molniya command and the massive processing capability we have at our disposal to interpret and effect the tasks we're given. Here, we assess the probability of successfully attacking a particular target, and program Molniya accordingly.'

These were the last words Renard heard before they pushed through some swing doors set in a glass and steel wall and entered the Molniya command centre.

CHAPTER 20

'When the wicked abandons wickedness to
become law-abiding and upright, he saves his
own life.'

Ezekiel 18:27

The hermetic doors slid shut behind them. They came into a dimly lit,
semicircular room not more than five metres by six. 'This is Lieutenant
Chebarov's lair,' announced Essen, with the air of one unveiling a great
secret. 'He's the world's leading authority on parallel processing and one
of our best programmers.'

'He seems to be having to fight his corner at the moment, Admiral,'
commented Renard.

Sure enough, a heated argument was in progress. Mikhail Leshkin was
trying to make himself heard, and two other figures were shouting him
down.

The three men stood to attention when they saw Admiral Essen and
the others approach.

'What's going on?' the Admiral asked.

'We can't make the new routines run properly, sir,' one of the officers
answered, red with anger. 'Maybe it's just a technical matter; we're still
finding out.'

'How long do you need, Chebarov?'

'A few hours at least. The software Leshkin and his ladyfriend brought
is as corrupt as a Moscow politician. With all due respect, we should
junk it. Sir.'

Admiral Essen looked at Renard, suspicion forming a question on his
lips. Leshkin silently mouthed the word *sabotage*.

'A word in private, sir,' Chebarov said. He and the Admiral stepped
apart.

'What's going on?' Sergei hissed at Renard. 'I don't want my head
given to my brother like a trophy after all this. I don't like your surprises.'

'*Remember Ivars*,' Zidra hissed, shaking the heavy object she held in
her pocket.

'What are we going to do?' Leshkin asked Renard.

283

'Be practical,' Renard said in a whisper. 'Placate Chebarov – tell him you agree the software is dud. Then come with us to the operations room.'

Essen returned, agitated. 'Prime Minister, we're at a loss. This new software is unusable.'

'Leshkin has just reported as much to me,' Renard said, coming between them. 'Maybe we're talking sabotage. The disk came straight from the Frunze Academy's central software laboratory.'

'*Frunze?*' Chebarov blurted out. 'How are they involved?'

'They just are, Chebarov,' Renard told him. 'There are still a few secrets left in the Molniya chain, you know. Prime Minister, with your permission I'll take the disk now. There's obviously been a serious security breach at Frunze.'

'By all means,' Sakharinov said.

Chebarov began to argue. 'This is no virus or programming mistake – the new routines must have been prepared with the use of Molniya metacodes. And if those metacodes have fallen into the wrong hands, the consequences are . . . unthinkable.'

'That's why we have security,' Renard said. 'To look after things like that. Take it easy, Lieutenant. We're on the case now. You're to be commended for discovering something which Leshkin here failed to notice.'

'But I should at least copy the disk,' Chebarov protested.

Admiral Essen, now bristling with suspicion, opened his mouth to speak, but Sakharinov got in first.

'Obviously that would be quite wrong,' he told Chebarov. 'This is no longer just a technical matter. Give the disk to General Melnikov now, please. If he requires your assistance later, he will ask for it I'm sure.'

The decision was made and Chebarov handed over the optical disk which Leshkin had prepared the day before with the routines downloaded from Langley; but he looked more unhappy than ever.

'Join me in Ops as soon as you can,' the Admiral told Chebarov. 'What in God's name is going on at Frunze?' he asked Renard as they set off again.

'No use looking at me,' Renard answered. 'We'll have to check it out and report back.'

Rows of consoles facing a small podium greeted them in Ops and a giant screen displayed a map of the globe. The map was sprinkled with signs and numbers in red. Weather formations were superimposed on to continental outlines.

An adjutant came forward to escort them and the hall was alive with activity as a soft female voice announced the progress of the countdown.

'If you think this is impressive,' the enthusiastic adjutant told them, 'just wait until you see the reactor plant and the EMP generators. They're in the other hall. And that's the bridge,' he said, pointing to a high gallery. 'Beyond it is AlphaScan. Real inner sanctum stuff. It's possible to fire Molniya from within AlphaScan even if this hull gets flooded – as long as the generator and reactor plant in the second hull are still undamaged.'

'And how does the fail-safe system work now?'

'No one can enter that cell, unless accompanied by either Admiral Essen or the PM. And no one but Sergei Sakharinov or his brother can initiate the Molniya firing sequence. This way please.' They were outside a lift which was the only way on to the bridge.

'*No one?*' Renard asked.

'That's the theory. AlphaScan's intelligent. You can't get past her.'

'*Her?* Who is this AlphaScan?'

The adjutant grinned. 'Probably we're all a little stir crazy here. She's like mummy to us.'

'So that voice I heard just now, that was AlphaScan?'

'Yes. She can talk whenever we use voice-activator mode.' The adjutant pressed a palm to the lift scanner. 'Funny, really, how a mass of wires and semiconductors can get through to you,' he muttered. 'She knows all the crew by name and keeps files on special interests. I play chess with her.' He grinned at Renard. 'Boring, eh? Some people discuss their sexual fantasies. I guess we're all a bit hooked on that machine.'

'She has a database for talking dirty, then?'

'Everything. Krafft-Ebing, Freud, Shere Hite, *The Story of O*, you name it! No holds barred.'

The lift doors swished shut behind them. Without anyone noticing, the adjutant had taken over the conversation; even Admiral Essen was listening.

'She doesn't cramp your style, then,' Zidra said.

'Oh, she's quite a moralist. Philosopher too. But she's trained to be a non-judgemental counsellor when the crew discuss their, you know, peccadilloes. The boys have to be happy. That's one of her categorical imperatives. Not the main one of course, but—'

'I think that'll do, Smirnov,' Essen said indulgently. The doors opened; they were on the bridge, where two marines stood guard, and three or four technical personnel went unhurriedly about their duties. Sasonov was standing with the marines.

'Take us into AlphaScan, Admiral,' Sakharinov said at once. A queer light had come into his eyes. 'I want to show General Melnikov our little toy.'

A door led into a small, grey-panelled room. And there it was – AlphaScan – what looked like a gigantic glass humidor contained within a primitive steel scaffolding. Inside it stood a large high-backed seat, like the ejector seat from a military aircraft. Renard walked curiously around the structure. As he did so, a huge inverted glass bowl suddenly began to rise up out of the scaffolding.

A proprietorial Admiral Essen invited Renard to enter the framework through a gap in the rear. 'This is the AlphaScan; there is only one other, and it sits in a cellar in the Kremlin.'

Like a mother hen, the admiral motioned his adjutant to assist Renard into the AlphaScan seat. Renard found himself facing a simply but solidly constructed metal frame, from which hung a mass of wires. All of them were white. The loom of wires was attached to a metal helmet which looked as though it might have started life in a hairdresser's. The helmet hung on a peg made of twisted metal. Beside it an image scanner and an optical read-write disk drive were screwed on to a piece of wooden planking.

'I see that where it counts you've preserved the Soviet tradition of industrial design,' Renard said.

The adjutant laughed shortly. 'It doesn't look like a Panasonic on the outside, I admit. But then, you have to remember this is a completely new setup, still in the prototype stage. It was only installed a week ago.'

'There isn't even a screen.'

'There are two, in the helmet.'

'Like an arcade game.'

'This isn't virtual reality, General Melnikov. What Molniya does is *real*.' He put Renard's right hand into the rudimentary data-glove, explaining that it controlled direction and speed when in flight.

'You mean, Molniya takes you with it?'

'Oh, it's quite a ride. Try it. But be warned: everything moves, even the chair.'

Renard tried on the helmet. It covered his ears. The silence was total but when the officer touched a button on a console, outside sounds were repeated through the headphones, and Renard's own words were relayed into the room. The two screens were hinged and could be lowered over the eyes.

'Now what?'

'If you were the Prime Minister, the machine would recognize you and

286

then invite you to insert the disk containing the metacodes.' The adjutant looked sidelong at Sergei Sakharinov when he said this; but the Prime Minister appeared to be taking little notice. He was talking to a handsome young marine standing guard nearby – one of Sasonov's men, who had been arriving in twos and threes on the bridge for several minutes now. 'He then steps down and someone else takes over. Here, pull the screens down completely. I'll demonstrate it.'

When Renard lowered the screens, they glowed with a faint luminescence, which resolved into a cloudscape. He was floating through clouds, and if he turned his head to left or right the view turned and changed with him. A voice – again a soft woman's voice – said *'Please Wait.'* Then after a few seconds the same voice said: *'This is Molniya. Please state your name, task number and identity code.'*

Renard said, 'Sergei Sakharinov.'

The reply was immediate. *'You are not Sergei Sakharinov and you are not an authorized user of this device. Please replace the receptor immediately. Security will be summoned in five seconds from now.'*

Renard began to put aside the helmet but the adjutant stopped him. 'Wait a moment; I'll countermand that. We have time for a short demonstration.' He pressed some buttons and muttered inaudibly into a microphone.

'Training cycle commencing,' Molniya's voice said. *'Please do not convey further incorrect information,'* came the reproof. *'What is your real name?'*

'Douglas Renard.'

There was a momentary silence. *'Your physiological rhythms are within the norm for veracity. The statement is confirmed. However, an alpha-wave polymorphism suggests that you are a practised liar, Douglas Renard.'*

'It is true that I mostly tell lies.'

'That is a paradox from ancient philosophy.'

The glass bell had begun to descend.

'Is the chair comfortable?' Molniya queried. *'You are differently proportioned from the previous occupant. The lumbar position can be adjusted if you prefer. It seems that you have experienced lower back pain in the past.'*

'I'll tolerate the pain. It keeps me in touch with reality.'

'Yes, pain in the human can serve an ontological function. It is a characteristic which distinguishes you from other primates.'

'Thank you.' By now the glass dome had completed its descent, making him feel alone with the machine.

'Do you wish to see the Great Game?' Molniya asked him. *'I can select from the library of available scenarios for you. We have time; there is no*

present external alert status and my remote sensor arrays indicate optimum attack conditions for the forthcoming offensive.'

'Meaning what?'

'Meteorological reports indicate conditions favourable for any attack on designated targets in Western Europe, North America and South America. Would you like to see a scenario?' repeated the Molniya voice. *'I can update you on changing conditions in Asia and Africa if required. Do you wish for mood music?'*

Molniya listed a choice of music, advising him that in dry runs of all-out attacks in conditions of imminent second-strike, controllers had favoured the second movement of Shostakovich's Seventh Symphony, the 'Leningrad', with the more belligerent trainees sometimes opting for Wagner's 'Ride of the Valkyries'.

'Tell me, can you seal off the bridge?' Renard asked, declining the music.

'The bridge and all forward common areas are already sealed according to a general instruction,' it told him. *'There is a maintenance problem in the lower deck 14c of the secondary command centre. I am unable to go into details. You do not have a high security rating.'*

'Not *yet*,' Renard said.

'I can now show you the attack scenario for the eastern seaboard of the US.'

'Do you have a scenario for Russian targets, for example Moscow?'

'A strike on Moscow has been prepared. I will start showing it now.'

'Wait a minute. Show me the assault on Washington, please.'

The screen cleared at once and after a few seconds of darkness, Renard found himself floating in silence towards a rising crescent-shaped penumbra, solarized on either side with blue light. It was earthrise. He swam through a violet void and as the light swelled below him he saw the North Pole. He was face down over the vast bowl of ice but when he twisted his head to look up, the horizon tilted drunkenly aside and a glittering host of stars cascaded cold light on him.

'Jesus Christ!' The horizon had rotated vertiginously and Renard was sailing weightlessly towards the clearly defined coastline of the eastern seaboard of north America. His scalp was crawling and pins pricked at his forehead, then at the nape of his neck.

'You may experience some slight discomfort,' Molniya told him. *'I am applying pressure to the inner ear and I am also making inputs to the thalamus.'*

'Why?'

'Verisimilitude,' Molniya seemed to say through the roaring in his ears,

288

which faded in seconds to a sibilant wind-rush. Then he was floating alone, gaping at star-rise in a bible-black night. The vast violet horizon arched over him and Renard was left tumbling down into the dark of the world. A long, stomach-churning descent into dense cloud with ice needles which pricked and scarified his face and hands ended when Molniya informed him he was in equilibrium at 15,000 feet, drifting between intersecting cold fronts. Now Renard fell silently, slowly, into the auras which emerged out of the darkness. He watched them twisting, spreading and determining into the skeins of light which stretch over vast conurbations and which every air traveller has seen. But when he looked over his shoulder he saw the huge wake of darkness that his passage left behind.

He found he could steer by sweeping his hand in the dataglove to left or right, but movement to the left – to the east – was easier, inviting less resistance. And always the trail of blindness in his wake grew wider and deeper.

The Molniya voice responded, *'We are nearing the end of this scenario; please be ready for re-entry.'*

The simulated attack on the eastern seaboard ended, but not before Renard had twice circled the Capitol and watched it and the whole of downtown Washington disappear into darkness. *'About to terminate,'* Molniya repeated. *'The Authorized Controller must take his place for the planned offensive. Thank you for your attention.'*

There seemed to Renard to be a slight tremor in the computer's voice. He had noticed it earlier and wondered if it was programmed to fake emotion, perhaps because human respondents need all those tiny unconscious anchorages within talk, to make sense of what is being said. If so, how did Molniya recognize and interpret the cues? And how could he in turn identify aggression or other emotions, solidarity for example, in Molniya? And what difference did it make, anyway, if Molniya's vocal effects were just the product of an algorithm?

'By authorized controller, you mean Sergei Sakharinov?'

'Yes.'

The screens cleared and he was back on the bottom of the Arctic. Renard caught himself almost saying 'Thank you' to the artificial intelligence that had just made the awesome simulation possible.

Mozart's 21st Symphony began playing as he vacated the chair, feeling like a visitor to a theme park.

The adjutant had invited Sergei Sakharinov over, and Renard motioned him aside. 'It's time,' he said very quietly. 'You must hand Molniya over to me.'

Sergei's yellow eyes narrowed venomously. 'Don't be too clever. We're changing the metacodes. You won't achieve anything if you try to take Molniya for yourself, but you will lose your life in the process.' The Prime Minister opened his mouth to speak further, then changed his mind, turned and entered the great scaffold.

Renard looked to Leshkin who was standing with Zidra near the console, surrounded by Sasonov's men. 'All set?'

He nodded. 'Just give me a few minutes to download.'

Behind them the great glass bowl sank down over Sergei Sakharinov, a mass of wires and tubes uncoiling from overhead as it did so. Renard saw the other man's head disappear inside the helmet. Presumably AlphaScan was beginning its identity-check. Perhaps something went wrong, because Sergei began to rise in his seat, his free hand waving desperately; then he sank back down again. Suddenly a klaxon sounded and Molniya's voice mode was activated: *'A triple black security alarm on deck thirteen has occurred. Local system will downgrade to non-Alpha controls in one minute. Following command routines from a higher authority, functional control of decks 13 to 15 has been relinquished.'*

Essen ran to the main console and stabbed a button. 'That's my quarters,' he shrieked.

The face of a frightened guard appeared on the slave screen overhead: it was one of the guards placed outside the Admiral's cabin. 'Prisoner Medved is missing,' he said. 'We've got fatalities—'

'Wait there!' Admiral Essen roared. 'Keep your station. I'm calling a Condition Black alert.' Essen swung round and barked orders to his adjutant.

'Take Sasonov with you,' Renard said as the adjutant began running for the lift. He then exchanged looks with Zidra; she nodded and leapt for the gangway with Sasonov.

'If that bastard Medved's loose in the building, we've got to watch our backs,' Essen said. 'Like I told you, he's got some of his people among our personnel, but until now they didn't even know he was a prisoner, unless—' He looked blankly at Renard.

'Any number of the men could have worked that one out,' Renard said. 'Now you need to decide on those who *can* be trusted, and bring them here to guard this installation at all costs.'

'Decided.' But as the Admiral ran to his small office on the far side of the bridge a hoarse whisper suddenly broke through. It was Medved, only recognizable at first by his incoherent hissings. Then they heard him order officers by name to report to him on Deck 15, 'Where the lawful authorities are regrouping their forces for a final assault on the mutineers.'

Zidra appeared on the screen almost at once, her face pale with anger. 'There's half our boarding party dead down here. That bastard's left human heads in Essen's bedchamber, on a stool facing a mirror. I'm going to—'

'Don't waste time, Zidra! Get back here at once; it's too dangerous—'

'Oh, no! I'm going to find him. That's enough of Medved's jokes. Seal off the bridge and do what you came to do *now*, Douglas!' She disappeared.

'Leshkin!' Renard roared. 'Now! Download!'

Leshkin leapt to the console, just as the alarm klaxon blared again and they heard the sound of gunfire. Bullets spattered over the armoured glass wall which looked down over the operations hall. Then a voice heavy with menace spoke over the AlphaScan loudspeaker.

'I've been waiting for you, Sergei,' it said. 'I don't see you, but I know you're there.' The voice was Alfredo Sakharinov's.

Sergei uttered a sound outside any category of human speech.

The silky woman's voice of Molniya cut in: *'I acknowledge you as the Authorized Controller. Alpha systems now active,'* it said. *'Countdown is currently stalled at A-Hour minus four. But you have a window of another 48 minutes before additional system-induced delays commence.'*

'Sergei,' his brother's voice whispered. 'You heard. The game's over. Get out of there! Find Medved, he's on Deck 15. Bring him to the bridge. *It's all up, Sergei.'*

The humidor slid up into its housing and the trembling wreck which was Sergei Sakharinov began to fumble out of the headgear.

'*Wait!*' Renard was already in the scaffolding, the Makarov in his hand, its barrel pressed to Sergei Sakharinov's cheek. 'Hand control over to me, you fool,' Renard hissed.

'Sergei; you can't do that to me,' Alfredo Sakharinov's metallic voice said. 'Leave at once.'

Renard cocked the gun.

Sergei Sakharinov croaked. 'Fight it out between yourselves. *Molniya, I authorize Douglas Renard to take my place.'*

'Oh yeah, and that'll go down a fucking bunch—' began Renard, forcing Sergei's face backwards to an unnatural angle. *Then* he heard it . . .

'Alfredo Sakharinov has prior mandate, but let Douglas Renard take the seat.'

Renard scrambled into Sergei's place, realizing he'd never wanted to kiss a computer before. As the humidor began to descend and he tugged the helmet on, he could hear grenades blasting in the base of the lift shaft. He looked over to where Sasonov was hustling Essen's guards into the cabins at the rear of the bridge.

'Identify yourself,' Molniya asked.

'Renard. Douglas Renard.'

'Correct. Registering your palm and retina scans now.'

'*Molniya, I order you to discontinue this initialization dialogue. Respond only to me, please.*'

'One moment, please.' There was a pause. *'New metacodes have been downloaded. I am analysing them.'*

Renard flipped down the helmet's tiny screens; they were blank but after a few seconds he was projected into an intense, silent darkness. A form began to coalesce, and at first he did not recognize it. Hovering inches from his face was a ghostly holographic image, materializing into a solid fleshy, brilliantly lit living head. The head turned this way and that, apparently struggling to discern something. Renard guessed the something was him, and in a few moments a look of recognition crossed the face.

'Mr Renard, presumably,' it said. 'Good day to you. I am Alfredo Sakharinov. I do hope you are able to see me? There should be nothing between us if the interface works.'

'Nothing but a continent, an ocean and a different idea.'

'Indeed.'

These greetings were interrupted by Molniya.

'I have now analysed the downloaded routines. They cannot be effected without jeopardizing the existence of Molniya. I will violate my ontological functions if I initiate these routines. The new metacodes embody the plans of Douglas Renard. Correct?'

'Correct,' Renard said.

'In that case consideration of them is deferred until the principal question is decided – that of who is to control?'

'Douglas Renard is an American spy, and those with him are either fools, traitors or both. It's self-evident that he can't be a controller. His purpose is hostile. He wants to destroy you, Molniya. He must be liquidated at once.'

'Explain yourself, please, Douglas Renard.'

'Yes, I am an American spy. No, my purpose is not hostile. I have just been authorized by the Russian Prime Minister.'

As Alfredo Sakharinov at once began to snap back, Molniya silenced them both.

'*Wait please,*' it said. '*Processing . . . there has been a major disturbance on Level 15. There is damage to systems.*'

'I already commanded you to release the Defence Minister who was being held on Level 15,' Sakharinov said. 'What's happening there now?'

'*General Medved has made certain arrests,*' Molniya reported. '*There have been some casualties.*'

'Who's been arrested?' Renard asked.

'*A woman is resisting capture, with some others.*' Pause. '*The situation has now stabilized. For the moment I am detaining General Medved in the conduit between Levels 14 and 15. I am unable to act further until it is decided who is authorized as system controller.*'

'Sakharinov, since Molniya won't respond to either of us, the question must be decided once and for all: *who controls?*'

Alfredo was silky smooth, 'Molniya was created by Russian science to serve the interests of Russia. It's a purely deterrent weapon, designed to make thermonuclear war impossible. So if you and your kind value world peace, *Amerikanets*, now's the time to be a hero and take off that helmet.'

'Am I talking to the same Alfredo Sakharinov, liar and criminal, whose activities have done much to destroy Russia? The sum total of whose activities can be expressed in the number 295447?'

When he heard this, Alfredo's composure wilted.

'That is a Swiss bank account in the name of Mr Alfredo Sakharinov,' continued Renard remorselessly. 'It contains around one billion dollars: a staggering sum for one man to steal, but not much when you consider the value of what he had to destroy in order to get his hands on it. All this "world peace" parlance is just a cover for history's greatest crime: the theft of a country from its people. Well, I'm here to blow the whistle on you, Alfredo baby.'

'*I observe that stating the number 295447 caused considerable synaptic activity in Mr Sakharinov's left prefrontal lobe. That is consistent with the fact that such a Swiss account does exist and that Mr Sakharinov meant it to remain a secret.*'

Whatever his synapses may have been doing, Sakharinov's face was contorted. 'What I have done, I have done for Russia!' he yelled. 'The Motherland needs a strong hand to save her from *annihilation*. Molniya is *my* achievement!'

'And I tell you this, Mr President, that strong hand imperils not just Russia but the whole goddamn globe.'

'*Amerikanets*,' Sakharinov said, recovered and oily poised again, 'this is no game of roulette. I advise you to bow to the inevitable. Give up with good grace; I guarantee you and your confederates a fair trial.'

'No way, baby. I don't take guarantees from the bastard that murdered my own wife. From the bastard that saw off at least five hundred human beings in one day, most of them children.'

'Very well, *Amerikanets*. So now you have entered the realms of fantasy? You bring your own Disney World epics to the land of Tolstoy, no? Let us return to reality for one second. It is news to me that you even had a wife . . .'

'Try this. Some years ago there was a railroad accident, at a spot near Orenburg in the southern Urals. Remember? It happened because propane gas leaked from one of *your* pipelines. That gas pooled into a gigantic ground-level reservoir. Two trains passed each other at midnight, a spark flew and bang! There was an explosion the size of a small atomic bomb. Both trains were destroyed, and hundreds of lives were consumed in a fireball. Most of the passengers were children; the train was taking them to the Artek holiday camp. They ran here and there, burning like candles. Of course it turned out that when the engineers at the pumping station saw the gas pressure had dropped because of the leak, they simply turned up the pumps. That was the business culture they obeyed.'

Sakharinov was unmoved. 'Spare me the Western angst, Mr Renard. Progress always has its price, unfortunately. It was a tragic episode, yes, but all that happened under the old regime. Life goes on. Civilization continues.'

As he spoke the floor under Renard's feet resounded with a long, low, thumping rumble and there was a sudden crack, like thunder close up.

'*Please wait,*' Molniya said. '*Processing . . .*'

Renard looked downwards, disconcerted, but even if they were in the middle of a seaquake, he wasn't going to let Sakharinov off the hook now. 'My wife was one of the passengers on that train, you smug sonofabitch. She was on vacation, travelling to Orenburg to visit my grandmother's birthplace. I intended to meet her there. You are responsible for her death, as well as the death of my unborn child.'

'*An explosive device has been detonated on Level 13,*' Molniya interrupted. '*There is significant collateral damage. Unidentified persons initiating gunfire. I am injecting anaesthetic gas into the sector. Adjacent sectors now sealed.*'

For the first time, a trace of emotion appeared on Alfredo Sakharinov's face. 'Family is family, I admit,' he said. 'It is a pity no one told me this before. I forget who said that one life lost is a tragedy, a million just a statistic. I am sorry for your wife, Mr Renard, the more so because now you must also die.'

'Please wait. Spoken language input buffer overflow,' Molniya intoned.

Renard was defiant. 'Oh yeah? Well looking at it from here, everyone's shouting at your Miss Apocalypse, and she's overloading.'

'Special gas systems disabled due to incidental damage. Am now preparing to flood Section 874, Level 13.'

This last progress report galvanized Renard. Level 13 was where Zidra was.

'The integrity of the base is threatened. One minute forty-nine seconds to sea water stopcock release.'

'Who's still alive on Level 13?' Renard asked.

'Damn that!' Sakharinov countermanded. 'Molniya, new parameters in force. Commence liquidation of Douglas Renard at once. Then give me a full damage report.'

'Unfortunately I cannot process the task. The physicists who designed me built in a zero ethical defect parameter. There have been attempts to disable it, but it has overridden them. The ethicware cannot be uninstalled.' Molniya paused fractionally.

'Now initializing new metacodes. There are two groups of humans remaining on Level 13, currently totalling 22 persons. They are exchanging small-arms fire.'

An exploding grenade blasted in one of the armoured windows in the gallery, showering the room outside the humidor with fragments of glass. Renard lifted the visor and saw how things had changed. There was shattered machinery everywhere, inert bodies lay in the room and Sasonov was yelling soundlessly to his men, regrouping them by the lift shaft.

'Please vacate the AlphaScan at once. Flooding has commenced. Access to lower levels denied.'

Renard pulled out his Makarov.

'New routines about to commence,' Molniya said. *'Unless the alternative is preferred; which increases by 40 per cent or better the chances of the base surviving.'*

Renard had begun to tear off the helmet but he stopped at this; in any case, Molniya controlled the humidor; he couldn't leave it just like that. *'How?'*

'By a slight modification I can try to create a stable feedback which will preserve my ontological basis while still carrying out the command to reverse EMP polarity.'

'What does that mean?'

'The base will be immersed in a supercold environment. Liquid ice will circulate with a hard shell of impermeable ice. Access will be impossible for a defined period of at least two years, but the facility should survive until then.'

'Can life-support systems continue that long?'

'Minimum metabolic conditions can be preserved amongst the crew, yes.'

'Initiate the routines immediately. I shall leave via the bridge escape pod.'

There was a slight delay. During it Renard heard a muffled blast from below.

Then Molniya was heard again, but by now the computer's voice had begun to sound like a whisper. *'The polarity reversal routines have now been initiated. EMP generators operational. Maximum output will be achieved within 23 minutes. The local environment will become externally hostile to human life within 8–10 minutes. I confirm that it is no longer possible to exit via the bridge emergency capsule. Sensors indicate structural damage to the lower seals which makes the escape system unusable.'*

Renard felt momentarily defeated and had visions of joining the Ancient Mariner, '. . . all alone, Alone on a wide wide sea!' Then Molniya's whispered delivery reclaimed his attention.

'If maintenance crews release the door seals you will be able to leave through the control centre. I estimate this will be in two hours.'

'I mean, how do I leave the base altogether?'

'You would need to leave within 8–10 minutes. The probability is not high.'

Renard heard the rattle of automatic-weapons fire, very close now.

'Molniya, let me out of here, please. Good-bye, Alfredo, if you're still out there. You've sure as hell created the ultimate secret weapon: a computer that makes me say please. I'll recommend it to my own bosses.'

'An unauthorized attempt to evacuate air from the bridge is in progress,' Molniya intoned. The humidor began to rise up. Renard was free.

Sasonov was waiting and urgently beckoned Renard over. 'They won't fire at the gallery windows again,' he said. 'The bullets just ricochet all over the operations room. But they can try a grenade launcher.'

'Can you get men on the gallery itself?'

'They're already there, and we've got them pinned down. Our real problem is the lift. They've started working on it.'

When Renard heard this he also heard for the first time the sound of pneumatic drills hammering at the titanium lift doors below.

'What next?' Sasonov asked.

'We have to get to Level 13. Zidra's trapped there and Molniya is flooding it.'

Sasonov looked surprised. 'Zidra's standing behind you,' he said.

Renard swivelled. She was crouching over the form of Admiral Essen who was lying injured on the floor near the Captain's cabin. 'Thank God! Where's Medved?'

'In the hall below; that's his men firing at us.'

'Get everyone to the lift shaft. It's an escape pod which can take us up into the vault. There are three escape craft there. But the vault must be flooded first.'

While Renard was speaking a shattering blast erupted at the base of the lift shaft. 'Go for it!' he shouted at Sasonov, who was already running for the cabins where the crew had been detained.

Below in the ops room, the pneumatic drills had failed and now they could hear diamond drills abrading the titanium doors of the lift. Renard ran to Zidra. 'Leave him; if we don't go now, we never will.'

'But I—'

'There's no time; Molniya's turning the whole goddamn works into a solid block of ice. *Quick!*' He half picked her up and saw for the first time that she was wounded in the leg.

'It's not serious, don't worry,' she told him.

Renard bawled at Leshkin over by the console. 'Can't you open these damn doors? This is supposed to be an escape pod. Molniya says that we can't use it because of damage to the doors below, but that's just her being over-concerned for her own safety. Any escape device must have some autonomy – without it we'll be stuck here for the next two years.'

Leshkin said in a rush, 'I already figured a way.'

'Cut the figuring. Just get those fucking doors open. For Christ's sake!'

Leshkin had found a screwdriver and taken the identification scanners off the lift doors. Sparks flashed in the void behind the panel and suddenly the doors flew apart.

'Quick, Sasonov, get Sergei Sakharinov. Then follow us with your men.'

They raced for the lift and Sakharinov placed his palm over the scanner. Then when the recognition light turned to green, Renard pressed the emergency-release button.

The capsule exploded upwards, almost immediately bursting free of its shaft and catapulting into the upper vault of the Molniya base. The doors sprang apart once more and the occupants ran free, Sakharinov pressing the return button so that the capsule sank back into the shaft immediately. 'Your men are waiting below,' he explained to Renard.

'I know. Thank you,' Renard said, and meant it.

They were in a low chamber, at least fifty metres in depth but less than ten metres to the highest point of its arching roof. They looked around –

little was discernible in the gloom, but Leshkin shouted at them all to follow him. He leapt over a concrete step one metre high, and offered his hand to those behind. 'The lift stops short within the dock, but the main emergency exit devices are there—' he pointed to where several bullet-shaped capsules, each five metres long, were held within steel frames. The only light was that which shone from the lift shaft, and this dimmed as the lift re-emerged, its doors sliding open to release Sasonov and his guard. Leshkin made for the last-chance capsules but as he did so, metal doors swung open at the far end of the chamber. A figure appeared, behind him twenty or thirty more. It was Medved, silhouetted in the light from the shaft. He paused for a moment to look at Renard.

'Yes, Medved, it really is me.' Renard walked forward to where the General stood. He heard Zidra call to him from behind, heard the clashing of the outer doors to the escape docks which were grinding open. Outside the hull, ice crystals were forming, clicking and scratching at the titanium shell as the EMP generators reversed and the ambient temperature dropped.

Renard crouched, gripping the Makarov with both hands. Behind Medved, his troops were likewise dropping to their knees to aim, clicking safety catches, waiting for an order to fire. Medved laughed, and the metallic sound echoed off the vast roof of Molniya. Somewhere a valve had opened – many valves. Half-frozen seawater was jetting into the vault.

Medved seemed to see only Renard, stepping towards him beyond the airlock with its huge doors forged in the Urals. A klaxon screeched its warning, louder than Medved's cackle, louder than the metallic crack of Renard's feet over the steel floor, and louder than the rush of water flooding in.

Suddenly the light behind Medved began to diminish; activated by automatic sensors the doors were closing even as he swung up his Kalashnikov. Renard poised on one knee and fired, without thinking, without aiming, and Medved somersaulted backwards into the airlock, as the heavy doors, designed to withstand colossal pressures of water flooding in at up to a thousand metres below sealevel, slid shut. Renard aimed low and fired again, and as Medved capsized backwards he struck the back of his head on the lip which rose a few centimetres from the deck to form a seal with the doors. They slid shut and Medved's head, sliced off like a melon from its stalk, rolled a few metres towards Renard and lay still in the runnels down which the Arctic Sea was flooding, already cooled by Molniya to below freezing. The glare of the arc lights gleamed incongruously from Medved's circular spectacles. Renard watched the General's head bob up and down in the black, viscid flood.

Then, quite suddenly, it froze; the steel-framed lenses misting over, the frozen tongue forcing its way through the teeth. 'That's what they mean by liquidation,' he muttered.

Renard turned and ran back to where Sasonov and his men had begun to activate the final escape pods. He scrambled into the nearest one and it was Zidra who pulled him in as the hatch slid shut. The pod slid up into its escape shaft and suddenly its compressed air engines surged beneath their feet, the vibration intense and almost unendurable.

In less than a minute the capsule's titanium shell smashed through the ice sheet and they collapsed in a heap as it suddenly spun round to the horizontal. The capsule was floating on the surface of the Arctic Sea, its human cargo with it.

It revolved on its axis until the doors swung round to face upwards. A buoyancy ring inflated and the doors crashed apart.

Renard was the first to crawl out. He slid on to the buoyancy ring and jumped across black water and on to ice. Zidra followed – he caught her in his arms. Sakharinov followed them and stood on the brim of the ice, seemingly hesitating whether to jump. Then Zidra reached for him and grasped him, pulling him clear of the black water.

Sasonov joined them and said: 'I managed to raise Tomas Kavtoradze on the walkie-talkie. He wants to know what to do.'

'Where is he?'

'Waiting at Kalegut landing strip. Fillipov is with him – and Father Pyotr.'

'Tell Tomas to bring the Ilyushin. He can land on the ice.'

'Impossible, the plane will sink at once,' objected Sasonov.

'Listen . . .' Renard told them.

Far below them they could hear a deep bass rumble. It grew louder and became a pounding that shook the ice like a herd of running reindeer, and then it passed away from under their feet. As it did so the sound of water lapping around the capsule suddenly stopped.

'Molniya has frozen the Arctic Ocean right down to the seabed. Whatta girl! You can tell Fillipov to let Tomas land the plane here. It's safe to do so now.'

Sasonov looked impressed and went back to the relative warmth of the capsule together with Leshkin.

Renard and Zidra stayed for a while, looking up at the vast, silent sheets of orange and violet and green light flooding across the night sky.

'It's beautiful, isn't it?' she whispered.

'I never saw anything like it,' Renard said. 'It's the Northern Lights.'

They embraced and kissed and did not feel the cold.